Pamela Evans was born and brought up in Hanwell in the borough of Ealing, London. She has two grown-up sons and now lives in Wales with her husband.

Close to Home

Pamela Evans

HEADLINE

First published in 2001
by HEADLINE BOOK PUBLISHING

First published in paperback in 2001
by HEADLINE BOOK PUBLISHING

4

ISBN 0 7472 6812 6

Typeset by
Letterpart Limited, Reigate, Surrey

Printed and bound in Great Britain by
Clays Ltd, St Ives plc

HEADLINE BOOK PUBLISHING
A division of Hodder Headline
338 Euston Road
London NW1 3BH

www.headline.co.uk
www.hodderheadline.com

To Martin, Simon, Julie, Millie and Max
with love

Chapter One

It was Friday night and a feeling of weekend exuberance was already flowing through the Flying Goose in the West London region of Shepherd's Bush, the steadfast efforts of the piano player barely audible above the sociable clamour.

Two young men stood chatting at the bar. On leave from National Service and having a boys' night out they'd stopped off here for a quick one on their way to the billiard hall. Both were in civvies, wearing traditional suits.

'Well, mate . . . only one more day of home comforts and we'll be back to spit and polish and food a stray dog would think twice about,' remarked Tom Hall, a tall, muscular man with piercing blue eyes and thick blond hair. His much-maligned army haircut didn't detract from his stunning good looks because his hair was so short at the back and sides it showed off his fine facial structure.

'Don't even mention it,' groaned his companion, Doug Scott. Doug was shorter than average, and had a chubby countenance and wayward brown hair that refused to be disciplined despite copious amounts of Brylcreem on the top. He had a good solid physique, though, a clear complexion and kind hazel eyes.

'No point in closing your mind to reality just because you're on leave,' opined Tom, taking seriously what had been merely a casual comment. 'We've both still got another year to do in the army and that's all there is to it.'

'We don't have to talk about it when we're out for the

evening, though, do we?' objected Doug. 'That subject is enough to turn the beer sour.'

'It isn't that bad,' Tom disagreed mildly. 'And we were lucky to be on leave at the same time.'

Doug nodded and took a sip of his beer.

'Going back to camp doesn't bother me, to be perfectly honest,' Tom confided, looking sheepish because mutual contempt for the army and its mindless discipline was something of a bond between peacetime conscripts.

'Don't let Ellie hear you say that,' warned Doug, whose sister, Eleanor, was engaged to Tom. 'She thinks that you're dreading it as much as she is.'

'Women make more of these things than we do, don't they?' Tom pointed out knowingly. 'I'll be sorry to leave her, of course.' For a moment he did look regretful. 'But since I don't have a choice in the matter, I might as well make the best of things while I'm in Germany.'

'I don't fancy going back to camp *at all*.' Doug had no problem admitting it.

A master of condescension, Tom gave Doug one of his most pitying looks. 'I can understand that too. It can't be much fun being stuck down in Aldershot.'

'Aldershot's all right.' Doug was on the defensive.

Tom supped slowly from his pint glass. 'Germany's the place to be,' he stated with authority, 'especially when you're there at the Government's expense.'

'We can't all get the dream posting,' Doug reminded him. 'It's the luck of the draw where you get stationed. Anyway, Aldershot suits me well enough.'

Up went Tom's brows. 'Really?' he said, as though Doug had just admitted to some embarrassing physical defect.

'Yeah, really. I'm gaining experience as an army driver, a job I'll enjoy doing after I'm demobbed,' he explained. 'And there's the added bonus of being able to get home more often than I could if I'd been posted abroad. You can't come home from Germany when you've got a weekend pass like you can when you're in Aldershot.'

'Home to see the steady girlfriend, eh?' Ostensibly this was friendly banter but undertones of serious ridicule were detectable to someone who knew Tom as well as Doug did.

A flush crept up Doug's neck, burning his face. Adulthood hadn't lessened Tom's power to destroy his self-esteem. No one could belittle Doug as effectively as Tom, not even the cruel and obnoxious army sergeants it had been Doug's misfortune to encounter during this past year of military service. 'That's right,' he said defiantly.

'Sounds to me as though Ann's got you where she wants you – well and truly under her thumb.'

Raised in the close proximity of their mothers' friendship, Doug and Tom might easily have grown up eschewing the enforced palliness of their childhood. But instead they'd become best mates, though they could hardly be more different. Tom was extrovert and ultraconfident; Doug was more gentle-natured and reserved. Tom had always had more of everything than Doug: more pocket money, gift of the gab, good looks and success with the opposite sex, even though he'd never seriously been interested in anyone except Ellie.

Doug was under no illusions. He guessed he owed Tom's friendship to the fact that he himself had nothing to offer in the way of competition. But his own credibility was greatly enhanced by his close connections with someone so self-assured and with an aura of wealth about him because his parents owned the corner shop in the poor neighbourhood of Shepherd's Bush where they'd grown up. Although plentiful employment was making ordinary people better off, in the autumn of 1953 the new age of prosperity didn't yet benefit everybody.

Although there were times when Doug loathed Tom for his arrogance and ability to manipulate Ellie and himself, he had never seriously considered breaking away. Old habits die hard, he supposed, and he did believe that he and Ellie could count on Tom's loyalty if it were ever put to the test.

But now he stood his ground as he responded to Tom's gibe. 'It wouldn't worry me if she had,' he told him. 'I like to get home to see her, anyway . . . and the family. As far as I'm concerned the army is a complete waste of time and the sooner I get to the end of my service the better.'

'We all feel like that about it,' Tom retorted hastily. 'But since we're forced to do it, it makes sense to cash in on the opportunities that come with it.'

'Which is exactly what I am doing,' Doug pointed out. 'When I get back into civvy street, I'll have my HGV licence so I can earn good money as a lorry driver. I'd much rather do that than go back into a factory.'

'I was talking more in terms of off-duty opportunities.' Tom didn't need to consider his future after demob because he would simply take up where he'd left off, running the corner shop with his widowed mother. 'I mean, Aldershot isn't exactly famous for its night life, is it?'

'Not really, no . . .'

'Whereas in Germany things are very different. They don't have such strict licensing laws, for a start. None of this closing at half-past ten nonsense. The beer halls are open till all hours out there, mate. Cheap beer, an' all.' He gave Doug a knowing look. 'The night clubs are something else. You should see the women.'

'Oi, this is your fiancée's brother you're talking to,' Doug cautioned him.

'You're Ellie's brother but you're also my mate.' Tom gave him a slow man-to-man grin. 'I got engaged to be married. I didn't take up holy orders.'

'Ellie thinks you're only half alive without her,' Doug reminded him.

'And I am,' Tom assured him. 'But moping around camp won't help.'

'If you say so.'

'I don't go out chasing women, if that's what you're thinking.' Tom didn't want Doug making trouble for him with

4

Ellie, whom he did actually love in his own selfish and cavalier way. 'I'm just saying that there's plenty of opportunity for those who want it.'

'Hmm.'

'You're only young once,' Tom was at pains to point out. 'If you can't have a few laughs when you're nineteen, when can you? I mean, when I get out of the army, it'll be the corner shop for me for the rest of my life . . . and marriage – in due course.'

'If marriage isn't what you want, why get engaged to Ellie?'

'It is what I want – *eventually*.'

Doug narrowed his eyes speculatively. 'You got engaged when your posting to Germany came through just so you could be sure of Ellie while you're away, didn't you?' he suggested.

'I won't deny that came into it, even though I know Ellie would never stray,' Tom admitted. 'Anyway, it made Ellie happy. It was what she wanted. And I do want to marry her . . . *when the time is right*. In the meantime there's no harm in grabbing a little fun and excitement, is there? You know I'd never do anything to hurt your sister in that way. Boozing with the lads, that's what I'm talking about.' He lifted his shoulders slightly and spread his hands. 'I might chat a woman up now and then for a laugh, but never more than that.'

'OK. There's no need to go on about it.'

Tom took a packet of cigarettes out of his pocket, offered one to Doug and lit one for himself. 'Anyway, this time next year we'll both be back in The Bush where the girls can keep their beady eyes on us,' he said, tipping his head back slightly before exhaling a cloud of smoke.

'That works both ways.'

Doug was actually joking but Tom chose to make an issue of it. 'I've no need to keep an eye on Ellie.' He sounded outraged at the suggestion. 'She'd never so much as look at another man.'

5

'No, she wouldn't,' agreed Doug, because his sister was the most loyal of women, and crazy about Tom.

'If you're having doubts about Ann,' said Tom, as though he was much older and wiser than Doug, 'marry her and get her pregnant. That'll clip her wings.'

'If Ann and I do decide to get married and have kids at some time in the future, it'll be a joint decision, not just a means of keeping her faithful,' Doug put him straight. 'Anyway, I don't have any doubts about her. She isn't the sort to play around.'

'You're too trusting,' chided Tom.

'So people are always telling me.' Doug drew hard on his cigarette, averting his eyes from his friend's disapproving stare and deciding to steer the conversation on to safer ground before an argument developed. He hated quarrels. 'I wonder if the girls are enjoying themselves on their night out together.'

'Bound to be, since they've gone to see the new Doris Day picture,' Tom mocked. 'Women can't get enough of those soppy, sentimental films.'

Tom was incredibly well informed about the opposite sex, considering Ellie had been his only serious girlfriend and he had no sisters, thought Doug, with uncharacteristic cynicism. '*Calamity Jane* is some sort of a musical Western, I think,' he informed him. 'I wouldn't mind seeing it myself.'

'You wouldn't catch me going to see rubbish like that,' snorted Tom.

'I've heard it's very good.'

'If you want to see it, you'll have to get Ann to sit through it again with you tomorrow night.' Tom paused, a thoughtful smile forming. 'Come to think of it, there are worse places to be than the back row of the pictures with your girlfriend on your last night of leave. If you know what I mean.'

'I'll wait and see what Ann wants to do.' Doug was noncommittal. 'As long as I spend my last night with her, I'm not too bothered about where we go.'

'Being serious, I wouldn't want to be with anyone except

6

Ellie on my last night either,' admitted Tom.

Doug drained his glass. 'In the meantime, let's go to the billiard hall, shall we?'

'There's no hurry.' Tom puffed on his cigarette. 'Let's have another drink first.'

'I'd rather go now,' Doug insisted. 'I don't want to spend the whole evening propping up the bar here.'

'Not do I.' Tom looked at the gold wristwatch his mother had given him for his eighteenth birthday. 'But there's plenty of time. It's still quite early.'

'We won't get a game tonight if we don't get there and book a table before they're all taken,' Doug pointed out. 'You know how crowded it gets down there on a Friday night.'

'What does it matter if we don't get a table?' Tom asked, irritation creeping into his manner. 'It's only a game of billiards. I'm not that bothered, anyway.'

'But we agreed to have a game.' Doug had a constant, uphill struggle to assert himself with this man. 'And I've been looking forward to it.'

Tension flared between them.

'I'm not leaving here until I'm ready.' Tom's voice was gruff with anger now, his eyes ice-hard. 'And I won't be ready until I've had another drink.'

'But—'

'Oh, stop being such an old woman, for God's sake,' interrupted Tom. 'You're really beginning to annoy me.'

Doug knew he shouldn't let Tom walk all over him; he also knew there was no point in trying to reason with him in this mood because it was a power game he was playing and he would accept nothing less than victory. Doug felt his courage dwindle under the force of the other man's personality, and hated himself for being so weak. 'Oh, all right, then,' he conceded, adding quickly, 'But only one more drink here. If you still don't want to come then I'll go on my own and find someone to have a game with when I get there.'

'Just one more, I promise,' said Tom, his amiable mood

returning now that he'd proved his was the superior will. 'Same again?'

'Just a half, please . . .'

But Tom wasn't listening. His attention had been diverted by the appearance of a young couple who came in and stood at the other end of the bar. They were both dark-haired and extremely striking in appearance. He was wearing a blue suit with a drape jacket; she had on a black suit with a tight-fitting skirt and perilously high-heeled shoes.

'I don't know who that Ray Brent thinks he is,' muttered Tom, looking resentfully towards the new arrivals. 'He must reckon he's a film star, or something, swaggering about in his flash clothes with his DA haircut.'

'He isn't doing us any harm.' Doug glanced towards the object of Tom's scorn. Both he and Tom knew the man only by sight because he was a little older than they, so had been in a different year at school. Ray Brent was very well known around Shepherd's Bush, though, because he was so noticeably good-looking and streetwise.

'It's all right for him,' Tom ranted on, looking surreptitiously at the dark-eyed Ray Brent, whose black hair was heavily greased and brushed into a high forward wave at the front. 'He can have sideburns and a quiff . . . he isn't in the army.'

'He's done his service, though,' mentioned Doug. 'I remember seeing him in uniform.'

'Yeah, well, maybe he has,' Tom admitted with reluctance, 'but he's still a creep.'

'You don't even know him to talk to. He's probably a nice enough bloke.'

'He's a flash git – anyone can see that,' insisted Tom. 'Look at him showing off.'

'How can he be showing off when he isn't taking any notice of anyone except his girlfriend?' Doug thought Tom's attack was totally unnecessary. 'Anyway, he's got as much right to be here as we have.'

8

'And look at the state of her,' Tom went on as though Doug hadn't spoken. 'It's a wonder she can walk in those shoes.'

'I don't suppose she intends to go out hiking in them,' observed Doug mildly.

'Common as muck.'

'She looks all right to me. And she's very attractive.'

'Of course she's attractive. Ray Brent wouldn't be seen dead with any girl who wasn't a looker.' Tom assumed the air of someone with special knowledge. 'His type has to continually prove that he can get one, you see. A beautiful woman on his arm is all part of his Mister Big act.' He puffed his lips out in a gesture of disapproval. 'Mind you, I wouldn't trust a woman who dresses like that. You'd never know what she was up to behind your back.'

'Depends on the woman, I suppose,' remarked Doug. 'Some girls like wearing what's in because they follow fashion, not to attract men. Ellie was saying only the other day that she'd like a pair of very high heels.'

'She's not going about in shoes like that,' announced Tom. 'I wouldn't allow it.'

'I don't see how you can stop her, if she really wants a pair.' Male dominance over women might well be the social norm but it wasn't something Doug felt comfortable with. It wouldn't occur to him to dictate to Ann.

'She'll do as I say,' stated Tom.

'That's between you and Ellie,' Doug decided wisely. 'Anyway, I don't know why you're getting so het up about Ray Brent. He and his girlfriend aren't interfering with us.'

But Doug did know why Tom was miffed. The green-eyed monster was rearing its head because of Ray Brent's good looks and charisma. One of the few advantages of being ordinary, Doug thought, was that you didn't have to worry about losing your place in the limelight.

'Did I say they were?' asked Tom.

'You're acting as though they are.'

'I don't like Ray Brent's type, that's all.'

'Forget him and get the drinks,' urged Doug lightly. 'It's your shout.'

'I'd rather leave,' announced Tom. 'Come on, let's get out of here, sharpish.'

'I thought you wanted to stay.'

'So I've changed my mind.' He was already moving away from the bar.

'There's no need to let Ray Brent drive you out of the pub,' muttered Doug, hurrying after him.

'No one drives me out of anywhere, mate.' Tom was most indignant.

'If you say so.'

'It's as you said,' explained Tom as they left the pub and headed across Shepherd's Bush Green. 'We won't get a game if we don't get a table booked.'

'You won't have any argument from me about that,' Doug told him, appearing to accept his explanation because it was easier.

Darkness had fallen and a haze of autumn mist shrouded the streetlights shining through the trees on the Green, the effect producing a soft orange cloud on the dark town skyline. The rattle of a tube train crossing the railway bridge added to the general rhythm of urban existence.

Doug was secretly thanking Ray Brent for speeding their departure from the Flying Goose. Despite what Tom said, Doug guessed he'd have put up more objections to leaving just to see if Doug really would carry out his threat and go without him. Thanks to Ray, Doug had got his way without the misery of an argument.

'Smashing film, wasn't it?' enthused Ellie Scott as she and her friend Ann left the cinema opposite Shepherd's Bush Green later that same evening.

'Lovely,' agreed Ann dreamily.

'Doris Day is so gorgeous, isn't she?' said eighteen-year-old Ellie, a tall, willowy girl with big blue eyes and a mass of red hair tied back in a ponytail. She was wearing a blue, loose-flowing coat and black ballet-pump-style shoes. 'I wish I looked like her.'

'Don't we all?' A well-rounded girl of Ellie's age with soft grey eyes and fair hair permed into a bubble cut, Ann added, 'But you look all right as you are.'

'With my red hair and freckles? Don't make me laugh.' The gingernut gibes of her childhood had left their mark on Ellie.

'Don't do yourself down,' Ann chided. 'Auburn hair might be in for a dig when you're a schoolgirl but it can be quite glamorous when you're older.'

'I'm not bothered, anyway,' smiled Ellie. 'Tom's happy with the way I look and that's all that matters to me.'

Passing the Shepherd's Bush Empire, they discussed its imminent closure as a variety theatre. 'My mum and dad won't half miss it,' Ellie remarked. 'They've always enjoyed a night out at the Empire.'

'It's going to be used as some sort of BBC studios, isn't it?'

'A television theatre, according to the local paper,' explained Ellie, glancing towards the foyer of the theatre that had been giving pleasure to audiences since 1903. 'They're going to be making TV programmes there in front of invited audiences, apparently.'

'How exciting!' exclaimed Ann.

Ellie looked at her, puzzled. 'How come, since we won't be invited?'

'We might get to see famous people going in and out when we're walking past,' explained Ann.

'There is that.' Ellie went on to say that she would walk to the bus stop with Ann, who lived in Acton so had to catch a trolleybus home. Ellie lived within walking distance of the Green.

'It's the boys' last day tomorrow,' mentioned Ann as they joined the bus queue.

'Don't remind me.'

'It's probably worse for you, as you and Tom are engaged,' Ann suggested.

11

'I must admit I hate the thought of his going back. But once he's actually gone, I get used to it again.' Ellie sighed, wanting to weep at the thought of being without her beloved Tom.

'Course you do.'

'No matter how far away he is, he's always here.' She pointed to her heart. 'And we've got through a year of being apart so we're on the homeward stretch.'

'It'll be over before you know it,' Ann encouraged.

'Yeah, course it will. I didn't think I could survive a day without seeing him when he first went away but somehow the time passed.' She looked mistily ahead. 'I live for his leaves, though.'

'It's a wonder you allowed him to go out with Doug tonight as you've so little time left together,' Ann remarked, pulling the collar of her tweed coat up against the damp autumn chill.

'Fat chance of my *allowing* Tom to do anything. He does what he wants,' she said, more with admiration than rancour. 'Anyway, I don't mind him spending time with his best mate. As long as I see him tomorrow night, you won't hear me complaining.'

'Anyone who interferes with the last night does so at their peril, eh?' smiled Ann.

'Not half.'

'Still, at least we can keep each other company while they're both away,' Ann suggested.

'Yeah, that'll be nice.'

Ellie and Ann had been strangers until Ann had started courting Doug just before he'd been called up. Being the same age and with similar interests, the two girls had struck an instant rapport. Ellie was fond of her reticent brother and delighted he'd found someone like Ann, who was slightly more assertive than he, but warm-hearted with it.

'Having you to chat to certainly helps me while Doug's away,' Ann confided.

Ellie gave her a close look. 'Is it getting serious between you two?'

'It is as far as I'm concerned but we'll just have to wait and see what happens when he comes out of the army and we're together more,' Ann told her. 'Because he went away soon after we met, it's been part-time courting up until now.'

'National Service is a flaming nuisance. It disrupts everything,' sympathised Ellie. 'It'll be a good thing when the Government phase it out.'

'Mm.' Ann leaned forward and peered through the mist to see if there was any sign of the bus. There wasn't. 'Have you set a date for the wedding yet?'

Ellie shook her head. 'I'd get married tomorrow if we could. But we have to get some money behind us first, so it'll probably be two or three years by the time we've saved up enough for the deposit on a place of our own.'

'Being engaged makes the waiting easier, though, I suppose?' her friend suggested.

'Oh, yeah,' confirmed Ellie. 'It makes you feel more secure.'

'How does it feel to be engaged to someone you've known all your life?'

'I've nothing to compare it with, of course, but it feels lovely. But then I've adored Tom for as far back as I can remember. It was a case of kid sister having a crush on big brother's best mate originally, I think. But I didn't grow out of it. It just got stronger.'

'How old were you when you started going out with him properly?' enquired Ann.

'Fifteen,' Ellie told her. 'I went to the pictures with him one night when Doug was ill and couldn't go.' Her eyes softened as she remembered. 'I think that was when Tom first began to fancy me. And it just sort of progressed from there. I can still hardly believe that I've got him. I didn't think I stood a chance, he being so gorgeous and everything.'

Ann made no comment.

'To marry Tom and have children with him is all I want from life,' Ellie went on. 'I've never wanted anything else.'

'You really should be more definite, Ellie,' laughed Ann, teasing her.

'I'm completely besotted, I know,' she confessed, smiling. 'I can't help it. I probably drive you all mad, always going on about how wonderful he is.'

'I don't mind. That's what friends are for, to listen to each other.'

'Tom can be a bit bossy but it's all part of his strong personality, and he's so sweet to me when he's in a romantic mood. So tender and caring,' said Ellie. 'I think my mum would rather I'd waited longer before getting engaged, though. She thinks I'm too young to tie myself down. Still, she hasn't made heavy weather of it.'

'What about his family?'

'There's only his mum,' Ellie told her. 'His dad died a couple of years ago.'

'Do you get on with her?'

'Yeah, we get on all right,' said Ellie. 'She dotes on Tom, though, especially since his dad died. He's an only child.'

'She isn't one of these clinging mothers who can't bear the idea of handing her son over to another woman, is she?' Ann looked anxious.

'She is a bit possessive of him at times but it doesn't really bother me. And she does seem genuinely pleased to be having me as a daughter-in-law,' Ellie went on. 'The fact that our mothers are such close friends has probably helped. Tom's mum has always been like an aunt to me. I suppose she feels less threatened by the idea of her son marrying someone she already knows.'

'You saw a lot of him when you were growing up, then?'

Ellie nodded. 'The two families were always in and out of each other's houses. We went on outings together, spent Christmas together . . . everything.'

'Very cosy.'

'Yes, it was, actually.' She pondered for a moment on the question of her future mother-in-law. 'I look at it this way – it must have been awful for Tom's mum to lose her husband so suddenly and it's only natural she would turn to her son for support. I would never try to come between them.'

'Course you wouldn't,' said Ann. 'You're not the type.'

The conversation was interrupted by the arrival of a trolley-bus, its trolley-wheel crackling on the overhead wires as it hummed to a halt. ' 'Bye, then,' said Ann, turning and moving forward with the flow of people.

'See you,' said Ellie.

Waiting until her friend had boarded the bus and waved from the window, Ellie began the walk home across the Green in a happy frame of mind.

Being of a generation largely sheltered from the horrors of the war by childhood and protective parents, she was as yet untouched by severe hardship. There had never been much money around at home but the Scotts had always got by, and now that the economy had improved generally, their standard of living was much less frugal than it had been in Ellie's childhood because the whole family was in regular employment. Ellie had a job as a clerk in a local insurance office, her father worked in an engineering factory, Doug was planning to be a lorry driver when he came out of the army, and her mother had a part-time job in a wool shop, which couldn't have been more appropriate because she was an avid knitter.

Ellie anticipated the future with a mixture of relish and impatience. It was wrong to wish your life away but it was difficult not to urge time onwards when you had so much to look forward to and the rest of Tom's army service still to be endured.

Comforting herself with the thought that she was officially engaged to him, she touched her engagement ring and counted her blessings.

Ellie's mother, Mary, was visiting Tom's mother that evening in her flat above the Chad Street corner shop. It was spacious living accommodation on two floors, well appointed but old-fashioned, with a dominant brownishness about it. Not for Pat Hall the brightly patterned carpet or jazzy contemporary wallpaper that had graced so many homes since the Festival of Britain in 1951 in stark contrast to the drabness of the years before. Nothing too colourful or daring for the conventional Pat.

'Well, it's been lovely having a chat and I'm really comfy sitting here but it's time I was going home,' announced Mary, putting her knitting down and covering a yawn with her hand. An accomplished knitter who could craft a garment while reading, listening to the wireless or having a conversation, she always had work in hand and never went visiting without it.

'Do you have to go so soon?' Pat hated to be alone.

'Afraid so,' said Mary, a blue-eyed redhead like her daughter, though currently the victim of a disastrous home perm that had gone frizzy.

'It's only just turned half-past nine.' Pat was a thin, angular woman with worried grey eyes and light brown, shop-permed hair that was set in symmetrical, scalp-hugging waves. 'You've got time for another cup of coffee, surely.'

'I'd love to but I really ought to be getting back.' Mary gathered her work and put it into a blue, leatherette knitting bag with a zip, her gentle eyes troubled because she knew her friend was lonely.

'But there's nobody in at home,' Pat persisted. 'You told me that Bob's gone down the Rose and Crown and the kids are both out. So why hurry back?'

'I've been here all evening, Pat,' Mary reminded her. 'And I want to make a bit of supper ready for when the others get in.' Pat already knew this but it suited her to pretend otherwise. 'Anyway, I don't want to be too late to bed because – as you know – I like to go out early on a Saturday morning to do the shopping before the market gets too crowded.'

'I'll put the kettle on for one last cup of coffee,' insisted the other woman. 'Come through into the kitchen and talk to me while I make it.'

Biting back a stab of irritation at her friend's ruthless determination to get her own way, Mary followed her into the kitchen, which had a grey mottled gas cooker, a deep sink with a wooden draining board, a small table and a kitchen cabinet painted a gloomy shade of dark green. Pat's kitchen did have one luxury item, though – a refrigerator, which thrilled Mary every time she saw it because Pat was the only person she knew who owned one. Pat had a television set too. She'd bought it for the Queen's Coronation earlier that year. Being the proprietor of a busy shop, she was better off than most of her neighbours.

'I really will have to go home soon, though, honestly.' Mary made it plain.

'When we've had this coffee, I'll throw you out,' said Pat, going against her nature and attempting humour in an effort not to seem too pressing. 'I've got to be up early myself in the morning to open the shop.'

'Tom sometimes does that for you when he's home on leave, doesn't he?' Mary asked.

'Yes, he's very good like that but I'll let him lie in tomorrow as it's his last day.'

'It doesn't hurt to give the boys a bit of spoiling when they're home,' approved Mary.

'It'll be a relief to me when he's finished with the army and can help me run the shop again so that I don't have to put up with staff from outside,' Pat confided. 'They don't have the same interest as family. You have to be behind them all the time.' She tutted, raising her eyes. 'I wouldn't trust Stan to be here in time to open up.' She was referring to her assistant, one of several she'd employed since Tom went away. They never stayed long. 'But then I wouldn't trust him with any sort of responsibility.'

'You can't expect an outsider to have the same interest in the shop as you have,' Mary pointed out reasonably.

'Which makes it all the more depressing because I know I won't find anyone suitable until Tom comes back.' Pat took a

17

bottle of Camp Coffee from the larder and measured the dark liquid into two fine china cups with a teaspoon, adding boiling water. She put a milk jug and sugar bowl on the tray with the cups and saucers and carried it into the other room.

'And talking of family, it won't be long before I'll be able to call you that, will it?' remarked Pat, continuing the conversation from an armchair.

A frown creased Mary's brow. 'I don't think the kids will be getting married for a long time yet,' she said.

'No, but when they eventually do . . .'

'Then we'll be as good as related.' Mary tried to share her friend's enthusiasm.

'It means a lot to me, you know, to feel closer to you and your family,' Pat told her.

Mary wasn't at all sure if the marriage of their children boded well for the friendship between herself and Pat. Might the leap from friend to family be a step too close? But Pat seemed keen and Mary didn't want to hurt her so she said, 'You and Tom are practically family anyway.'

'Ellie and Tom are lovely together, aren't they?' said Pat, waxing lyrical. 'Like two hearts beating as one, you might say. Completely right for each other.'

Her friend wasn't so sure about that either. Tom was a decent enough boy – he'd never been yobbish or in trouble – but he was noticeably short on humility and too overbearing in his attitude towards Ellie; he crushed her spirit somehow. Anyway, Mary thought, her daughter was far too inexperienced to commit herself to anyone. The only boy she'd ever been out with was Tom.

Being the easy-going type, Mary didn't make issue unless it was absolutely necessary, and hadn't seriously opposed the engagement because she thought it unlikely that the love affair would reach fruition at the altar. Ellie adored Tom but her adoration was a thing of youth which Mary hoped would run its natural course and end quite painlessly. But she said, 'They certainly do seem to be very fond of each other at the moment.'

'It'll be so much nicer for us, as the parents, to be coming together rather than finding ourselves linked with strangers, don't you think?'

Mary said what she knew Pat wanted to hear. 'Yes, course it will.'

The two women had been friends since infants' school; through childhood and adolescence, marriage and childbirth, their friendship had endured. They knew a lot about each other, told each other things, had shared their troubles and pleasures over the years. But the strength of their affection lay in their keeping a certain distance and respecting each other's privacy. Even though they lived within walking distance of each other, there had always been a tacit line over which neither had ever passed.

Theirs was an unlikely alliance, given their contrasting personalities. Mary had a relaxed, light-hearted attitude to life and no pretensions. Pat was grimly serious, with thinly veiled implications of superiority and uncompromising views on everything from the Government to the morality of the nation. But somehow the relationship had worked; they accepted each other's faults and tolerated them – most of the time, anyway.

But Pat had been hard going this past two years since her husband, George, had fallen victim to a fatal heart attack. She just didn't seem to have the mettle to cope with widowhood. People were sorry for her, of course, but her overt self-pity and abrasive attitude kept them at a distance. So, as her only real friend, Mary found herself cast in the role of sole comforter, needing to have succour constantly on tap. She accepted the task willingly and wanted to be kind but it wasn't always easy to stay patient with someone as difficult as Pat could sometimes be.

'I understand the young lovers have gone their separate ways this evening,' Pat was saying as Mary came out of her reverie.

'That's right.'

'I'm surprised they could bear to tear themselves away from

each other as Tom's so near to the end of his leave.'

'They've got the rest of their lives to look forward to,' Mary reminded her. 'And it will do the boys good to have a night out together as they happen to be on leave at the same time.'

'Ellie didn't mind then?'

'Of course not.' If Mary was any judge, Ellie hadn't had a say in the matter since Tom ruled the roost in that relationship. 'You know Ellie, she's easy-going like me.'

'A lovely girl.' Pat sipped her coffee.

'I think so,' said Mary proudly.

'You're so lucky having a daughter.' Pat's voice became heavy with discontent. 'I wish I'd been blessed in that way. I wouldn't be so lonely now if I had.'

'Daughters, as well as sons, have their own lives to lead, you know.' Mary's tone was meaningful. 'It's no good relying on your children for company when they're grown up.'

'Fat chance of my relying on Tom as he's away most of the time,' said Pat, missing the point. 'That's why I'm so glad I've got good friends like you and Bob.' Before Mary could respond, she added, 'I do appreciate your support. I hope you know that.'

Consumed with guilt for feeling impatient, Mary said kindly, 'Yes, I know you do, dear.'

They fell silent, drinking their coffee, each lost in her own thoughts.

'Have I told you how delighted I am to be having Ellie as a daughter-in-law?' asked Pat.

Ad nauseam, thought Mary, but said, 'Yes, you have mentioned it.' Being brutally honest, Mary suspected that Pat's ardent approval of Ellie had its roots in self-preservation. Pat was hoping to keep Tom close to home by making a friend of his intended. While Mary couldn't blame her for this, as the mother of the intended she was uneasy. She could see trouble ahead for Ellie, and her maternal instinct was stronger than her pity for Pat.

'George would have been so pleased to welcome her into

20

our family.' Pat sounded on the verge of tears now.

'Yes, I think he would,' agreed Mary lightly. 'He always liked Ellie.'

'I miss him so much I don't know how I get up in the mornings some days,' Pat confessed, her voice breaking. 'And it's been two years.'

'I'm sorry you're having such a bad time, dear. I'm sure it'll start to get easier soon.' Sympathy only seemed to make things worse so Mary decided on a little plain-speaking. 'Perhaps you should try to concentrate on the positive side.'

'Is there one?'

'There usually is if you look for it. You've got your health, and at least George left you well provided for,' Mary reminded her. 'You've got a good business so you don't have to worry about how to make ends meet.'

Even in her depressed state Pat couldn't resist seizing the opportunity for one-upmanship. 'Oh yes, there's no problem there. It would be far worse for someone . . . well, someone like yourself to be left on their own.'

Just when Mary's conscience was making itself felt, Pat reminded her why she was sometimes driven to seething impatience. 'I dare say I'd manage,' she said tartly. 'We might not be in the same league as you financially but Bob's a great believer in life insurance.'

Pat shot her a look and Mary saw fear in her eyes. She was afraid she'd go too far and lose her only close friend. 'I wasn't suggesting he isn't,' she explained. 'I meant—'

'I know exactly what you meant and it doesn't matter.' Mary forced a smile to keep the peace. If she'd let this side of Pat's nature seriously affect her, their friendship would never have got past the starting post. She finished her coffee, put the cup and saucer on a small table and stood up, clutching her knitting bag. 'But now I really must go.'

'Have I upset you?' asked Pat.

'Just a little,' Mary admitted frankly. 'Your suggestion that Bob and I are on our uppers didn't go down too well.'

'I didn't mean that.' She looked worried. 'I'm sorry if I've upset you.'

'Apology accepted.' Her tone was still slightly cooler than usual.

'Thanks for coming.'

She seemed so downcast and vulnerable, Mary relented, her tone resuming its normal warmth. 'Thanks for having me. I enjoyed it.' A slight distortion of the truth was justifiable under the circumstances, she thought. The loss of a husband was not an easy thing and Pat needed all the support she could get. 'I'll see you over the weekend sometime.'

'I hope so.'

They went down the stairs to the street door, which was next to the shop entrance.

''Night, Pat.' Mary gave her a friendly peck on the cheek.

''Night, Mary.'

Mary strode off into the night, relieved to get away and a little ashamed of that. Nostalgia for happier times, when Pat had been easier company, imbued her as she turned the corner into Marsh Road and approached the small Victorian terraced house she'd lived in for most of her married life. It was situated within serried ranks of others – modest dwellings with bay windows and tiny front gardens fringed with low walls and privet hedges. She walked up the path and turned the key in the lock, glad to be home.

'Time, gentlemen *please*,' shouted the landlord of the Flying Goose, becoming impatient at having to make a fourth announcement. 'Come on now, folks . . . haven't you got homes to go to?'

Most people had gone; there were just a few stragglers, among them Ray Brent, his girlfriend, Maria, and a very drunk young man called Keith Wilkes. An argument was in progress between Ray and Keith on account of Keith openly leching after Maria for most of the evening.

'Are you deaf or something?' growled Ray, scowling at the

other man. 'How many more times must I tell you to clear off and stop pestering the lady?'

'He's not doing any harm, Ray,' put in Maria. She was a terrible flirt and Ray suspected she might have been leading Keith on just for the fun of it. With his black-and-white check jacket and drainpipe trousers, crepe-soled shoes, and his hair greased and quiffed, Keith looked the business. 'He's had too much to drink, that's all.'

'She's not complainin', are you, darlin'?' Keith's speech was very slurred.

Ray had his arm firmly fixed round Maria's shoulders. 'Go on, then,' he said, looking at her. 'Tell him to get lost. If he hears it from you it might sink in.'

'You'd better go, Keith.' She wasn't very assertive.

'Just a kiss,' he begged.

'You're drunk,' she said, pushing him away none too convincingly. 'You don't know what you're talking about.'

'I do, you know.' He gave Ray a boozy look. 'And I know that you're too good for him.'

'You're asking for a smacking,' warned Ray.

'And who's gonna do it, eh, Brent?' enquired Keith.

'Me,' Ray informed him.

'You ain't got the bottle,' the other man mocked.

'We'll see about that . . .'

'You think you're such a big man around here, don't you?' muttered Keith. 'The King of Shepherd's Bush. Well, you don't frighten me.'

'Now then, lads,' admonished the landlord, who was washing glasses behind the bar. 'We don't want any trouble in here. Go outside if you want to settle your differences.'

'Come on, then,' Ray challenged Keith.

'No, Ray, no fighting.' Maria put a restraining hand on his arm, looking alarmed.

'He's asking for it,' was Ray's reply to that.

'Just lay off him, will you?' implored Maria. 'The bloke's had a few too many and doesn't know what he's doing.'

23

Ray looked at her. She was indisputably gorgeous with her dark hair, smooth complexion and voluptuous figure. She was a bit lavish with the make-up but the thick mascara and bright lipstick made her look even more deliciously exotic. Of Italian extraction, she reminded him of Gina Lollobrigida. But as lovely as she was, Maria wasn't easy to have as a girlfriend. Ray felt permanently threatened because of the male attention she attracted wherever they went. But he was mad about her. No matter what trouble she caused him, he still wanted her.

'Are you sure you're not encouraging him?' He threw her a shrewd look.

'Course I'm not,' she assured him. 'You know I've got eyes for no one but you.'

'That had better be true,' he told her.

'You leave her alone,' ordered the drunken Keith.

'Mind your own business,' Ray retaliated.

'You don't own her.'

'Oh, I've had enough of this.' With one swift action, Ray grabbed the man's arms and marched him to the door. 'Now get out and stay out,' he commanded.

'All right, I'm going,' mumbled Keith, and staggered through the door, uttering some ripe invective.

Back at the bar, Ray assured the landlord they'd be leaving shortly and drained his glass, idly chatting to Maria. On the way out, she went to the ladies, arranging to meet him outside.

'See you in a minute, then,' she said.

'OK.' He left the pub and went out into the misty autumn air, glad of the opportunity to cool off after the heated altercation with Keith Wilkes.

The market was buzzing with the terrible news the next morning. Mary couldn't believe it. Something like that happening around here! It was shocking! She was so shaken, she hurried home before finishing her shopping, deciding to go out later for the rest, when she'd calmed down.

'You'll never guess what's happened,' she said, bursting

24

into the kitchen where Ellie was at the sink washing the breakfast things and her father was sitting at the table drinking tea.

'Whatever's the matter, love?' asked Bob, a heavily built man with a shock of curly grey hair and big hazel eyes.

Ellie turned to look at her mother, drying her hands on the tea towel. 'You're as white as a sheet, Mum.' She was very concerned. 'What's happened?'

'It's so awful,' she told them, her voice quivering. 'Absolutely terrible.'

'What is?' asked Bob.

'There's been a murder,' Mary blurted out, putting her shopping bag on the floor and sitting down at the table, cheeks flushed, eyes fraught with worry.

'There's always been murders, love,' her husband pointed out in an effort to soothe her. 'No point in upsetting yourself about what you read in the papers.'

'I didn't read about it in the paper. Everybody's talking about it down the market.' Her gaze darted from one to the other. 'It was here – in Shepherd's Bush.'

The tea towel fell from Ellie's hand; her father put his cup down so shakily the tea spilled on to the table in a puddle.

'You're having us on,' he said incredulously.

'Would I joke about a thing like that?'

'No, course you wouldn't,' he conceded. 'It was just such a shock to hear you come out with it.'

'It shocked me having to say it, I can tell you.'

'When was this murder and where?' Ellie enquired.

'Last night, outside the Flying Goose,' Mary informed them gravely. 'A young fella from Acton – I think someone said his name was Keith Wilkes – died after a fight.'

'Oh my God.' Ellie turned pale.

'No wonder you're looking queasy, Mary,' sympathised Bob. 'Hearing about something like that when you're out shopping is enough to turn anyone's stomach.'

Ellie poured her mother a cup of tea and put plenty of sugar in it. 'Drink this, Mum; it's supposed to be good for shock,' she urged her, putting a comforting arm round her shoulder.

'Well, I hope they get whoever did it, and pronto,' declared Bob heatedly. 'We don't want any murderer on the loose around here.'

'They've already arrested someone, apparently,' Mary informed him.

'Thank God for that. We can do without scum like that walking the streets in our neighbourhood,' he said. 'Coming in from other areas and making trouble.'

'It wasn't anyone from outside,' she explained shakily.

'A local man?' Bob couldn't believe it.

Mary drank her tea thirstily, her mouth dry with nerves. 'It was Alfie Brent's boy, Ray,' she informed them gravely.

'Never!' exclaimed Bob.

'It's true,' she confirmed. 'He was arrested and charged last night. An open-and-shut case, apparently. A fight over a girl, according to local gossip.'

'Bloody hell,' gasped Bob.

'My thoughts exactly,' said Mary.

Ellie sat down quickly as a quivering in her knees threatened to take her legs from under her. She wasn't personally acquainted with Ray Brent, but knowing an alleged murderer even by sight made her feel very peculiar.

Chapter Two

'I suppose you've heard about the murder, Mrs Hall?' said a customer at the shop.

'Ooh, not much,' Pat told her with irony. 'Only from everybody who comes in. Nobody's talking about anything else this morning.'

'Shocking, isn't it?'

'Worse than shocking.' The two women were having this conversation while Pat sliced a wedge of Cheddar with cheese wire, picked it up with a sheet of greaseproof paper and placed it on the scales.

The customer sucked in her breath, looking doom-laden. 'A bit too close to home for my liking,' she proclaimed with a woeful shake of the head.

'You and me both,' agreed Pat.

'You don't expect something like that to happen on your own doorstep, do you?'

'Course you don't.'

'Makes you realise it isn't safe to walk the streets,' declared the woman, pulling her dismal brown coat further round her and tucking in the curlers poking out the front of her headscarf.

'Oh, I wouldn't go so far as to say that.' For the sake of her own sanity, Pat didn't want the incident blown out of all proportion. A murder in the neighbourhood could do terrible things to your nervous system when you lived alone. 'From what I've heard it was a fight that got out of hand.'

'It's still murder.'

'They *have* got the man responsible, though,' Pat pointed out. 'And it isn't as if he's suspected of killing anyone before now.'

'It's frightening just the same.' The woman was determined not to lessen the drama by allowing any positive aspect into the conversation. 'It makes you wonder what will happen next.'

'I should try not to let those sort of thoughts take a hold if I were you.' Sympathy and advice were all part of the job of a small shopkeeper and Pat issued both as a matter of course. 'It's just a one-off – not the forerunner to other awful things.'

'He's claiming he didn't do it, o' course, like murderers always do.' The customer was now in full flow and enjoying every moment, Pat guessed. Gossip of this calibre was almost unprecedented in this neighbourhood and the woman was milking it for all it was worth. 'My friend's sister's mother-in-law lives near the Brents, and the word is that Ray's father, Alfie, reckons his boy is innocent too.'

'Oh?' Pat paused in what she was doing and looked up. 'But I heard that Ray Brent was actually caught in the act, so to speak – that he was with Keith Wilkes when he died.'

'He was. But according to Alfie Brent, Keith Wilkes had already been in a fight and was dying when young Ray found him,' the customer explained.

'He would say that, wouldn't he?' opined Pat.

'Exactly,' agreed the other woman with barely concealed excitement. 'No one can blame any father for not wanting to believe the worst of his son. None of us wants to think bad of our kids, do we?' She drew a deep breath and let it out slowly with a sage movement of the head. 'But Alfie Brent is kidding himself if he thinks anyone else will believe his boy's story.'

'Mm,' nodded Pat, wrapping the small piece of cheese in the greaseproof paper.

Several other items were requested – a quarter of tea, a pound of Rich Tea biscuits, a tin of pilchards. Having worked through her shopping list, the woman returned eagerly to the topic. 'Mind you, I've seen that Ray Brent around the town,' she said, clearly relishing her own disapproval, 'and he looks like a right heathen with his drainpipe trousers and fancy haircut.'

Pat didn't pass comment; just concentrated on adding up the customer's bill.

'Does your Tom know him?' enquired the customer, as she handed Pat a two-shilling coin.

'Not as far as I'm aware,' Pat told her. 'But obviously I don't keep tabs on all his friends.'

'Of course you don't. I only asked because they're a similar sort of age,' the busybody explained. 'Still, it's all for the best if he doesn't know him. You don't want him mixing with riffraff like that, do you?'

'Certainly not.'

'Tom still home on leave?' she enquired chattily.

'Going back tomorrow.'

'Not helping you out in the shop this morning, then?'

'I'm letting him take it easy this morning as it's his last day.'

'A bit of spoiling never hurt anybody, I say,' the woman approved, looking around. 'Has Stan got the day off?'

'He's phoned in sick.'

'That's a nuisance for you, especially on a Saturday, your busiest day.'

'Friday is my busiest day, as it happens,' Pat corrected. 'People go to the big stores and the market on a Saturday.'

'Yes, I suppose they would,' said the woman, sounding bored with the subject.

Within seconds, however, she was back in her element when a sudden flurry of customers provoked further discussion about the murder, everyone far more interested in that than being served with their groceries. Pat was used to her shop being used as a local meeting point.

'Do you know the Brents at all, Pat?' enquired a woman who eventually managed to drag herself away from the debate for long enough to ask for a tin of baked beans and some custard powder.

'No, I don't know them.' She lowered her eyes as she spoke because what she was saying was an extremely economical version of the truth. She didn't know the Brents *now* and she didn't know Ray at all. But she had once known Alfie Brent – very well indeed.

'Poor old Alfie Brent. He must be in a right state, having had his son arrested for murder,' remarked Bob Scott that same day over a family lunch of stew and dumplings. 'Young Ray's everything to him.'

'You know Ray Brent's dad?' Ellie hadn't realised.

'Yeah, I know him. We were at school together,' her father confirmed.

'Do you still see him?' asked Ellie.

'Yeah, he's in the Rose and Crown every now and again. We sometimes have a chat. He's a decent bloke.'

'Alfie Brent had a bit of a crush on Pat Hall once, years ago.' Mary looked at her astonished daughter. 'There's no need to look quite so surprised.'

'Sorry . . . it's just that it's so hard to imagine Tom's mum being young and having the boys after her.' Ellie was being frank, not malicious.

'For your information, madam,' her mother admonished lightly, 'Pat hasn't always been Tom's mum. Your generation didn't invent love and romance, you know. We've had our moments too.'

'Before or after the Battle of Hastings?' teased Ellie.

'You watch it, young lady,' warned Mary, but she was smiling and taking it all in good part.

Bob wasn't smiling, though. He was still dwelling on what had happened last night outside the Flying Goose. 'Poor Alfie,' he said again. 'He's worked hard to give his son a decent upbringing and that's how he repays him – by killing someone.'

'Hey, hang on a minute, Dad,' reproached Ellie. 'Aren't you supposed to be innocent until proved guilty in this country?'

'That's what they say, yes,' her father admitted. 'But there isn't much doubt about Ray Brent's guilt in this case. I was talking to the bloke next door and he knows someone who was in the Flying Goose last night and he reckons that—'

'You've been listening to too much gossip,' interrupted Mary. 'Ellie's right. Innocent until proved guilty, that's the principle of British justice. All these stories that are flying about the neighbourhood are just conjecture.'

'Come off it, Mary,' argued Bob. 'Ray Brent was found with the dying man with his blood all over him. And not only that, there were witnesses who saw him arguing quite heatedly with Keith Wilkes inside the pub. The landlord heard Ray threatening to beat him up and saw him force him out through the door. Ray was seen going outside soon after that, apparently. If that isn't conclusive proof, I don't know what is.'

'I admit it does seem cut and dried,' his wife was forced to agree. 'But we don't know all the facts.'

'It'll be all over the papers soon enough, anyway,' Bob pointed out. 'We'll find out more about it then.'

'They won't have the full story, though, I bet,' was Mary's opinion. 'We'll have to wait until the trial before the whole truth comes out. Until then I don't think we should make assumptions and be too quick to judge.'

'You won't stop people gossiping and drawing their own conclusions,' said Bob. 'It's only human nature.'

'And they'll have Ray Brent hanged even before the case is heard,' Mary pointed out.

'Hanged!' The idea was repugnant to Ellie: it always had been. 'They won't do that, will they?'

'It depends on the evidence and the verdict,' her father told her.

'The thought of anyone being executed turns my stomach,' said Ellie.

'Because you're a naïve young woman with very little

31

experience of the world,' preached her father. 'A lot of people are all in favour of a life for a life. Keith Wilkes's family are probably of that opinion this morning.'

'Yeah, yeah, I know all about that side of the argument,' she said. 'But I'm entitled to my opinion.'

'Anyway,' her father went on, 'I should think it's more likely to be a long stretch in prison for Ray Brent, as the killing was the result of a fight. The charge will probably be manslaughter.'

The nature of the conversation curbed Ellie's appetite and she pushed her plate away.

Sitting next to her, her brother looked peaky too. Pale and heavy-eyed, he laid down his knife and fork.

'Is all this gory talk putting you off your food too, son?' asked his mother.

Doug nodded absently.

'I'm not surprised,' she said. 'It's a wonder any of us can eat anything with all this awful talk of murder and people getting hanged.' She threw her husband a look. 'Change the subject, Bob, for goodness' sake. We're trying to have a meal here.'

'You're too squeamish.'

'Sorry, Mum,' said Doug, looking woefully at his mother. 'It's no reflection on your cooking but I just can't eat any more.'

'But it's your favourite.' Mary set great store by the food intake of her family; she saw it as a barometer of their health and wellbeing. 'And you usually have such a good appetite.'

His father threw Doug a shrewd look. 'Except when he's got a thumping hangover,' he grinned. 'You look like death warmed up, mate.'

'I don't feel too good,' Doug admitted.

'A hangover? That's not like you,' commented his mother. Doug was the most moderate of men.

'I thought you and Tom went out to play billiards last night, not to get drunk,' Ellie put in.

'We did play billiards,' confirmed Doug.

'They would have had a few drinks as well, though,' Bob pointed out to his daughter. 'Billiards and booze go together like meat and gravy.'

'Any excuse for a booze-up.' Ellie was playfully bantering rather than making a serious point. She looked at her brother. 'I suppose the pair of you got plastered.'

'We had a few drinks.'

'Well, I hope Tom's not still feeling fragile when I see him tonight. It's our last evening together for a long time and I want to make the most of it.'

'He'll be fine,' muttered Doug distantly.

'Which is more than can be said for you, son,' observed Mary. 'Go and lie down.'

'Don't fuss, Mum.'

'A walk in the fresh air will do you more good,' claimed his father. 'Or a hair of the dog.'

'I'm feeling a bit queer actually.' Doug's face was ashen. 'Sorry about the meal, Mum, but . . .' The sentence remained unfinished as he rushed from the room.

'Poor lad,' sympathised Mary.

'Poor lad, my arse,' Bob disagreed good-humouredly. 'He's just paying the price of self-indulgence.'

Despite Mary's censorious comments, the conversation eventually drifted back to the murder after Doug had gone.

'I've seen that Ray Brent around the town,' Ellie mentioned as her mother served up semolina pudding and stewed apples. 'He seems very sure of himself and is a bit of a sharp dresser. But he isn't rough . . . doesn't look the sort to get involved in a fight. He certainly doesn't look like a murderer.'

'They come in all shapes and sizes, love,' her father pointed out. 'If they had a particular look about them, they'd all be taken off the streets.'

'You know what I mean,' said Ellie. 'He looks tough but not violent.'

'Looks can be deceiving,' he pointed out.

'Not always, though,' Ellie disagreed. 'The bother boys who

33

regularly fight outside pubs on a Saturday night have got trouble written all over them.'

'Yeah.' Her father couldn't deny that. 'I'm just saying that a violent streak isn't always obvious.'

'I suppose not,' Ellie conceded. 'Anyway, whatever Ray Brent has or hasn't done, he isn't short of female admirers. I know plenty of girls who fancy him rotten.'

'Are you one of them?' teased Mary.

Ellie raised her eyes disapprovingly. 'Mu-um,' she admonished, 'you know I don't fancy anyone but Tom. Anyway, Ray Brent only goes out with really gorgeous women.'

'He won't be going out with any women, gorgeous or otherwise, for a very long time,' stated Bob. 'Alfie's been a good father to him, an' all.' He was seeing the whole thing through a parental eye. 'He brought the boy up on his own too.'

'Why?' enquired Ellie.

'His wife died when Ray was a baby.'

'What a shame,' she said.

'It was too,' agreed her father. 'Alfie's a bit rough around the edges but he's a good man. Definitely the sort to have taught his son the difference between right and wrong.'

'I suppose the fight got out of control and right and wrong didn't come into it,' suggested Mary.

'It gives me the creeps,' responded Ellie.

'I'm not surprised. It's enough to scare anybody,' said her father, adding quickly, 'But you're quite safe, love. They've got him in custody. There are no maniacs on the loose.'

'There will be if Tom's still hungover when I see him tonight.' Ellie was making a conscious effort to lift the atmosphere. 'And it'll be me. I'll be *that* mad with him.'

They all laughed and the gloom dissolved. It had been a weird sort of a morning, though, Ellie thought.

Ellie and Tom went out dancing that night at the Hammersmith Palais. Ellie was determined to enjoy herself but she had her work cut out because Tom wasn't in the best of moods – liverish as a result of his hangover, she guessed. He seemed preoccupied and distant, hardly surprising with his leave at an end.

'I suggested to Doug that he and Ann join us tonight,' she mentioned casually when they were upstairs in the bar, having a drink at a table by the balcony which overlooked the dance floor. 'But he didn't seem to fancy it.'

'He probably wants to be on his own with Ann,' Tom suggested.

'Of course he does, and so do we want to be on our own,' she agreed. 'But Ann likes dancing so she might have wanted to come . . . and it isn't as though we'd have all been together while we're dancing or after we leave here. But he didn't appear to be paying attention to anything I was saying, to tell the truth. Mind you, he's had the most awful hangover. Probably that's what's making him miserable.'

'He's going back off leave tomorrow,' was Tom's scathing reply. 'Work it out for yourself.'

'All right, Tom,' she responded quickly. 'There's no need to get cross.'

As though realising that he'd been offhand with her and now wanted to rectify that, he leaned across the table and took one of her hands in both of his, looking into her eyes. 'Anyway, I'm glad they didn't come with us. I'd rather have you to myself for the whole of the evening.'

'Yeah, me too.' Her eyes were shining, red hair, looking darker in the dimly lit bar, falling loose to her shoulders. She was wistful as she added, 'I wish you didn't have to go back.'

'It's a pain for us both.'

'You'll write lots, won't you?'

'Course I will.'

They stared at each other, transfixed. 'You look lovely tonight,' he said softly at last. She was wearing a white blouse with a turned-up collar tucked into a circular skirt in green felt with a wide elastic belt. The style showed off her slim figure.

'You look nice too.' She paused, reaching forward to touch his cheek. 'You're a bit pale, though. Still suffering from the effects of last night?'

'Last night?'

'You can't fool me,' she said in a tone of playful reproof. 'I told you, Doug had the mother of all hangovers this morning, which accounted for the mood he's been in for the rest of the day, so if you tell me you aren't suffering from the effects of overindulgence last night, I won't believe you.'

'I did have a bit of a thick head this morning,' he admitted.

'Well, you don't need a lot of booze to have a good time when you're out with me so you'll have a nice clear head tomorrow morning.' Her manner was light-hearted. Being in such thrall to Tom meant that she never dared assert herself towards him in any serious way, though she acknowledged secretly that it wouldn't be like Tom to admit too readily that he couldn't take his drink.

He didn't reply and seemed to drift off into his own thoughts.

'You seem a bit quiet,' she said. 'Is it because you've got to go back?'

'Of course. You know I hate leaving you.' He raised a gallant smile, but Ellie could see the misery behind the brave show and she loved him all the more for it.

In an effort to dispel the gloom in the air, she said brightly, 'Come on, let's go and dance.' She was none too happy herself with his departure clouding everything but she managed to smile as she stood up and gave him a twirl, her stiff petticoats rustling. 'It's a slow one and the lights are low so let's make the most of it.'

'What a very good idea,' Tom said, brightening and giving her a loving smile.

They danced every dance after that, and wrapped their arms round each other in the Last Waltz. A passionate good night was said in the darkest corner of the alley behind her house, followed by a more demure one at her front door, for the benefit of her parents just in case they weren't asleep.

On Sunday afternoon Ellie went to the tube station with Tom to see him off to Liverpool Street Station where he was to get the train to Harwich and then the boat to the Hook of Holland en route for Germany. Their goodbyes had already been said so they didn't make a big performance of it now, just gave each other an affectionate hug and reaffirmed their love.

'You take care of yourself now,' he said with a half-smile, his handsome face brightly suffused with pink from the cold wind.

'And you take care of yourself too.' Her cheeks were glowing, the blue of her eyes vivid against the cornflower-coloured knitted scarf around her neck. 'That's an order.'

'I'll tell the sergeant to tuck me up in bed at night, shall I?' he said waggishly.

'Oh, Tom,' she admonished with an emotional giggle.

'Don't worry about me,' he told her. 'If nothing else, the army toughens you up.'

'Love you,' she said.

'Love you too.'

After a final embrace, he headed for the platform and she walked out of the station and along the main road towards the Green. The shops were shuttered and silent, the market closed, pigeons outnumbering people in the quiet of a Sunday afternoon.

Ellie blew her nose, comforting herself with optimistic thoughts of the future. The grinding tension had gone now that the actual parting was over; it was just a question of letting time pass with as much patience as she could muster. Ann was coming to the house for a chat later, after she'd seen Doug off. So that would help them both through the first lonely evening. Thank heavens there wouldn't be many more of these heart-breaking wrenches.

A chilling headline on a board outside a newsagent's shop jolted Ellie out of her reverie: 'Local murder – man arrested and refused bail.' A shiver ran up her spine. It was an odd feeling to think that headline news had been made so close to home. She doubted if she'd ever be able to walk past the Flying Goose again without remembering what had happened there.

Returning to the more immediate problem of life without Tom, she decided to visit someone who would also be feeling a bit lost this afternoon. His mother could be irritating at times with her strong opinions and cloying attitude towards Tom, but it must be lonely for her in the aftermath of his departure.

Feeling better for having focused her thoughts on someone else, Ellie headed for the Chad Street corner shop.

Ray Brent had thought he was beyond shock after what he'd been through this past three months, since his life had taken such a cruel and unexpected turn. But when he heard the foreman of the jury pronounce him guilty of manslaughter, his blood turned to ice.

He was still reeling as he heard the judge sentence him to ten years in prison. He felt sick and dizzy; for one awful moment he thought he was going to disgrace himself in front of the court by passing out cold. Ten years! Bloody hell! The three months he'd already spent in custody would be taken into account, but even so . . .

Dressed in a dark drape suit with a clean white shirt and best bootlace tie, his hair cropped prison style and bearing no resemblance to the fancy hairstyle he'd had before his arrest, he managed to stay on his feet despite swirling giddiness and nausea that brought him out in a cold sweat. Gripping the brass rail at the front of the dock for support, he lifted his chin resolutely and looked directly at the judge as he told the warders to 'Take him down.'

Keeping a firm hold on his self-respect had been enormously important to Ray throughout this whole ordeal. No matter how tough it got, he was determined not to be broken by what had happened. Shifting his gaze to his father in the public gallery, he met his eyes and lifted his head even higher to show him that he wasn't defeated. He actually wanted to weep at the pain in his father's eyes but showed no sign of weakness.

Despite his own trauma, Ray found room in his heart to be concerned for his father, who looked pale and exhausted. This terrible business had knocked the stuffing out of him. But, like his son, Alfie Brent wouldn't be beaten by it.

Ray and his father had always been close. Alfie was the person Ray cared about most in the world. Maria was no longer in the picture. She'd ended their relationship by letter almost immediately after his arrest. It had hurt a lot. But she had spoken up for him in court when she'd been called as a witness. She'd said that in all the time she'd known Ray he'd never committed any act of violence, and had always struck her as a thoroughly decent type. Her character reference hadn't swayed the verdict in his favour but it had left him feeling a little kinder towards her.

But now he could feel a firm grip on his arms. After one final agonising look at his father, he allowed the police to take him down to the cells.

It was the week before Christmas and Bob Scott was ensconced with a group of cronies in the public bar of the Rose and Crown. The men were commiserating with each other about the unfathomable nature of the female psyche. It was generally agreed that women were a strange breed at any time of the year but in the run-up to Christmas they were completely beyond the pale. This being the public bar it was mercifully free of them.

'You're better off getting out of the house and leaving 'em to it,' declared one man, gloomily.

'It's not safe to stay in,' said another.

'They make extra work for themselves and then complain because they've got too much to do,' said a balding man with a ginger beard. 'This, that and the other's got to be done before the big day. I've never understood why all the curtains have to be washed just because it's Christmas.'

''Cause you get more visitors, I suppose,' suggested some knowing soul.

'Who's gonna bother to look at the curtains at Christmas, I ask you?' was another comment.

'Christmas Eve is hell on earth while all the baking's going on,' said someone glumly.

'And God help you if you want a nibble of something festive a bit early,' said the ginger beard. 'There'll be three million sausage rolls and mince pies coming out of the oven and you're not allowed so much as a bite until everything's ready and she gives the word to say that Christmas has officially started.'

'Still, once the festivities are underway and the women have calmed down, we all have a whale of a time, don't we?' put in Bob. 'And all thanks to them. There would be sweet bugger all for Christmas if it was left to us men.'

There was a murmur of agreement and they moved on to a subject they did understand: football. They were discussing the recent performance of Fulham Football Club when a sudden silence descended over the bar. Following the gaze of the other men, Bob was startled to see the reason for it. Alfie Brent had just come in and was standing uncertainly by the door.

Every eye in the room was focused on Alfie as the place came to a standstill. The bar staff stopped serving, the punters stopped drinking. Then gradually heads were turned away from Alfie and the tense silence was broken by a mumble of disapproval.

'I know what you're all thinking.' Alfie's gravel tones filled the room, making heads turn back towards him.

'Bugger off,' shouted some nasty piece of work.

'No I won't,' retaliated Alfie defiantly. 'I haven't been in here for a drink since my boy was arrested because of people like you. I've been hiding away when I had no cause to.'

'Go back home to your bolt hole,' called out another

spiteful man. 'We don't want your sort in here.'

'I've as much right to be here as you have, and I've finished with hiding away,' announced Alfie. 'It's time I had my say, and you're going to listen whether you like it or not.'

The atmosphere was so tense Bob could almost hear his own heartbeat echoing across the room.

'You can say whatever you like but you can't make us listen,' said an unsympathetic character.

'My son didn't do it.' Alfie's voice boomed across the bar. 'He didn't kill Keith Wilkes.'

Into the ensuing silence the nasty piece of work said, 'More fool you if you've let your boy con you into believing that. But we're not that gullible.'

'You'd stand by him whatever he'd done,' said a cynic at the other side of the room from Bob.

'Yes, I would. I won't deny that and I'm not ashamed of it,' admitted Alfie, a tough-looking man in his forties, with expressive dark eyes, strong features and bushy black hair heavily peppered with grey. Even in adversity he cut an impressive figure. 'But I hope I would also be man enough to admit it if he was guilty. But he isn't. Keith Wilkes was already dying when Ray went out of the pub that night. He found him injured and was trying to help him. I don't care if you believe it or not, but *don't you dare* treat me or my boy like dirt under your feet.'

For a moment no one said anything.

'How do you know what happened? You weren't there,' someone challenged eventually.

'It's all down to something called faith,' replied Alfie. 'My son has told me what happened that night and I believe him. I'd know if he was lying.'

'Credit us with some intelligence,' said the cynic, with blistering disapproval. 'It's common knowledge that your boy was arguing with Keith Wilkes in the pub that night. The bloke was lusting after his girlfriend and Ray didn't like it. Any fool can work out what happened.'

There was a loud chorus of support from the heartless crowd in company with the cynic.

Bob decided it was time to make an intervention. 'Come on, chaps, be fair,' he said towards the gathering. 'Let the man have his say.'

'Yeah, give him a chance,' echoed one of Bob's mates to general agreement from the others.

Alfie nodded appreciatively towards Bob, then turned towards his critic. 'What you say is true,' he continued, his voice ragged with emotion. 'Ray was having an argument with Keith Wilkes in the pub but he didn't kill him.'

'Who did then? The invisible man?' mocked the cynic. 'There was no one else around.'

'I don't know who killed him and neither does Ray,' admitted Alfie. 'But it wasn't him.'

'Surely you wouldn't expect him to admit it,' said the cynic.

'If he'd done it, sure I would,' replied Alfie. 'But you'll find out. The truth will come out one day. Until then, how about showing me some respect? My boy's doing time for something he didn't do. What more do you want?'

There was a confused muttering. The crowd of cynics looked away in disgust. Others seemed awkward, as though they didn't know quite what to do.

It wasn't in Bob's nature to be spiteful and he didn't like it when other people were. In an impulsive action, he got up and went over to Alfie. 'What are you having, mate?' he said, raising his voice to reach the far corners of the room.

Alfie looked at Bob in surprise, as though he couldn't quite believe what he'd heard. 'You're offering to have a drink with me?' he asked.

'Well, I'm not offering you a three-course meal,' grinned Bob to ease a difficult moment.

'Thanks very much, mate.'

Bob saw the face so taut with stress soften with relief.

As the two men walked towards the bar, the tension in the room lessened and the hum of normal conversation resumed.

Following Bob's example, several other men came up to Alfie and offered words of support. Bob's friends were among them.

'You seem to have worked some sort of a miracle,' commented Alfie, and Bob noticed the dark circles under his eyes, the grim set of his mouth. 'I appreciate it.'

'Most of the blokes are all right. There's always one or two who like to think the worst when something happens they're not sure about,' Bob told him. 'It just needs one person to take a stand and the rest soon follow.'

'I didn't want to hide away as though I've got something to be ashamed of,' Alfie explained.

'And why on earth should you?' Bob encouraged. 'Take no notice of those few troublemakers. They get their kicks out of making bother.'

'Your having a drink with me means a lot,' Alfie confided. 'I've been pretty much alone this past few months.'

'I can imagine.' Bob gave him a sympathetic nod. 'Still, now that you've broken the ice there'll be no need for you to stay at home on your own every night, will there?'

'Thanks to you, no.'

Suspecting a potential misunderstanding, Bob knew he must speak his mind. 'Listen, mate,' he began, his kind heart making this difficult for him, 'just because I've given you my support here tonight, that doesn't mean I share your belief in Ray's innocence.'

'I suppose not.'

'How can I when I can't possibly know the truth about what happened that night?' Bob didn't want Alfie to be hurt later on because he'd read more into Bob's gesture of support than there actually was.

'Don't worry about it, Bob. I understand.' Alfie looked disappointed, though.

'But I do know that whatever happened that night it had nothing to do with you,' continued Bob. 'And I'll be proud to have a drink with you in here any time you like.'

'That's nice to know,' said Alfie.

Bob shrugged his shoulders casually. 'So what's it to be then?'

'I'll have a pint of bitter, please,' said Alfie, managing a half-smile.

'A pint coming up.' As Bob turned away towards the bar, he felt choked with compassion that he daren't let the other man see. Alfie was a proud man and would be offended by anything even resembling pity. It was respect he was after, and rightly so. Bob admired him for having the courage to stand by his son in such appalling circumstances.

Alfie Brent was a strong man but anyone could see that his heart was breaking. 'Two pints of bitter, please,' Bob said thickly to the barman.

Chapter Three

When Elvis Presley became a household name in an explosion of controversy in 1956, Ellie thought he was wonderful. Her mother flew in the face of her own generation by admitting to enjoying his music, Tom claimed that the singer was a talentless git, and Pat, predictably, thought that both Elvis and his eloquent pelvis should be banned from public exposure altogether.

'The man is thoroughly offensive . . . not far short of obscene,' she complained. 'A bad example to young people. Openly encouraging them to be immoral.'

'Such a fuss everybody's making,' objected Mary mildly. 'He's only a singer.'

'But he doesn't *just sing*, does he?' Pat was keen to point out. 'It's the message he conveys with his lyrics and his disgusting gyrations that are causing such offence. If he did what he does on stage on the street, he'd be arrested.'

'If the police could get to him through the crowds of adoring young women,' grinned Mary, deliberately making light of it because Pat was being so pompous. 'He's an entertainer and it's all part of his act.'

'As an entertainer he has an influence on people, especially the younger generation. They make idols of pop singers these days,' Pat went on heatedly. 'Anyway, I don't know why a woman of your age is supporting him.'

'And I don't know why you're getting so het up about it,' Mary told her intolerant friend. 'It isn't as though you've any teenage children who might be affected by him. And Tom certainly isn't likely to be corrupted.'

'I was thinking in terms of the general good,' was Pat's curt explanation.

'Well, I like his music and I don't mind admitting it. It's new and different,' said Mary. 'And I do actually think he's got a very good voice. OK, so he's a bit near the mark, but he certainly knows how to put a song over.'

'Tuneless, incomprehensible drivel,' snorted Pat. 'He should have stuck to driving trucks.'

'A lot of people are very glad he didn't.' Mary was determined to stand her ground. 'Anyway, he's just the latest craze. This time next year the youngsters will be drooling over someone else.'

'In the meantime, what sort of example is he setting to young people . . . young women like Ellie?' Pat was as resolute to make her point.

Mary chuckled at that one and couldn't resist a little devilment to bring Pat down off her high horse. 'Ellie is nearly twenty-one and soon to be married. If her knickers come off, it won't be any fault of Elvis Presley's.'

'Really, Mary,' objected Pat with scathing disapproval. 'Do you have to be so crude?'

'You do rather ask for it, dear,' Mary said sweetly.

Not only was 1956 a good year for 'that husky young truck-driver from Memphis', it was also an excellent one for Ellie. Having saved up enough for the deposit on a house, she and Tom got married in the autumn, just after her twenty-first birthday. She had the wedding she had always wanted, with a long white dress, church bells, and a reception at a hotel with dancing in the evening for all her friends and relatives. Now engaged to Doug, Ann was a bridesmaid and Doug the best man.

A good time was had by all. As Mary had been proved wrong in her predictions about the romance, she respected the couple's love for one another and did all she could to make the day unforgettable for her daughter. When it was the moment for the couple to depart for their honeymoon the band was playing Elvis Presley's worldwide hit 'Heartbreak Hotel'.

'Ours won't be a heartbreak hotel,' Ellie said to Tom as they left the reception in a shower of confetti. 'Ours will be a hotel of happiness and love.'

In fact, it wasn't a hotel at all but a shabby guesthouse in windswept, out-of-season Clacton-on-Sea. The nearest thing to ensuite facilities was a jug and bowl on a hideous washstand, the bathroom being located on a lower floor along a creaky landing and down some rickety stairs.

The sour-faced landlady, Mrs Daly, made it clear on their arrival that guests weren't welcome in the house during the day and that she locked the front door at night at ten thirty on the dot. Breakfast was at eight o'clock sharp and high tea at precisely six. You missed them at your peril.

'It sounded really nice in the advertisement,' said Ellie gloomily. She and Tom had chosen the honeymoon accommodation together from the holiday ads in the local paper. Now they surveyed the musty bedroom with disappointment, observing its ugly furnishings, out-of-date décor and absence of the much-vaunted seaview in the advertisement.

'I can't see us lasting the week out here with Dracula's mother downstairs, can you?' Tom asked miserably.

'Not really.'

'I reckon we'll be so fed up we'll head for home in a day or two,' he predicted.

But they didn't. Despite the cold wind, sheeting rain and the snarling presence of Mrs Daly at their lodgings, they were blissfully happy. In between showers they braved the seafront with their arms entwined, and sheltered from the rain in cafés and coffee bars, drinking coffee and longing for the night when they could snuggle up together in the high double bed with its icy starched sheets and mattress that dipped in the middle. Mrs Daly, whom they nicknamed 'Drac', became a source of private amusement to them. They parodied her disapproving manner, going into fits of laughter under the sheets then making sweet, satisfying love.

Ensconced in her new husband's arms in the lumpy bed in the draughty room with the windows rattling from the force of the elements, Ellie was totally content. She had waited a long time to be Tom's wife and it was worth every moment.

One Friday evening a few weeks after their return from honeymoon, Ellie hurried home from the office and set to work enthusiastically in the kitchen of the little terraced house in Fenleigh Gardens that she and Tom had bought. Situated some ten minutes' walk from their parents, it was an old property but they had modernised the kitchen and furnished it in contemporary style, having saved steadily throughout their long engagement.

In a happy mood, she was humming a tune as she chipped some potatoes, seasoned steak and prepared some mushrooms and a salad. Being a Friday there was a feeling of incipient holiday, even though Tom had to work on a Saturday, and they were having steak as a treat. Cooking and keeping house was still a novelty to Ellie and she thoroughly enjoyed it.

Serving the food on to the plates, she heard his key in the door. 'What perfect timing,' she said, turning to smile at Tom as he came into the kitchen.

Looking towards her culinary creation on the worktop, he frowned. 'Is it?'

'I've done something special for us, as it's the weekend.' Her happiness faded as she perceived his filthy mood.

'So I can see.'

'I'm glad you're so thrilled about it.' Disappointment drove her to sarcasm. 'What's the matter?'

'We're eating at my mother's this evening,' he stated categorically.

'Oh, really? Who says?'

'I do.'

'How come I knew nothing about it until this minute?'

'It was a spur-of-the-moment thing that I arranged just before I finished work,' he explained. 'Mum seemed a bit down and I thought she could use some company.'

Ellie wanted to be a friend to Pat, and tried never to come between her and Tom. Throughout her relationship with him she had been almost fanatically dutiful towards his mother, at pains to make sure she didn't feel excluded. But this evening she wanted her husband to herself.

'Well, you'll just have to go round there and tell her we can't go, won't you?' It was almost unheard of for Ellie to object to anything Tom had arranged. 'Because I've already cooked a meal for us.'

'Too bad.'

'You shouldn't have made arrangements without telling me,' she admonished.

'I thought I'd be home before you started cooking.' His irritation was obvious.

'That isn't the point,' Ellie said coolly. 'You shouldn't have arranged it without talking to me about it first. I wouldn't do that to you. I would never just go ahead and assume you would be willing to do a thing without checking with you first.'

'Oh, stop going on about it, for God's sake, woman,' he snapped. 'I've had an exhausting day and the last thing I want is a load of earache from you.'

'I haven't been sitting about contemplating my navel either,' she retorted.

'Don't make me laugh. Your job's a holiday compared to mine, sitting down all day in a nice comfortable office. I wouldn't mind it, I can tell you,' he said nastily. 'I've been rushing about all day, delivering orders and standing behind the shop counter serving queues of yakking women. Friday is our busiest day and I've been on my feet with hardly a break.'

'All right, so you've worked harder than I have and you don't want an argument.' His domination of her had begun at such an early age subservience was ingrained in her. Even this minor rebellion was giving her palpitations and nausea. It was only anger that was driving her on. 'Well, I don't want an argument either. But nor do I want to go to your mother's. Even apart from the fact that I've already cooked us a meal, I don't actually *feel* like going to see her tonight.'

His eyes darkened with fury. 'Well, that's just too bad because we're going. And that's all there is to it.' There was such brutal harshness in his tone, she was inwardly trembling.

'And what am I supposed to do with this?' She waved her hand towards the food.

'I've no idea,' Tom said with blatant disinterest. 'Save it for tomorrow and warm it up, I suppose.'

'You can't warm up steak and chips,' she informed him angrily. 'It'll taste foul.'

'You'll just have to chuck it away then, won't you?' was his cutting retort. 'It's only a bloody dinner, Ellie . . . it isn't a matter of life and death.'

This issue went deeper than just wasted effort and unwanted food. This was about his casual disregard of her feelings. 'But it's your favourite.' Annoyingly, she could feel tears smarting. All had been sweetness and light between them since the wedding – Tom had been especially kind and loving, and setting up home together had been such fun – which made this first married argument all the more painful. 'I cooked it specially because I know you like it. The steak cost a fortune.'

'You shouldn't have bought it if it was too expensive,' was his ungrateful retort.

'I won't again, don't worry. It's the last time I'll put myself out for you.' They both knew she didn't mean it.

Tom emitted a sigh of seething impatience. 'Look . . . I'm sorry you've gone to the trouble of cooking a meal that isn't needed.' There wasn't a hint of contrition in his tone. 'But my mother is feeling lonely and I offered her our company for a few hours this evening. Is that really too much to ask of you, a couple of hours of your time? You and I have each other. She's on her own. It isn't easy for her now that I've left home.'

Now Ellie was ashamed. She felt selfish, like some awful clinging wife who was jealous of her husband's affection for his mother. 'I'm sorry.' She bit back the tears she knew would annoy him. 'I was so disappointed because I was looking forward to an evening on our own, I just lashed out.'

'Yeah, I know.' His tone was softer now but there was still no sign of a genuine apology. Remorse didn't feature in Tom's vocabulary.

'I was being selfish,' Ellie said, putting herself in the wrong, as usual. 'I'll clear this food away and we'll go to your mum's. As you say, she's on her own. We can be together any time.'

'Come here.' He opened his arms and she went into them without hesitation. He won every argument simply because she could never stay angry with him for long.

'I hope you hadn't already cooked something before Tom told you you were coming to me, Ellie dear,' said Tom's mother as they sat down to sausages and mash with tinned peas in Pat's dismal dining room. 'I wouldn't want to put you out.'

Ellie thought about the meal she had taken such care with, now moulding away in the rubbish bin. 'No, I hadn't started anything,' she fibbed, to save Pat's feelings.

'That's all right then.' Pat shook the pepper pot over her meal and turned to her son. 'You ought to have the phone put on at home, you know, Tom,' she suggested. 'There would be no problem letting Ellie know about any last-minute change of plan then. It would make it so much easier for us all to keep in touch.'

'That's a good idea, Mum.' He was full of enthusiasm. 'I think I'll do that.'

Not a word to Ellie about her opinion on the subject, she noticed. 'I think you'll have to wait quite a long time to get it put on,' she said to show them that she did actually have a voice. 'I've heard that the GPO have a very long waiting list.'

'The sooner we apply the better then,' enthused Tom, who'd

been accustomed to being on the phone at home because of the shop. 'I must admit I have been feeling a bit cut off since I moved out of here.'

'I'd be happier knowing you were there on the end of the line if I needed you,' mentioned his mother.

I bet you would, thought Ellie, hating herself for such vicious thoughts but unable to stem the flow.

Tom turned to Ellie. 'It'll be good being on the phone, won't it?' he said excitedly. 'You'll be able to ring all your friends up for a good old natter.'

'Not many of them have telephones,' she pointed out.

'They soon will have, though. More people are getting wired up all the time,' he announced with an air of authority. 'It's the demand that's causing the waiting list. I don't know why I didn't apply for one as soon as we moved in.'

'I suppose we've had other things on our mind,' said Ellie with emphasis on the 'we'.

This little reminder that they were actually a partnership was lost on Tom, who was busy deciding on the location of the telephone in their home.

'Most people seem to have them in the hall, I think,' mentioned Pat.

'That's probably the best place for ours then,' he decided, sounding pleased with himself.

Discussion of the enormous advantages of the telephone dragged on for a while between mother and son, until they drifted on to the shop, a subject which also excluded Ellie and lasted until the end of the meal.

'Sorry, Ellie dear,' apologised Pat, after some tedious dialogue about stock, wholesalers and competition to the corner shop from the big self-service stores that were opening everywhere. 'Tom and I get carried away once we start talking business.'

'That's all right,' she said, trying not to sound cross.

'You should come and work with us, then you'd be a part of it all.' Pat's manner suggested that this was all Ellie had ever wanted. 'We could do with another assistant and I'd like to keep it in the family.'

Guessing that such an arrangement would mean dogsbody status for Ellie while those two lorded it over her, she said, 'I'm quite happy with the job I have, thanks.'

'But you're one of the family now,' persisted Pat. 'And this *is* a family business.'

'I'd rather stay where I am, if you don't mind.' For the sake of her sanity as well as her marriage Ellie knew she mustn't allow herself to be bullied into this. The strain on both would be too much. 'But it was kind of you to offer.'

'Oh.' Pat's brows crept up in dismay. Ellie guessed she'd expected her to be overwhelmed with delight about it. 'It's your decision, of course.'

'Nice of you suggest it, though,' said Ellie politely.

Pat shrugged dismissively, then turned her attention to her son. 'You go in the other room and put your feet up in front of the telly, dear. Ellie and I will clear away and do the dishes. We'll bring you in a nice cup of coffee when we've finished.'

Having been indulged by his mother all his life, Tom needed no second bidding and wandered off into the other room.

As Ellie helped Pat to clear the table, she was feeling tense. What she'd regarded up until now as mild interference from a lonely woman was beginning to seem more like manipulation by a determined one as Pat insinuated herself more confidently into their marriage. She'd rule their lives completely if Ellie didn't put her foot down.

But that wasn't a simple matter. If she mentioned it to Tom he would deny that it was happening. And she had a horrible suspicion that if she openly opposed Pat he would take his mother's side against his wife.

The compassionate side of her nature was proud of him for taking his filial duties so seriously. The part that was so desperately in love with her husband and wanted their marriage to work, rebelled against it. Trouble was, there wasn't much she could do without hurting someone.

A week or so later something happened, or rather didn't happen, that pushed all else to the back of Ellie's mind.

'You can't possibly be pregnant,' was Tom's reaction when she told him that her period hadn't arrived. 'We've only been married five minutes.'

They were about to go to bed and she was sitting at the dressing table brushing her hair while he was already in bed. 'I'm almost certain I am,' she told him, her hair crackling and flying with static electricity as the brush went through its thick wavy locks. 'I'm never so much as a day late. Anyway, there are other symptoms too.'

'That's just your imagination because you're so worried you might be pregnant,' he said dismissively, lying back against the pillows frowning.

'I'm not worried,' she corrected. 'I'd love to have a baby. Wouldn't you?'

'Eventually, I suppose. But not yet,' he said adamantly. 'We've only just got married.'

'It must have happened on our honeymoon,' she pondered, getting into bed beside him. 'I remember we were a bit careless one time.'

He stared into space, mulling over the possibility. 'You'd think you could be reckless just once without getting caught, wouldn't you?'

'Some people probably get away with it for ages,' she smiled, 'but judging by the way I feel, we haven't.'

'Don't start looking at prams yet,' he advised hopefully. 'It might be just a false alarm.'

It wasn't. Ellie's pregnancy was confirmed and the birth expected the following summer. Ellie was thrilled. Tom was initially furious but warmed to the idea once he got used to it, albeit not with quite the same fervour as his wife. 'Having a kid might be all right, I suppose. It's nice for a man to have a son,' was the way he saw it.

'It might be a girl.'

'Yeah, there is that,' he said as though this were only a distant possibility. 'But I'd rather have a boy.'

Ellie felt so complete within herself and full of plans for the future and motherhood, issues that had bothered her before now paled into insignificance: Pat's possessiveness of Tom; Tom's domineering attitude towards herself. It all went over her head as she revelled in the thought of the new life she was carrying, and waited for nature to take its course.

Fortunately it hadn't taken its course sufficiently in February to prevent her from being matron of honour to Ann when she and Doug got married. She just about managed to squeeze into the blue satin dress that Ann had made for her.

The newly-weds set up home just a few minutes' walk from Ellie and Tom, which was convenient for the whole family. As spring turned to summer life fell into a blissful pattern for Ellie. Six weeks before the birth she gave up work to become a full-time housewife with no desire or plan to return.

When the pregnancy snailed towards the final stages, the days seemed endless. The weather was warm and Ellie lethargic. She didn't have the energy to do much more than lumber through her domestic chores and sit around knitting. Her mother had taught her how to do it as a child and she'd enjoyed it but had lost interest during her teens. Now she knitted furiously for her baby – matinée coats, leggings, hats, mittens, jumpers. With her mother busy making baby clothes too, the new arrival would have an extensive wardrobe.

'I don't know how you can do that so fast without looking at it. You're like a blooming machine,' remarked Ann one warm summer evening. Doug and Tom had gone out for a game of billiards so the two women were keeping each other company at Ellie's. They were sitting in the living room with the french doors open. It was a light, pleasant room with pale walls, greyish-blue patterned carpet and contemporary furniture in a soft shade of grey. The scent of lilac wafted in from the small back garden.

'My technique is bound to have improved because I've done such a lot of knitting since I've been pregnant,' replied Ellie, who was radiant with health, eyes bright and clear, face lightly tanned and freckled from having time to sit in the garden. Pregnancy suited her and she looked attractive in a loose flowered top and royal-blue maternity trousers. 'It's something I really enjoy. I take after my mum in that way. She's always clacking away, as you know.'

'I admire you both.' Ann was looking cool in a navy and white spotted summer dress, her fair hair short and layered. 'I can't knit to save my life.'

Ellie shrugged. 'Each to their own.'

'Exactly.' Ann gave her friend a close look. 'Anyway, I expect you're sick of people asking you, but how long have you got to go now?'

'Two weeks according to the doctor, a week according to my reckoning,' said Ellie. 'But the midwife said it could come any time now.'

'Still set for a home birth?'

'Yeah. There are no problems so the doctor is quite happy for me to have the baby at home,' she explained. 'Thank goodness for that. I hated the idea of having to go into hospital.'

'You look really well,' Ann complimented her.

'Fat, you mean,' laughed Ellie.

Ann grinned; she had the most pretty smile that put dimples in her cheeks. 'At least you've got an excuse for it,' she said, glancing towards her own chubby proportions. 'I hope you feel as good as you look.'

'I feel heavy, exhausted, constantly wanting to pee, and plagued with indigestion.' She giggled at her own catalogue of doom and added, 'But it's all worth it because I'm looking forward to this baby *so much*.'

'I'm quite excited about it too,' confessed Ann warmly,

finishing her coffee and putting the cup and saucer down on an occasional table.

'I hope you're planning on providing it with a cousin quite soon,' Ellie said lightly, knowing that her friend wouldn't see her remark as an intrusion. 'It'll want some company later on.'

'You never know.' She pushed her fingers through her hair, leaning back slightly in a relaxed manner. 'We're not intending to leave it too long. Doug's earning decent money, especially on the long-distance runs so it won't be the end of the world for me to give up my job in the builder's office.'

'We weren't planning on having this one so soon but now it feels as though it's all we ever wanted.'

'Tom's happy about it now, then? I remember you saying he wasn't too pleased at first.'

'He wasn't ready, wanted us to have more time on our own, that's all,' Ellie explained. 'But he's fine about it now. It isn't quite the same for men, though, is it?'

'And talking of men, there's something I want to talk to you about.'

'Oh?' Ellie's heart lurched because Ann's mood had become serious, her soft eyes clouded with worry.

'I'm worried about Doug,' she told her.

'Why? Not ill, is he?'

'No, not physically, anyway,' Ann replied. 'But I think he's deeply troubled about something and it's affecting his mental health.'

'In what way?'

She bit her lip anxiously. 'Bad dreams and moods of melancholy.'

'Oh dear. Might it have something to do with the fact that he has to go away for his work?' suggested Ellie. Doug was away from home when he was on long-distance runs. 'He's always been a bit of a home bird.'

'No, it isn't that.' Ann didn't sound in any doubt.

'What makes you so sure?'

'The violent nature of the dreams. He wakes me up,

shouting and screaming and punching the air. When he comes to himself he's shaking like a leaf. Being away from home now and again wouldn't affect him like that, surely?'

'I shouldn't have thought so,' agreed Ellie. 'But what could it be that's causing him such distress?'

'He says he doesn't know.'

'But you think he does?'

'I'm sure he must do.' Ann was thoughtful. 'You know yourself that dreams usually linger for a while in your mind after you wake up, even if you can't remember a thing about them later on.'

'Mm, I suppose so,' agreed Ellie.

'I can hardly interrogate him about the content of his dreams, can I,' Ann continued, 'since a dream is such a personal thing. But he's obviously troubled or he wouldn't be having nightmares. And the worst thing is, he won't talk to me about it.'

'What sort of things does he say when he's shouting in his sleep?' Ellie enquired.

'It's barely comprehensible,' Ann told her. 'Seems to be shouting and swearing mostly.'

'That's odd in itself,' mused Ellie, 'since you don't often hear him use bad language when he's awake.'

'That's what I thought.'

Ellie was thoughtful, casting her mind back. 'I've just remembered something,' she said. 'He used to talk in his sleep sometimes when he lived at home. His bedroom was next to mine and I used to hear him yelling through the wall.'

'He's been prone to that sort of thing all his life then?' probed Ann.

'Oh no, not all his life. I don't recall him doing it when we were children,' she said, trying hard to remember. 'I seem to recall it starting when he was in the army.' She paused, giving it more thought. 'Yes, I first noticed it when he was on leave once. I know it was then because I remember thinking I wouldn't be disturbed when he went back.'

'So at least we know when it started,' remarked Ann.

'I used to tease him about it the next morning,' Ellie told her. 'He always just laughed it off and I didn't want to embarrass him by prying.'

'He makes light of it now too,' said Ann. 'He'd deny it was happening at all if he didn't wake me up so that I see him in such a state.'

'It's strange,' murmured Ellie. 'But if it doesn't worry him, why not just try to live with it?'

'Because it isn't normal to have nightmares, and I'm sure they are happening because he's desperately worried about something.' Ann paused. 'And, as I said, it isn't just dreams. He gets these dark moods every so often as well, goes all quiet and withdrawn . . . sort of shuts himself off from me.'

'He's always been the quiet type,' Ellie reminded her.

'This is more than just quiet,' Ann told her. 'This is downright moody. When we were courting he used to be moody. As far as I can remember it started during the latter part of his army service.'

'About the same time as he started talking in his sleep then,' Ellie remarked.

'It must have been about then,' said Ann. 'But it's only since we've been married that I've got to know about the nightmares because I'd never spent a night with him before that. And, of course, now that I'm living with him I'm more aware of the moods because we're together all the time.'

'Perhaps something upsetting happened when he was in the army that left a lasting impression on him,' Ellie suggested. 'National Service can be very traumatic for some of the boys, what with the sergeants constantly trying to break their spirit to make men of them. There have been attempted suicides in some of the camps, so I've heard. That sort of brutal environment could be very damaging to a gentle soul like Doug.'

'Yes, you hear all sorts. That seems highly likely to me. But you can't ask a man about that sort of thing, can you? I mean, if they had had trouble coping with all that macho stuff, they'd never dare to admit it for fear of seeming weak. Which, of course, is the whole root of the problem. Two years in the army, having a rotten time and not able to confide in anyone. It's not healthy to bottle up your fears. They're bound to come out sometime.'

'I'm sure you're right.' Ellie adored both Doug and Ann and hated the idea of anything being wrong between them. 'Is everything OK apart from that?'

'Oh, yes,' Ann assured her. 'He's a good husband and I love him to bits. And we're very happy most of the time. It's just this one thing that's coming between us. If there's something troubling him, I want to help him, and it's hurting me that he's shutting me out.'

'It would do,' sympathised Ellie. 'And apart from anything else you're losing sleep so you're tired the next day.'

'Exactly.'

'I suppose he goes back to sleep and you're left wide awake, worrying?'

'I am, yes, but Doug doesn't go straight back to sleep. He usually goes downstairs and sits in the kitchen drinking tea and smoking for ages, which tells me that he's more upset than he cares to admit,' she explained. 'I've tried to help but he doesn't want me with him. He's made that very clear.'

'I can understand how upsetting it must be for you, but if he won't talk about it the best thing you can do is try not to worry too much,' advised Ellie. 'Maybe he'll tell you about it in his own good time. Or it might stop. It's a shame to let this one thing spoil your marriage.'

'I suppose you're right,' said Ann. 'I certainly feel better for having talked about it. Can we keep this between us, though?'

'I won't say a word,' promised Ellie. 'Now can I get you another cup of coffee?'

'You stay where you are,' commanded Ann, getting up. 'I'll make it.'

'If you insist,' said Ellie graciously. 'I might as well make the most of being pampered. I won't get much chance once young junior arrives.'

'Only two weeks left, so push your luck for all you're worth until then,' laughed Ann.

'I intend to,' smiled Ellie.

As it happened Ellie didn't have two weeks left. In the early hours of the following morning she went into labour. After a gruelling twelve hours of indescribable agony she gave birth to a daughter in the marital bedroom from which Tom was banished by the midwife throughout the entire confinement.

'Isn't she the most beautiful thing you've ever seen?' Ellie effused to Tom when the authoritative nurse finally allowed him into her hallowed domain.

'Yes, she is,' he agreed, keeping his distance as he peered rather awestruck at his perfect little daughter sleeping in Ellie's arms, wrapped in a shawl, her eyes just slits in her pink mottled face. 'I think she looks like you.'

'Only because of her hair,' Ellie said, because her daughter's tiny head was covered with downy red hair. 'The first hair always falls out, apparently. The second lot might come through the same colour as yours.'

'Really?'

'Yes. I hope it does,' she told him. 'I wouldn't wish ginger hair on anyone. At school they'll call her carrots and ginger nut.'

'It didn't do you any harm,' Tom said, sitting on the edge of the bed.

'I suppose not.' She gave him a searching look. 'You're not disappointed because she isn't a boy, are you?'

'No, course I'm not,' he assured her, grinning. 'We'll manage a boy next time.'

'Give over,' she chuckled. 'I don't fancy going through that again for a while.'

'When we're ready, I mean.' He leaned across to take a close look at his daughter. 'She's a little smasher. Well done. I'm proud of you.'

'Why, thank you.' Ellie was taken aback because Tom wasn't given to sentimental talk. Just when she thought she knew him, he managed to surprise her. Propped up against the pillows with her baby in her arms and her husband by her side, she thought this must be her finest moment.

The arrival of Donna Jane Hall caused a great deal of excitement in the family, being the first grandchild on both sides. Ellie's mother had arranged to take time off from the wool shop when the baby arrived and came during the day to help Ellie while she recovered from the birth. Pat came to visit in the evenings.

'I can see something of Tom in her, you know,' said Pat one evening when they were all there.

'She's the image of Ellie,' disagreed Bob.

'There's a lot of Ellie in her, I agree,' conceded Pat, 'her red hair being the most striking similarity. But I can see Tom around the cheekbones.'

'Mm, maybe,' agreed Mary as they clustered around the crib. 'But there's a lot of our family in her too.'

Ellie and Tom exchanged looks. Competition in the granny department had already begun.

One evening a few days after Donna's birth, when Ellie was still confined to bed, the baby asleep in her carrycot and Mary downstairs in the kitchen preparing a meal, Tom came home from work and said he had a surprise for Ellie.

'Come and have a look,' he said, helping her out of bed and drawing her to the window.

Looking down into the street she didn't see anything unusual except a shiny black car parked outside the house. 'There's a car outside – has the doctor come to see me?'

'No.'

'Someone ill next door?'

'The car's mine, Ellie.'

'Yours?'

'I bought it this morning,' he informed her excitedly. 'It's second-hand but in very good condition. Isn't it fantastic?'

'Well, yes,' she muttered, looking puzzled. 'But we had no plans to buy a car. You use the shop van to get to and from work.'

'I've been thinking about getting a car for a while,' he told her. 'And I was talking to Mum about this Ford Consul I'd seen that I liked and she said why not go ahead and buy it, so I did.'

Ellie felt hot tears rush into her eyes. Not just because he had discussed it with his mother and not his wife. Not even because it was always me and never us, and mine and never ours. But suddenly, unexpectedly, the fact that he never consulted her over major decisions seemed hugely important. They were a family now. Surely these things should be discussed with her.

'I didn't realise you could afford it,' she said coolly.

'Mum gave me a bonus.'

'In other words, she paid for the car,' Ellie suggested.

'No, not really. I work hard at the shop,' he retorted. 'I run the place for her. I earned every penny of the bonus.'

'But the bonus came out of the blue because she knew you wanted a car, did it?' she said dully.

'More or less,' he stated proudly. 'When I told her what a good buy it was she said it was time I had something to reward me for all my hard work.'

Ellie hadn't even been aware that a car was in his plans for the future, let alone an immediate priority, and she felt excluded. 'I see,' she said flatly.

'I thought you'd be thrilled,' Tom scowled.

'Did you?'

'Of course I did. We'll be able to go out places at weekends with the baby.'

'Mm.'

'And not only that,' he went on excitedly, seeming not to notice that his wife was upset, 'I'm going to teach you to drive as soon as you're out of that bed. We can get started right away. You'll be up and about next week, won't you?'

Ellie had just had a baby, was still basking in the early glow of motherhood and trying to get used to her awesome new role. Learning to drive a car was not high on her list of priorities. 'Me, driving a car?' she said, bemused.

'Yeah, why not? It isn't unheard of for a woman to drive these days.'

'It might be quite common among the better off but it's still unusual among people like us,' she objected.

'Come on, Ellie, a modern woman like you – I thought you'd jump at the chance,' he chided.

'And normally I would.' Learning to drive a car would be rather exciting – when the time was right. But she found herself instinctively reacting against Tom's bullying tactics now that she had a child to consider. 'But I'm going to be busy with the baby and I can't think about anything else at the moment. She must be my first priority for the next few weeks.'

Tom tutted impatiently. 'You're not expected to stop doing everything else except look after a baby when you become a mother, you know,' he said scornfully.

'No, but you *are* expected to give the child all your attention at first,' she pointed out. 'All I'm saying is that I'm not sure if this is the right time for me to take on something as major as learning to drive a car. Maybe it would be better to leave it until Donna's a little bit older. Or at least give me time to get used to looking after her before you start arranging for me to have lessons.'

'Trust you to have a negative attitude,' he blasted at her hurtfully. 'There's no reason why we can't start your lessons as soon as you're up and about again.'

'We have a baby now, Tom,' she reminded him. 'I can't just go swanning off when I feel like it.'

'You're just making excuses.' His voice rose with temper. 'There are plenty of people who'll be willing to look after the baby while I give you lessons – my mother, your parents. Ann 'will probably be only too pleased to help out as well.'

'Let's see how it goes, shall we—'

'We're the first people in the street to have a decent car,' he cut in. 'The few who do have wheels have only got old bangers. So not only will I be the first to have something better than a clapped-out old banger but my wife will be the first woman around here to drive.'

His wife. So this had nothing to do with her as a person. It was all about his ego, which seemed to Ellie a trivial consideration compared to the importance of being a parent. His bullish manner shouldn't have upset her since she was accustomed to it but she felt dangerously close to tears. Hormones must be on the march, she thought, bewildered by her feelings. 'You know I've never been interested in trying to go one better than the neighbours,' she reminded him.

'But I am and you'll do as I say.' The unveiled cruelty in his tone made her nervous. 'Anyway, prestige isn't the only advantage to be had. There are practical considerations too. Your being able to drive the car will be useful to me in the business.'

'That's convenient for you.'

'There's nothing wrong with a wife helping her husband in his work,' he snapped. 'And a half-decent wife wouldn't even query where her duty lies.'

'I don't think there's any question of my not knowing where my duty lies,' she defended.

'Stop being so difficult about it then,' Tom said irritably. 'If you have a driving licence you'll be able to do shop errands . . . go to the wholesaler's if we need something urgently, and stuff like that. You can even do the odd delivery if I'm too busy to do it myself. Now that you're going to be at home all day, you might as well do something useful with your time.'

'Looking after a baby is about the most useful thing anyone can do,' she defended.

'Yeah, yeah, point taken,' he said dismissively. 'You can

65

take her with you when you go out on errands for me.'

What Tom said was perfectly valid. It was his attitude that was so infuriating. 'If you say so,' she said dully.

'She'll be perfectly all right in the carrycot on the back seat.' His mouth was set in a grim line. 'You're just making a silly fuss over nothing.'

'All right, Tom,' she said wearily. 'You've made your point. There's no need to go on about it.'

He glared at her. 'For Christ's sake, Ellie, anyone would think I'd just told you I was having an affair with another woman to see your sour face,' he growled. 'When all I've actually done is bought a car that will make our lives better, and suggested that you learn to drive the bloody thing. Isn't that what you women want, more equality with men? Isn't that what that Pankhurst woman and her cronies chained themselves to railings for?'

It was so women could have a say in things which I'm certainly not having now, she thought. His decision to buy a car and teach her to drive it was about as democratic as the British class system. But it was no use pointing this out to Tom because he simply wouldn't listen and would fly into a rage, which Ellie felt too weak and vulnerable to cope with so soon after giving birth.

'All right. You win, Tom. Once I'm back on my feet, we'll see about driving lessons,' she said.

His mood changed the instant he knew that victory was his. 'That's my girl,' he said, beaming at her.

Ellie felt as though her new world of motherhood had been violated by his lack of sensitivity towards it. She had always accepted his assertiveness because it was in the nature of the man she loved, but today she was beginning to see just how unequal the situation between them really was, and viewed her own compliance as self-betrayal.

It wasn't just hormones causing these new feelings, it was motherhood. Already it had changed her. The fierce, humbling devotion she felt for her baby, and the instinct to protect, had heightened her self-awareness and made her realise what a doormat she was to Tom. She hated herself for it but knew she was powerless to change things.

Feeling tears swell beneath her lids as she went back to bed, she turned her face from Tom and hastily wiped them away before he noticed. He would be irritated by what he would see as an unnecessary display of feminine emotion.

Chapter Four

Learning to drive a car didn't in itself present Ellie with too much of a problem. It was the tyranny of Tom's tuition she found so discouraging.

'Pay attention to what you're doing, for God's sake, woman,' he bellowed when she stalled the engine while trying to pull away from traffic lights.

It was a warm summer's evening and Tom was putting her through her paces around the Shepherd's Bush area.

'I am,' she uttered shakily.

'Don't make me laugh,' he argued. 'You wouldn't be making such a mess of it if you were. You should listen properly to my instructions.'

Tom in bullish mood was bad enough under normal circumstances. With the elevated status of driver over novice, he was crushing to the point where her confidence was in ruins.

'Sorry,' she said meekly.

'Use the clutch more smoothly,' he lectured as she tried again to get the car moving. 'You're much too heavy with it. That's why you keep stalling. You'll wear the damned thing out with that sort of treatment.'

'Sorry.'

'Don't keep apologising,' he puffed with seething irritation. 'Just get this car moving. We're holding up the traffic. Everybody's honking.'

'I had noticed.' Intimidated to the point where she could barely function, Ellie exerted too much pedal pressure and succeeded only in revving the engine up.

'Gently,' he shouted. 'Use a bit of finesse.'

'Oh dear,' she muttered feebly.

'Being pathetic isn't going to help,' he ranted. 'Just do what I've taught you and the car will move forward.'

After a couple more unsuccessful attempts, there was movement at last; it wasn't the smoothest of take-offs but at least she hadn't stalled again. She'd just managed to build up her courage a little when Tom destroyed it again by cowering back in his seat with his hand clutched to his brow. 'Watch out for that bus coming toward us!' he screeched. 'God Almighty, we're going to hit it.'

They passed the bus without incident. 'I *was* in control, you know; there was no chance of us hitting it.' Her voice was quivering, her mouth dry.

'Why were you heading straight for it then, you stupid bitch?' he yelled. 'It's enough to frighten anyone out of their wits.'

'I was nowhere near it.' That much she was sure of. 'I was well clear of it.'

'You'll kill the pair of us if you carry on like this.' He shook his head disbelievingly. 'Talk about incompetent!'

'That really isn't fair, Tom,' she objected strongly. 'I *am* just a beginner.'

'No chance of my forgetting that.'

'Anyway, it was your idea for me to have lessons so soon,' she reminded him. 'I was in no hurry to learn to drive.'

He sat upright in his seat and she could see him glaring at her out of the corner of her eye. 'I'd never have suggested it if I'd known you were going to be so hopeless. You should be making some sort of progress by now. The way you're going, it'll be years before you're ready to take your test.'

'It might help if you were to stop wrecking my confidence with a constant barrage of criticism.' Her hands were damp, her heart thumping. He was making her so distressed, she couldn't think straight. 'Your shouting at me is making me so nervous, I'm not functioning properly.'

'*You're nervous!*' he exploded. 'What about me? I'm in fear of my life here. Your hair-raising performance is enough to make anyone shout.'

'You could try to be a bit more patient,' she suggested.

'You've stretched my patience to the limit.'

'I'm doing my best.'

'Driving a car is a simple enough matter, for heaven's sake,' he continued. 'I don't know why it's taking you so long to get the hang of it.'

'Since Donna's only a month old, it can't be that long,' she pointed out. 'I think this is about my fourth lesson.'

'Yeah, well . . . stop yakking and watch what you're doing,' he ordered as they cruised along the Uxbridge Road. 'Turn right at the traffic lights.'

'OK.' Her nerves were jangling as she waited at the red lights, praying she could get the car to move forward without another humiliating mistake.

'Well, go on then,' he said the instant they turned to amber. 'They've changed. Are you colour-blind or something?'

'Shut up, Tom.'

'Oh, no, I don't believe this,' he wailed. 'You've only gone and stalled it again.'

It seemed to Ellie at that moment as though the entire motoring population of Shepherd's Bush was engaged in a protest against her via the motor horn; the noise was deafening. 'Oh God . . .' she muttered weakly.

'We'll have a riot on our hands in a minute,' tutted Tom. 'You're a highway menace.'

Completely unnerved, her mind went blank. 'What shall I do?' she asked in desperation.

'Start again,' he told her. 'Turn the engine back on and use the pedals – *smoothly*.'

'Right.'

Eventually the car moved, albeit jerkily, and they turned the corner into a side street. 'About bloody time too,' Tom said. 'It took you long enough to get it right.'

Damp with perspiration and trembling all over, Ellie drew the car into the kerb.

'What are you doing?' he wanted to know. 'I didn't tell you to pull in.'

'I know you didn't.'

'So why—'

Switching off the engine, she turned to him. 'I'm not prepared to put up with any more of your bullying,' she explained. 'So you can change places with me and drive us home.' It was a statement, not a request and she was amazed at her own audacity.

Judging by his manner, Tom was surprised too. 'Don't be so daft, Ellie,' he admonished, but some of the fierceness had gone out of his tone. 'You can't give up now.'

'I don't have a choice because your attitude is making it impossible for me to learn,' she told him, opening her door. 'It's dangerous, the way you carry on.'

'I'm dangerous!' He was astounded. 'You're the one who's dangerous.'

'Only because your constant criticism is making me into a nervous wreck and impairing my judgement,' she informed him, courage fuelled by her firm belief that there was a safety risk to their continuing. 'You don't have a suitable temperament to be a driving instructor and there will be an accident if we carry on with the lessons.'

'Oh, so it's my fault that you can't get the hang of it, is it?' he said, affronted.

'Frankly, yes.'

'It's no good blaming the teacher just because you can't do it,' he taunted.

Ellie was thoughtful, mulling over a sudden idea. 'If you want to boast about your wife being the first woman driver in the street, and you also want me to drive around doing shop errands for you, then you'll have to pay a professional to teach me,' she announced. 'Because the only way I'll continue with

72

lessons is with a qualified instructor.'

Before he had time to respond, she was out of the car and on her way to the passenger door. Stunned by her forcefulness, he did as she'd told him and moved into the driver's seat.

'How are you, son?' Alfie Brent was speaking to his son across a table in the prison visiting room where several other inmates were talking to their visitors. A large presence of warders stood watchfully in the background.

'Mustn't grumble, Dad,' said the indomitable Ray.

He rarely did, though he had every reason to, and Alfie was full of admiration for him. Even in the early days of his sentence, when the horrors of prison life and being locked in at night with a dirty blanket and a slop bucket were new to him, and resentment had been visible in those striking dark eyes, he'd kept his complaints to himself.

As time passed, Alfie had perceived a kind of plucky resignation in his son. It was as though Ray had accepted the fact that nothing could be done about his plight and decided to take the line of least resistance.

'You look well, anyway.' Ray had lost a lot of weight since he'd been in prison. At first he'd appeared gaunt, especially with the prison haircut. But he'd been looking better lately, and Alfie thought it suited him to be slimmer.

'I'm fine,' confirmed Ray. 'You all right, Dad?'

'Not so bad.'

'How's work?'

He made a face. 'As boring and repetitive as ever.' Alfie worked on the assembly line in a box-making factory where Ray had also been employed prior to going to prison. 'But it feeds me and pays the rent so I'm not complaining.' He gave him a wry look. 'Compared to what you have to put up with, it's a doddle.'

'It would be nice if you could do something you enjoyed though,' said Ray.

'It's regular employment, son, that's the main thing.'

'There is that,' agreed Ray.

They chatted generally for a while until Alfie asked, 'How are you getting on with those metalwork classes you were telling me about last time I came?'

'Very well.' Ray looked pleased. 'I'm getting to be quite a dab hand at welding.'

'That's really good, son,' his father enthused. 'What sort of things are you making?'

'Ornamental stuff mostly. Candle-holders, pot-holders, lanterns, that sort of thing. I'm hoping to make some fancy steel gates when I'm better at it. That'll be something to get my teeth into.'

'Does this mean I'll be getting a fancy holder for my pot plants?' joked Alfie.

'Sorry, Dad. Everything we make goes to charity if it isn't needed at the prison,' Ray explained.

'And so it should,' approved Alfie, his expression becoming more serious. 'I'm dead chuffed that you've found something to take an interest in.'

'Me too. It makes a break from the grind of prison life, having a lesson once a week,' confessed Ray. 'I think I might have found something I can be good at if I stick with it.' He grinned. 'It seems an odd place to find a new skill, though.'

'You won't be the first person to learn something new in prison,' his father told him.

'I know,' agreed Ray. 'You hear of people writing books, doing academic courses, all sorts.'

'And if you've found a new hobby it's all to the good,' enthused Alfie.

'Actually I've been thinking that I might like it to be more than just a hobby, eventually.'

'Oh?'

'I quite fancy doing ornamental metalwork when I get out, as a job.' He made a face. 'Though it's such a long time ahead, I can't consider it seriously.'

'You're getting there, though,' his father encouraged. 'You've done four years.'

'It sometimes feels more like forty.' A look of bleakness passed fleetingly across his face. 'And I'm still not even halfway through the sentence.'

'You might be, if you get remission for hard work and good conduct,' his father pointed out. 'You can get as much as a third off your sentence for that.'

'That's what I'm hoping for, but I can't bank on it.' Ray's expression became grim; his eyes gleaming with anger. 'I don't think I'll ever take anything for granted again after the way things have turned out for me.'

'I should think remission is a strong possibility, though. You've been a model prisoner, from what I can make out – working hard, keeping out of trouble.'

'I'm trying to get through the sentence with as little fuss as possible, and I am hoping for the best about remission,' Ray confessed. 'But nothing is guaranteed, is it? I thought I had my life sorted once before and look where I ended up.'

'Keep a grip, son,' Alfie said.

'Don't worry, Dad.' Ray became determinedly hearty again. 'You know me, I don't let things get me down.'

'That's a fact,' said his father, wanting to weep he was so proud of him.

'Wasn't she a little love in the church?' Mary was sitting on the sofa nursing little Donna at her christening party at the home of Ellie and Tom one Sunday in October. 'Not a peep out of her, not even when the vicar sprinkled the water on to her.'

'An absolute angel,' agreed her equally adoring paternal grandmother, who was seated beside Mary, chucking the baby under the chin and being rewarded with a wide, toothless smile. 'Look at her laughing, the little duck.'

They were still ensconced on the sofa paying homage to their small relation when Ellie appeared, looking smart and attractive in a blue fitted jersey suit that brought out the colour of her eyes and enhanced the gold tones in her red hair, which she wore in a casual style just above shoulder length.

'Shall I take her off you now, Mum,' she offered, 'so that you can go and get yourself something to eat?'

'No, she's all right here with me, love.' Mary didn't want to let her go. 'If you could get me a sandwich, I'll manage.'

'Sure.' She looked at her mother-in-law. 'Can I get you anything, Pat?'

'A couple of those little salmon rolls would be nice, dear.'

'Coming up.' Ellie swung off towards the dining room where a buffet tea was laid out.

'She's taken to motherhood like a duck to water, hasn't she?' remarked Mary proudly.

'She certainly has,' agreed Pat.

'It's a big upheaval,' Mary went on. 'But she doesn't seem to have had any trouble adapting.'

'Tom's a good father too,' Pat put in determinedly. 'He's very proud of Donna.'

Pat had an annoying habit of capping any positive remark Mary might make about Ellie with one about her son, as though, in complimenting her daughter, Mary was in some way criticising Tom. But Mary refused to let it rankle. Today was a time for celebrating their good fortune in having such a beautiful granddaughter.

'Yeah, they're a nice little family. May they have many happy years together,' she said amicably.

The christening party was drawing to a close. The nonrelated guests had departed, leaving only the family at the house in Fenleigh Gardens. Ellie was in the kitchen with Ann, who was helping her with the dishes while the others chatted in the living room.

'How are you getting on with the driving lessons now?' enquired Ann chattily.

'Pretty good,' Ellie replied. 'Actually, I've been given a date

76

for my test. It's at the beginning of December.'

'That soon?'

'Yeah. My instructor seems to think I'll be ready by then so I'm going to give it a try. I don't know if I'll pass first time but some people do.'

'It doesn't seem to have taken you long to get to grips with it,' remarked Ann.

'Once I started lessons with a proper instructor I came on in leaps and bounds,' Ellie explained. 'I don't think I'd ever have learned with Tom.'

'They say driving lessons are a recipe for divorce, don't they?'

'They were certainly a disaster for us. Tom can't help the way he is, bless him. But he doesn't have the patience for teaching, especially if I'm the pupil. I suppose it could work for some couples – you and Doug, for instance. Doug isn't so quick to fly off the handle.'

'We're thinking of getting a little car soon, as it happens, so I might put him to the test.'

'Getting a car, eh?' remarked Ellie, pleased.

'It'll only be something old,' Ann told her, 'but it'll be nice to have our own transport.'

'It's very convenient when you've got a baby,' enthused Ellie. 'Half the house goes with us when we go out. It's great, being able to pile it all into the car.'

'Actually,' began Ann, drying a cup and putting it away in the cupboard, 'we haven't said anything to anyone yet but we've got a little one on the way.'

Ellie dropped the dishcloth in delighted surprise and dried her hands. 'Oh, that is good news, Ann. I'm so pleased for you.' She hugged her. 'When's it due?'

'May.'

'Lovely.' Ellie turned back to the dishes in the sink. 'No need to ask if Doug's pleased.'

'He's thrilled.'

'I've been meaning to ask – is he still troubled with bad nights and so on?'

'Not so often lately,' Ann was pleased to tell her. 'He seems to be having a calm patch at the moment. No funny moods, and nice peaceful nights.'

'That's good.'

'It's always been intermittent,' explained Ann, 'so I don't know if something might trigger it off again.'

'Let's hope fatherhood will cure him altogether,' said Ellie. 'He'll certainly have more to occupy his mind, and he'll probably be too shattered to dream when he goes to bed, with all those disturbed nights that new babies bring.'

'Don't, Ellie,' laughed Ann. 'I'm trying not to think about that side of it.'

'There's nothing more exhausting than having a new baby in the house, believe me,' said Ellie. 'They turn your world upside down when they first arrive. But it's worth every minute.'

'I can't wait,' smiled Ann.

Ellie had to admit to being pleased with herself when she passed her driving test. Even apart from the sense of personal achievement, it was good to be able to prove to Tom that she wasn't as useless as he'd made her out to be.

But for all that she was now qualified to take to the road, she felt she needed more practical experience before she should drive with the baby on board.

'That's ridiculous,' was Tom's scathing reaction to her comments on the subject when they were out for a Sunday afternoon spin a couple of days after her test. 'There's only one way to gain driving experience and that's to get on and do it.'

'I agree with you and I will do it,' she told him. 'But not right away – not when Donna is in the car, anyway.'

'But you're a qualified driver now. That means you're fit to drive, regardless of who's in the car with you,' he stated. 'You should be able to take over at the wheel from me any time I ask you without giving it a thought.'

'And I will do, in time,' she assured him. 'But I'm not doing it with Donna in the car until I'm more confident.'

'What difference will Donna make?' he queried. 'It isn't as though she'll start climbing about or anything. The worst she can do is cry and that shouldn't put you off since it's what babies do and you're used to it.'

'She's small and helpless, Tom.' Ellie's feelings about this were so intense it seemed odd that he didn't understand why she was concerned. 'Her life is in the hands of whoever is driving, which is why I want to make sure I'm in control before I take her out in the car. I know it seems silly to you—'

'You're right, it does.'

'But it's the way I feel.'

'You should throw yourself in at the deep end,' he persisted. 'That's the best way to cure beginner's nerves.'

It was a sunny December afternoon and they were heading for Richmond Park over Kew Bridge. Tom liked to take the car further afield on a Sunday to 'open her up a bit'.

'I accept that that's the right thing for most people, but I'd rather do it my way, if you don't mind,' she said. 'It's a personal thing and I really hope you'll respect my wishes about this.'

'You've passed your driving test, Ellie.' His tone carried equal measures of persuasion and irritation. 'There's no reason why you shouldn't drive this car, with or without the baby.'

'Tom, please . . .'

'You must have more confidence in yourself.'

Not easy when you're married to a man who habitually tramples on other people's self-belief, she thought, but said, 'Passing the test is just the beginning. A course of lessons and twenty minutes in front of an examiner may be enough for some people. But I feel I need a few trips out without Donna before I take the plunge with her in the car.'

'Oh, really . . .'

'A bit of practice, that's all I ask, Tom,' she persisted. 'I'm not talking about months or even weeks, just the chance to get some experience of coping with the traffic before I drive with Donna in the car. A reasonable enough request, I would have thought.'

But Tom was relentless. 'The examiner gave you a piece of paper that clearly states you are fit to drive, so you've got to get behind this wheel and do it.'

'And I will, when the time's right.'

'You can drive us home,' he suggested.

'Leave it, Tom, please,' Ellie entreated. 'Let's drop the subject and enjoy our afternoon out.'

'Have it your way,' he shrugged, but she knew she hadn't heard the last of it.

Arriving at Richmond Park, Tom put the car in one of the car parks and they headed briskly towards Pen Ponds with Donna asleep in her carrycot on wheels. The weather was cold but bright, the heatless sun illuminating the winter beauty of everything, the bare trees etched against the sky and reflected in the brown, gently undulating surface of the water. There were plenty of people about: boys kicking footballs, dog walkers, people on bikes, children feeding the ducks under parental supervision. Ellie found herself anticipating with pleasure the time when Donna would appreciate the large population of ducks, geese and swans here. Her daughter had given her so much to look forward to.

Tom was very quiet – sulking, she assumed, because she wouldn't agree to what he wanted. Honestly! No sooner had he stopped pressuring her to pass the driving test than he was trying to force her to drive the car with the baby on board before she was ready.

Ellie still loved Tom as she always had, but no longer with the immaturity that had either blinded her to his faults or made them endearing. She knew that his feverish insistence that she drive under his terms was simply to feed his power over her since there was no urgent practical necessity for her to do the occasional shop errand for him. His behaviour wasn't whole-some. Neither was it a male supremacy thing because she'd seen him do the same sort of thing to Doug. She did hope he wasn't going to continue to badger her because she found it very wearing.

Her hopes about this were dashed when they got back to the car park. After he'd put the baby in the car and loaded the carrycot wheels into the boot, he handed Ellie the car keys.

'I'm not driving,' she told him.

'You are.'

'I've told you I don't want to do it with Donna in the car,' she reminded him.

'You're driving us home and that's all there is to it.' It was a categorical statement.

'I'd really rather not, Tom.' She was worried now, and very nervous. 'You know how I feel about this. I've asked you to respect my feelings. Please do it.'

'You're being absolutely pathetic and I'm not having it,' he declared. 'I didn't pay all that money for lessons just so you could sit in the passenger seat.'

'Don't force me into it, Tom . . .'

He clamped his hands to either side of her face and held it so that her gaze was fixed on him. 'Listen, I am *not* driving you home,' he said slowly, as though she were hard of hearing. 'So unless you want a very long walk, you'll have to do it.'

He knew she didn't have any money with her to get the bus or train. She never took her purse when she went out with her husband. They were miles from home and it was cold for Donna to be out for too long.

'You really are being cruel, Tom.'

'It's what's known as being cruel to be kind.' He was adamant. 'You're the sort of person who needs someone to give you a shove to make you do things. You'll thank me for it later.'

'I really don't think this is wise . . .'

His eyes blackened with hostility. 'Just get on and do it and stop whining.' She knew from the tone of his voice that he would take no more argument. 'You'll be perfectly all right once you get going, believe me.'

Ellie searched for another solution but there wasn't one. She needed to get the baby home and Tom knew that. He had pushed her into a corner and she hated him for it.

'It seems I've got no choice,' she said coldly.

'That's right,' he confirmed. 'So get on with it and stop making such a fuss.'

It was with extreme caution that she drove the car out of the car park and headed for home. Her eyes were fixed on the road ahead, all her senses heightened by the added responsibility of having Donna in the car.

'Get some speed up,' Tom urged her after a while. 'You're driving like an old woman.'

'This is a built-up area,' she pointed out. 'There's a thirty-mile limit along here.'

'Nobody takes any notice of that.'

'Well, I'm going to,' she stated firmly, and continued to drive within the law.

'The lights are green,' he informed her a bit later on as they approached some traffic lights. 'Put your foot down and you'll get across before they change.'

'I'd rather not.'

'Just do it, Ellie.'

'It doesn't matter if we have to stop for a few minutes,' she said without increasing her speed and continuing to stay within the legal limit for the area. 'We're not in any particular hurry.'

'That isn't the point,' he nagged. 'Why stop when we don't have to?'

'Will you stop giving me orders, for heaven's sake!' she snapped, her nerves raw. 'You've forced me to drive the damned car. At least you can let me do it in my own way. If we miss the lights it really doesn't matter.'

'Of course it matters,' Tom argued. 'It's a question of

anticipating what's ahead and acting accordingly.'

'Which is exactly what I am doing,' she said in frustration. 'I'm slowing down and preparing to stop if I have to.'

'Do what I say and put your foot down. Quickly, go on, do it now,' he instructed.

Tension knots drew ever tighter in her stomach, despite all her efforts to stay calm. 'Shut up, for goodness' sake, will you, Tom?' she blurted out.

'Don't you dare speak to me like that,' he yelled.

'Stop interfering then,' she retaliated. 'You're driving me mad.'

They had reached the lights now and as they were still green Ellie was able to proceed. But the car was never to reach the other side of the junction . . .

The dull crunch of metal and the tinkle of splintering glass rent the air as the car crashed to a halt and spun round, throwing Ellie against the door.

'What the hell . . .?' she muttered, gathering her wits sufficiently to realise that a vehicle to the left had jumped the lights and gone into the side of them. The passenger door had been pushed in and Tom was slumped forward with his head on the dashboard, which was sticky with blood. Afraid to touch him for fear of making things worse, Ellie cried out, 'Tom! Tom! Can you hear me? Please say something.' He was silent and ominously still.

The sound of the baby screaming in the back stabbed into Ellie's consciousness. 'Donna, darling,' she gasped. 'Mummy's here, baby.'

Concern for her husband and her daughter filled Ellie's mind to the exclusion of all else; she barely noticed that her own face was smarting with cuts from the flying glass, and was almost oblivious to the chaos erupting around them as the traffic was held up in all four directions of this busy crossroads. People were running towards her and crowding around the car.

Common sense told her that Tom shouldn't be moved until professional help arrived. With her heart pounding and blood running down her face, she scrambled out of the car and climbed into the back to get to her screaming baby.

By some miracle, Donna was unhurt and Ellie's injuries were only superficial. It happened that way sometimes in road accidents, the nurse who dressed her wounds told her. It was all to do with the angle of the impact, apparently. Occasionally one passenger took the brunt and the others got off scot-free.

Tom had certainly taken the brunt of this one. He was still unconscious and Ellie had been told that the doctors couldn't be sure yet of the extent of his head injuries or, indeed, if he would regain consciousness at all.

Ellie's family and Tom's mother were all at the hospital. Wanting to spare Pat the shock of receiving the news by telephone or from a policeman at her front door, Ellie had managed to get a message to her brother, whose neighbour was on the phone. Doug had broken the news to Pat and brought them all to the hospital in the Austin he'd bought recently.

But now Ellie had finished in casualty, having had her cuts treated and a general examination. The doctor had also given Donna a thorough going-over and said she was fine and could go home. Mary offered to take her.

Acutely vulnerable after what had happened, and very much aware of the fact that she could have lost her precious daughter in the accident, Ellie said with a sob in her voice, 'I don't think I can bear to part with her, Mum.'

'I know how you must be feeling, love. But this is no place for a baby and you need to focus all your attention on Tom,' Mary said kindly. 'Donna will be fine with me. Doug will take us home, won't you, Doug?'

'Course I will.' Doug looked terrible; he was whey-faced, his eyes bloodshot and swollen. His friendship with Tom went back a long way. Ellie could understand how anxious he would be.

Having been given various instructions relating to Donna, Mary left with Doug, who promised to come straight back to the hospital. Ellie's father and Ann insisted on staying and waited in the reception area while Ellie went to join Tom's mother in the side-ward they kept for patients who were on the critical list.

Pat was sitting at her son's bedside, holding his hand when Ellie entered the room. She was struck by the fact that Pat looked worse than Tom did. There was a grey tinge to her skin and she was visibly trembling. Although Tom's head was bandaged and he was on a drip, he looked extremely peaceful, his cheeks suffused with pink, his fine features composed; it was as though he were simply enjoying a deep sleep instead of fighting for his life. Ellie's heart went out to him and she prayed silently.

Knowing she must stay strong and positive for Pat, however, she stifled her own feeling of hysteria and put a comforting arm round the other woman's shoulders. 'Why don't you go and get a cup of coffee?' she suggested kindly.

'No,' Pat said dully.

'I'll stay here with Tom,' Ellie assured her. 'They've finished with me in casualty and Mum's taken Donna home so I'm free now to sit with him.'

'I can't leave him.'

'A break will do you good,' urged Ellie gently. 'I'll come and get you if anything happens.'

Pat turned to face Ellie, her face blotchy, her features twisted with agony. 'Oh, Ellie,' she said, in a low strangled voice, 'he's my only child and I can't bear to lose him.'

Ellie could see that she was on the point of breaking down but was grimly containing herself. With extreme gentleness, Ellie led her outside into the corridor and held her while she sobbed, the thin body heaving.

'There, there,' she soothed, unable to stem the flow of her

own tears. 'He's going to get through this. We both have to believe that.'

'He's in an awfully bad way,' wept Pat.

'Yes, he is,' said Ellie thickly, 'but it'll take more than this to finish Tom off. He's young and strong – he'll come through.'

'He seems so helpless.'

'And he is at the moment,' she was forced to agree. 'But once he comes round—'

'Please God that he does,' sobbed Pat.

'Doctors can do wonderful things these days,' said Ellie, managing to stay positive even though Tom's prognosis wasn't good. 'He'll be all right, you'll see.

Ellie felt Pat's body loosen and her weeping subsided. 'Sorry, Ellie,' she muttered, her voice thick with tears. 'I know this must be terrible for you too.'

'It is.' Ellie couldn't deny it. 'But we're here for each other and that's something that'll help us both.'

Pat blew her nose, seeming a little calmer. 'We'd better go back in there.'

'I'll go back in,' said Ellie. 'You do as I suggested and go to the cafeteria and get some coffee. You can bring some back for me. I'm gasping.'

'Thank you, Ellie,' she said, her voice shaking. 'I don't know what I'd do without you.'

They had never been close but were now united by mutual anxiety. 'You'd manage if I wasn't around,' she told her warmly. 'But I am here and I'm not going anywhere.'

The other woman nodded and trotted off, a sad figure in a tweed coat and brown hat. Ellie went back into the ward and sat down by the bed looking at her husband. It hurt to remember that the last words they'd spoken to each other had been angry ones. Why had she let him force her into driving the car before she was ready? Why hadn't she stood up to him with more force instead of allowing him to wear her down?

Would he be fighting for his life now if he'd been at the driving wheel himself?

Of course, if that had been the case Ellie would have been in the passenger seat so would be the one in intensive care now instead of Tom. But even as she thought this, Ellie reasoned that an experienced driver might have anticipated the recklessness of the other driver and avoided the accident altogether somehow. It was a disturbing thought, and one that lingered in her mind.

The police came to see Ellie at the hospital that evening to get her statement, apologising for bothering her so soon at such a dreadful time, and explaining that they needed her version of events. They assured her that there was no question of the accident being her fault. They could tell by the position of the two cars that the other driver had gone through a red light, and there were several witnesses to verify that. He'd been drinking, apparently.

The man had sustained only minor injuries and had already been discharged from hospital, but would almost certainly be facing criminal charges for dangerous driving. The police officers were very kind to Ellie and told her she wouldn't have any trouble with any insurance claim she might make. Tom's car was expected to be a write-off. Ellie wasn't bothered about that. It was the least of her worries.

Her anger with the other driver was diminished by her own sense of guilt. Despite everything the police officers had said to assure her that she wasn't in any way to blame for the accident, she couldn't stop wondering if it would have happened if she hadn't been driving the car. The guilt began to fester and take a hold; she was powerless against it.

Both Pat and Ellie stayed at the hospital all night. Ellie remained in the chair by the bed but managed to persuade Pat to go to the relatives' room for a while.

Tom's condition remained unchanged. He showed no sign of regaining consciousness that night, or the next day, or the one after that. They were told his condition was reasonably stable but the doctor in charge of his case pointed out to them that his coming round was by no means assured.

Although ostensibly Ellie was strong for Pat, her own nerves were in shreds. She lost track of time and hardly saw Donna; the baby was being looked after by her mother, who had indefinite leave from her job at the wool shop. Normal life became a memory as everything revolved around Tom. Pat even closed the shop until further notice because she had no one to stand in for her and had neither the heart nor the energy to look for anyone.

After the first few days, Ellie and Pat began to go home at night, though they continued to stay with Tom during the day. The sister in charge of the ward suggested that this would be the most sensible arrangement for them all as the two women needed their rest and the hospital staff needed to maintain their routine.

One early evening a couple of weeks after the accident, Ellie had just got home after collecting Donna from her mother's when she received a telephone call from the hospital. It was good news. Tom had regained consciousness at last. But the nurse conveying the message had been instructed to tell Ellie that the doctor would like to see her before she next saw Tom, and would be very grateful if she could get there before he went off duty.

Warm with relief, and remembering that Doug wasn't away on a long-haul job this week, Ellie contacted him by telephone through his neighbour. He and Ann came over right away. Ann agreed to stay with Donna while Doug drove Ellie to the hospital. Some sixth sense warned her not to tell Pat about this new development until she'd seen the doctor. But she was, none the less, full of joy on the way to the hospital.

In the doctor's office, however, Ellie's spirits plummeted as she listened to what he had to say. When he'd finished and she headed for the ward to see Tom, Doug went with her to offer moral support, but he was almost as nervous as she. Her legs were shaking so much she hardly knew how to put one foot in front of the other. But she forced herself to be strong. She had to be to face this new ordeal . . .

Chapter Five

'Hello, Tom,' said Ellie, taking his hand and holding it in both of hers lovingly.

His total lack of response tore at her heart. Silently, he stared at her without a hint of recognition.

Doug stepped forward. 'Wotcher, mate.' He was being studiously normal. 'How are you feeling?'

Tom responded with a blank stare. Not only did he fail to recognise them, but he showed no interest in who they were or why they were here.

'It's good to see that you're awake at last.' Ellie was struggling to sound ordinary. They had been asked to keep the conversation simple and not to appear shocked by the fact that his behaviour wasn't as before. 'How's your head?'

He pointed to his bandages. With obvious difficulty he uttered a guttural sound that Ellie assumed to be something to the effect that his head was hurting, but his speech was so badly distorted it was just a guess.

'You've got a headache, have you?' she said sympathetically, managing to conceal her horror of the fact that her husband had become a stranger. 'I'll ask one of the nurses to give you something for it.'

Muttering something incomprehensible, Tom started to cry suddenly, loud uninhibited sobbing, eyes and nose streaming unchecked. Ellie rummaged in her handbag for a handkerchief and mopped his face in the way a mother would for her child. He wept with increased vigour, apparently oblivious of the fact that this was a general ward and he was causing a disturbance.

'Steady on, mate,' said Doug kindly. 'We'll get the nurse to give you something for your headache.'

'Shush, Tom,' Ellie soothed, taking his hand again. 'Don't cry. It'll stop hurting once you've had some medicine.'

As suddenly as it had begun, the crying stopped, and he wiped his nose on his pyjama sleeve, mumbling something unintelligible, which seemed to be an objection to their suggestion of medicine.

'All right, Tom, don't upset yourself,' said Ellie, giving his hand a reassuring squeeze.

Without warning he became violently distressed, ripping his hand from Ellie's grasp and cowering back from her, shaking his head and shouting, 'No, no, no . . .' in his strange warped manner.

'Calm down, Tom.' She was profoundly troubled but managed not to show it. 'No one's going to force you to have medicine if you don't want it.'

Wildly flapping his arms at Ellie, he made a roaring noise she deduced was a request for her to go away. Keen to do what was best for him, however, she ignored this and moved closer to him, eager to provide the succour she believed he needed. But his clenched fists came shooting towards her face with such viciousness she instinctively backed away.

Alerted by the commotion, two nurses hurried on to the scene. Devastated, Ellie stood aside, watching as they held Tom down and put a needle in his arm. The injection had an almost immediate effect and he lay back with his eyelids fluttering, then becoming still. Her strong, domineering husband had become as powerless as a baby. It was heartbreaking.

'I think it'll be best if you leave, Mrs Hall,' suggested one of the nurses, anxious to restore order on the ward. 'Your husband will sleep for a long time now. You can come and see him tomorrow at visiting time.'

Biting back the tears, Ellie left the ward with her shocked brother trailing behind her.

'I can't bear to see him like that, Doug,' she said as they headed through a maze of corridors towards the exit.

'Me neither.' He put a comforting arm around her.

'The doctor told me that brain damage had reduced his mental age to that of a child of five and warned me what to expect,' she went on. 'But actually seeing him like that . . .'

'I know. It gave me a hell of a shock too,' Doug confessed gravely.

'It didn't seem real, did it?' she continued. 'I almost expected him to revert back to his old self at any minute and say he'd just been kidding.' She paused and added sadly, 'But, of course, I knew that wasn't going to happen.'

'Did the doctor say if there's anything that can be done for him?' Doug enquired.

'He was noncommittal about that but there's sure to be something they can do.' Ellie needed to believe this. 'Now that he's conscious and they know for certain that there is brain damage, they're going to do tests to find out the extent of it and whether or not it's operable, apparently. But the doctor seemed more concerned about preparing me for the shock of the way Tom is now than talking about his future prospects.'

'Doctors never commit themselves until they're sure about something anyway,' Doug pointed out.

'For all that he prepared me, it still broke my heart when I saw Tom.' Ellie felt sick with sadness and worry. 'And heaven knows how his mother's going to cope with this blow. The poor woman will be devastated.'

'She's bound to be,' Doug agreed.

'And to think that if I hadn't let him make me drive the car that day it might never have happened,' she said.

'The accident was *not* your fault, Ellie,' Doug told her emphatically. 'You must know that in your heart?'

'Yeah, I know that technically I wasn't to blame,' she conceded, 'but I can't help thinking that if a more experienced driver had been at the wheel, perhaps it could have been avoided.'

'There's only one person to blame for the accident and that's the bloke who drove through the red light.' Doug's tone became hard. 'But, anyway, Tom shouldn't have bullied you into driving when you didn't feel ready.'

'I haven't said that he *bullied* me into it.' The circumstances preceding the accident had come out in conversation but Ellie had not said anything derogatory about her husband.

'You didn't have to. I know what Tom's like when he wants his own way.'

'It isn't like you, Doug, to speak ill of someone when they're down.' She was surprised by his attitude.

'I don't normally and I shouldn't have now,' he admitted. 'But you've got quite enough to worry about without blaming yourself for the accident which you couldn't possibly have caused as well. You were not to blame, *right*!' She had rarely seen him more forceful. 'And as for fretting about whether you should have let Tom force you into driving the car, that's plain stupid. I know Tom and I know how he can make people do things against their will. So stop punishing yourself.'

'Not easy, but I'll try,' she promised as they left the hospital building and walked out into the cold night air.

'At least Tom's alive,' Doug pointed out. 'We have to thank God for that.'

'And I do . . . every minute of every day.' She paused. 'But what sort of a life is he going to have if he stays as he is?'

'They'll do something for him, don't worry.'

'Yeah, I know,' Ellie said. 'That it should happen to Tom of all people, a man so much in control of himself and everybody else – to lose his dignity like that.'

'The way he is now, though, he doesn't know what dignity is, let alone that he's lost his, so he can't be upset by it, can he?'

'There is that.'

'We mustn't be too gloomy.' Doug was trying to stay

positive for her sake but he was equally as worried. 'It's still early days. And doctors are in the business of getting people better. Once they've done the tests and know what can be done for him, they'll get on and do it.'

Ellie wiped her tears and blew her nose. 'I must pull myself together,' she resolved. 'Especially as I have the job of breaking the news to Pat.'

'I'll take you round to her place straight away, if you like.'

'Thanks, Doug. I'm dreading it but the sooner I get it over with the better.'

'It was just as well you decided to see him before telling her he'd come round,' he approved. 'At least you can get her used to the idea before she sees him.'

'Exactly. And, as you say, it's still early days. There might be a drastic improvement by the time she gets to see him tomorrow.'

There wasn't an improvement of any kind. Tom was as lacking in recognition of his mother as he'd been of Ellie and Doug. Poor Pat was beside herself with grief. Her handsome, confident son had become like a retarded five-year-old, inarticulate and unable to respond to the mother who had doted on him all his life. Ellie could feel Pat's pain as her own.

As the days passed Tom began to treat Ellie and Pat as benevolent aunts when they visited him, usually bearing gifts of fruit, sweets, squash. Such were the limitations of his memory span, he often didn't recognise them from one visit to the next. He seemed to function within a world of his own, muttering to himself almost constantly.

Occasionally he behaved like a sweet child, but usually he was difficult and demanding. His temper tantrums were frighteningly violent and sedation was often administered to calm him while his visitors were there. But through it all he retained his striking good looks, noticeably so when the heavy bandaging was replaced by a smaller dressing as his wound healed. Somehow, this made his behaviour all the more poignant.

Visiting Tom was as exhausting as it was depressing. He upset the other patients and his behaviour was disruptive to the extent that the ward staff could barely manage him. Ellie couldn't help wondering how she would cope with him if there was no improvement by the time he was discharged from hospital, especially with the baby in the house.

Christmas passed in a blur. They all went through the motions but no one was in the mood for celebrating. Had Donna been of an age to understand such things, Ellie would have made sure it was special for her, but as things were, it seemed right to let the holiday pass with the least amount of fuss. She was thoroughly relieved when it was over.

As the new year got underway, she waited for news from the hospital of test results and plans for surgery or special treatment for Tom. Whilst his mental state didn't change, his physical condition improved steadily. His dressings were removed and his hair began to grow back so that he looked much the same as he had done before the accident. Ellie comforted herself with the thought that he didn't appear to be suffering. While his loved ones lost weight and sleep worrying about him, he was perfectly content, living from day to day in the routine of hospital life.

Ellie pointed this out to Pat in the hope of consoling her. 'At least he's happy, Pat, and is blissfully oblivious of what we're going through or that he isn't leading a normal life.'

'That's what upsets me, that his life isn't normal,' she told her.

'But he doesn't know that, does he?' Ellie reminded her. 'Life is wonderful as far as he's concerned. He doesn't have a care in the world now that his head has stopped hurting – no worries, no responsibilities. He has regular meals, nurses to look after him, everything he needs.'

'I pray to God he won't be like this for the rest of his life,' said Pat.

'Me too. I suppose we have to face the fact that he may never be exactly the same as he was before, though,' Ellie mentioned with necessary candour. 'But they're bound to do something to improve on the way he is now.'

'We should get some news soon.'

'Yes,' agreed Ellie. 'But in the meantime I think we ought to get some normality back into our lives. I have a baby to look after and you have a shop to run. Now that Tom's out of danger we should return to doing it.'

'I really don't feel up to running the shop,' Pat told her. 'I feel so weak.'

The trauma had physically weakened Ellie too, so she could sympathise with Pat. 'I'm not exactly bursting with energy either but I think we'll both feel better if we get back to some sort of a normal routine – as far as we can, anyway. In my case it's a necessity. Now that I don't have Tom to provide for Donna and myself, I shall have to get a job. I can't expect you to carry on paying Tom's wages indefinitely when he isn't working.'

'How can you go out to work when you have a baby to look after?' Pat queried.

'I shall have to find someone to mind her,' Ellie said. 'Mum's been brilliant while I've been at the hospital so much but she's got her job to go back to so I can't ask her. She only works part-time so she'll probably be willing to have Donna when she isn't on duty but I shall have to get a full-time job so I'll need someone to look after Donna the rest of the time.'

Pat pondered for a moment. 'Why not come and work for me at the shop?' she blurted out. 'I need an assistant to stand in for Tom while he's out of action.' She paused, searching Ellie's face for her reaction. 'You can bring the baby with you.'

Ellie was extremely doubtful about such an arrangement but she needed a job urgently, and not having to farm Donna out while she was at work was a big consideration. Also, she thought, it would be better for Pat to have someone she knew helping her at this vulnerable time, rather than a stranger.

She took a deep breath and cast her doubts aside. 'That sounds like a good idea,' she said. 'When would you like me to start?'

Ellie often found herself in the role of manager rather than assistant at the Chad Street corner shop. Not only was Pat depressed, she was also emaciated through not being able to eat properly since the accident. So she spent a large part of the day upstairs in the flat. Ellie accepted the responsibility with a willing heart and was soon ordering stock, cashing up and doing the banking.

Having thought she would never again have the courage to drive a motor vehicle, she was forced behind the wheel of the shop van because there was no one else to do the deliveries. Pat herself couldn't drive and had no intention of learning. So it fell to Ellie to do it. Initially she was terrified but her confidence gradually built up, especially as she was driving on familiar territory.

Going to the shop every day wasn't ideal for a baby but the arrangement worked out well enough for the moment. Donna still slept for a large part of the day, and Mary called in regularly to take her for walks in her pram. This being a neighbourhood shop, everyone knew Ellie and made a great fuss of her daughter. It wasn't unknown for a customer to give Donna her bottle, take her for a walk or lift her out of her pram and give her a cuddle if she was crying.

Although Ellie enjoyed the community atmosphere, she knew within days of starting the job that she didn't want it to be long-term. If she was going to have to be the family breadwinner on a permanent basis, she'd rather do something else. She wasn't sure what that might be but she knew it wasn't this.

For now, though, she needed the money as much as Pat needed her. So she took each day as it came and was glad to be busy. It took her mind off Tom, whose condition remained unchanged. She was still waiting for news from the hospital of some sort of breakthrough for him.

News came in February.

One evening when Ellie arrived on the ward – on her own because Pat had been to see Tom during the twice-weekly afternoon visiting hour – Dr Wright called her into his office.

'Sorry we've kept you waiting so long for any definite news about your husband's long-term prospects,' he said. 'We wanted to explore all avenues before we made a final decision. But I am now in a position to give you the result of our assessment.'

'Oh?' Her heart was like lead because it was obvious from his grave expression that she wasn't going to like what she heard.

'Not the sort of news you were hoping for, I'm afraid,' he confirmed.

'No?' She was so tense she could hardly breathe.

'After a great deal of deliberation, we have decided that Tom's condition isn't operable.'

'What, not at all?' she cried. 'Surely there must be something you can do for him?'

'Yes, there is, and everything that can be done will be done,' he assured her.

'Such as?' she demanded.

'His condition can be controlled with drugs. But surgery is not an option.'

'Controlled, not improved,' Ellie snapped. 'You'll keep him sedated so that he doesn't get violent and harm anyone, and leave him to spend the rest of his life as a vegetable.' Despair was making her unreasonable. She'd pinned all her hopes on medical science. 'That's what it boils down to, isn't it?'

'I can understand your being upset, Mrs Hall.' The doctor stared at his hands for a moment. 'But we have done thorough tests and discussed your husband's case at length, which is why we've been so long giving you any definite news. The damage to your husband's brain is so severe that surgery would be too much of a risk to his life.'

'And what sort of a life is that?' she asked through dry lips. 'For a grown man to live as a backward child who doesn't know his loved ones and can't even speak properly?'

Dr Wright took her fury in his stride, his cool grey eyes meeting hers. This sort of thing was all in a day's work to him. 'We've done all we can for him here,' he went on to say, without answering her question. 'So we'll be transferring him to St John's in North London at some time in the next few days.'

'A mental hospital?'

'Yes, that's right. Specialist psychiatric care is what he needs now. Physically Mr Hall is in pretty good shape, considering his injuries. So that's something to be grateful for.'

'What exactly will they do for him at St John's?'

'They'll find the right drugs for him; encourage him to do occupational therapy; try to give him some purpose to his life. He'll be with people trained to cope with someone with his particular disability.'

Ellie gave the doctor a sharp look. 'I get the impression this isn't going to be a short-term thing.'

He sighed, studying his fingernails for a moment before looking up. 'I should think he will be a long-stay patient. But that will be up to the doctors there.' He paused, giving her a kindly look. 'You've seen how he is. You must have been expecting something like this, my dear.'

She sighed, her anger abating as she accepted the inevitable. 'I suppose I just didn't want to face up to it. I think I've been hoping for some sort of a miracle. I just assumed he would be coming home when he was discharged from here.'

'Oh no, that's out of the question. His behaviour is far too unpredictable for him to live in a home environment. Even with sedation he's still a danger to himself and other people. We have to section him.'

'Poor Tom,' Ellie said sadly.

'He'll be well looked after, you know,' the doctor pointed out.

'Institutionalised, though,' she murmured, almost to herself.

He gave her a studious look. 'Surely you must have known you couldn't have him at home, that you wouldn't be able to cope with his violent behaviour?' he said. 'He's a big man with enormous physical strength.'

'I was worried about that part of it, mostly because of the baby,' Ellie was forced to admit. 'I suppose I was hoping his condition would improve.'

'He will improve up to a point with the right drugs,' he informed her. 'But . . .' he paused as though choosing his words carefully, 'he won't ever be much different from how he is now in terms of his mental age. His behaviour should become more stable but his brain isn't going to grow like that of a child. So we have to treat his condition as a permanent one and do what's best for him as he is, rather than thinking in terms of a change. I'm afraid you'll have to accept that the damage is irreversible.'

'So he'll have to live in an institution for the rest of his life?'

'Who knows what might happen in the future?' He leaned back, putting his forefingers under his chin. 'Medical science is advancing all the time. All I can say is that with the treatment that is available at the moment, a mental hospital is the only option.'

Throughout the entire bruising experience of the accident and its after-effects, Ellie's concern had focused on Tom, his wellbeing, his recovery. Now, as she faced up to the fact that there wasn't going to be a recovery, her own situation came sharply into view. To all intents and purposes she was on her own now, a single parent. Every decision must be hers, every responsibility. It was a daunting realisation, all the more so because Tom had always been such a dominant presence in her life.

Turning her attention back to Tom's plight, she said, 'The thought of my husband having to spend the rest of his life in a mental hospital is awfully grim. Is there really no alternative?'

The doctor tapped his fingers against his chin thoughtfully. 'There is but it's in the private sector,' he explained.

'A nursing home?'

'Yes, but there's more to it than an ordinary nursing home. It's a specialist unit in the country near Senbridge in Surrey, not far from Dorking. Greenlands is a large country house converted into a nursing home for people with special problems like Tom's. Quite a few of the residents are accident victims, some of them young.'

'What can Greenlands give them that an ordinary hospital can't?' she wanted to know.

'A better quality of life,' he informed her. 'Because it's smaller and they have more staff, the patients get more individual attention. They can't cure their condition but they can give them privacy and more specialist care.'

'In what way?'

'They encourage them to have hobbies and to take part in sporting and social activities – within their own capabilities, of course. They offer them a challenge and a chance to stretch themselves at Greenlands.'

'Sounds nice.'

'It is,' he said. 'It's set in extensive grounds and is in a lovely spot. Patients really thrive in those surroundings. Of course, there is a disadvantage in that it's outside of London so visiting isn't so easy for many of the relatives.'

He reached into one of the drawers in his desk and pulled out a brochure which he handed to Ellie. 'This will give you an idea of what the place has to offer.'

Looking at pictures of a country mansion, Ellie was impressed but what really made an impact was the smiling faces of the people pictured in the sunlit grounds, talking together in groups, some in wheelchairs. A few young men were playing football. 'The patients all look so happy,' she remarked.

He nodded.

She flicked through the brochure again. 'I can't see the price anywhere,' she said.

'It differs with individual needs.'

'I suppose it costs the earth,' Ellie guessed.

'It isn't as expensive as other private nursing homes because it's partly funded by a charity,' he explained. 'But it is outside of the National Health Service and is therefore a fee-paying establishment. If it were within the NHS I would already have recommended Tom for a place there because it would be absolutely ideal for him.'

'I think it would be too,' she said wistfully.

'Maybe one day there'll be places like Greenlands available to NHS patients,' he remarked.

Ellie didn't reply. She was preoccupied with the beginnings of an idea. 'Could you arrange a place there for Tom if I could afford to pay for it?' she asked.

'Of course, but . . .'

'You're right to look doubtful; I can't afford it at the moment,' she admitted with a strong note of determination in her voice. 'But I might be able to in the not-too-distant future.'

The doctor's brows rose but he didn't dismiss what she said. 'It would be wonderful for Tom if you were able to manage it,' he enthused.

She appreciated the fact that he appeared to be taking her seriously since she obviously wasn't from the sort of background that ran to private medical care. 'It won't be for lack of trying if I can't,' she told him, her mood now buoyant with fresh hope. 'He'll have to go to St John's for the moment but I shall do everything I can to get him into Greenlands as soon as possible. I want the very best for him.'

'Would you like me to find out if there's a waiting list?' he suggested kindly.

'Yes, please,' she said in a positive manner. 'It would be useful to know the situation as regards that.'

★ ★ ★

'Have you noticed how the customers have stopped asking about Tom now that he's in St John's?' Pat said to Ellie one morning in the early spring, during a quiet period in the shop.

'They haven't stopped asking,' corrected Ellie, stacking some tins of baked beans on to the shelf behind the counter. 'Only this morning, someone enquired about him.'

'They're not asking as often as they used to, though, are they?' insisted Pat, who was working most of the day in the shop now but still left a lot of the responsibility to Ellie.

'That's probably because he's off the danger list,' suggested Ellie. 'People don't stop caring but they have other things on their minds, problems of their own to worry about.'

'It isn't that,' said Pat, emptying a bag of copper into the till drawer. 'It's because he's in a mental hospital, or loony bin as they call it. They think he's mad.'

'People are embarrassed about mental illness, for some reason, that's true,' admitted Ellie. 'But in Tom's case I really believe it's because they know he isn't seriously ill now. The accident isn't front-page news around here any more. They know he's going to be all right.'

'Out of sight out of mind, more like it,' Pat said bitterly. 'The poor boy is stuck there in St John's with no one of his own to look after him. Thank goodness the place is near enough for us to visit on a regular basis.'

Ellie had mentioned nothing to Pat about Greenlands and didn't intend to until she had something definite to say. 'Tom doesn't care if we go to visit him or not,' Ellie pointed out frankly. 'He's in a world of his own.'

'I think he is pleased to see us, you know.' Pat was an expert at self-delusion when it came to Tom. 'I know he doesn't appear to bother one way or the other but we don't know what he's feeling inside, do we?'

'I think we can get a pretty good idea,' replied Ellie. 'He's happy enough whether we go to see him or not.'

'It twists my heart every time I think of him being in that terrible place,' Pat went on.

Ellie had to admit that going to St John's was an extremely depressing experience. There were some very tragic cases in the ward with Tom: poor disturbed souls of all ages, senile dementia patients who wandered about in bewilderment talking to themselves; manic depressives who stared silently into space; hollow-eyed overdose patients brought back from the brink of suicide. It certainly made Ellie count her blessings.

There had been a particularly upsetting incident during a recent visit when Tom had wet himself in the day room. This had brought ridicule and fury from the other patients.

'Dirty bugger,' one patient had said. 'He ought to be in a locked ward, not fit to mix with decent people.'

Ellie had been hurt on his behalf; had been protective of him. But Tom hadn't been touched by it. He'd simply allowed himself to be led away by a nurse for a change of clothes. The incident had been on Ellie's mind for days afterwards. She couldn't stop thinking about his loss of pride and dignity. Fortunately Pat had had a heavy cold that day so hadn't been able to go with Ellie to visit. She'd have been very upset. Ellie had spared her feelings by keeping it to herself.

Now Ellie replied, 'St John's is a bit grim, but the staff do the best they can for the patients. It's a difficult job.'

'At least it's near enough for us to visit regularly and keep an eye on things,' said Pat.

Ellie didn't say anything; just nodded.

'I can't tell you what a relief it is for me to have you working with me,' Pat said with a kind of morbid enthusiasm. 'You've been my salvation since the accident.'

'I haven't done anything,' was Ellie's modest reply.

'You've been here by my side. I couldn't have faced a stranger stepping into Tom's shoes here at the shop.'

As well meant as this sort of talk was, it made Ellie feel trapped; there was rather too much of it lately. 'I'm sure you'd have got used to it eventually,' she said.

'Thank goodness I didn't have to.' Pat was eager to convince Ellie.

A customer came in for some streaky bacon and Ellie got busy at the bacon slicer.

'How's the baby?' asked the customer.

'She's lovely, thanks,' said Ellie. 'Asleep in the back at the moment.'

'They're easy to manage at that age but you'll have your work cut out when she starts running around, won't you?' remarked the customer in a friendly manner. 'With you being behind the counter, I mean.'

'I certainly will,' agreed Ellie, who was only too well aware of the difficulties she would face when Donna became mobile. 'I shall have to make proper arrangements for her then.'

'Ellie and I will manage between us,' said Pat matily. 'We make a good team, don't we, dear?'

These constant references to Pat's reliance on her were beginning to feel threatening, but Ellie's compassion for Pat was unabated. To have your only son become so tragically disabled was a terrible burden for anyone to live with, though it was becoming obvious that Pat used pity as a tool in her bid for self-preservation.

There were times when Ellie suspected that Pat blamed her for the accident. Something in her eyes when Ellie had expressed her own doubts about this had made her feel uneasy. But Pat never came right out and said it. Ellie wasn't sure if she held back for fear of losing Ellie's friendship or if she herself were imagining things because she was so full of guilt.

Ellie weighed the bacon in greaseproof paper, then wrapped the paper around it and put it into a bag. She then added a bag of sugar, some self-raising flour, currants and tinned peas to the collection of purchases on the counter.

'Got any frozen peas?' the customer asked.

'No, we don't do frozen food,' Ellie told her.

'That's a nuisance,' the woman tutted. 'I shall have to go all the way to the town to the self-service store to get some.'

'Humph,' snorted Pat. Self-service store was a thing you mentioned to her at your peril. 'There's plenty of fresh veg outside.' She kept a modest selection of fruit and vegetables under the awning outside the shop.

'It's too early in the year for fresh peas,' the customer pointed out, 'and frozen ones are the next best thing.'

'We've plenty of tinned peas,' said Pat.

'No, I want the frozen ones,' insisted the customer, who was a long-standing regular. 'They're almost the same as fresh ones and very quick to cook. You can have them all year round too.'

'Yes, I've tried them and thought they were nice,' added Ellie sociably.

'Are you going to be stocking them in the future, Mrs Hall?' enquired the customer.

'I've no plans to,' said Pat stiffly. 'People around here haven't got fridges, and you need the ice-box section to store frozen food.'

'You'd be surprised how many have got fridges now, and more people are buying them every day,' the customer disagreed. 'Anyway, you don't need a fridge to have frozen peas if you cook them straight away.'

'I'm not planning to stock them.' Pat stood her ground.

'It might be worth your while considering it, love,' said the woman, who wasn't shy about making suggestions. 'Frozen food is getting to be very popular. The kids love fish fingers. Anyway, I'm off to get some frozen peas down the town.'

The customer was spared a sharp retort from Pat by the sound of the baby crying in the back room. Before Ellie had a chance to respond Pat pre-empted the situation, leaving Ellie serving a sudden rush of customers. The shop was empty when Pat reappeared. 'Is she all right?' Ellie asked.

'She's fine.'

'What was the matter with her?'

'She'd lost her dummy,' Pat explained. 'I found it on the floor and she's gone back to sleep. Dipping the dummy in the sugar works wonders.'

'Oh, Pat.' This was very awkward for Ellie. 'You know I don't like you to do that.'

'It doesn't do any harm,' said Pat. 'And she loves it.'

'Too much sugar isn't good for her,' Ellie explained.

'That little bit won't hurt.'

'That isn't the point.' Ellie tried not to mind. This was a small thing, trivial on its own, but an irritation when it was one of many incidents in which her mother-in-law completely disregarded her wishes. Ellie knew that she must be firm about these little issues or she'd be in danger of having Pat take over her daughter's upbringing altogether. 'You know I don't approve. I really would rather you didn't do it.'

'It's coming to something when a grandmother can't give her own grandchild a bit of comfort.' She was full of pique. 'She is my grandchild. I do have some rights.'

'But she's my daughter and therefore my responsibility,' Ellie returned.

'I'm only trying to help.' Pat was very downcast. 'Since the accident I've done my best for you and Donna. I pay you almost as much as I used to pay Tom so that you can live decently and pay all your bills.'

Ellie curbed the impulse to point out that she worked every bit as hard as Tom had, and carried far more responsibility than any shop assistant could reasonably expect. Everything from customer deliveries to buying stock fell to her and she often ran the shop single-handed for long periods when Pat was upstairs in the flat, nursing her broken heart over the fate of her son.

Pat had the same power as Tom had once had to bend the will of those who opposed her. But what he had achieved with bullying tactics, his mother gained by inspiring pity. She looked utterly forlorn, lips trembling, small grey eyes brimming with tears, shoulders bent forward.

'Yes, I know you've been good to us and I really do appreciate it.' Ellie felt heartless but knew she must establish her point, however difficult. 'But it would help me if you could do what I ask when it comes to Donna.' She tried to soften the blow by being chummy. 'You know how us new mums are with our babies. I expect you were the same when Tom was little. We all want to do things our own way.'

Pat shrugged and took her handkerchief out of her overall pocket and sniffed into it.

'Don't let's fall out over this.' Ellie was being totally sincere. 'We're bound to have different ideas about what's best for Donna. It's only natural.'

But Pat was having none of it. 'In future,' she said haughtily, the rigid stance of her shoulders indicating the extent of her umbrage, 'I won't do anything for the child at all unless I get permission from you first.'

This was her way of trying to make Ellie feel bad enough to back down and give her a free hand with Donna. Ellie felt utterly wretched but wasn't prepared to be bullied into doing that. 'Obviously there's no need to go that far,' she told her.

'That way I can't do wrong,' was her cool response.

'Please don't be hurt,' urged Ellie.

'Of course I'm hurt. I'm not made of stone,' she said mournfully. 'But don't worry, I'll do what you want.'

'Thank you.' Ellie effected a swift change of subject to defuse the situation. 'I was wondering,' she began, 'if it might be worth your while thinking about getting a freezer cabinet and stocking a small range of frozen food. Judging by the number of people who ask for it, there must be a growing demand.'

Pat looked around the shop, which wasn't organised to maximum efficiency. Too much space was taken up with cartons of tinned food that wouldn't fit in the stockroom, and dry goods such as toilet rolls and cleaning materials. 'We don't have the space for it,' she stated.

''We would with a little reorganisation,' Ellie suggested keenly. 'All we need to do is move things around.'

'I can't be bothered,' said Pat gloomily. 'I don't have the energy even to think about it.'

'It might be just what you need,' enthused Ellie. 'Something new to take an interest in.'

'There would be all the expense of getting a deep-freeze cabinet.' Pat was completely negative. 'This shop has always stocked traditional lines.'

'Frozen food is fast becoming a traditional line. Anyway, it's always a good idea to move with the times when you're in business,' Ellie pointed out. 'As the customer said, even people without fridges buy frozen peas for immediate use.'

'No, I don't want the bother,' said Pat.

'Look at it this way,' Ellie persisted. 'If someone has to go to the self-service store to get a packet of frozen peas they might end up getting everything else there too. Then where would you be?'

Pat pondered on the question. 'There is that,' she sighed. 'All right, I'll think about it.'

'Good.' Ellie looked at her watch. 'Well, I reckon it's about time we had a cup of tea, don't you? Before we get inundated with customers again.'

'Yes, that would be nice.' Pat's manner was still chilly but Ellie detected a slight softening.

'I'll put the kettle on then, shall I?' said Ellie, who never took anything for granted and always kept in mind the fact that she was Pat's employee as well as her son's wife.

'If you would, dear.'

Ellie was still feeling tense as she put the kettle on in the staff room at the back of the shop. Talk about a new business venture seemed to have calmed the waters for the moment, but she sensed more trouble ahead. Working with a relative wasn't always a good idea.

It was just after lights out and Ray Brent lay on his bunk staring into the darkness and listening to the sound of stifled sobs from the new arrival in the bunk below. Kenny had only been here a day or two and was finding it hard going. He was only twenty-one.

Guessing that the other man wouldn't want Ray to acknow-ledge the fact that he was weeping, he said nothing and tried to block out the painful sound, staring at the shadow of the barred window on the wall caused by the lights outside shining through it. He could look at that image now without an adverse reaction but for a long time after he'd come in he'd had to keep his eyes tightly closed against it. The sight of the bars had given him panic attacks, reminding him that he was locked in. His heart would thump and he'd be in a cold sweat for most of the night. The screws seemed to slam the cell doors hard to make sure you didn't forget. That was a long time ago, though. Since then he'd learned to cope with the claustrophobia. Discipline of the mind was the answer. Plenty of that was needed in prison.

He'd never forget those early days: the beatings he'd taken from hardened villains, reminding him who ran things around here, until he'd learned to keep out of their way; the retching from the stench of the slop bucket, and the sheer dehumanisation of prison life.

But now Kenny continued to sound distressed and Ray decided that an intervention was necessary.

'Here, turn it in, Kenny,' he said in a low voice. 'We have to be up early in the morning, mate, and they keep you on the go all day. You'll need your sleep.'

'Sorry.'

'That's all right, son,' Ray said kindly. 'But you'll have to learn not to let it get you down in here.'

'Yeah, I know.' The young man's voice was thick and shaky.

'It's hard for you to imagine at the moment,' Ray continued, 'but you do actually become used to being in here and it gets easier.'

There was no reply and Ray knew Kenny was weeping again, despite his best endeavours to conceal it. Ray climbed down and sat on the edge of the other man's bunk. Kenny turned on to his side away from him.

'We've all been there, you know,' Ray told him. 'We've all

been through what you're going through now.'

'It's stinking in here, not fit for human beings.' His voice was muffled.

'Yeah, well, it's a place of punishment, isn't it?' Ray pointed out. 'They're not likely to put us up in a posh hotel.'

'You know what I mean.'

'We all know what it's like at first, even if some of the blokes would never admit it,' said Ray. 'I was in a terrible state when I first came in.'

There was a silence, then Kenny rolled over slowly on to his back. He was a pimply, unprepossessing young man with crooked teeth and small, deep-set eyes. 'Not you, Brent,' he said in surprise. 'I can't imagine you letting it get to you.'

'Of course it got to me,' Ray told him. 'What do you think I am – some hardened villain who's lost the need for decent living conditions?'

'No, course not. But you seem to be sorted . . . seem to know your way around.'

'Only because I've been here a long time,' Ray explained. 'You toughen up after a while.'

'What are you in for?'

'Manslaughter.'

'Blimey.'

'What about you?'

'Robbery. Me and some other blokes did a post office job.'

'That sort of thing's a mug's game.'

'I realise that now it's too late,' Kenny admitted. 'Some mates I know organised it. I didn't wanna go on the job in the end.'

'Why get involved?'

'Got caught up in the thrill of it, I suppose,' he confessed with a sigh. 'When I tried to back out at the last minute, they threatened to put me in hospital.'

'That would have been better than coming in here,' said Ray. 'It would have been shorter, anyway.'

'I didn't know we weren't gonna get away with it, did I?'

Kenny said. 'I was more afraid of what they'd do to me than getting caught. Seems stupid now.'

'We're all wise after the event.'

Kenny put his hands behind his head, looking at Ray and seeming calmer now. 'So, who did you kill?' he enquired.

'They reckon I killed a bloke in a fight.'

'Meaning that you didn't do it,' said Kenny, knowingly. 'Everyone in here reckons they didn't do the crime they were convicted of, according to one of the screws. "This prison is full of innocent men," he said, the sarky git.'

Ray wasn't prepared to take the discussion any further along that road as far as his own circumstances were concerned. He'd learned a long time ago that there was no point. 'He's right to some extent. Denial is rife in here.'

'Well, I won't deny what I did but I don't know how I'm gonna get through another day,' confessed Kenny.

'You'll get through it because you don't have a choice, son,' Ray advised him. 'Day follows day no matter how bad you feel and somehow you live to tell the tale.'

'Easy for someone tough like you.'

'I'm good at *pretending* to be tough,' he corrected.

'Same thing, innit?'

'No, not at all,' replied Ray. 'I learned early on that you don't do yourself any favours in here by showing any sign of weakness. It doesn't matter how feeble you feel or how scared you actually are, you have to act strong. You can be crying for your mother inside your head but you don't let anyone know that.'

'Is that right?'

'Yep. Keep out of trouble and take any opportunity that prison offers, is my advice to you.'

'Opportunity? In prison? Don't make me laugh.'

'There are classes,' Ray told him. 'I've made use of them and learned a new skill.'

'No thanks,' Kenny said. 'I couldn't stand school as a kid. I'm not gonna go back to it now.'

113

'It's up to you, of course,' Ray went on, 'but it helps to pass the time.'

'I'll give that one a miss, thanks.'

'Fair enough. One thing I will say, though,' Ray went on, 'you'll make things worse for yourself if you try to buck the system. The screws will have it in for you if you make trouble for them and it isn't a good idea to make enemies of them.'

'I'm more worried about the other prisoners,' Kenny told him. 'There are some real hard cases in here.'

'Yeah, there are. The majority of the blokes are all right, though,' said Ray to reassure him.

'Plenty of corruption, I bet.'

'Bound to get that in a prison. Just keep your nose clean and don't be too trusting. Some of the so-called hard men will have you beaten up as soon as look at you if you cross them.'

'Thanks for cheering me up.'

'Just giving you a friendly warning,' explained Ray. 'Look strong and don't get stroppy and you'll be all right. Once they know you're no threat to them the hard men will leave you alone.'

'Thanks, Brent,' said Kenny. 'I feel a lot better now we've had a chat.'

'Good. Now, is it worth my going back to my bunk or are you going to start blubbing again and keep me awake all night?' Ray asked good-humouredly.

'No, I'll be all right now.'

'Thank God for that, because we both need some shuteye,' said Ray, climbing back to his own bunk. 'Night, mate.'

'Night, Brent.'

Poor bugger, thought Ray, lying down and pulling the rough, smelly blanket over him. He was glad he didn't have to go through the terror of those early days again.

As the cell fell silent, Ray turned his mind to a less depressing topic: the future and his plans for when he became a free man again. That day couldn't come quickly enough for him. But he was under no illusions about it. He knew it wasn't going to be easy to build a new life after a prison sentence. Many a man's good intentions fell apart under the harshness of society's attitude towards ex-cons.

'Anything wrong, love?' Bob enquired of his wife one evening over their meal of toad-in-the-hole. 'You've got that worried look about you.'

'It's Ellie,' she sighed.

He tensed. 'What's happened now?' he asked.

'Nothing new.'

'So what are you worried about?' His voice was warm with relief. 'Ellie's doing fine, coping really well. I'm proud of her.'

'So am I. She's a brave girl, getting on with her life without a fuss even though it's obvious she's feeling dreadful,' said Mary. 'But I'm not sure if the full impact of what happened to Tom has sunk in properly yet, the fact that he's never going to get better, that she's lost the love of her life for ever. God knows what she's going to feel like when it does.'

Putting down his knife and fork, Bob reached across the table and put a comforting hand on her arm. 'Ellie's a fighter, she'll come through it,' he reassured, 'and we'll be here for her if she needs us. So stop worrying.'

'I'll try.' She managed a smile but knowing that her daughter was suffering was almost a physical pain to Mary.

Chapter Six

In May Ann gave birth to a son.

'Well done,' Ellie congratulated when she came to visit one evening soon after the birth. She peered at the rumpled little face of her new nephew sleeping in his mother's arms. 'He's absolutely beautiful.'

'You won't hear me disagreeing with you about that.' Ann was beaming.

'Have you decided on a name for him yet?'

'We've more or less agreed on Matthew.'

'I like that,' Ellie approved. 'It'll be nice when he grows up too.' She grinned. 'I must say it's very obliging of you to have done what I asked and provided Donna with a cousin. They'll be glad of each other in a few years' time.'

'I'm pleased that they're near enough in age to grow up together too.'

Sitting at the side of her sister-in-law's bed, Ann having had a home delivery, Ellie thought how serene and pretty she looked, propped up against the pillows in her pink bedjacket, eyes shining, skin seeming to have a new bloom to it. Doug was downstairs in the kitchen seeing to some refreshments.

'Doug's bursting with it, isn't he?' Ellie said. 'I don't think I've ever seen such a proud dad.'

'He is chuffed,' Ann confirmed. 'I suppose most men are when their first child is born. I expect Tom was the same when Donna arrived.'

'He was pleased, of course,' said Ellie. 'But Doug's like a man reborn.'

'The baby does seem to have given him a new lease of life.' Ann became solemn. 'He was really knocked back by Tom's accident, you know, even though he did his best not to show it. He's been depressed ever since . . . until now.'

'It was bound to have had an effect on him,' Ellie remarked. 'They'd been mates a long time.'

'He's been having bad nights on and off ever since the accident,' Ann continued. 'But now that his nibs has arrived, he seems full of beans and I'm hoping the dreams will stop.'

'I hope so too.'

They chatted about babies and childbirth for a while. Ann asked Ellie who was baby-sitting for her this evening. She said her mother was.

'How's Tom?' Ann enquired conversationally.

Ellie's features tightened, a fleeting moment of worry dulling her eyes. 'He's all right,' she replied. 'Well . . . about the same really. Happy in his own little world.'

'Is something wrong, Ellie? I mean something else?'

'No.'

'That isn't the impression I'm getting.'

Ellie forced a smile. 'I'm fine, honestly,' she assured Ann. 'Don't worry about me.'

'If you say so.' Ann wasn't convinced but didn't pursue the matter because she didn't want to intrude. 'How's the job going?'

'Not too bad.' Ellie smiled as she thought of something. 'Actually we've had a bit of excitement this week because Pat's splashed out on a deep-freeze cabinet. As from yesterday, we're stocking a modest selection of frozen foods.'

'Wow,' laughed Ann. 'The Chad Street corner shop really is moving into the modern world.'

'At least it's given Pat something else to think about besides Tom,' Ellie confided.

'It was worth doing just for that then.'

'It certainly was,' agreed Ellie. 'I think it'll be a commercial success too. It's doing well already.'

Doug came in carrying a tray of tea and biscuits. He was grinning widely. 'Well, what do you think?' he asked Ellie, glancing towards the baby before putting the tray down on the dressing table.

'A masterpiece,' was her heartfelt verdict. 'You can both be very proud.' She gave him a wicked smile. 'I didn't think my shy, retiring brother had it in him.'

'Watch it,' he riposted.

'Just kidding,' she said. 'I expected nothing less of you than a bouncing baby boy.'

'That's more like it.' He looked at her enquiringly. 'So how are things with you?'

'Fine.'

'How's Tom?'

Again Ellie tensed. 'About the same, Doug. But he's OK . . . seems quite happy.'

He gave her a sharp look but knew better than to probe. If his sister wanted him to know what was bothering her, she would tell him in her own good time. 'That's all right then,' he said, and turned his attention to the refreshments, taking the baby and lifting him gently into his carrycot so that Ann could drink her tea.

'I'm enjoying being waited on,' smiled Ann. 'I could become accustomed to having a slave.'

'Don't get too used to it,' laughed Doug affectionately. 'Things will revert to normal once you're on your feet again. I'll be the slave-driver again.'

'That'll be the day,' was Ann's light retort.

They chatted pleasantly until Ellie said she had to go, sooner than they'd expected. 'Don't want to keep Mum out too late,' she explained.

After he'd seen Ellie out, Doug went back upstairs to the bedroom to keep his wife company.

'Unless I'm very much mistaken Ellie's worried about something,' said Ann.

'I wasn't fooled by her beaming smile either,' agreed Doug, sitting on the edge of the bed.

'She looked odd when I mentioned Tom,' Ann remarked. 'And the same thing happened when you asked her how he was.'

'I hope he hasn't taken a turn for the worse and she's keeping it from us so as not to spoil our big event.' Doug looked anxious.

'I wondered if it might be something like that too.'

'Oh well, if it's anything serious we'll find out in due course,' said Doug.

Ann nodded in agreement and they both turned their attention to a more immediate problem as an agitated grunting sound from the carrycot built quickly to a loud, resonant wail.

As soon as her brother closed the door behind her Ellie's expression darkened. She was worried about the daunting task that lay ahead of her. It had been on her mind all evening but she hadn't wanted to burden Ann and Doug with her problems at a time of such personal joy for them.

She hadn't previously planned to go ahead and do it tonight but had decided at some point during the last hour or so that as the dread of it was shadowing her life, it made sense to get it over with while she had the opportunity. Contrary to the impression she'd given her brother and his wife, her mother wasn't actually expecting her back yet. So she had time.

With knots of nervous apprehension pulling tight in her stomach, she headed for Chad Street.

'Surrey!' exclaimed Pat, her eyes wide with shock. 'You're having Tom moved to some nursing home in the back of beyond?'

Ellie took a sip of coffee to moisten her dry mouth. They were in Pat's living room, sitting either side of the unlit hearth.

Ellie had been to Greenlands last Sunday to look round and meet the staff, but she had only been able to impart to Pat a little of what the place had to offer and how it was now possible for Tom to go there, before she'd been interrupted by Pat's explosion. 'I've come to talk to you about it, to see what you think.'

'You've already made up your mind,' accused Pat.

In all honesty Ellie couldn't deny it. 'I do think it would be the best thing for Tom, yes, I admit that,' she said, smarting from the fury in Pat's eyes but knowing she had to stand her ground for Tom's sake. 'But I'd like you to be happy about it too.'

'How can I possibly be happy about it when it means I'll never see him,' Pat wailed.

'You *will* still see him.'

'Not so often.'

'No, not so often,' Ellie was forced to agree. 'But we'd still visit him regularly. We'll go together . . . say once a month or so, on the train. I wouldn't dream of not going to see him just because he's further away.'

Pat lapsed into a sulky angry silence. Her face and neck were suffused with scarlet patches, which indicated that she was genuinely distressed and not just making a fuss to draw attention to the importance of her position as Tom's mother and her right to have a say in his future. 'Insurance money, you say,' she muttered, fiddling nervously with the collar of her dreary navy-blue summer dress that had the shapeless look of an overall about it.

'Yes, as I've just explained, I put a claim into the insurance company after the accident as soon as it became obvious how seriously injured Tom was, based on the fact that he is going to need special care for the rest of his life,' she informed her. 'And because the accident was the other driver's fault and there is police evidence to prove that, they've paid the claim in full so I can afford to let him go to Greenlands.'

Pat emitted an eloquent sigh. 'I see,' she said.

121

'I haven't touched the money myself,' Ellie went on to explain. 'I've had it all, even the amount they paid for the car to be replaced, put into a trust fund for Tom. I want him to have the best care I can afford. Honestly, Pat, I don't think he'll do better than Greenlands.'

'All this time you've been planning and scheming to get poor Tom out of the way, and not a word to me, his mother,' Pat lashed out, her eyes burning with hostility. 'I didn't even know you were trying to get money from the insurance company.'

'I'm not trying to set this up because I want to get Tom out of the way and I didn't say anything about the insurance claim because I didn't know if the company would pay up.' Ellie knew Pat had resorted to calumny because she was desperate, and tried not to be too hurt by it. 'I wanted to be in a position to do something definite before I mentioned Greenlands to you. But now that I am, I'm here to discuss it with you. I haven't signed anything yet. I thought you might like to go with me to have a look at the place before I actually set the wheels in motion for him to go there.'

'I'm not going to look at it. As far as I'm concerned it's a terrible idea and I don't know how you can even consider sending Tom somewhere miles away from the people who love him.'

'I'm not keen on that side of it either,' Ellie confessed. 'But we have to do what's best for Tom, not what's best for us.'

'The best thing for Tom is to be somewhere that's easily accessible to his relatives,' insisted Pat. 'The poor boy won't have anyone of his own to see him every week if he's stuck out in Surrey. He'll think we've abandoned him.'

Ellie took a deep, calming breath. Being a mother herself she could fully empathise with Pat. She could hardly bear to imagine how she would feel if in twenty-odd years' time her darling Donna became a broken human being who didn't even know her own mother. 'We both know that those sort of thoughts aren't possible for him,' she said soberly.

'All right. But I'll think it; *I'll* know we've abandoned him,' Pat's voice quivered.

'But we won't have, either of us,' Ellie told her. 'I know it's hard for you to accept this but Tom's happiness lies with the medical staff and the other patients, not us. Whether we go to see him or not makes no difference to him. It will be exactly the same if he goes to Greenlands but better for him because he'll have a higher level of personal attention and more things to interest him.'

'You're going to have him sent there whatever I say, aren't you?' Pat's voice was breaking.

'Please try to understand that, as his wife and next of kin, it's my duty to give Tom any opportunity within my means,' Ellie entreated. 'But you're his mother and your opinion means a lot to me.'

'Huh!'

'It's true whether you believe it or not.' Ellie spoke from the heart. 'If only you could bring yourself to open your mind to the advantages Greenlands has to offer Tom, I'm sure you'd be as keen as I am for him to go there.'

'Oh, what's the point of my saying anything?' Pat said in a tone of bitter resignation. 'You've obviously made up your mind. I don't have any control over my own son's future. Just imagine how you'd feel if this was Donna.'

'I already have, believe me,' Ellie told her with a sad shake of her head. 'But when it comes to the crunch I'm the one who has to make a decision on Tom's behalf. Surely you can't really think it's been easy for me?'

'You don't seem to have had too much trouble.'

'You're not being fair,' Ellie defended. 'Don't you think I miss Tom and hurt for him, and need him by my side, knowing that he's never going to be there again? God knows, Pat, there isn't much we can do for him. Don't let's deprive him of the little we can do. Don't let's stand in the way of his having a better quality of life just because we won't see him so often.'

123

But Pat seemed unable to view the matter logically. 'You won't get round me with pretty speeches,' she ranted, her eyes bright with angry tears. 'It's wrong to have your sick husband stuck out miles away from anywhere.'

'Greenlands is in Surrey, not the Australian Bush,' Ellie pointed out. 'We can get there by train and bus.'

'And how long will that last, eh?' questioned Pat, her eyes narrowed venomously on Ellie. 'You'll soon get fed up with all that travelling. It'll be out of sight, out of mind, and Tom left to rot in the country.'

Because Ellie knew how traumatised Pat was, she was managing to hang on to her temper but the strain of the other woman's belligerence was taking its toll. 'If you really do believe that, you don't know me at all,' she said wearily.

'I don't know you,' was Pat's acid reply. 'I thought I did but this proves what a stranger you really are.'

'I've loved Tom for the whole of my life, and that's something you *do* know if you'll only allow yourself to admit it.' Ellie's tone was firmer now. She couldn't allow Pat to trample all over her. 'And my life as well as yours has been shattered by his accident. Not a moment goes by when I don't long to have him back as he was. Maybe it's worse for you as his mother – I don't know. I doubt if such things can be measured.'

Pat shrugged in reply.

'If Tom hadn't got married, you would be the one making the decisions,' Ellie continued. 'As it is I have to do it. Sure as hell poor Tom can't do it for himself. And I couldn't live with myself if I just sat back and let him rot away at St John's when I have the means to make things better for him.'

'Better for you, more like.'

Ellie counted to ten. 'Look, Pat,' she began, 'Tom has seven days a week to live through and our visits are a very tiny part of his week, a part he won't miss since most times he takes no notice of us at all, and that's something you can't deny. I want a general improvement for him and I know he'll get that at Greenlands.'

'You just want shot of him,' Pat said, her voice rising hysterically. 'He's a nuisance to you now.'

'How can you say that?'

'Oh, get out!' shrieked Pat, leaping up, openly sobbing now. 'Go on, get out of my home. Go away and leave me alone. You're nothing but a cold-hearted bitch.'

Ellie was crying too as she made her way downstairs and left the premises.

Because Ellie was so distressed when she got home, she bared her soul to her mother. 'What am I supposed to do, Mum?' she said, her eyes red and swollen from crying. 'I must do the right thing for Tom, but Pat's in such a state about it, I feel I can't give her another blow after all she's been through.'

'She has had a tough time,' agreed Mary, 'what with losing George, then Tom's accident. But it hasn't exactly been a bed of roses for you lately either.'

'This isn't about me, or Pat,' cried Ellie. 'This is about Tom. I could leave him at St John's and he wouldn't know any different. But that isn't fair to him when I have the money to get something better for him.'

'There is no question but that you must go ahead with your plans for him to go to Greenlands,' Mary stated categorically. 'Pat will come round when she's had time to think about it.'

'I'm not so sure,' disagreed Ellie miserably.

'We'll just have to wait and see, won't we?' Mary put her knitting into her bag and got up purposefully, slipping her hand-knitted white cardigan on over her colourful summer dress. 'But I'm sure she'll see sense. So try not to worry.'

'Thanks for sitting with Donna,' said Ellie.

'A pleasure, love,' Mary assured her. 'There hasn't been a sound out of her so I didn't have to do anything.'

'Good.'

'Oh, by the way,' said Mary, as they headed for the front door, 'you know that knitting machine I ordered from my next-door neighbour's mail-order catalogue?'

Ellie nodded.

'It arrived this morning so I'm going to try it out when I get home.'

'How exciting,' Ellie managed to enthuse. 'I bet you can't wait to get home to get started.'

Mary hesitated for a moment. 'That's right, dear,' she said.

'I'd like to have a go myself the next time I come round, if you'll let me,' said Ellie. 'There are a stack of things I want to knit for Donna, but it takes so much time.'

'They say you can knit ever so fast on these machines. Some of our customers at the wool shop have got them. They don't half get through some wool.'

'Yes, I've heard they're good,' commented Ellie. 'I'll be interested to know how you get on with yours.'

'I'll keep you posted,' Mary promised.

'Night, Mum.'

'Night, love.'

Mary turned at the gate. 'Now don't you lie awake all night worrying about Pat,' she advised. 'She'll see it your way when she's calmed down.'

Ellie nodded. 'Have fun with your new toy.'

'Yes. See you soon.'

Mary headed down the street, but she didn't go straight home to her knitting machine as she'd led Ellie to believe. There was something far more important she had to attend to first.

Wearing a red dressing gown and pink hairnet, Pat was scowling when she answered the door to Mary. 'Oh, it's you,' she grunted.

'I know it's late but we need to talk,' Mary explained.

'I suppose you're here on your daughter's behalf, to try and talk me round about this wretched place she wants to send Tom to in Surrey,' she said accusingly.

'I've come because I think you might need a friend,' Mary corrected.

'Oh.' There was no mistaking the relief in Pat's eyes, though Mary knew she'd rather die than admit it.

'So, do I get to come inside or are we going to talk out here on the doorstep?'

'Ellie's told you what I think of the idea, I suppose,' Pat said as they sat down in the living room with some coffee.

'Yes, she's told me,' confirmed Mary. 'But before you start jumping to conclusions and thinking she came running to me with tales, that isn't how it was. She was obviously upset when she got back from here so, naturally, I asked her what was wrong. She poured her heart out. If she hadn't been so distressed she probably wouldn't have said a word.'

Staring at her hands, which were trembling, Pat said, 'I'm not feeling any too grand myself, to tell you the truth. This Surrey idea for Tom has knocked me for six, Mary.'

'That's perfectly understandable.' Mary paused for a moment, looking at her. 'You and I have been friends long enough to be honest with each other, haven't we?'

'Which sounds to me as if you're about to tell me that I'm wrong and Ellie is right,' Pat surmised.

'I hope I have a little more sensitivity than that,' Mary told her. 'But I am going to ask you to give some serious thought to the responsibility to Tom that Ellie has. I also want you to know how important your approval is to her.'

'Huh! My approval is the last thing she needs. She's obviously capable of making up her own mind about what happens to my son.'

'You wouldn't say that if you'd seen the state she was in when she got home from here.' Mary was determinedly gentle. She knew that Pat was suffering.

'Oh.' Pat lowered her eyes, drinking her coffee, her hands shaking. She didn't say anything for a long time and when she did speak it was as though all the fight had gone out of her. Her cynical face crumpled into despair. 'I know Tom isn't the man we knew any more, but he's still my son, whatever his condition.'

'Of course.'

'I'm afraid I'll lose him altogether if he leaves London.' Pat's voice was weak and shaky. Mary had never seen her look so vulnerable. 'While he's nearby and I can just hop on a bus to see him, I still feel a part of his life even though he hasn't a clue who I am. If he goes away to Surrey, I'll lose that contact. You can't imagine what that feels like, Mary. What I went through when George died was bad enough but this is a thousand times worse.'

Mary swallowed hard. 'I can understand your fears, dear, but I think you're worrying unnecessarily,' she said kindly. 'You'll still be able to visit. I know that Ellie intends to see him on a regular basis so you can go together. And wouldn't it be a comfort to you to know that he's having a better life at Greenlands than they can give him at St John's?'

'Yes, I suppose so,' Pat admitted with a sigh of resignation.

'It'll be lovely for him,' Mary enthused, 'being in a smaller, more personal environment with people who'll have more time to pay attention to him.'

'In my heart I know all that, of course I do,' Pat confessed. 'But when Ellie told me about it, all I could think of was him being so far away. It seemed like just one blow after another.'

'It's difficult for Ellie too,' Mary pointed out softly. 'But she really does want the best for him, you know. I think she's had a good few sleepless nights over this decision.'

Pat put her empty cup down on the table and lowered her head. 'I said some terrible things to her,' she said, putting her hand to her brow.

'I'm sure it was nothing that can't be put right,' Mary encouraged. 'Ellie would have realised you were upset and didn't mean what you said. I'm sure she'll forgive you.'

'I don't want to lose her.' Pat looked frightened now.

'And you won't,' Mary assured her. 'Ellie isn't the sort to bear grudges.'

'I could cut my tongue out . . .'

'Now stop being so bloomin' melodramatic and come here,

you daft bat,' smiled Mary, standing up and opening her arms to her friend.

Pat was so profuse in her apologies the next morning when Ellie arrived at work, the young woman was rather over-whelmed by it.

'I shouldn't have sounded off at you like that,' she said, as she put the float in the till prior to their opening the shop. 'It was very wrong of me. All I could think of was Tom being so far away. I really am very sorry. I didn't mean all those terrible things.'

'It doesn't matter,' said Ellie. 'Forget it.'

'Thank you, dear.'

'Does this mean that you really do think Greenlands will be the best thing for him?' Ellie enquired. 'Or are you just trying to keep the peace between us?'

'No, it isn't just that,' Pat said. 'I'm still not happy about him being so far away but I can see that he'll benefit from the sort of care they can give him at a place like Greenlands.'

'I can get it arranged with your blessing then?' asked Ellie, buttoning her white nylon overall.

'Yes, you can.' Pat paused with the copper bags in her hand. 'Actually, I've had an idea.'

'Oh?'

'I think it might be sensible for me to sell the shop van and get an estate car that you can have for private use as well as shop business.' Her voice was high-pitched with enthusiasm, most unusual for Pat. 'An estate car will be just as good for deliveries and so on, and handy for you to get about with Donna outside of working hours. As you've put all the money you got from the insurance company into the trust fund for Tom, you won't be able to replace his car, will you?'

'No.' Ellie gave a wry grin. 'And an estate car will also be handy for me to drive us to Surrey to see Tom.'

'Well, yes,' Pat admitted, having the grace to turn pink. 'There is that.'

Ellie didn't blame Pat for looking after her own interest whilst appearing to be altruistic but it worried her that she was prepared to go to such lengths. 'Having to use public transport won't put me off going to see Tom, you know,' she felt she must point out. 'There's no need to supply me with transport to make sure I go, because I shall go anyway.'

'I know that,' Pat was quick to make clear, 'but having your own transport will make it more convenient for us both. And it will make your life a lot easier outside of shop hours.'

'It isn't necessary, Pat, honestly.'

'Just count it as a perk of the job.' Her enthusiasm was tinged with the hard edge of determination. 'You've worked hard; you deserve some sort of a reward.'

'I get paid for what I do.'

'But I want to give you something extra,' Pat insisted. 'To show my appreciation.'

It wasn't that Ellie wasn't grateful because she was, *very*. It would be an enormous help having the use of a car. It wasn't even the fact that Pat was guaranteeing her own travel arrangements with this act of generosity that made Ellie uneasy. It went deeper than that. The use of the shop car was a means of persuading Ellie to stay in the job by making it not worth her while to leave. She and Donna were the only family Pat had left, in a manner of speaking, and she wanted to keep them close. But Ellie wasn't without compassion or understanding so she said, 'It's very kind of you. Thank you very much.'

'I'm glad the two of you made it up,' said Mary.

'So am I,' said Ellie. 'It would have been miserable for us both if we hadn't.'

'Mm.'

It was the evening of the same day and Ellie had called on her mother after work. They were in the back room where Mary was trying, unsuccessfully, to demonstrate her knitting machine to her daughter. It was a single-bed machine with a ribbing attachment, and Mary had it set up on the table, which was littered with scraps of knitting and balls of wool that she was using to practise.

'So, how many sweaters have you knitted so far?' Ellie asked jokingly.

'Give us a chance,' said Mary, holding the wool across the needle bed over some selected latch needles which had been pulled out into the working position. 'I've only had it since yesterday.'

'I've heard you can knit an adult sweater in a couple of hours on one of those things.'

Mary had her eyes fixed on the machine in concentration. 'You probably can when you've had some practice,' she said absently. 'But that seems very far away to me at the moment.'

'You being the whizz knitter that you are, I was expecting to find a whole range of new knitwear waiting for Donna and me,' teased Ellie. Looking down at her daughter, who was sitting on her lap, she added, 'Isn't that right, baby?'

Donna chuckled.

'Right. Keep your fingers crossed.' Mary was now about to pull the cam box across the needles and cast on. Instead the work came off the needles altogether. 'The damned thing's done it again,' she wailed. 'It keeps coming off when I'm trying to cast on.'

'Not as easy as you thought then,' suggested Ellie.

'It's a bugger of a thing and I can't get the hang of it at all,' Mary confessed miserably. 'If I do manage to cast on and do a few rows, the wool still comes off. Oh, what a fiddle. I wish I'd never bought it. I'd sooner stick to hand knitting.'

'Let's have a look,' offered Ellie. 'You hold Donna.'

Having carefully read the user instructions, Ellie pulled out a number of latch needles, attached the wool to the machine, set the tension and carried out the same procedure as her mother.

'Oh, I've done it! I've cast on!' she cried excitedly, repeating the process and knitting another row and another until she had a sizeable piece of work in just a few minutes. 'It's absolute magic. I could really do things with this.'

'Why doesn't it work like that for me?'

'I was just lucky, I suppose.'

'I've been at it for hours and I still can't get it to work properly,' complained Mary, picking up some scraps of knitting and looking at them with disapproval. 'This is all I've got to show for a whole afternoon's work.'

'It'll take a while to get used to it,' said Ellie. 'My doing it right first time was just a fluke. It's like anything new – you need practice. Once you've cracked it, I bet you'll wonder how you ever managed without it.'

'I hope so because I'll be making the weekly payments for a long time to come,' mentioned Mary worriedly.

'I think it's great,' enthused Ellie. 'Can I have another go just for the fun of it?'

'Course you can, love,' Mary agreed readily. 'I've got to check things in the kitchen anyway. Your dad will be in from work in a minute.'

'I'll have to go home soon too.'

'You're welcome to stay for a bite to eat with us,' invited Mary. 'There's plenty.'

'Thanks, Mum, I'd love to,' said Ellie absently; she was absorbed in the instruction leaflet.

'Well, I might not have taken to the machine but it's certainly taken your mind off your troubles,' remarked Mary, standing up and putting the struggling Donna on the floor; she was at the crawling stage and into everything.

'Mm,' muttered Ellie vaguely, looking up at her mother. 'It's absolutely fascinating.'

Mary was smiling as she left the room with Donna on all fours at her heels. For the first time since before Tom's accident she'd seen a sparkle in Ellie's eyes.

It was a September Sunday afternoon. Sunshine bathed the lawned gardens of Greenlands, which was sheltered from the road by ancient elms, oaks and poplars. A rambling old red-brick house which had once been a family home, with a turreted roof and ivy climbing the walls in places, it was, on the outside, a charming picture of olde worlde charm.

But inside it was a miracle of practicality with the benefits of modern invention. It was equipped for people with special needs of both sexes and had adapted toilet facilities, lifts to the upper floors and bright and cheerful bedrooms. The men's sleeping quarters were at one side of the house, the women's on the other, but they shared the communal facilities.

As well as various staff offices, medical rooms and a dining room on the ground floor, there was also a room for occupational therapy, a recreation hall with facilities for table tennis and snooker, and card tables, and a television lounge. An indoor swimming pool added to the amenities.

Ellie and Pat were sitting under a tree in the garden near the house, having tea. The grounds were dotted with patients and visitors on this lovely afternoon. Tom was wandering about muttering to himself. He never stayed put anywhere for long. His attention span was so short it was nothing for him to walk away when someone was in mid-sentence.

Watching him from across the garden, Ellie found herself observing how magnificent he looked. He had been here for three months and his blond hair had been bleached to pale gold by the sun and fresh air, his London pallor replaced by a rich golden tan. As he strode towards them, tall and fit and upright, in a sports shirt and light trousers that Ellie had recently brought for him, it was as though nothing had happened. You'd never guess from looking at him that he'd lost his adult intellect and for obvious reasons his natural urges had to be curbed too, with drugs. He looked just like the man Ellie had married. Reality came crashing in as soon as he opened his mouth, however.

'Lo,' he said in the distorted way they had come to understand.

'Hello, Tom,' said Ellie.

'Are you all right, son?' asked Pat.

He nodded vigorously, running on the spot and pointing to his feet.

'You're going to have a game of football,' Ellie translated.

He nodded again.

'That'll be fun,' encouraged Ellie.

'Yeah,' was his guttural reply.

Pat handed him a bag containing sweets and fruit. 'We've brought you a few things, dear,' she explained.

He looked in the bag and jumped up and down with excitement.

'There's some fruit in there as well as sweets,' Pat mentioned. 'It's better for you than sweets.'

Standing still suddenly, he frowned darkly. 'Matron,' he mumbled.

'I'm sure you're allowed to have one or two without asking Matron first,' suggested Ellie. Although she was used to his being subject to other people's rules and regulations, it sometimes caught her off guard and filled her with dismay.

'Matron,' he repeated.

'There's no need to go and see her now,' said Ellie, who constantly strived to improve her communication with him. 'Come and sit down and talk to us for a while.'

Tom scuffed the grass with his foot and didn't reply.

'What have you been doing since we last saw you?' enquired his mother.

He shrugged and uttered a barely recognisable version of 'Dunno.'

'How are you getting on with your reading?' Ellie asked. He was being taught to read in the same way as a child but would only ever reach a certain standard.

He shrugged again.

'Never mind,' said his mother.

His mood changed so suddenly it startled Ellie even though she had seen it happen so many times since his accident. He began chanting, 'Dunno, dunno, dunno.'

'All right,' Tom,' she said, getting up and taking his arm to comfort him. 'It doesn't matter, darling. Don't upset yourself. Shush, shush, now.'

With the full force of his strength he wrenched away from her and pushed her so hard she fell against the iron garden table and sent the tea things flying.

'Calm down, Tom,' she urged him, regaining her balance and moving towards him.

'No . . .'

'Stop that, Tom,' intervened his mother worriedly.

'Now then, Tom,' admonished one of two male attendants running up to them, alerted by the disturbance. He looked at Ellie. 'What's going on here?'

'I'm not sure. He just flew into a rage,' began Ellie, but was silenced by a heavy blow to the face, making her see stars. She reeled back, holding her head, blood dripping from her nose, her eye already swelling.

The two men held Tom away from her but he was struggling to get at her, punching the air with his fists and shouting incomprehensibly.

'If you go inside, Mrs Hall,' said one of the attendants quietly, 'someone will see to your face.' And they marched Tom towards the house.

Too shocked to move, Ellie stood where she was. 'Your poor face,' muttered Pat shakily, taking her arm.

'I'll be all right.'

'Come on, dear, let's go and get it seen to,' she suggested.

Both women were trembling as they walked across the garden towards the house, all eyes upon them.

Only after Ellie had put Donna to bed that night, did she finally give in to her feelings. Alone in her living room she sat in an armchair and sobbed until there wasn't a tear left in her. Her head throbbed and her bruised eye hurt, but her physical pain was nothing to the mental agony of today. She cast her mind back to this afternoon in the matron's office at Greenlands after Tom had been given a sedative and Ellie's eye had been treated.

'I think it might be kinder,' the matron had said to Ellie and Pat, 'if you don't visit Tom again.'

'What!' Pat had been aghast.

'That's a bit harsh, Matron,' Ellie had added. 'How on earth can we stop coming to see him?'

'It might seem harsh but I really believe it would be in everybody's best interests if you were to keep away from Greenlands,' Matron had continued. She was a plump, wholesome woman of about fifty with a scrubbed complexion, shrewd brown eyes and short greying hair showing beneath a white starched cap which she'd worn with a navy-blue uniform. 'For the time being, anyway.'

'But we can't just abandon him.' Ellie had been distraught.

'Of course we can't,' Pat had echoed.

'And you wouldn't be abandoning him,' Matron had pointed out.

'Seems like it to me,' Ellie had said.

'You can telephone us as often as you like to find out how he is but . . .' The matron had paused and looked gravely from one to the other, 'quite frankly, we can do without any more incidents like the one we had here this afternoon.' She'd focused her gaze on Ellie's eye. 'And I'm quite sure you can.'

'I can't let something like that stop me from coming to see my own husband,' Ellie had protested.

'I really think—' Matron had begun.

'He isn't well,' Ellie cut in. 'He didn't mean to hurt me. He wouldn't do that.'

'You can't stop me seeing my son,' Pat had argued, angry. 'That's nothing short of wicked.'

'I'm not telling you you can't come, Mrs Hall,' Matron had corrected smoothly. 'I am *asking* you to stop visiting him for a while. I really do believe it would be the best thing for Tom, as well as yourselves.'

'It was me who seemed to upset Tom,' Ellie had been thinking back on the incident, 'not his mother. So surely she doesn't have to stop coming?'

'It would be better if neither of you came.' The matron had been quietly adamant.

Something had been puzzling Ellie. 'Tom doesn't even know who I am,' she'd said, 'so why would I upset him in particular?'

'It wasn't you, as such.'

'No?'

'No. Any visitors disrupt his routine, which is why I am asking you both not to come,' the matron had explained. 'When he's in a regular routine he feels safe. Anything out of the ordinary throws him off balance and he's frightened of that feeling. When he gets frightened he gets violent and lashes out at anyone who happens to be around. Your black eye is the result. It could be more serious next time.'

'He hasn't harmed me before,' Ellie had pointed out.

'Only because you were too quick for him,' Matron had reminded her. 'I've seen his notes, my dear. I know that he's had violent temper tantrums and tried to attack you before when you've been visiting him at St John's and at the hospital before that.'

Ellie had made a face. 'I've tried to put those out of my mind,' she'd confessed.

'Which is perfectly understandable. But the truth of the matter is that your visits do Tom more harm than good the way he is at the moment.'

'I see,' Ellie had said glumly.

Pat had just nodded miserably.

'We aim to keep him on an even keel here,' Matron had gone on to explain. 'It makes it very hard for my staff when he's being difficult.' She'd paused as though bracing herself to impart something particularly unpleasant. 'The fact is, if he becomes too disruptive, we won't be able to keep him here. He'll have to go back to St John's, where they have secure wards.'

'Oh, no!' Ellie had cried.

'Oh dear.' Pat had been equally concerned.

'We are a relatively small unit here offering specialist care,' Matron had continued. 'We encourage the patients to get along, to socialise with one another. A friendly atmosphere is the whole point. So if one patient upsets the others with his behaviour too often, we can't keep him.'

'I appreciate that.' Ellie had run a worried hand over her brow. 'It just seems so cruel not to visit.'

'You're not being cruel to Tom, you can rest assured of that,' Matron had been at pains to point out. 'Anyway, I'm not saying that you can never come again. Maybe in a while he'll be more able to cope with visitors. But at the present time it undoes all the hard work my staff put in on him.'

Beginning to accept the inevitable, Ellie had turned her mind to practical matters. 'What about clothes and other things that he needs?' she'd asked. 'I usually bring them with me.'

'We'll take care of that here, don't worry,' the matron had offered. 'We'll let you know what he needs, get your approval, then send you the bill after the purchases are made.'

They'd left soon after that, having agreed not to visit again until they were told otherwise. They'd both been too miserable to say much on the way home in Pat's estate car that Ellie had the use of. Pat had been close to tears when Ellie had dropped her off at the flat.

Now Ellie dried her eyes and went to the kitchen to make some coffee. Today had been a watershed. It was time to accept the situation fully and get on with her life as it was and stop clinging to the hope that one day she might take up her role as Tom's wife again. She realised now that she'd never stopped hoping he'd eventually be back, the old Tom bossing her around and taking control.

She would never stop loving him and as soon as it was deemed wise by the matron for them to resume visiting, she would do so. But her marriage was over as surely as if Tom had died, and all things associated with it had gone: the loving, the planning, the shoulder to lean on, the sex. She'd been hanging on to false hopes. Now she must let go.

As she brushed a floppy lock of her red hair from her brow with her hand, she accidentally touched her swollen eye and winced. The pain strengthened her resolve. The man Ellie had married had had plenty of faults but he'd never raised a hand to her. Her beautiful hero, the man she had loved all her life, no longer existed.

Chapter Seven

Mary didn't grow any fonder of her knitting machine.

'It's a mystery to me why you can't get on with it,' remarked Ellie one Wednesday afternoon a few weeks later when she called at her mother's house. 'I liked it from the start. And now that I'm more used to it, I think it's fantastic.'

'I don't know why either, but I just can't take to it. It's nothing but an aggravation to me,' declared Mary. 'Knitting is supposed to be a pleasure, not a punishment.'

'Machine knitting is a pleasure for me,' said Ellie, who borrowed the machine regularly from her mother. 'It's exciting because you get such fast results.'

'Excitement isn't the feeling it inspires in me.' Mary was gloomy. 'Fury more like. My nerves are in tatters after a session on that thing. It's a relief to get back to my two needles of an evening when I'm sitting in my armchair.'

'Surely the evening would be a good time to get to grips with the machine,' Ellie suggested, 'when the work of the day is done and you've got time to put your mind to it.'

'Blow that for a lark,' Mary proclaimed. 'I can't work on it in the living room because it makes such a noise your father can't hear the telly. And I don't want to spend the evenings sitting at a table in another room on my own. I know where I am with hand knitting. I should never have bought the wretched thing.'

'Why not get some tuition?' suggested Ellie. 'I believe there is some available from the manufacturers.'

'I could take lessons from you as you're so good at it. But that won't make me like it, will it?' Mary pointed out. 'The problem isn't that I don't know how to use it but that I don't *like* using it.'

'You're not going to give up on it altogether, though, are you?' Ellie enquired.

'I wish I could, but I suppose I'll have to persevere as I'm still paying for it,' was Mary's mournful reply. 'I can't just write it off.'

'I'm sure you'll get the hang of it eventually.' Ellie paused and gave her mother a persuasive look. 'And in the meantime, may I borrow it again? I've got some things I want to make and I enjoy doing it in the evenings when Donna's in bed.'

Mary threw back her head and laughed. 'Keep it for as long as you like, love,' she offered. 'If it isn't in the house I won't feel guilty for not trying to master it.'

'Thanks, Mum.'

'Anyway, let's forget the dratted thing now and have a cup of tea.' She smiled at her granddaughter, who was sitting on the sofa beside Ellie nursing a doll. 'And some milk and biscuits for you, eh, little one?'

'Bickie, please,' requested Donna, a sweet-faced child with her mother's red hair and big blue eyes. She didn't have much of a vocabulary yet, but she knew how to ask for anything of a sugary nature.

The three of them trooped into the kitchen and Mary put the kettle on. Ellie and her mother usually got together on a Wednesday afternoon because it was half-day closing at both the corner shop and the wool shop, so neither was on duty.

'I just happened to mention to Ann that it's getting to be quite difficult having Donna with me at the shop all day now that she's running around,' Ellie remarked conversationally as they waited for the tea to brew, 'and she offered to take her off my hands whenever I need it.'

'That's kind of her.'

'She says that if I get a pram seat, she can sit her on

Matthew's pram and take her with them when she goes shopping or to the park.'

'Ann's a good sort.'

'She is. It's a comfort to know that the offer is there,' Ellie continued. 'I shan't bother her unless I absolutely have to, of course. And I won't need to every day because you take Donna off for a break from the shop when you're not working. But having a toddler around for the whole day isn't exactly conducive to efficiency. It worries me that Donna is so restricted too.'

'Pat still doesn't seem to mind her being there, though,' Mary assured her. 'She's often said as much to me.'

'Oh yes, I'm lucky in that way,' Ellie was quick to agree. 'I wouldn't be able to have her with me at all if I worked anywhere else. I think Pat is after a close bond with her granddaughter from an early age.'

'And who can blame her?'

'Exactly,' agreed Ellie.

'How is Pat?' Mary enquired. 'I haven't seen her for a few days. Is she still fretting about the visiting ban at Greenlands?'

'She hasn't said much about it lately,' Ellie told her. 'I suppose she's accepted the fact that we can't see Tom for a while and that's all there is to it.'

'Don't take this the wrong way,' Mary began cautiously, 'but I was wondering if it might be rather a relief to you to have a break from visiting. It must be a terrible strain, going to see someone who doesn't know you and isn't pleased to see you.'

'It is difficult,' Ellie confessed. 'The frustration of not being able to communicate with Tom has been awful. I've got used to him not being Tom any more, of course, but it still hurts to see him like that. So, yes, I suppose a short break might do me good, as long as the ban doesn't go on for too long.' She gave her mother a wry look. 'It seems such a terrible thing to admit to . . . makes me feel so guilty.'

'You're only human,' replied Mary. 'I think it's wonderful

143

the way you've coped, taking it all in your stride.'

Ellie hadn't told her mother about the long sleepless nights or the times she'd fallen apart inside, and been terrified she might crack up. Neither had she mentioned the guilt that still plagued her because she'd been driving the car at the time of the accident. 'It's nice of you to say so. The support I've had from you and the rest of the family has helped me to cope,' she said graciously, lifting her daughter on to a chair and putting her bib on.

Sitting in an armchair in her living room the following evening, Ellie was finishing off some embroidery on a sweater she'd knitted for herself on the machine. The embroidered ornamentation was something of an experiment. Working the last stitch on a motif of white daisies on a blue background, she held the work out in front of her and studied it, pleased with the finished effect.

The machine restricted her to plain knitting and ribbing with the attachment, so a spot of embroidery gave the garment a look of individuality. She'd made up her own design, drawing the pattern on a sheet of graph paper beforehand and keeping it by her to work from. She'd learned to embroider as a child, and had done quite a bit of it when Tom was away in the army and she'd had such a lot of time on her hands. Her mother had always been a good needlewoman, as well as a brilliant knitter, and had encouraged her with that sort of thing from an early age.

Now, seeing how well this had turned out, she was eager to do something similar for Donna, whose wardrobe had already benefited from Ellie's enjoyment of the machine.

Glancing at the clock, however, she noticed with astonishment that it was nearly midnight. Since Tom had been away, the clocks seemed to stop in the evenings. But not tonight, thanks to her absorbing new hobby.

Flushed with success and full of ideas, she put her work basket away in the other room, where she kept the machine, and made her way upstairs. She was pleasantly tired and hopeful that she might sleep well for a change. For the first time in ages, she felt relaxed as she got ready for bed. Machine knitting might be the bane of her mother's life, but it was therapeutic for Ellie.

'I like your sweater, Ellie,' complimented Ann at the weekend. The family were gathered at Mary and Bob's for Sunday tea. 'Where did you buy it?'

'I made it on Mum's machine,' Ellie told her.

'Really?' She was very impressed. 'I noticed how unusual it was but it's so neat and professional-looking, I thought it must be shop bought.'

'No, it's all my own work. I got all creative . . . thought a bit of embroidery on the front might make it look special,' explained Ellie, enjoying the praise.

'And it works really well,' Ann enthused, casting a close eye over the garment. 'Something a bit different, and a whole lot classier than some of those in the shops.'

'I think it's nice too,' added Mary. 'She's a clever girl, getting to grips with the monster machine. It's more than I can do.'

'But you make beautiful things by hand,' Ellie complimented her, 'whereas I like the speed with which I can do a garment on the machine. Instant satisfaction, that's what appeals to me.'

'It isn't instant when I try to do it,' grinned Mary. 'I could knit a pair of gloves by hand in the time it takes me to cast on on that damned machine.'

'Now you really are exaggerating,' laughed Ellie.

'Well, speaking as someone who can't knit a stitch, I'm full of admiration for you both,' Ann told them.

The three women were having this conversation in the kitchen while they waited for the kettle to boil. Home-made apple pie and seedcake were laid out on the kitchen table, ready to be transferred to the living room along with several plates piled high with sandwiches. There were also tinned peaches, jelly, blancmange and a jug of evaporated milk.

Doug appeared, carrying Matthew, a pink-cheeked child, with soft hazel eyes like his father's.

'What's all this? A mothers' meeting?' enquired Doug in a jovial manner.

'We're just admiring Ellie's sweater,' Ann informed him. 'Do you like it?'

'Yeah, it's all right,' he said, with typical male indifference to that sort of thing.

'She made it.'

'Well done, you,' said Doug to his sister. 'You should teach Ann to knit.' He gave his wife a wicked grin. 'She needs something to do with her time.'

He ducked to miss his wife's hand flicked in his direction.

'With a six-month-old baby and you to look after, as well as a house to run, I'm sure she's sitting about all day contemplating her navel,' said Ellie with irony.

'You men just haven't got a clue,' Ann told him lightly.

He handed their son to her. 'I think he's been busy in the basement,' he explained.

'Thanks for pointing it out.' She tutted towards the two other women, raising her eyes. 'Men! Funny how they come over all helpless when a nappy needs changing, isn't it?' she laughed.

'Ignorance is bliss, I reckon,' said Ellie good-humouredly as Ann headed towards the door with her son in her arms. No one seriously expected Doug to involve himself in what was considered to be strictly a female domain.

They were all laughing when Bob appeared at the kitchen door with Donna clutching his hand. 'What's going on out here that's so funny?'

'Just Doug pretending to be incompetent because it suits him,' Ellie explained.

'But now it's time for tea,' announced Mary as the kettle began to whistle. 'So get cracking, Ellie. Take all the food and put it on to the table in the other room while Ann changes the baby.'

After an enjoyable family tea with plenty of jokes and joshing, the visitors prepared to take their offspring home to bed.

'I was wondering, Ellie,' began Ann, when they were at the front door about to depart, 'if you'd consider making me a sweater something like yours . . . different colours and embroidery but the same sort of thing.'

'Of course I will.' Ellie was flattered to be asked.

'I'll pay you of course,' Ann added, 'for making it as well as for the materials.'

'We'll talk about that another time,' said Ellie, slightly embarrassed by the idea of taking money from a relative for something she enjoyed doing.

'I won't take any argument about that,' said Ann in a tone that didn't invite debate.

'OK,' Ellie conceded. 'You decide which colour you want and what sort of thing you want embroidered on it and I'll get the wool and get started.'

'Smashing.' Ann was delighted. 'I'll give it some thought and pop round to your place for a chat about it one evening next week. I'll welcome suggestions too.'

'I'll look forward to it,' said Ellie, fastening Donna's coat.

She was thinking about it all the way home in the car, working out different colour matches and embroidery patterns.

One evening a few weeks later, Ann telephoned Ellie. 'I was wearing that sweater you made for me when I went to see my mother today and she loved it,' she told her. 'So much so she's asked me to ask you if you can make one for her.'

'Oh.' Ellie was taken aback but thrilled. 'Well, yes, I don't see why not.'

'And when you can fit it in, I was wondering if you could do me a jacket for Matthew, similar to that blue one you made for Donna,' she said.

'I'd love to.' She was even more excited now. 'Any idea what sort of embroidery pattern?'

'I want the jacket in royal blue with something suitable for a little boy on it,' Ann explained.

'What about a red and white train?' suggested Ellie. 'Or a boat or a kite?'

'A train would be lovely.'

'No problem. But what about your mum?'

'I'll tell her to contact you direct, shall I?' Ann suggested.

'That'll probably be best.'

Ann could hear Matthew asserting himself. 'Must go,' she said. 'Baby's crying. See you.'

'See you.'

Ellie's eyes were shining as she replaced the receiver; she was imbued with a new sense of purpose.

'I've got a proposition to put to you.' Ellie confronted her mother the next day in her lunch break when she took Donna to be minded for the afternoon.

'A proposition?' Mary wore a hearty grin. 'Ooh, it's a long time since I've had one of those.'

'I'm being serious,' Ellie admonished jokingly, 'so stop mucking about.'

'OK, dear, I'll pay attention,' she agreed cheerfully. 'Fire away.'

'I've been thinking that as you don't use your knitting machine and it spends most of its time at my place, why don't I take it off your hands altogether?'

Mary's eyes lit with interest but she waited for Ellie to tell her exactly what she had in mind.

'Take over the weekly payments, I mean,' Ellie explained. 'And if you work out how much you've already paid on it, I'll pay you that too . . . but it'll have to be over a period of time because I can't manage a big lump sum.'

'You can forget what's already been paid. I'll put that down to experience,' Mary told her. 'But are you sure you can manage the payments on what Pat pays you?'

Ellie told her about the orders she'd had for knitwear recently. 'If I'm going to get paid for what I do for other people, either I pay you for the use of the machine to cover your payments or I take them over from you altogether.' She'd given the matter careful consideration and was quite definite about it. 'It wouldn't be fair to carry on using it on such a regular basis while you're still lumbered with the repayments.'

'I must admit it would be a relief to be shot of it,' said her mother. 'Machine knitting isn't for me and I know it never will be. I should never have been tempted into buying it. I've been worried to death about wasting money on a whim.'

'So if I take it off your hands, we'll all be happy.' Ellie's excitement was growing.

'Consider the deal done,' agreed Mary, picking up Donna, who was standing at her feet with her arms raised towards her. 'Ooh, Donna, your gran feels like a new woman.'

Donna chuckled and Mary threw her up in the air, then smothered her with kisses.

Ellie went back to work smiling.

Ellie had heard of the power of word of mouth but hadn't realised just how effective it could be until news began to spread about her hand-embroidered knitwear. After Ann's mother came Ann's mother's friend. Then someone Ann knew at the baby clinic wanted a jacket like Matthew's for her little boy. Ellie's neighbour ordered two plain navy-blue school jumpers for her son as well as a sweater for herself with roses embroidered on the front. And so it went on. The orders were so regular, Ellie had to open an order book and start a waiting list because she was working at the shop all day and only had the evenings after Donna was in bed to spend on her knitwear.

She enjoyed the work enormously, and the extra money came in very handy. The only drawback was finding enough time actually to produce the knitwear. As people were paying her, she wanted to provide a professional service but this just wasn't possible the way things were at the moment.

It was an unexpected incident one day early in the new year that set her wondering if perhaps she could turn an enjoyable hobby into a full-time job . . .

'That's a pretty dress your little girl's wearing,' said the assistant in a children's shop near Shepherd's Bush market. It was Ellie's Saturday off and she was choosing a new coat for Donna in the sale. 'It's so cute and really unusual. I haven't seen any of those about around here.'

'I made it for her on my knitting machine,' explained Ellie, observing her daughter with pride. She looked beautiful in the blue dress with white daisies embroidered round the neck, sleeves and hem.

'Really?' The woman was fortyish and well groomed, her blonde hair worn in a short feathery style, slim figure clad in a fitted black suit. Her interest in Ellie's work seemed to grow by the second. She came up to Donna to have a closer look, inspecting the embroidery and fingering the material between her finger and thumb. 'It really is lovely.'

'Thank you,' said Ellie. 'I'm glad you like it.'

'Do you do much of that sort of thing?'

'Quite a bit.'

'Just for yourself?'

'No, not now,' Ellie replied. 'I get quite a few orders from other people.'

'Do you do children's cardigans and sweaters too?' the woman asked.

'I do whatever customers ask me for,' Ellie told her.

'Would you be interested in making some stuff for me to sell in the shop?' the woman enquired, stroking her chin thoughtfully.

'It's your shop then?' Ellie had assumed the woman just worked there.

'That's right.' She smiled and thrust her hand forward. 'Rene Morris.'

'Ellie Hall,' supplied Ellie, shaking her hand.

150

'Well, Mrs Hall, I reckon your knitwear would do very well in my shop.' Rene Morris was very enthusiastic. 'People are always looking for something a bit different and your work is certainly that. The embroidery gives the garments that something extra.'

'That's what I aim for,' Ellie told her.

'There's still a demand for anything handmade, you know, despite the wide variety of cheap mass-produced garments that are available in the shops these days.'

'Let's hope there always will be,' said Ellie.

'Indeed.' Rene Morris turned her attention to business. 'So, what about cost?'

'I work out my prices by charging by the ounce for the knitting, allowing time also for the embroidery, and adding that to the cost of the materials,' Ellie informed her.

'Obviously, as a retailer I'd expect some sort of a discount to allow me to make a profit,' Rene Morris pointed out. 'But I'd order strictly on a firm sale basis, not sale or return.'

'I'll do some costings and give you some definite prices.' This was so exciting for Ellie, she was quite overwhelmed by it. 'What sort of things do you have in mind to start with?'

'Sweaters at first, I think. In a few sizes and for both sexes, in light colours ready for the spring,' she said thoughtfully. 'And a few cardigans and knitted jackets which sell all year round. I'd like them in one of the new man-made fibres – Orlon or Bri-nylon, something like that. Can you do that?'

'Sure.'

'Good. Being a mum yourself you'll know how popular easy-care clothes are for children.'

'I certainly do,' confirmed Ellie. 'The man-mades wash like a dream and come in lovely colours.'

Rene Morris nodded. 'It's too late in the season for knitted dresses,' she said, casting an admiring eye over Donna's again, 'but if the other stuff goes well, I'll order some later in the year for next year's winter stock.'

A sudden slug of reality brought Ellie down to earth. She'd

been too caught up in the thrill of it all to pay attention to the practicalities. This wasn't a friend of a friend wanting a jumper knitted when Ellie could manage to find the time. This was serious business. Rene Morris would want something that Ellie couldn't give her – a firm delivery date.

'Look, I think we'd better slow down a little,' Ellie told her. 'As much as I'd love to take the work on, I'm going to have a problem finding the time to meet the order. I have a full-time job, you see.'

'That's a shame.' The woman was obviously disappointed.

'Can I think about it and let you know?' Ellie didn't want to close the door on this opportunity, but she needed time to work something out.

'Certainly,' said Rene Morris, adding a touch briskly, 'but don't leave it too long if you want to catch the spring trade. I'll be putting the first of the new lines on show when the sale's finished. I like to buy my stock well ahead.'

Suspecting that the proprietor was telling her in so many words that she wouldn't lose sleep over the deal if it didn't happen because there was no shortage of manufacturers vying for the retail space in her shop, Ellie said, 'I'll definitely let you know one way or the other by the end of next week.'

'Fine.' The woman turned her full attention to the business in hand and smiled at Donna. 'Now, young lady, let's get you fixed up with a nice new coat, shall we?'

Rene Morris's order was on Ellie's mind all evening and she lay awake most of the night mulling it over. She knew she was being offered a life-changing opportunity that she should grab with both hands. But how could she when she had a full-time job which she couldn't give up because she had a child to support?

There must be a way around this; there *had* to be some way she could accept this order and use it as a test case as well as a commercial enterprise. By the time she finally fell asleep, she knew exactly what she must do.

★ ★ ★

'You're early,' said her mother when Ellie and Donna arrived on her parents' doorstep the next morning while they were still having breakfast, a full fry-up as it was Sunday.

'I'd have been here even earlier if it wasn't for the fact that I know you have a lie-in on a Sunday,' she told them. 'I've been awake half the night.'

Mary looked at her granddaughter. 'Oh dear, have you been playing your mummy up?' she smiled.

'No, it wasn't her,' Ellie explained. 'It's me. I was too excited to get to sleep.'

'Excited, eh?' said Mary. 'That sounds promising. I'll do you some breakfast and you can tell us what's happened to get you into such a tizz.'

Having assured her mother that she and Donna had already had breakfast and couldn't manage another, Ellie helped herself to a cup of tea and sat at the kitchen table with Donna beside her, munching a piece of toast. Ellie's father had been reading the Sunday paper when she arrived and it was open on the table at the page containing an article about the American pop singer Buddy Holly's tragic death the previous week; the small plane he'd been travelling in to do a show had crashed. He was twenty-two. They talked about this briefly, then Ellie got to the point of her visit and told them about Rene Morris's order.

'That sounds good,' was her father's positive response.

'Yes, well done, love,' added Mary.

'I'm really thrilled.' Ellie turned to her mother. 'I've got a proposition for you, Mum.'

'Another one!' exclaimed Mary. 'Blimey, my luck has really changed. So, what is it?'

'Well, because I'm at work all day, I can't possibly accept Rene Morris's order unless I have some help with the knitwear,' she explained. 'They're children's garments so the knitting won't take as long as for adults. But it's still a lot of work.'

153

Mary's brow furrowed. 'I'd love to help you but I'm hopeless with that dratted machine, you know that,' she said regretfully.

'You're not hopeless with a sewing needle, though, are you?' Ellie's voice was high with enthusiasm.

Her mother eyed her questioningly. 'Ah, I see. You want me to help with the sewing up?'

'Exactly. I'd pay you for it . . . a percentage of what I get paid.'

Mary looked offended at this. 'I couldn't take money for doing my own daughter a favour,' she protested. 'But of course I'll do some sewing up for you.'

'There's all the pressing to do first, remember, because the knitting curls up,' Ellie pointed out. 'That will take time, and the sewing-up is very time-consuming.'

'I still don't need paying, though,' Mary insisted. 'I'll do it as a favour.'

'It won't be just a favour,' Ellie was keen to explain. 'If things go as I hope they will, this won't be just a one-off. It'll be an ongoing thing. So I need to know if you would be willing to do sewing-up for me on a regular basis.'

Mary squinted at her daughter. 'What exactly are you getting at, love?'

'I'm thinking of doing knitwear on a full-time basis,' Ellie told her parents. 'If Rene Morris's order goes well and she shows signs of wanting more, I shall think of turning my hobby into a proper business, giving up my job at the shop and knitting full-time for adults and children.'

She waited for the gasps of horror, the warnings and the criticism. But they didn't come. Both her parents stared at her with a bemused expression.

'Come on then, tell me I'm crazy and I mustn't take a chance like that,' challenged Ellie.

'It's a big step, of course,' said Mary, 'but basically I think it's a good idea. If you can make a living doing something you enjoy, it can't be bad.'

'Would you get enough work for a full-time living, though?' Bob was more circumspect now he'd heard the full story.

'I think so but I can't be absolutely sure until I actually do it. I'm in an awkward situation at the moment. I can't take on any big orders because I won't have the time to do them because I'm at the shop all day. And I won't know if it's going to work until I've done a reasonable sized order.'

'You can do a spot of homework, though, can't you?' suggested Mary. 'There's nothing to stop you making enquiries in shops where they sell knitwear, showing them some samples of what you can do. See what reaction you get.'

'Exactly,' Ellie agreed. 'I thought I'd call at some retail outlets locally to see if there's any interest. Here again, time is the problem, though. Being at work all day, I need the evenings to do the knitting after Donna's in bed. And while I've got Rene Morris's order to do I'll need my half-day off from the shop to work on that. But I'll find the time to test the water somehow.'

'I'll help with that in any way I can,' offered Mary. 'I'll look after Donna while you go and see these people.'

'You're a diamond, Mum.'

'You ought to make sure you have enough to live on for a while before you give up your job at the shop,' warned her father. 'Just in case there's a gap before your knitting money starts coming in.'

'I've been saving the money I make from the knitting,' Ellie explained. 'And I'll make quite a bit on Rene Morris's order. When I have enough put by to live for a couple of months, and a good supply of orders ahead of me, that's the time I shall take the plunge and give up my job.'

'Sounds as though you've thought it through sensibly,' Bob approved.

'There's no way I can do this thing without taking a chance. If I try and I fail I'll just have to go back to work for someone else. There's plenty of jobs about.' She paused, her eyes shining with resolve. 'I really want to make a success of this.'

'I can see that,' said Mary.

'I'll want your help with the sewing up, Mum, but you can see now how I'll need to pay you.'

'It does put a different light on it,' Mary conceded. 'It's going to be a regular job rather than just the odd bit of sewing now and again.'

'That's right,' confirmed Ellie. 'And when you're doing a job you get paid for it. But don't say yes if you don't fancy it. I know you have your work in the wool shop to consider.'

'That's only two days a week,' said Mary. 'I should be able to manage the two things.'

'Even so, it wouldn't be right for me to put pressure on you just because I want to set up in business. If you don't want to commit yourself, I'll just have to find someone else.' She paused. 'But I'd love it to be you because you're such a brilliant needlewoman and also because I think it'll be such fun working together.'

'Count me in,' said Mary.

'Wonderful,' said Ellie, going over to her and hugging her. 'I'll go ahead and tell Rene Morris I can take the order, then.'

'Yes, you do that, love,' said Mary.

Meeting Rene's delivery date was worrying, exhausting, terrifying and enormously satisfying. Ellie's arms and shoulders ached at the end of every evening.

'I'm getting huge muscles in my arms from pulling that cam box to and fro,' she said to her mother.

Working into the small hours most nights, she produced knitwear with embroidered flowers, dolls, chicks and bunnies; for the boys there were footballs, trains or sailing boats woven into the front. There was a wide selection of colours and designs, all with a label bearing the name 'Ellie Hall Knitwear' sewn into the back. She'd had the labels made by a firm of garment label manufacturers recommended to her by Rene, who had advised her to sew a maker's label into all her knitwear now that she was selling commercially.

The first order was ready by the end of February, as agreed, and Rene was delighted. The whole thing gave Ellie a terrific sense of achievement.

It also proved to her that working in her spare time on this venture wasn't going to be suitable if she were to make a successful business of it. She'd made a few enquiries, shown her samples round the shops and had received strong interest. But she couldn't take any firm orders until she was in a position to give delivery dates. It wasn't possible to stay up half the night working on a permanent basis because she was exhausted during the day. And that wasn't fair to her daughter, or her employer.

For the second time in her life, Ellie was faced with a major decision over which she knew she must trust her own judgement. The first had been when she'd had Tom transferred to Greenlands, the second was deciding to go into business for herself.

Before she took this drastic action any further, however, there was something important she had to do. Something that even the thought of made her tremble.

'Leaving!' gasped Pat. 'You're leaving the shop?'

Ellie chewed her bottom lip, racked with guilt. She'd guessed Pat would be devastated. Apart from the fact that she liked to keep Ellie and Donna close to her, she was going to have trouble finding another suitable assistant because she was so difficult to get on with. 'I'm afraid I don't have a choice if I'm to make a success of my knitwear business.'

'But knitting isn't a job,' Pat stated dismissively. 'It's a thing people do in their spare time.'

The shop was closed for the lunch period and the two women were sitting at the table in Pat's living room having scrambled eggs on toast. Donna was with her other granny for the afternoon. When Ellie had told Pat she wanted to have a chat, she'd been invited to join her for lunch.

'Usually it is a hobby,' Ellie agreed. 'And it was for me until recently. But the knitting machine has changed everything and I want to focus my attention on it. I need to give it one hundred per cent if I am to make a go of it.'

'It's the maddest idea I've ever heard,' Pat said cuttingly.

'Why?'

'Who in heaven's name do you think is going to buy home-made knitwear?' Pat mocked. 'I admit the things you make are quite attractive but you'll never compete with the shops. There's a terrific selection of things available these days.'

'I don't intend to try to compete with the shops,' explained Ellie, trying not to be crushed by her attitude. 'I'm hoping to sell *into* the shops as well as knitting orders for individuals.'

'Even if you were to get the shops to buy from you, there won't be much profit left for you once they've taken their cut,' Pat was keen to point out.

'There won't be as much in it for me as selling direct to the public, of course,' agreed Ellie, 'but I shall still get a fair price, and I hope to work in both sectors.'

'You can't give up a secure job when you have a child to support,' Pat went on. 'It isn't right.'

'I know it sounds irresponsible,' admitted Ellie, 'but it isn't just a whim. I've given it a lot of thought, and I really do believe I can make a go of it.'

'You ought to bear in mind the fact that you have a child to feed.' Pat wasn't going to give up.

'She won't suffer by it.' Ellie remained firm. 'I can assure you of that.'

Pat pushed her food away. She was very pale and had tell-tale red blotches suffusing her neck. 'What about me in all this?' she demanded. 'Have you thought about how I'm going to manage in the shop without you?'

'Yes, I've thought about it a lot,' Ellie told her truthfully. 'And I'm really sorry to cause you any trouble but—'

'You're not sorry at all,' Pat argued.

'I am, truly I am,' Ellie tried to convince her. 'I feel awful about leaving but I can't let this chance pass me by. I might never get another opportunity like it.'

'You, you, you and bugger the rest of us.' Pat's voice was shaking with fury.

'I was hoping you might find it in your heart to be pleased for me,' Ellie said sadly.

'I might have been if it was something sensible you were about to go into.'

Ellie didn't believe that. She knew Pat would be difficult whatever Ellie's reason for leaving. 'I don't mind staying on until you've found a replacement for me in the shop,' she offered co-operatively.

'After all I've done for you,' Pat went on as though Ellie hadn't spoken. 'I gave you a job when you needed one. I even provided you with transport. And this is how you repay me.'

'I've said I'm sorry.' Ellie's patience was beginning to wear thin. 'But giving in my notice isn't exactly a crime.'

'That's gratitude for you,' Pat snapped. 'It's the last time I'll help you out.'

'I didn't ask you for a job and I certainly didn't ask you to give me transport,' she felt compelled to point out. 'You wanted me working in the shop to replace Tom because it was better than having to work with a stranger. And you gave me the use of a car so that I could drive you to Greenlands to see Tom.'

'I gave it to you because I thought it would make your life easier,' Pat insisted, 'and you throw it back in my face.'

There was no point in trying to reason with her when she was in this mood, Ellie knew that from past experience. 'Whether you believe it or not, I really am sorry to have upset you,' she said. 'It's a chance for me, Pat. Can't you try to see it from my point of view and be just the tiniest bit pleased for me?'

'Certainly not. You can rot in hell for all I care.' Pat's voice had risen to a shout. 'So just get out and leave me alone.'

'I'll go downstairs and get ready to open the shop,' suggested Ellie. 'It's almost time.'

'Don't bother.' Pat was beyond rational thought. 'I want you out of here as from now. I've got to manage without you so I might as well start right away.'

'But—'

'See how you get on without a regular wage and the use of a car to run around in, madam,' she sneered. 'You'll soon come running back. Well, you'll be out of luck because there will never be a job for you here again.'

'Please don't be like this,' begged Ellie, guessing that the other woman was hurting even more than she was. 'Let me help you by staying until you've found someone else, someone you'll feel comfortable working with.'

'No. Get out!' she screamed. 'I don't want to see you again . . . ever.'

Gulping back the tears, Ellie left the room and hurried downstairs; trembling slightly, she took off her overall and hung it on the peg, put on her coat and left the premises.

Mary called on Pat at the flat that same evening. 'You've done it again, haven't you?' she said, having heard all about it from Ellie. 'You've cut off your nose to spite your face. Not only have you thoroughly upset Ellie but you've left yourself with no help in the shop, as well as the possibility of not seeing your granddaughter again.'

Pat looked awful – grey and gaunt. She lowered her gaze sheepishly and didn't reply.

'You did the same thing to Ellie when she told you about Greenlands,' rebuked Mary. 'What's the matter with you? Are you trying to make sure you spend the rest of your life in splendid isolation or something?'

'Don't go on at me.'

'Someone has to,' Mary told her. 'You'll lose Ellie and Donna for good if you carry on like this.'

'I was so disappointed when she said she was leaving, I just blew my top, couldn't stop myself,' confessed Pat. 'Because I just don't know how I'll manage without her.'

'You'll get a new assistant, that's how you'll manage,' Mary told her firmly.

'How will I get anyone like her?'

'By advertising for one, or getting in touch with the Labour Exchange, of course.' Mary was taking no nonsense. 'As much as I love Ellie, even I have to admit that she isn't the only good shop assistant in the world.'

'But I haven't worked with people who aren't family for any length of time,' Pat moaned. 'None of the assistants I had when Tom was away in the army stayed for long.'

'Now's the time for you to make a new start, then,' advised Mary. 'With a little give and take you might even prefer working with a non-family member once you get used to it. At least if you fall out over something at work, your personal life isn't affected.'

Pat gave Mary a sheepish look. 'Do you really think Ellie will stop me seeing Donna?' she asked.

'You've told Ellie you never want to see her again,' Mary reminded her. 'That's hardly the way to ensure regular access to your granddaughter, is it?'

'I didn't mean what I said.'

'You'd better go round to Ellie's and tell her that then, hadn't you?' Mary suggested.

'I'm not sure if I can face her.' This was typical of Pat. Brave with rage but feeble in the aftermath.

'Don't talk wet, woman, of course you can. Get round there and tell her you're sorry and wish her well in her new venture,' advised Mary firmly. 'And while you're at it, ask her to stay on at the shop until you find a suitable replacement. Otherwise you'll be complaining that you can't manage.'

'I'll go round there right away,' agreed Pat.

'One of these days you're going to push Ellie too far, you know,' Mary warned her with a wise shake of the head. 'And

me too if it comes to that. I might reach the point where I get
fed up with being peacemaker.'

'Oh, Mary, don't say that.' Pat looked frightened.

'Make sure you don't put me in that position,' lectured
Mary. 'Don't lose your temper when things don't go your way.
Try to be a bit more sensitive to Ellie's feelings.'

'You're a good friend, Mary.'

Mary sighed. 'And you, my dear Pat, are your own worst
enemy.'

'I'll go and put things right with Ellie now,' Pat said. 'I'll
beg her to forgive me if necessary.'

'Good,' approved Mary. 'And having done that, make a
promise to yourself that you'll never let this situation arise
again.'

'I'll try,' Pat promised. 'I really will.'

Chapter Eight

Because the common perception of fledgeling entrepreneurship was one of dire hardship and anxiety, Ellie expected to be wringing her hands in the early days, wondering where her next meal was coming from.

But, astonishingly, Ellie Hall Knitwear got off to an energetic start and flourished throughout the spring and summer of that year. It didn't just happen, of course, and was a result of high-quality work and dogged marketing. Any retail outlet with even the most tenuous potential as a stockist received a visit from Ellie, armed with a case full of samples and a steely resolve to display them. Clothing shops, drapery stores, fabric sellers – she even persuaded the owner of a shoe shop to rent her some space in their window with a few examples of her knitwear and some advertising material.

Her reputation continued to spread by word of mouth too. She preferred working for individual customers. Even aside from the fact that the work was more lucrative, she enjoyed the personal contact and the chance to discuss the style of garment, embroidery patterns and so on.

Being home-based was a boon in that it allowed her to spend more time with Donna. Naturally there were times when motherhood and money earning didn't mix, but with a little expediency and a whole lot of determination she usually managed to meet both obligations in the course of a day.

Her day began early. She tried to get at least a couple of hours in at her machine before Donna woke up, and also made full use of the time when the child had her daytime nap. Domestic chores were done at odd times and with great velocity. If she was feeling fraught, she reminded herself of the stalwart women of earlier times who'd taken in washing or made matches at home to feed the family, often with several small children under their feet and none of today's modern conveniences. Donna was a very contented child anyway, and was happy to play with her toys while Ellie knitted.

Flexibility was another advantage of homeworking. Time lost in necessary daytime diversions such as shopping, visiting the park or seeing friends and relatives to give Donna social contact, could be made up at night after she was in bed. Ellie was enormously grateful to her mother and Ann, who took care of Donna when Ellie had business calls to make.

She also received help from an unexpected source . . .

Pat was so eager to get back into Ellie's favour after her initial reaction to Ellie's resignation, she offered her the continued use of the shop estate car when Ellie's replacement – a man called Les, whom Pat didn't like, but whom she employed in the absence of any other applicants for the job – didn't need it for the deliveries. This made Ellie's operation a lot more efficient and was especially useful in delivering stock to the shops. Transport was essential and she planned to get her own car as soon as she could afford it.

Because Pat no longer saw Donna on a daily basis, she asked Ellie if she could have her on a Wednesday afternoon when the shop was closed. Ellie agreed without hesitation, glad there hadn't been a rift between her and Pat. She'd have hated for Donna to lose contact with one of her grannies.

Visits to Greenlands resumed in the early summer. But Ellie and Pat were asked by the matron to keep them short and undemanding to avoid any trouble. Seeing her husband continued to be a tense, heart-rending experience for Ellie but she was comforted by the fact that he was well cared for and happy.

The success of Ellie's business meant that Mary was kept

busy too. As well as sewing up the garments and stitching in the labels, she also helped with the embroidery, made pattern suggestions and was generally involved. Everything Ellie knew about knitting and sewing she'd learned from her mother, so she was always confident that Mary's work was of a high standard.

Mary was even thinking in terms of giving up her job at the wool shop. She was earning as much with Ellie, and things looked set to get even busier in the future. Rather than be too hasty, though, they decided that if business continued as it was for another three months Mary would resign from the wool shop and pour all her time and energy into Ellie Hall Knitwear.

Then, in August, everything changed.

The breathtaking rise to success of Ellie Hall Knitwear was matched by its sudden dive towards failure. Every order in hand was delivered, all the regular customers had everything they needed for the time being, and the phone remained stubbornly silent.

'Delayed teething troubles,' was Ellie's explanation.

'It did seem too good to last, I must admit,' Mary remarked. 'But what's caused it to stop so suddenly?'

'My lack of business experience and foresight.' Ellie was in no doubt about that. 'I knew before I went into this that I would have to learn as I went along; that I could only prepare up to a point.'

'I don't see how your lack of experience could have caused this sudden famine of orders, though,' her mother pondered.

They were drinking tea in Ellie's back garden, the air soft and fragrant with the scent of garden flowers. The days were all warm in this glorious summer of 1959, which had so far been an endless stream of sunshine punctuated by cool balmy nights. Dressed in a blue gingham dress, the sun gleaming on her auburn hair, Donna was pedalling up and down the path on the tricycle Ellie had bought her for her second birthday recently.

'Indirectly, I mean,' Ellie explained, mulling it over. 'I suppose I got so caught up in the excitement of seemingly endless orders, I didn't look far enough ahead. Had I been experienced in this business I'd have realised that the regulars would reach saturation point and not need anything for a while.'

'What could you have done if you had anticipated it?' Mary was curious to know. 'You can't be in two places at once – out getting new orders and at home making the knitwear.'

'That's the problem,' agreed Ellie. 'But I should have found the time somehow.'

Mary was noncommittal about that.

'Anyway,' Ellie continued, 'now that we have hit this slack patch I must use the time to spread the net wider, get our knitwear into outlets further afield so that someone will always want something from us. I've only ever targeted West London. It's time I did some marketing in other London regions.'

'Mm.'

'Trouble is,' Ellie frowned at the practicalities of the situation, 'it's going to take a while for any success I have in that direction to filter through into actual money in the bank. And I need cash quickly. I can't afford to have nothing coming in for any length of time.'

'Of course you can't,' her mother agreed. 'Not with a little one to feed.'

Ellie was thoughtful for a while; then a sudden sparkle came into her eyes. 'I've just had an idea,' she said excitedly.

'I guessed you'd come up with something,' grinned Mary, who had been confident her daughter would overcome this setback. 'So, come on, let's hear it.'

'I could make a cheaper range of knitwear, using less expensive wool and with only a small, simple piece of embroidery on the front, and sell it at the market,' she suggested. 'It'll be autumn soon; people will be buying winter woollies.'

Her mother had doubts about this. 'It's a good idea, but mightn't it cause a problem with the shops you supply if they see Ellie Hall Knitwear being sold from a market stall?'

'You do have a point, but I think I can probably overcome that by making the cheaper range under a different label.'

'Of course you can,' said Mary, brightening. 'I didn't think of that.'

'I'm only thinking of the market as a temporary thing,' Ellie pointed out, 'and I'd only do it once a week, on a Saturday, which will give us time to make enough stock, and also allow me to get out and about promoting the Ellie Hall range. If I can get that side of the business back on track, I'll drop the market.'

'My, my, you *are* getting a good head for business,' Mary complimented her.

'Something to do with necessity being the mother of invention, I suppose,' smiled Ellie.

'It certainly seems to work like that for you.' Mary paused, her brow furrowing. 'I've just thought of a possible snag, though. I think Shepherd's Bush market is made up of established stallholders. I'm not sure if you'll be able to get a casual Saturday pitch there. Even if they do have them, they'll be like gold dust.'

'You can rent a stall for a day at Napp's Road Saturday market in Hammersmith, though,' Ellie informed her gleefully.

'So you can,' said Mary. 'I'd forgotten about that.'

'It isn't as big or well known as ours here in The Bush but it draws the crowds. I've been a few times and it's always been busy.'

'Good thinking, love.' Mary was delighted. 'It's Saturday tomorrow. If I were you I'd get down there and have a word with the market inspector first thing in the morning. I'll look after Donna while you go.'

'Thanks, Mum.' Ellie was filled with fresh hope now that she had a definite scheme in mind to save her business.

Ellie had to wait a few weeks to be allocated a pitch so it was September by the time she set up shop for the first time in Napp's Road Saturday market. She was there early, setting out her stall, spreading the cellophane-wrapped jumpers out on display and hanging one of each colour on the rail. Her hands were shaking and she was sick with nerves, never having done anything like this before. But she was excited too, and ready for a challenge.

It was a misty morning with autumn chill in the air and the promise of sunshine, though the sun had yet to appear. Ellie was warmly clad in a black three-quarter coat over a bright blue polo-necked sweater and black slim-line trousers. A blue hat and muffler she'd knitted specially for the occasion added the finishing touch to her practical outfit.

'Wotcher,' said a gravel-voiced man of about thirty, dressed in a black donkey jacket. He was short and wiry, with small, speculative brown eyes and a greasy mop of chestnut curly hair.

'Hello,' Ellie smiled.

'Syd Bell's the name,' he introduced himself, a cigarette in his mouth. 'I noticed we'd got a newcomer; thought I'd pop over and make myself known.'

'That's kind of you,' she responded with a warm smile. 'I'm Ellie Hall.'

'Nice to meet you,' he said. 'I do kitchenware – pots and pans and stuff. Any problems or anything you want to know, just give me a shout.'

'Thank you.'

'I've been doing this market for years,' he told her proudly. 'Everyone knows me around here.' He pointed towards the street. 'My stall's just down there between the pie stall and the bloke selling china and glass.'

'I'll bear that in mind,' Ellie told him, glad of a friendly face among strangers.

'Ain't seen you around on any of the other markets,' he remarked casually, holding the cigarette between thumb and forefinger now and taking occasional puffs. 'I work different ones during the week in and around London. You see the same faces.'

She told him this was her first time at any market and admitted to feeling a bit nervous.

'You'll be all right once you get started,' he said, his mateyness tinged with superiority. He was being perfectly pleasant to her but there was something about him she didn't like. 'Stand firm and don't put up with any nonsense from the punters.'

'Bartering, you mean?'

He nodded. 'However low your prices are they'll try to knock you down even more. It's the reason they shop in a market,' he informed her knowingly. 'They'll have the stuff off you for nothing if you don't watch yourself.'

'Oh dear.' He was making it sound so grim, she was wondering if she'd done the right thing in coming.

'Make sure you don't lose all your profit in the thrill of a sale,' he advised. 'It's easily done when you're new to the game.'

'I'll remember that.'

'You'll soon get used to it.' He picked up one of the wrapped sweaters and looked at it. 'These look like decent gear. Did you get 'em local?'

'I made them.'

'Ooh, classy.' His gaze lingered on her face. 'You're not just a pretty face then.'

'Well, no . . .'

'You married?'

'Yes.' It was a relief to be able to say that and she deemed it wise not to give him the grim details of her marriage. He seemed the type who would automatically assume she was sex-starved and appoint himself rectifier.

'Oh.' His thick brows rose. 'Well, perhaps we can have a drink together sometime, anyway?'

He seemed harmless enough but Ellie sensed a harshness

beneath that congenial manner. 'Perhaps.' She was non-committal but kept her manner friendly. She didn't want to make enemies on her first day.

'Best o' luck then,' Syd said, moving away. 'And don't forget . . . if you need anything, Syd Bell's your man.'

'Thanks, Syd.'

'A pleasure.' He swaggered off to talk to another stallholder.

Fortunately the other market traders Ellie spoke to weren't quite so self-promoting. At one side of her were a married couple selling towels and bedlinen, and at the other was a middle-aged man with a mouth-watering selection of sweets – some home-made by his wife, he told Ellie. The street was a sea of colour, stalls as far as the eye could see, topped with bright awnings in a variety of shades and patterns. Everything from gramophone records to greengrocery was on offer here, and as the punters began to arrive the atmosphere buzzed with noisy vitality.

Having grown up in Shepherd's Bush, Ellie was no stranger to markets – as a customer. But being a stallholder was a different thing altogether and nerve-racking in the extreme, especially with the survival of her knitwear business depending on her success here today.

Infected by the gaiety of the ambience, however, she soon forgot her nervousness. With so much potential business about, the air was filled with promise but she had to wait until mid-morning for her first firm sale; a women's red sweater with a single white embroidered daisy. She was thrilled. And when she'd managed to shift three-quarters of her stock by the end of the day, she was even more buoyant.

'You've had a good day then.' Syd Bell sauntered over when she was packing up.

'Not half.' She was all smiles now. 'How about you?'

'Pretty good,' he told her. 'Business is usually booming at this time of the year, up until Christmas.'

'That's encouraging.'

'How about coming out for a drink with me tonight to

170

celebrate the fact that you've had a good day?' he suggested with a slow smile, his gaze resting on her persuasively. 'Tell the old man you're going to see your sister or something.'

'I don't have a sister.' She deliberately misunderstood him. 'But I do have a two-year-old daughter so I shall be at home looking after her this evening.'

He gave a casual shrug. 'Some other time, perhaps,' he said in a manner to suggest that it was her loss.

She nodded at him, smiling. She didn't particularly like or trust him, but nothing could dampen her spirits at the close of business today.

Ellie was still full of it when she got to her parents' house to collect Donna. They all went into the living room, Ellie sitting on the sofa with Donna on her lap, having first smothered her with kisses.

'Well done,' congratulated Mary. 'Fancy selling most of your stock on your first day. You've got off to a wonderful start.'

'It's better than I hoped for, I must say,' admitted Ellie.

'You'll be going again then?'

'The market inspector said that as long as I turn up when I've booked the pitch and run my stall in a decent manner, I can have the pitch for as long as I want it,' Ellie explained. 'So if you're willing to look after Donna, I'll carry on for a while. It won't be for ever, as I've said, but I need to continue until the other side of my business picks up.'

'Any time,' Mary offered. 'And if I can't do it for any reason, I'm sure your dad will stand in for me, or Ann. We'll work it out between us.'

'Thanks, both.' Ellie gave her parents an appreciative smile.

Mary chuckled. 'You realise that it's in my own interests to help you get your business back on course,' she pointed out. 'If you're earning money, so am I.'

Knowing that personal gain was the last thing on her mother's mind when she offered assistance, Ellie was smiling as she said, 'There is that.'

Her father made an observation from his armchair by the fire. 'Sounds as though you've thoroughly enjoyed yourself as well as making a few quid.'

'I have.' She was glowing with enthusiasm. 'I was in a terrible state when I got there this morning, though – actually shaking with nerves. But once the trading was underway, I loved it. There's a terrific feeling of camaraderie among the stallholders.' She paused, remembering. 'There was one bloke who was a bit of a bighead but the others were all smashing. They chat to you when they're not serving, and keep an eye on your stall while you answer a call of nature, or go and get a cup of tea or coffee. It was all very sociable.'

'I expect they were all talking about the big news from around here, weren't they?' mentioned Bob, frowning. 'People all over London will be talking about that.'

She looked puzzled. 'It was all market talk, Dad,' she told him. 'Nobody mentioned anything about Shepherd's Bush. Why? What's happened?'

'Ray Brent's been released from prison,' he announced.

'Ray Brent . . . Cor, that seems to have gone quick,' she remarked absently. 'Has he done his time already, or did they find out that he didn't do it or something?' She was still preoccupied with her day at the market and not giving the subject her full attention.

'Neither. He got remission for good behaviour,' her father informed her. 'He's only served six years of his ten-year sentence.'

'Really? I bet his dad will be pleased,' she said, remembering that her father knew Ray's father. 'He'll be out celebrating with his son tonight, I bet.'

Bob frowned. 'If people will let them celebrate,' he muttered solemnly.

'You reckon there'll be trouble, do you, Bob?' asked Mary.

'Bound to be,' he said gravely. 'Some people will go out of their way to make Ray Brent wish he was back inside.'

'Why would anyone want to do that?' Ellie queried. 'He's

done his time so now he should be allowed to get on with his life without interference.'

'He hasn't done his time, though, has he? Not all of it,' Mary reminded her. 'And some people won't like that.'

'He's done his time as far as the law is concerned,' insisted Ellie, her interest in the subject growing as she became drawn into the discussion. 'The powers that be must think he's learned his lesson and that he isn't a danger to the public or they wouldn't have let him back into society.'

'That's quite true,' agreed Bob. 'But it doesn't stop some people being up in arms about it.'

'Seems daft to me. I mean, it isn't as though he's done any other crime.' Ellie found herself becoming heated at the unfairness of it. 'As I remember it, it was a fight that got out of hand. It could have gone either way.'

'All right, love, there's no need to get worked up about it,' admonished her father. 'I'm only telling you what the feeling is among some of the locals. It isn't necessarily my opinion.'

'I'm not getting worked up,' she denied. 'It makes no difference to me personally what people think of Ray Brent. I don't even know the man. But I don't like to think of anyone having a vendetta against him. It's unfair.'

'There's those who think his release isn't justice,' Bob went on. 'They just see that a man is dead and he's responsible.'

Mary had the local paper in her hand. 'Enough of all that, you two,' she said, folding the paper over at a particular page and handing it to Ellie. 'There's something in here that might interest you.'

'Oh?' Ellie stared at the page.

'The bit about the cockle and whelk stall man,' her mother informed her. 'The one who has a stand outside the Talisman pub on the Green.'

'Yeah, I see,' said Ellie, glancing at the photograph of a familiar local face. 'How has he managed to get himself in the paper?'

'The *Gazette* is running a special feature about local

173

people who've made good,' explained Mary, her voice rising excitedly. 'Ordinary people who have set up in business for themselves or succeeded at something against all the odds. The cockle stall man is doing very nicely, apparently. Started with nothing and now he's got people working for him all over London, selling cockles and whelks outside pubs. This bit of local publicity won't do him any harm, either.'

Ellie read the article. 'Mm . . . interesting,' she muttered thoughtfully. 'You wouldn't think you could earn a decent living selling cockles and whelks except at the seaside, would you?' She handed the paper back to her mother.

'According to that you can,' said Bob.

'You ought to take a leaf out of his book,' suggested Mary.

'What, get out there selling cockles and whelks?' Ellie said, teasing her. 'Not really my thing, Mum.'

Both her parents roared with laughter.

'Get yourself in the local paper, I mean,' tutted her mother, grinning.

'If it was that easy everyone with anything to sell would be in there.'

'I realise that, but because of this special feature, they want to hear from people with an interesting story to tell,' said Mary. 'It's a golden opportunity for you. You and your knitwear business will make a nice human-interest story . . . how you turned a hobby into a full-time job and are keeping a roof over your head with it, sort of thing. You can certainly do with the publicity at the moment.'

'Something like that is worth more than any amount of advertising,' added Bob.

'Mm . . .' Ellie was pondering.

'If you get them to put your telephone number in as well, you're bound to get some enquiries.' Mary's voice was high-pitched with enthusiasm.

'OK, I'll give it a go. I'll ring the paper on Monday morning,' Ellie told them, warming to the idea more by the moment. 'I don't know if they'll be interested in me but there's no harm in trying.'

The *Gazette* were *very* interested in Ellie and did a piece about her a couple of weeks later, with a photograph of her at her knitting machine. It was great fun having the journalist come to the house with a photographer.

Having put herself forward for this, Ellie felt obliged to answer some personal questions, which meant telling them about Tom, though she didn't go into detail. To add human appeal to the story the feature mentioned the accident and the fact that Ellie was supporting herself and her daughter from her knitwear business. It was all done tastefully and, when the article appeared in the paper, she felt like a celebrity.

She didn't exactly have customers jamming her telephone line but she did have enough enquiries to make the exercise worthwhile. Most interesting of all was a telephone call she had from a most unexpected quarter.

'Have you just had Cliff Richard on the phone or something?' asked Ann, who just happened to be visiting with Matthew when Ellie took the call. 'You're looking *that* pleased with yourself.'

'Hardly,' laughed Ellie, 'but it was an exciting sort of call in a way.'

'Come on then,' urged Ann. 'Tell me who it was.'

'It was some bigwig from the local branch of some women's guild,' Ellie told her. 'She saw the article about me in the paper and wants me to go along to their next meeting and give a talk to the members about my knitwear business. There'll be about two hundred people there.'

'Wow!' Ann was impressed.

'I'm thrilled to be invited, naturally,' said Ellie, 'but I don't know if I can do it. Public speaking's out of my league.'

'It isn't now because you've been asked to do it,' Ann pointed out encouragingly. 'And you won't know if you can do it unless you get out there and try.'

'There is that.' Ellie was thinking ahead. 'But supposing I stand up to speak and my legs turn to jelly or my mouth dries up?'

'Then you'll have to ask for a chair and a drink of water, won't you?' grinned Ann. 'Where is it, anyway?'

'In a church hall in a street off Wood Lane.'

'Oh, that's not so bad,' said Ann. 'It isn't as though you've got to stand up on stage at the London Palladium or anything, is it?'

'Still a bit scary, though.'

'I hope you didn't turn the invitation down,' said Ann.

'You know me better than that.' Ellie gave her a beaming smile. 'Not only are they going to pay me a fee, but I can take samples of my work to show after the talk, and take orders,' Ellie informed her. 'So I'll do it even if I'm half dead with nerves. I'm not going to let a chance like this pass me by.'

There was a sudden shriek from the back room. 'Mummy . . . Mummy . . . come and see what Matthew's doing,' called Donna.

They hurried to the scene to find Matthew, now an adorable horror with a gift for destruction and a tendency to ransack everything within reach, busily unwinding a ball of wool that had been in a bowl on the floor beneath the knitting machine and was attached to the work in progress.

'Oh, Ellie, I'm so sorry,' apologised Ann, hastily removing her son before any more damage could be done.

'No harm done,' Ellie assured her. 'He hasn't pulled the work off the machine, just unwound the wool from the ball.'

'Thank God for that,' said Ann.

'It's my own fault,' admitted Ellie, shaking her head at her own carelessness. 'I should remember to keep that door shut when I'm not in there.'

'That's what fame does for you,' giggled Ann, teasing her. 'It takes your mind off ordinary things.'

'Don't be daft,' protested Ellie, but she was smiling. Being in demand had done wonders for her confidence.

176

★ ★ ★

Everything was all right until Ellie actually stood up to speak . . .

Oddly enough, she'd been more excited than nervous when she'd set off in the car in exuberant mood, leaving Mary at home with Donna. She'd still felt on good form when she'd unloaded her samples from the car and was greeted by the talk organiser on entering the hall.

But when she got to her feet on the small stage in the crowded hall, and realised that every eye in the room was on her, her heart thumped so hard she couldn't breathe, and the room spun around her. Fortunately, she'd been given a table so she gripped the edge of that, remembering what her mother had told her about deep breathing.

Worse followed. She opened her mouth and nothing came out. Her skin was on fire and she was soaked with perspiration. For a moment she thought she might collapse.

Then the most astonishing thing happened. She heard herself saying in a rapid, nervous tone, 'I believe it's customary for a speaker to take questions when they have finished their talk but I thought I would do something a bit different tonight.' She'd never experienced real silence until that moment. It was terrifying. Her mouth was so dry it didn't seem possible to continue. But somehow she did. 'I'm going to reverse the procedure and have questions now to set the ball rolling. This way you'll get to hear the aspects of my work which most interest you.' Her tongue felt like a dehydrated pork pie but at least she managed to swallow. 'So, may I have the first question, please?'

Two hundred faces stared at her from rows of chairs lined up in the hall. Not a word was uttered. The silence was so intense it actually hurt and Ellie thought they must hear her stomach churning. Why on earth had she started question time when she'd arranged with the organiser to do a forty-five-minute talk with questions at the end? Desperation was the answer to that.

Realising in a flash of rational thought that the members of the audience were probably as nervous as she was about speaking out in front of everyone, she was about to open her mouth and hope for the best when a lady in the front row said rather shakily, 'How did you get started?'

It was a lifeline and her answer was not so much a reply as the beginning of a story which broke the ice and got the talk underway. When she'd finished with the first question she found herself fielding more from all over the room. 'Were you a good knitter before you had your machine?' asked one. 'Do you do all the embroidery yourself?' enquired another. 'Have you always been good at sewing and knitting?'

As the questions came thick and fast, her nervousness dissolved. She began to feel like a professional, an expert in her particular field. It was more like a discussion group than a formal talk, and she could feel the rapport with the audience, warm and sweet, a personal triumph. Her jubilation was heightened when she was presented with a bouquet of flowers at the end. Elated, she thanked the audience for listening, after which she was surrounded by women wanting to speak to her personally, look at her knitwear and place orders.

'You went down a storm,' said the organiser when the crowd eventually dispersed and the women began chatting among themselves.

'Thank you,' said Ellie graciously. 'I really enjoyed it.'

'May I recommend you to other branches of our organisation?' the organiser requested. 'I'm sure some would be keen to book you to speak at their meetings.'

'Certainly,' said Ellie, delighted.

'Do you ever do demonstrations on the machine?' enquired the other woman.

'I haven't up until now but I'd be quite prepared to.'

'Maybe you could come along again, when some time has elapsed, and do a demonstration for us instead of a talk,' suggested the organiser, a slim woman in a red twinset and a navy-blue pleated skirt.

'I'd love to.'

'I'm sure that would go down well with our members,' she went on. 'We're always on the lookout for speakers. We like to have people who do something a little bit out of the ordinary and it's so difficult to find someone different every month.'

'It must be,' said Ellie politely.

'Your husband must be so proud of you,' the woman remarked chattily as Ellie gathered her things, ready to leave.

Ellie didn't reply. She felt cold suddenly.

'The way you've built up a business from nothing,' the woman continued to effuse.

A polite nod was Ellie's reply.

The organiser touched Ellie's arm in a sympathetic gesture. 'I understand from the article in the paper that your husband was injured in an accident,' she said.

'That's right.'

'I know it can't be easy for you, my dear,' she continued in a compassionate tone, 'but it must cheer him up to know how well you are coping.'

This wasn't the time to put a stranger in the picture as to the nature of Tom's injuries, so Ellie just nodded. The other woman's attention was elsewhere anyway.

People were leaving and goodbyes were being said. 'Thank you again for coming,' said the organiser. 'See you in the not-too-distant future, I hope. I'll be in touch.'

'I'll look forward to it.'

Loading her things into the car, Ellie felt the euphoric glow of success slip from her grasp. The mention of Tom had been a hefty reminder of reality and the dull thud of guilt took up residence, casting a shadow over everything. At first she couldn't understand why she should be suddenly struck by compunction at this time, then realised it must be because she was out enjoying herself while Tom was confined to a nursing home. Five-star comforts notwithstanding, it was still an institution.

She took herself in hand, determined not to let guilt about

this aspect of the situation take hold. She'd had quite enough of that to contend with already. All she had done was enjoy a job of work, for heaven's sake.

The organiser's assumption that Tom would be proud of his wife stirred something inside her too – an unpleasant thought that refused to be suppressed. It wasn't just that poor Tom was incapable of feeling anything for her now, though that was sad enough. This was more to do with the depressing realisation that were he still in full command of all his faculties, he wouldn't feel pride in his wife's achievement. Jealousy was the emotion that would flow naturally in him. It had always been for Ellie to be proud of Tom, not the other way round, and he would hate it to be otherwise.

It was a moment of painful clarity for Ellie, and she set off for home feeling glum, her evening spoiled.

Chapter Nine

When Ellie arrived at the market one cold and misty morning in November, she immediately sensed a change in the atmosphere. Instead of the noisy ebullience that usually greeted her as the traders set up their stalls, talking and calling out to each other, there was a curious hush; tension was tangible in the air.

Groups of stallholders were standing around gossiping in low voices. Her neighbours – Joe the sweet-seller, and the towel vendors – weren't at their stalls. She spotted them with a gathering of others further down the street, engaged in conversation with Syd Bell, who seemed to be holding forth about something quite heatedly, judging by the expressive way he was using his arms.

'What's going on?' Ellie enquired of Joe when he returned to his stall and got busy putting his confectionery on display.

'Syd Bell's organising some action,' explained Joe, a large, weatherbeaten man of about fifty with a corpulent middle, dark, thinning hair and a droopy moustache.

'Action?' She looked at him speculatively. 'What sort of action?'

'A protest against Ray Brent.'

'Oh, no!' she cried impulsively. 'Honestly, I don't know why people can't just live and let live, and mind their own business.' Ellie had come across plenty of prejudice against Ray Brent since his early release two months ago. 'Why would the traders want to take action against him anyway?'

'He's been given a pitch on this market, that's why we're

not minding our own business,' Joe told her sternly, obviously miffed by her criticism.

'I see,' she said. 'What's he selling?'

'Ornamental metalwork, fancy lanterns and plant holders, that sort of thing,' Joe informed her.

'It's unusual anyway.'

'He makes them himself, apparently. He's got a stall up the end. His dad's helping him.'

'They're not muscling in on anyone else's territory, are they?' Ellie pointed out. 'There's no one else doing that sort of thing on this market.'

'The Brents won't be doing it for long either,' declared Joe, setting up his brass scales and weights. 'Once they know they're not wanted here, they'll soon sling their hook.'

'That seems very unkind,' Ellie blurted out.

'Yeah, well, he's a murderer, isn't he?' Joe reminded her, his voice rising as he set out trays of coconut ice and various kinds of toffee, all freshly made by his wife. 'Syd's right when he says we don't want his sort on this market. He'll drive the punters away.'

'I don't believe that's true at all,' Ellie felt bound to say. 'If people are affected at all by his being here, which I very much doubt, since they come here because they like the goods on offer, they'll be even more likely to come and bring their friends too, to have a nose. Someone who's been in the papers always draws the crowds, no matter what they've done.'

Joe shrugged, then concentrated on lifting large glass jars of boiled sweets on to the stall – aniseed balls, pear drops, sherbet lemons, humbugs. He stood back, surveying his stall, which was becoming more irresistible by the moment. 'To be perfectly honest, I don't care who works here from a personal point of view,' he admitted, looking at Ellie gravely, 'but, as Syd pointed out, earning a living is hard enough as it is on the market, without having the tone of the place lowered by a murderer.'

'Is Syd going to put notices up all over the market saying

that convicted murderer Ray Brent is working here then?' Ellie wasn't normally facetious but what she was hearing brought out her combative spirit.

'He won't need to because Ray Brent won't be working here once he hears what Syd has to say,' was Joe's sharp response.

'Sounds to me as though Syd Bell is a real troublemaker.'

'He isn't afraid of an argument, it's true,' admitted Joe, who was a nice enough man but easily led. 'He's always been the one who organises things around here outside of the market inspector's jurisdiction. Most people can't be bothered.'

'Well, I hope he isn't expecting me to join his lynch mob.' Ellie was adamant.

'He's expecting everyone on the market to support him,' he informed her, his fat crumpled face wearing a worried expression. 'He told me to pass the message on to you. He wants us all to stand united against the Brents.'

'I want nothing to do with it.'

'Oooh . . .' Joe took a sharp breath, shaking his head. 'Syd won't like that.'

'Then he'll just have to lump it,' she announced, 'because I'm not joining a hate campaign just because Syd Bell gets his kicks out of making trouble for someone who's done none of us any harm.'

Joe gave her an anxious look. 'Syd's a big man among the traders, Ellie,' he warned her. 'People around here do what he tells them.'

'Well, I'm not going to.' It was a categorical statement.

He looked at her gravely. 'Oh, well, that's up to you,' he told her. 'Personally, I'd rather not cross him. It's safer that way.'

'I'll take my chances.' Ellie thought Syd Bell's clout was being grossly exaggerated. He was only a market trader, the same as all the others.

Even as they spoke, stallholders were deserting their posts and heading in the direction of Ray Brent's stall. 'Syd wants the Brents off the market before it opens for business,' Joe explained. 'So if you're not joining us, I'll see you later.'

'OK.'

He hurried away, leaving Ellie loading her stock on to the stall, and putting her float in the money pouch she wore around her waist under her coat. This part of the street was deserted now. Even the market inspector was nowhere to be seen. She wasn't near enough to see or hear what was being said at the Brents' stall but the distant sound of raised voices drifted in her direction in the damp morning air. On a sudden impulse, she headed for the action.

'I'll tell you again, shall I, Brent?' Ellie could hear Syd's gruff voice from where she was standing at the back of the crowd. 'We don't want scum like you on this market. So, on your way. Take your stock and your father and bugger off.'

Infected by the prevailing mood set by Syd Bell, there was a ripple of support from the other traders. 'Yeah, we don't want your sort around here,' added someone.

Ray Brent's rich, husky voice resonated through the crowd. 'Sorry to disappoint you, folks,' he told them in an even tone, 'but my father and I aren't going anywhere.'

'That's right,' added his father with equal firmness. 'We've as much right to be here as you have. You're not going to drive us away so you may as well clear off and get on with your work.'

'How many more times must I tell you?' Syd sounded exasperated. 'You're *not welcome here*.'

'We're here to do business, not win a popularity contest,' was how Ray Brent put it. 'We're sorry you don't like us but it's your problem, not ours.'

'He's got some front, ain't he?' jeered Syd, looking at the others and firing them up.

'He has, an' all,' agreed someone. 'It's a bloody cheek, if you ask me.'

'I think it's time we showed these two that we mean what

we say, don't you?' Syd shouted to the crowd.

About half the traders answered in the affirmative. The others stood by in silence, looking worried. Ellie was heartened by the fact that Syd Bell's views weren't shared by everybody.

'If you don't leave of your own accord, we'll move you by force and chuck your lousy stock where it belongs, on the rubbish dump,' threatened Syd. 'And as there are a lot more of us than there are of you, you'd be wise to be on your way if you don't want your stuff ruined.'

Although it was obvious to Ellie that the men under attack were not easily intimidated, they were hugely outnumbered here and she could feel the heat rising. Fearing that violence was about to erupt, her natural impulse for justice compelled her to act. She pushed her way through the crowd and turned to them.

'What's the matter with you people that you want to stop someone earning a living?' she asked in a rousing tone. 'The man has done his time – why can't you just let him go about his business? His being here isn't going to hurt any one of us. You'd think he was about to take the bread out of our mouths the way you lot are carrying on.'

The silence was breathtaking. Ellie looked at Ray Brent, who was standing behind his stall next to his father. He grinned at her, put his head at an angle and winked. He barely resembled the flash Teddy Boy she remembered seeing around the town years ago. He'd matured well. Gone were the greased hair and sideburns, the drape jacket and drainpipe trousers. His black hair was now worn short and brushed back, emphasising his square jaw-line, and he was wearing a dark casual jacket over a cream, polo-necked sweater.

He looked like a hard man but she sensed that was more to do with his muscular build and positive attitude than his features, which were clean-cut. It was the first time Ellie had seen him in such close proximity and she hadn't realised until now that he had such striking dark eyes.

'Well, well,' said Syd in a mocking tone while Ray and his father stood by, watching the scene with interest. 'Do we have a traitor in our midst?'

'Oh, really . . . talk about dramatics,' said Ellie with blistering scorn. 'I think you've been watching too many gangster films, Syd. Well, I've got news for you, mate. This is real life and we are all here to earn a living. So why don't you let us get on with it in peace, instead of stirring up trouble?'

'What's it to you, anyway?' demanded Syd. 'Do you know the geezer or something?'

'No, I don't know him. But I do know about fairness.' Ellie looked towards the gathering. 'Are you really, in your hearts, bothered about someone who's been in prison working on the market?'

There was a confused muttering.

'Well, if you are, you're not the sort of people I believed you to be,' she went on. 'I had you down as folks with a bit of heart and humanity.'

'The man is a murderer,' put in Syd Bell.

'As far as we're concerned, it doesn't matter what he's done,' insisted Ellie. 'He's paid his debt to society and he should be allowed to get on with his life. My God, it's no wonder so many ex-cons end up back inside, if this is the sort of treatment they get when they come out.'

'She's right,' said one brave soul.

'Mm,' mumbled another, followed by others as the tide began to turn.

'Well, you lot can do what you like,' Ellie said, hoping that she'd gained some support. 'I'm going to get ready to open up shop. But I urge you to think about what I've said. There but for the grace of God and all that.'

And without looking to either side of her she elbowed her way through the crowd and went back to her stall. Outrage at the injustice had given her the courage to speak out. Now that she had done she was trembling all over. But seeing people drift back to their stalls gave her encouragement. Some even stopped by and told her they admired her for standing up to Syd, and they had decided to defect from the hostilities.

'Are you completely thick or what?' demanded Syd Bell, appearing at Ellie's stall a few minutes later; he was white with temper, his eyes hot with rage.

'Not that I know of,' she replied.

'Well, you can't have much between your ears or you'd know that when I organise something, I don't expect to have some mouthy bird mess it up for me,' he raged. 'I don't like it. *Understand?*'

'Don't kid yourself, Syd,' she said. 'Your miserable campaign would have fallen apart without any intervention from me. The majority of the stallholders didn't want to take part, anyway, and only went along with it because you got them all worked up.'

'Rubbish!'

'You don't give a damn what Ray Brent was in prison for,' she went on. 'You're just frightened of the competition. You're scared he might have more power around here than you, once he gets established.'

'What a load of drivel.'

'You can deny it all you like but I know what you're about,' Ellie insisted. 'Ray Brent is a powerful presence, a threat to your authority among the traders. That's why you want to get rid of him – in case people are drawn to him rather than you. Well, your fan club obviously isn't as strong as you thought it was, or they would have stayed with it.'

'They only came away because they needed to get ready to trade,' he argued.

'You didn't achieve your aim and move the Brents off the market before it opened, though, did you?' she challenged.

His beady eyes met hers in a clash of hostility. 'There'll be other times,' he said, his brows rising a fraction. 'I'm not about to be beaten by the likes of you and Ray Brent.' He paused, staring at her grimly. 'You'll soon find out just how much influence I do have around here.'

The viciousness in his eyes made her blood run cold. But she managed to compose herself, determined not to give him the satisfaction of knowing he was frightening her. 'You don't scare me,' she bluffed.

'You'll be more than scared by the time I've finished,' he declared.

'Are you threatening me?'

'You can take it whatever way you like,' he told her, 'but I don't enjoy being made a fool of.'

'Oh, go away and leave me to get on with my work,' she said, assuming an attitude of boredom to hide the fact that he was making her nerves jangle.

He looked at her with pure hatred. 'I'm going. But you haven't heard the last of this.'

Joe had been listening to the conversation and was worried about her. 'You'd be wise not to make an enemy of him,' he advised when Syd had gone. 'He can be an evil bugger when he's riled.'

'I'd rather take my chances than go along with his mindless prejudice,' Ellie told him.

'Just be careful, that's all,' warned Joe.

'Afraid he'll beat me up in some dark alley one night, are you?' she suggested.

'No, that isn't Syd's style.'

'That's all right then.'

'But keep your wits about you and watch your back,' Joe advised her in a chilling tone. 'I'll say no more on the subject than that.'

Ellie had a visitor at lunchtime. Ray Brent came over to her stall to thank her for her efforts on his behalf earlier, and to ask if he could buy her lunch as a thank you. He explained that his father was covering for him on the stall. The fact that Ray had taken the trouble to find out her name pleased her, for some reason.

'Thanks for offering but I don't take a proper lunch break,' she told him.

'Why's that?'

'I don't like to ask anyone to cover for me for that long,' she explained, 'so I just have a sandwich here at the stall.'

'How about joining me for just a drink, then?' He gave her the most melting smile. 'I'm sure one of the others will keep an eye on things while you take a short break.'

He was awesomely attractive – not prettily handsome like Tom, but robustly masculine, a hint of vulnerability showing through that tough exterior and adding to his appeal. Without further argument, she found herself asking Joe if he'd be kind enough to look after her stall for half an hour, then headed off through the market crowds by Ray's side.

The pub was packed to the doors with market people. A tense silence crept through the bar when Ellie and Ray went in. All heads were turned in their direction. It was extremely disconcerting but Ellie took Ray's lead and appeared to ignore it, and the place soon hummed into life again.

They managed to grab a table by the window when someone left. He had a pint of beer, she just had a shandy because anything stronger would make her sleepy and she wanted to be fully alert for the afternoon's business. 'They'll soon get used to having you around,' Ellie said encouragingly.

'They'll have to because I'm not going to disappear.'

'I realise you might find this hard to believe but they are actually a friendly bunch – apart from spiteful Syd, of course,' she said. 'The trouble this morning was all his doing.'

'Don't worry about me,' Ray assured her. 'I've had worse things to deal with than a few stroppy market traders.'

She studied his face, observing the premature lines around his mouth, the hard glint in his eyes, despite the warm smile he was giving her. 'Yes,' she said seriously. 'I expect you have.'

'It was very kind of you to stick your neck out for me this morning, and I was touched by it,' he told her, 'but I can look

189

after myself. There's no need for you to get on the wrong side of anyone on my account.'

'I acted on impulse.' It was hard to imagine anyone who seemed as nice as he did actually killing someone; it was a chilling thought but she wasn't at all frightened of him. Syd Bell seemed far more menacing. 'Just put it down to my natural dislike of prejudice.'

'And I admire you for it. But I don't think it's a good idea for you to upset Syd Bell.' His brow was taut, his eyes clouded with concern. 'He seems like a nasty piece of work to me.'

'There's no need to worry your head about me,' Ellie assured him. 'I'll be all right.'

He still seemed concerned. 'You just mind how you go,' he said with a sober expression.

'Yeah, I will,' she said to ease his mind.

'The irony of all this is that I didn't actually do the murder,' he said darkly.

'Oh?' Ellie stared at him, waiting for him to continue.

'Still, there's no point in going on about that now. It's all in the past.' He obviously regretted his comment and effected a swift change of subject. 'Did I see something about you in the local paper recently?'

'That's right.'

'I thought it was you,' he said. 'You're from my neck of the woods, then?'

'Yeah. Shepherd's Bush born and bred.' Her mood had lifted with the change of topic and she gave him a warm smile.

'And famous with it,' he grinned, picking up on the altered atmosphere.

'Not as famous as you.' As soon as the words were out she regretted them. 'Sorry, I didn't mean to bring that up.' She put her hand to her mouth in a gesture of regret. 'Me and my big mouth.'

He didn't seem to mind. 'Don't worry about that,' he said amiably. 'It's quite true. Six years ago you couldn't open a newspaper without seeing my face splashed all over it.'

'I remember.' She swiftly steered the conversation on to safer waters. 'Whereas my claim to fame was just a little piece in the local rag which gave my business a much-needed boost. That's the only reason I put myself up for it.' She went on to tell him about the knitwear orders and the opportunity for public speaking that had come about as a result of the publicity. 'Giving that talk did wonders for my confidence. All those people listening to what little old me had to say. I never thought I would ever do anything interesting enough to be asked, let alone enjoy it. That sort of thing had always been a world apart, until now.'

'That's great.'

'I was pleased.'

Giving her a studious look, he said, 'I believe they mentioned something in the article about your husband being seriously injured in a car accident.'

Ellie's mood saddened. 'Yes, the journalist asked me about my background to give the piece more human interest, I suppose.' She was embarrassed to feel tears rushing into her eyes. 'Poor Tom will probably spend the rest of his life in a nursing home.'

'I'm so sorry.' Ray asked more about it in a conversational rather than a probing manner, and Ellie felt so easy with him, she found herself telling him about Greenlands, though she didn't go into detail about Tom's condition.

'Sounds like a really good place,' he approved. 'But not very convenient for you to visit.'

'That is a bit of a drawback but I manage.' The depth of her sorrow about Tom's situation was far too personal to discuss with a stranger; he seemed to sense this and didn't continue along those lines.

'It must be hard for you,' he commented. 'Almost like being a widow, I suppose.'

'I've often thought the same thing.' She paused as something occurred to her. 'As you're from around our way, you might know my husband.'

'I thought I might too when I read the article, but the name didn't ring a bell,' he told her. 'It said in the paper that he's twenty-five. I'm twenty-nine so I wouldn't have known him at school. We'd have gone around in a different crowd.'

She agreed and they chatted generally in the way of social exploration. He asked her more about her business; she asked him if he'd always done ornamental metalwork.

'No, I learned it while I was a guest of Her Majesty, as a matter of fact,' he explained.

'Really?'

He went on to tell her about his dead-end job in the factory. 'As I was doing a long stretch I thought I might as well make use of my spare time in prison to learn something new. It was originally meant to be just a hobby but I knew it wouldn't be easy to get a decent job after my release, so it made sense to make use of my new skills and turn it into a full-time occupation. I set up on my own soon after I came out.'

'Quite a brave step,' Ellie remarked.

'Finding a job seemed to require more courage,' he confessed with a wry grin.

'I think I can understand that.'

'My father's been a great support to me,' Ray went on to say. 'He found a workshop for me while I was still inside so that I could get started right away. Fortunately, the setting-up costs were quite low – just advance rent on the workshop, a small welding plant and some materials. Dad lent me what I needed. He's an absolute rock . . . They don't come better than him.'

'Is he in the business with you?'

'No. He just helps out in his spare time. He's in the factory where I used to work during the week so he's only free at weekends. He enjoys working with me . . . it makes a change for him.'

'What other methods do you have of selling your work besides the market?' Ellie enquired chattily.

'Advertising in London local papers mostly,' he told her.

'The small stuff will be sold mainly through the market but I want to take on bigger projects as soon as I can – gates and speciality stair-rails, that sort of thing. I'd also like to do some restoration work. Once I get properly established, I'm hoping my reputation will be my best advertisement.'

'By restoration work, do you mean the ornamental gates they have on big country houses?'

'That's right. There's plenty of work about in and around London, in the posh parts' – he pointed out – 'gates, fancy railings and so on.' His voice radiated enthusiasm when he spoke about his craft.

'Sounds to me as though you've found something you really enjoy,' she opined.

'I have,' he confirmed. 'It's a damned sight more satisfying than working on the assembly line in a factory, I can tell you. And I'm absolutely determined to make a go of it.'

'You've got the right attitude anyway,' she encouraged. 'I'll have to pop over to your stall and have a good look at your work. I only caught a glimpse this morning.'

'I'd like you to see it.'

'I will come over, I promise.' Looking at her watch, she was startled. 'Heavens above,' she gasped. 'We've been here nearly an hour. Joe will think I'm really taking liberties.'

'I must go too,' Ray said, draining his glass. He stood up to put his coat on, looking at her uncertainly. 'Er . . . I was wondering if I could thank you properly for this morning. Take you to the West End for a meal one evening, perhaps.'

Ellie was taken aback. 'You've already thanked me,' she said. 'There's no need for anything more.'

'I'd like to.'

'I don't think so.'

His face muscles tightened, his expression becoming hard. 'I see . . . yes, I quite understand,' he said dully.

Realising that he had misunderstood her, she assured him, 'My answer has nothing to do with your past.'

'Don't worry about it,' Ray said tightly. 'I realise that an alleged murderer isn't an ideal dinner companion. I shouldn't have suggested it.'

'You're far too quick to jump to conclusions,' was her hasty response. 'The reason I can't accept is because I have a small daughter. My relatives are brilliantly supportive, but they already look after her when I'm out working so I'd rather not ask them to sit for me again in the evening while I go out socialising.'

'Of course.' He looked contrite. 'I remember there was something in the article about your having a daughter. I didn't think it through properly.'

'Anyway, you've bought me a drink and I've enjoyed our chat,' Ellie said. 'That'll do for me.'

'Fair enough.'

They walked back to her stall together and he departed. Whatever the truth about his past, he was terrific company. She'd felt so at ease with him, she could have happily chatted to him all afternoon. She found herself regretting having turned down his dinner invitation. But, even apart from her domestic responsibilities, Ellie had enough complications in her life as it was. The emotional uproar that could possibly result from a date with a man, even if it was only a one-off to say thank you, was something she could definitely do without. The feeling that she had missed out on something important lingered in her mind, though.

Later that same afternoon she had a visit from Ray's father, who introduced himself to her as Alfie Brent. Like his son, he was extremely striking in appearance, with the same firm features, dark eyes and muscular physique, but Alfie's bushy hair and eyebrows were now completely white. He thanked her profusely for what she'd done that morning.

'It was nothing,' she assured him. 'As I told Ray, I would have done the same thing for anyone. I'm one of these irritating people who can't keep their nose out when some-one's being unfairly treated.'

'Well, it warmed my heart anyway, ducks,' he was keen to

tell her. 'Made me feel as though the whole world isn't against us.'

'I'm glad.' She looked at him. 'I'll tell my dad that I've seen you. He's Bob Scott. I believe you sometimes see each other in the Rose and Crown.'

'You're Bob Scott's daughter!' Alfie's face lit up. He remembered how her father had stood up for him in the pub one night soon after Ray had been sent down. 'Now I understand where you get your good nature from.'

'Thank you.'

'And thank *you* for your support,' he said again. 'Anything we can do for you at any time, you only have to ask. I must get back to work. Ta-ta for now.'

'Ta-ta, Alfie,' Ellie said, and felt oddly privileged for having met the Brents.

That evening Ray Brent was soaking in the bath in his father's flat where he was staying temporarily until his business was up and running. The arrangement suited them both for the moment. His dad enjoyed the company and it was useful to Ray not to have the expense of a place of his own while his business was still in its infancy. Sharing the rent and the bills allowed them both to live more cheaply.

Leaning back with the sponge under his head, he ran over the events of the day at the market. After a slow start, business had been steady. They'd shifted a lot of plant and candle holders, probably because they were quite cheap and made good presents. He needed to produce a lot more to make the most of the run-up to Christmas. It was bound to be slack for a while in the new year.

His thoughts drifted on to Ellie Hall. He was angry with himself for asking her out even though it had just been as a token of his appreciation. But it hadn't been just that, though, if he was really honest with himself. He'd only used that as an excuse to get to know her better. The instant he'd clapped eyes on her he'd known she was really special.

The memory of her gave him a warm feeling and he found himself smiling as he recalled her leaping to his defence so wholeheartedly. She'd stood there with her cheeks glowing, red hair all over the place and blue eyes blazing, as she told the market traders what she thought of them. What a woman! Phew. And how different to Maria, who'd made such a hasty retreat from his life immediately after his arrest. The last he'd heard of her, she was getting married and moving right away from the area.

Sociable company wasn't something Ray had a great deal of these days. Some of his mates had been loyal to him while he'd been inside; others had drifted away. Six years was a long time to be out of circulation. Most of them were married now anyway, and busy with their wives at weekends.

Still, he could usually find someone to have a game with at the billiard hall; or he might even talk his father into going to one of the town's livelier pubs with him unless Dad had anything special on at the Rose and Crown.

Ray certainly had no intention of staying at home on a Saturday night just because he didn't have anywhere in particular to go and had to face the possibility of verbal abuse whenever he went into a pub. After six years living with villains it would take more than a few loud-mouthed trouble-makers to put him off.

One thing he mustn't do was to chase after Ellie Hall just because he needed a woman. She was gorgeous and he fancied her rotten. To all intents and purposes she was on her own but she was actually married and therefore off limits. He'd asked her out on impulse. It mustn't happen again.

Oh well, he thought, emerging from the soothing hot water and reaching for the towel, a few pints and a game of billiards would do nicely for tonight. Unless, of course, there was a spare woman about and he got lucky. He was a normal, healthy man. Ellie Hall was out of the question, so he had to make the most of any other opportunities that came his way.

'Wotcher, Bob,' greeted Alfie the next day when he saw Ellie's father in the Rose and Crown during the Sunday lunchtime session. 'I was hoping I'd see you in here.'

'How's it going, Alfie?'

'Mustn't grumble. Yourself?'

'Pretty good, thanks,' answered Bob. 'How's that son of yours getting on?'

'He's all right.' Alfie told him all about Ray's new business.

'I'm glad to hear he's doing well,' said Bob.

'The reason I wanted to see you, Bob, is to compliment you on that daughter of yours. She's a diamond and no mistake.'

Bob beamed proudly. 'I know that, mate, but what's she done to make you realise it too?'

The other man gave him a detailed account of events at the market the previous day. 'You should have seen her, it was a real treat,' related Alfie with admiration. 'Talk about taking the fire out of their argument. She really went to town on 'em. The whole thing fizzled out after she'd finished. Cor, what a woman. You must be very proud of her.'

'I am.' Bob looked worried but Alfie was too busy effusing about Ellie to notice.

'Let me buy you a drink,' offered Alfie, 'to thank you for bringing up your daughter to be such a lovely person.'

'That's very kind of you,' Bob accepted politely. 'I'll have a pint of bitter, please.'

'Coming up.'

As Alfie turned away from him towards the bar to order the drinks, Bob's brow creased into a frown. He didn't want to spoil things for Alfie by mentioning it, but he wasn't best pleased to hear that his daughter was taking the side of an alleged murderer against her workmates. That wasn't a wise move on her part at all. Bob had defended Alfie when Ray was arrested but when it came to his daughter's well-being he viewed things differently. Ellie was just starting market trading and she was an outsider in Hammersmith. She'd do well to tread very carefully indeed.

★ ★ ★

There was the usual gathering at Mary and Bob's house in Marsh Road for Sunday tea that afternoon: Ellie and Donna, Ann, Doug and Matthew. As they all began to congregate in the living room, Ellie was amazed to find herself under attack from her father.

'I don't know what you think you're playing at,' he bellowed at her from his armchair.

She stared at him with a puzzled expression. 'What have I done?'

'Fancy getting involved in a ruckus at the market and taking the side of a convicted murderer against all the other stallholders,' he rebuked sternly. 'You must want your head examined.'

'Ah . . . I see,' she said. 'You've been talking to Alfie Brent in the pub?'

'I'll say I've been talking to him,' he blasted at her. 'He's singing your praises to the heavens. Seems to think that you're some sort of heroine.'

'I can't help that.'

'Of course you can help it. It's because you stuck up for his son,' he fumed.

'Well, I—'

'And I notice you didn't tell us that there'd been any trouble when you came to collect Donna after the market yesterday,' he interrupted.

'It didn't seem important. I was thinking of other things that had happened during the day, and paying attention to Donna,' Ellie said truthfully. 'I suppose I just didn't get round to it.'

'You kept shtoom because you knew we wouldn't approve, more like,' he growled.

'No, Dad, it wasn't like that,' she disagreed hotly. 'I had other things on my mind when I got back. I was preoccupied with Donna and I was more concerned with telling you what a good trading day I'd had.'

'Oh well,' he mumbled, 'be that as it may, you shouldn't have got mixed up in trouble.'

'But the stallholders were being manipulated by this one troublemaker and treating Ray really badly,' she told him, sitting next to Ann on the sofa, the children playing on the floor unconcerned with the adult conversation. 'I couldn't just stand back and watch them ganging up on someone. It was so unfair.'

'Don't you realise the danger you've put yourself in by taking the Brents' side?' Bob glared at his daughter.

'I thought you liked Alfie,' she said, almost as though that one fact automatically guaranteed her father's loyalty towards the Brents.

'I do like him but that doesn't alter the fact that his son's been in prison for murder.'

'Ray claims he didn't do it.'

'Don't they all?'

'Oh, come on, Dad,' Ellie argued. 'Ray Brent didn't seem in the least bit dangerous to me. He's a really nice bloke, as a matter of fact.'

'That isn't the point I'm trying to make,' Bob went on. 'I'm not saying that Ray Brent will hurt you in any way, or that he did the murder, but other people might turn against you if you get friendly with him. You'll make enemies among the other stallholders by going against them and taking his side. And you could find yourself in trouble because of that.'

'It wasn't me against *everyone else*,' she corrected. 'Not in the end anyway. A lot of them could see that I was right. As I've said, it was a man who sees Ray as a threat who stirred up the trouble. I just wasn't prepared to go along with it, and I don't think you'd be very proud of me if I had. Not when it comes down to it.'

'Ray Brent doesn't need you to clear his path for him,' Bob went on. 'He's tough, but you're not. You're only a young woman; he's seen more of life than you ever will. He can look after himself.'

'Which is exactly what he said to me in the pub,' she informed him.

Bob clutched his head as though in pain. 'You went to the pub with him?'

'That's right.' She saw no reason to be ashamed of it. 'He wanted to thank me for standing up for him so he bought me a drink at lunchtime.'

Now her mother made an intervention. 'I should keep well away from him if I were you, love,' she advised.

'That's what I'm telling her,' added Bob.

'Honestly, anyone would think the man was in the same league as Jack the Ripper to hear you talk. I went for a drink with him, not for a weekend in Brighton,' she said, imagining their reaction if she happened to mention that he'd invited her to go out with him for a meal.

'This is nothing personal against him,' her father was keen to point out. 'Your mother and I are only concerned about the enemies you may make by taking his side. They could make things very awkward for you on that market if they wanted to. And you can't afford that sort of trouble. You've got young Donna to think about, you've got to be careful.'

'I appreciate your concern but I'm not some harebrained teenager.' She was beginning to get irritated now.

'Nobody is suggesting that you're irresponsible,' Bob said, 'but you can't expect us to stand back while you put your safety and your business at risk.'

'Come on, Dad,' Ellie urged him. 'I'm a big girl now. I can look after myself.'

'I'm very well aware of the fact that you're a grown woman,' he told her, 'but your husband can't look out for you and Donna so it's up to us to do what we can to see that you're all right.'

She softened towards him. 'I know you mean well but you can't expect me to go against my instincts for fair play just to save my own skin.' She paused, looking from one to the other. 'I'm certain you would have acted in the same way as I did if you'd been there.'

'You could be right but that isn't the issue,' Bob said sagely. 'If you know what's good for you you'll steer well clear of Ray Brent and all the complications that go with him.'

Up until now Doug had been sitting quietly on the sofa beside his wife, listening to the conversation. Suddenly he made a heated interruption. 'I don't believe I'm hearing this,' he said angrily. 'Will you just listen to yourself, Dad? You and Mum have brought Ellie and me up to have a social conscience and to stand firm in our beliefs, yet here you are condemning her for trying to see that justice is done.'

There was a tense silence. Doug wasn't given to losing his temper so they were all shocked by this outburst.

'It's a hard world out there, Doug,' preached his father, 'and your sister is meddling in things she knows nothing about.'

'She knows enough to run her own business and she certainly knows unfairness when she comes across it.' His voice was shaking with rage, his face and neck suffused with high colour. 'And those are the important things. Frankly, I admire her for having a go.'

'And so do we, of course,' Mary was quick to add. 'All we're saying is that Ray Brent could be a dangerous man to get friendly with because of the trouble it could cause Ellie with her workmates.'

'What right have you to condemn him?' Doug demanded, his voice rising.

It was so unusual for Doug to make a stand, they all stared at him aghast.

'He's been in prison for murder, Doug,' his mother said at last.

'It wasn't murder, it was manslaughter. And he denied it throughout his trial,' insisted Doug. 'How do you know he wasn't telling the truth?'

'I don't, and I wouldn't dream of pretending to know what happened that night,' Mary made it clear. 'I've told you, this isn't about him personally. I just don't think it's a good idea for Ellie to upset people on his behalf.'

'Sounds to me as though you've got it in for him good and proper,' accused Doug.

Mary gave her son a sharp look, an angry flush suffusing her cheeks. 'You know perfectly well that I'm not a malicious person,' she said brusquely. 'I just think Ellie should be aware of the consequences of getting friendly with Ray Brent if the others are against him. Any parents worth their salt would feel the same as your father and I do. Anyway, whether he killed a man or not is beside the point, it was a long time ago. It's water under the bridge.'

'Exactly. So why make out the bloke is public enemy number one when he's done his time and is trying to get on with his life?'

'Ellie is our daughter,' said Mary. 'We're bound to be concerned about her.'

'And she's my sister. Personally, I'd be far more concerned if she'd just stood back and said nothing at the market yesterday,' he carried on. 'Mob rule and easily led fools – is that what you'd rather Ellie were part of?'

'I've told you that we admire her guts.' Mary's manner was brisk. 'But we don't want her getting into any trouble unnecessarily. Without a husband to look after her, she's vulnerable.'

Doug turned to his sister. 'Well done, sis,' he said. 'You're a star in my book.'

She leaned across and put her hand on his arm, concerned to see him so distressed. 'Nice of you to say so, Doug. But calm down, eh? Mum and Dad are only thinking of me and Donna.'

'Just the same—'

'I don't know why you're in such a temper about it, anyway,' Bob cut in with a querying look. 'It isn't even as if Ray Brent is a mate of yours.'

'You don't have to know someone to feel for them when they're not being treated right,' he retaliated.

'I accept that,' agreed his father.

202

'It must be hard for anyone to make a new start when they come out of prison,' Doug continued. 'And it makes my blood boil to hear that some people are spiteful enough to make it even harder.'

'So you'd have your sister put herself at risk for the sake of your principles then, would you?' accused his father, angry now at the criticism.

'You know me better than that,' Doug objected. 'Anyway, I don't think she has put herself at risk. You've blown the whole thing out of proportion. All she did was stand up for what she believes in. And if she has any trouble at the market we'll all help her sort it out. So there isn't a problem.'

'All right, Doug, you've made your point,' intervened Ann gently. 'Now can we please change the subject?'

'What a good idea, Ann,' approved Mary, getting to her feet. 'I'm going to put the kettle on and I don't want to hear another word about Ray Brent when I come back.'

Doug sat down next to his wife and seemed to calm down but he hardly said a word for the rest of the afternoon. Ellie knew he hated arguments and would still be smarting from this one. He evidently felt very strongly on the subject to have quarrelled with his father about it. Still, no one could object to Doug's principles and, Ellie reflected, seeing the children playing at their feet, perhaps those principles had been honed by Doug having a son of his own. She thought of Alfie and how he had stood up for Ray. How precious families were – even if they didn't always agree.

Chapter Ten

Because parking was strictly limited in Napp's Road on market day, Ellie left the car in a side street, usually managing to get the same space each week. Transferring the stock from the car to the stall was a bit of a drag because she had to make several trips lugging cumbersome cardboard boxes packed with knitwear.

The Saturday morning following the unpleasantness over Ray Brent's presence, the job seemed particularly laborious because the weather was bitter, an overnight frost making it slippery underfoot. She picked her way carefully to the stall, eager to divest herself of the first load.

She wasn't pleased, therefore, to find a young man in a duffel coat setting the stall up with gramophone records.

'What's going on here?' Ellie asked, peering at him over the top of the carton of sweaters she was carrying.

He looked at her blandly. 'What ja mean?' he enquired, chewing gum vigorously.

'This is my stall.'

Unconcerned, he continued to stack records. 'I wouldn't be setting up here if it was, would I?' he pointed out without looking up.

'But this is my regular pitch . . .'

'I know nothin' about that,' he said, glancing at her briefly. 'All I know is, this stall's been allocated to me. The market inspector, Reg Cox, brought me here himself.'

'But I'm here every Saturday,' she protested.

Pausing in his work and paying more attention to what she was saying, he chewed thoughtfully, looking at her. 'I dunno what's happened then. He must have moved you to another pitch or something, because he definitely told me to set up here. I wouldn't have done it otherwise.'

'That's peculiar.'

'I should go and see Reg Cox about it, love,' he suggested. 'Find out what's going on. Nothing to do with me. I'm just doing what the man told me.'

'He must want me to work another pitch, I suppose,' Ellie muttered worriedly. 'Heaven knows why.'

'That's management for you, innit? They're a law unto themselves.' He was warming towards her now that it was becoming obvious that this was an 'us and them' situation. 'You can leave that box of stuff here while you get it sorted, if you like,' he offered helpfully. 'Save you dragging it about with you.'

She thanked him and was about to go in search of Reg Cox when Syd Bell swaggered on to the scene.

'What's this?' He gave Ellie an unctuous smile. 'Someone stolen your pitch?'

'Rex Cox must have moved me,' she said absently, too preoccupied with the problem to pay much attention to Syd. 'I'm just going to see him, to find out about it.'

'You'll be wasting your time,' he advised her, eyes gleaming victoriously.

'Why?'

'There won't be a pitch for you anywhere on this market – not today or any other day,' he informed her smugly.

It took a few moments for the implications to sink in. Then: 'You've done something, haven't you?' she accused, her eyes narrowed on him. 'You've fixed it to get me off the market.'

'Would I do a thing like that?' He was playing with her and enjoying every moment.

'With the greatest of relish,' she replied angrily. 'Well, you won't get away with it.'

206

Turning away from the record seller, Syd took Ellie's arm and led her out of earshot, speaking in a low voice so close to her ear she could feel his warm breath, a nauseating miasma of stale cigarette smoke. 'I already have,' he told her, 'and there's not a damned thing you can do about it.'

'Oh, no?' she challenged. 'We'll soon see about that.'

'I told you you'd be sorry you crossed me and you're about to find out just how sorry.' He put some bruising pressure on her arm but in such a way as to be unnoticed by any onlookers. 'I'll teach you who calls the shots around here. Nobody messes with me and gets away with it.'

She pulled away from him. 'I'm going to sort this nonsense out right away,' she declared.

'Have you got cloth ears or something, woman?' Syd asked, emitting a raucous laugh. 'I've just told you you'll be wasting your time.'

'I'll be the judge of that,' she said, and hurried off in search of Reg Cox, Syd's horrible laughter ringing in her ears.

She found the market inspector in the crowded café tucking into a great doorstep of a bacon sandwich. Dressed in a tan-coloured suede coat, he was a big man of about forty, with greying brown hair and insipid grey eyes that protruded slightly beneath wild, tangled eyebrows.

Fortunately for Ellie he was alone at the table so, without preamble, she joined him. Deeming it wise at this initial stage to behave as though the meeting with Syd Bell hadn't taken place, she asked Reg why someone else had been given her stall.

'First come first served,' he said in a disinterested manner. 'You know the rules. The other trader got here before you so he got the stall.' As though anticipating the next question, he added, 'And there isn't a spare pitch to be had anywhere.'

'That isn't how it works for regulars,' she disagreed, still playing it straight. 'When I started here you assured me that as long as I turned up every week, paid my dues and conducted my business in a fair and honest manner, the pitch would be reserved for me for as long as I want it.'

'I don't remember saying any such thing,' he denied, lowering his eyes. 'Now if you don't mind, I'm having my breakfast and I'd like to do so in peace.'

Ellie didn't move; she stayed where she was, fixing him with a studious look. He was a strong, assertive man who ran the market with a firm hand. He certainly wasn't the type to be intimidated by the likes of Syd Bell, so the incentive had to be money. She decided it was time for her to come clean and get to the point. 'I know that Syd Bell is behind this,' she announced in an even tone.

'Syd Bell?' He looked suitably puzzled.

'He's been shouting his mouth off about it so there's no point in your denying it,' she informed him, omitting to mention that Syd hadn't mentioned any names. 'I must say I'm surprised at you. I thought you were as straight as a die, which just goes to show what a fool I've been.'

'You wanna watch—' he began.

'You just couldn't resist getting your sticky fingers on an extra few quid, could you?' she interrupted, determined to have her say. 'You're too greedy to say no to a backhander from Syd to get me off the market.'

'You wanna watch what you're saying,' he finished at last with a convincing show of affront. 'I don't like having my good name called into question.'

Ellie fiddled with the brown sauce bottle for a moment. 'I'll do more than damage your reputation if you don't find me a pitch on this market immediately,' she said, meeting his eyes in a cool stare. 'I'll see to it that you lose your job.'

'Oh, yeah?' He was predictably cynical.

'I'll report you to the council for interfering with a trader's livelihood for your own financial gain,' she announced briskly. 'They won't keep you on after that.'

A momentary widening of his frog-like eyes betrayed his unease, despite his efforts to conceal it. He'd obviously thought he was safe to go along with Syd's scheme in the mistaken belief that Ellie wouldn't dare to oppose him, being a woman and a relative newcomer to the market. 'Do what you like,' he challenged her with an air of indifference. 'It'll be your word against mine.'

'They'll be obliged to look into what I have to say because I shall make it an official complaint and it'll show the council up in a bad light if they let it pass,' she pointed out. 'And naturally I shall make sure the other stallholders know about it.'

The bacon sandwich was now sitting on his plate half-eaten; he'd apparently lost his appetite. 'Go ahead, and see how far it gets you,' he said, taking a packet of cigarettes out of his pocket and lighting one.

'I intend to. I shall be at the council offices first thing on Monday morning,' she informed him. 'And I shan't leave there until I've had a meeting with someone in a position of authority about what's going on in the management at Napp's Road market.' She stood up purposefully. 'Now I'll leave you to finish your breakfast . . . if you still feel hungry.'

She marched to the door and was about to open it when she felt Reg's hand on her shoulder. 'Look, surely we can work something out between us without any bad feeling,' he said feebly.

'That's up to you,' she replied, turning to face him. 'You know what I want.'

'Perhaps I might have been a bit hasty in letting your pitch go to someone else this morning,' he admitted.

'That's one way of putting it.'

'This market has always had good relations between management and traders,' he told her. 'There's no need for you to worry the powers that be at the office, not when we can sort the problem out between ourselves.'

This volte-face confirmed his guilt. But she didn't want to be unnecessarily vindictive and have him lose his job if she could get what she wanted a more peaceable way. Better to teach him a lesson without involving anyone else. 'Are you saying that if I stay away from the council I can have my regular pitch back?' Ellie asked.

'I'm not admitting to taking a bribe. I want to make that perfectly clear.' He was adamant. 'But maybe I shouldn't have let your pitch go to someone else.'

'Will you tell the record seller to move his stuff, or shall I?' she enquired.

'I can't move him off there today, as he's already set up.' Reg looked extremely worried. 'But you can have it back on a regular basis from next week.'

'So what do I do today? I can't afford to lose a day's trading.'

He scratched his head, then drew hard on his cigarette. 'Let's go and have a look round to see who hasn't turned up.' He glanced at his watch. 'Anyone who's coming will be here by this time. If we can find a spare stall you can have it instead of one of the casuals who are waiting around on the off chance.'

He was already leading the way, his breakfast apparently forgotten. They found an empty stall at the end of the market. 'Will this do you, just for this week?' he asked.

She nodded.

'And no more talk of the council offices?'

His need for reassurance was extremely incriminating but Ellie was prepared to let it go. 'Provided I don't find myself without a stall again at any time in the future.'

'You won't.'

'We'll say no more about it then,' she said. 'Now if you'll excuse me, I have to go and get my stock.'

'I'll give you a hand,' he offered.

'Thank you.'

It was satisfying to see how co-operative the guilty became when exposure loomed, Ellie thought wryly, as they headed for the car to get her knitwear.

'Oh, there you are,' said Ray Brent later that day, appearing at her stall. 'When you weren't in your usual place this morning, Dad and I thought perhaps you were giving it a miss today.'

'Chance would be a fine thing,' she said, determinedly cheerful. 'I can't afford to take a day off.'

'Why the change of position?' he enquired chattily.

Recognising genuine concern in his eyes, Ellie decided to spare him the truth, given the origins of her trouble. Ray was the sort of man who would feel bad, would see it as his duty to act on her behalf in retaliation to Syd Bell and Reg Cox, which could land him in all sorts of trouble. She'd kept quiet about the bother she'd had to the other traders for the same reason.

'Some sort of a mix-up with the stall allocations,' she fibbed. 'It's just a one-off. I'll be back in my usual place next week.'

'That's all right then.'

The conversation halted while she served a customer, then she asked him what sort of a day he was having.

'Not too bad at all,' he told her cheerfully. 'The candle holders and ashtrays are virtually walking off the stall. They make good Christmas presents. Cheap and cheerful, just what people want at this time of year.'

'I'm glad you're doing well,' she remarked. 'It's always nice to hear.'

He gave her an anxious look. 'Are you OK?'

Actually she felt ghastly. Delayed reaction from this morning's trauma was making her feel disorientated and shaky. But she said, 'Yeah, I'm fine.'

'You don't look too good.'

'Charming.'

'You know I didn't mean it like that,' he assured her with a chuckle. 'I just wondered if anything was wrong. You look a bit pale and worried.'

'Standing here all day in the freezing cold is enough to make anyone pale and worried,' she grinned, making a joke of it. 'But apart from the frostbite I'm fine, honestly.'

'Good.'

They chatted about other things, both stamping their feet and hugging themselves against the weather. He told her about some glass-topped coffee tables with fancy ironwork frames that he'd made and was trying on the stall. He'd sold two out of three already. She said they sounded lovely and she would pop over and have a look. After some more pleasant discourse, he went back to work, happily ignorant of her troubled morning.

Mulling it over, Ellie decided it would probably be best not to tell the family about the incident either. Not only would it cause her parents to worry, it would also be another stick for them to beat Ray Brent with. And she felt quite violently opposed to that.

By the end of the afternoon's trading Ellie was feeling better altogether. She'd shifted quite a lot of stock and that was always uplifting. Her state of calm didn't last long, however. She was thrown into turmoil again when she was packing up.

'I see you're still here then,' commented Syd Bell nastily. 'I thought we'd seen the last of you on this market.'

'You underestimated me if you thought I'd give up that easily,' she said, putting some unsold sweaters into a box. 'So you'd better get used to seeing me around because I'm not going anywhere. In fact, I'm having my old pitch back next week.'

It was obvious from the look on Syd's face that Reg Cox hadn't told him. 'Is that right?' His mean little eyes blazed with anger.

'You threw your money away on Reg,' she told him. 'Loyalty to you didn't stand a chance against the fear of losing his steady job with all its perks.'

Syd gave her a harsh look. 'This isn't over, you know,' he warned her.

'I think it is.'

'You just won't get the message, will you?'

'I don't give in to vicious threats, if that's what you mean.'

'And I don't give in at the first hurdle,' he warned her in an evil tone. 'I want you off this market, and that's what will happen, I can promise you that.'

'Yeah, yeah.' She managed to sound indifferent but she actually felt completely out of her depth in this chilling world of double-dealing and implied violence. 'Now if you'll excuse me, I have to get my stuff back to the car. It's been a long, cold day and I want to go home.'

He lapsed into thought for a moment, then smiled suddenly. 'Don't let me stop you,' he said.

'I won't.'

Instead of moving away, he stood watching her pack the knitwear into the boxes for a while before finally departing. It was very unnerving.

Ellie was still feeling uneasy as she made her way to the car. She told herself to stop worrying. There's only one way he can get you off this market and he's tried that and it's failed, she told herself. Idle threats, that's all they are. But Syd Bell was on her mind all the way home.

When she drew up outside her parents' house, however, and saw Donna waiting for her at the window, all thoughts of Syd Bell and the market disappeared from her mind.

It was frosty again the following Saturday when Ellie drove to the market and parked the car. As she got the first of her boxes of stock out of the back and trudged to the stall with it, treading carefully so as not to slip, she was glad of the extra clothes she'd put on, because the cold was that penetrating sort that bit into your bones and turned your breath to steam. Two of everything except her bra made her feel a bit bulky but it was worth it, though God knows how she was going to survive the day in this weather.

'You'll need a hot-water bottle strapped to your bum today, Ellie,' grinned Joe, who was already at his stall, stamping his feet and blowing on his mittened hands.

'That would be lovely but I'll have to make do with two pairs of drawers,' she said jokingly.

He laughed and Ellie was still smiling as she trekked back to the car to get the next box of stock. But her smile faded as she went to unlock the back doors of the estate car to find that the locking mechanism was broken. Someone had tampered with it.

'Oh, my God!' she cried, opening the doors and looking inside to see a heap of junk that had been good-quality knitwear just a few minutes ago. All her stock had been slashed to ribbons, beautiful hand-crafted sweaters now a pile of ragged scraps of knitting. 'Syd Bell . . . How can he have done such a terrible thing?'

The shock made her light-headed and giddy, her legs threatening to buckle beneath her. Too weak to stand, she sank down on the front wall of a nearby house to recover, her brow damp with icy perspiration.

It was in this sorry state that Ray and his father found her, having just arrived and parked up nearby.

'Ellie,' said Ray, leaping out of his grey car and running over to her. 'Whatever's the matter? Aren't you feeling well?'

'Why are you sitting there, love?' added his father gently. They were both obviously very concerned about her. 'You'll catch your death of cold. You've got to keep moving to keep your circulation going in this weather.'

She didn't say anything, just waved her hand towards the car, inviting the two men to look inside.

'Christ Almighty!' gasped Ray.

'Bloody hell,' said Alfie.

'Who's done this to you, Ellie?' asked Ray grimly.

Still she didn't speak but got up and forced herself to take another look at the ruins of her work. 'I feel as though I've been raped,' she said quietly.

'The first thing to do is to get you warm,' suggested Ray, taking her arm and not pressing her for more information at this stage. 'Let's go to the café and get you a hot drink.'

'You need a cup of hot sweet tea for the shock,' added Alfie. 'You go with her, Ray. I'll set the stall up. Don't rush, take as long as you need. I'll see to everything on the market.'

Already in a state of raw emotion, she felt tears spring to her eyes at their kindness.

The café was warm and steamy, the air heavy with the savoury aroma of fried food. Though normally pleasurable to Ellie, it turned her stomach this morning, because of the shock to her nervous system. Ray got a mug of coffee for himself and tea for her with plenty of sugar in it.

'Your stock has been trashed because of me, hasn't it, Ellie?' he said when they were settled at the table.

'Don't be daft.'

'It's because you stuck your neck out for me that first day,' he insisted.

'Ray . . .'

'It's Syd Bell's revenge on you for going against him on my behalf, isn't it?'

She stared into her tea mug, still fearing that Ray would make trouble for himself if she told him the truth, but seeing no way round it. 'He's taken against me and wants me off the market,' she told him, still fudging the issue. 'Because his plan to that end didn't work, he trashed the stock to pile on the pressure and try to force me out. He thinks I'll be frightened away.'

'And he wants you off the market because you took my side. I know it's true so you might as well admit it,' he said. 'I wasn't born yesterday. I know exactly how people like Syd Bell operate.' He paused, thinking about what she'd just said. 'What plan didn't work?'

Heaving a sigh, she said, 'If I tell you, you must promise you won't do anything.'

He shook his head. 'I can't do that, I'm afraid,' he stated frankly. 'It isn't in my nature to stand back and let someone get hurt on my account. Syd Bell needs sorting.'

'You'll be playing into his hands if you try,' she advised

him. 'He'd just love the chance to rubbish you and set people against you again, like he did that first day.'

'Tell me what's been going on, Ellie,' he entreated. 'I won't do anything silly, I promise.'

Since she now realised that he would make it his business to find out anyway, she told him.

He listened in silence. 'I knew something was wrong last Saturday,' he told her. 'I didn't really believe your story about a temporary change of pitch.'

'I thought if I told you, you'd go after Syd and Reg and land yourself in trouble,' she said.

His eyes were soft as his gaze rested on her face. 'Why did that matter to you?' he asked.

Because you touch something deep inside me, she thought, but said, 'It wasn't only you. I didn't tell any of the other stallholders either in case they felt obliged to intervene on my behalf and got into bother.'

'Oh, I see.' He sipped his coffee. 'You're quite a woman, do you know that?'

She'd taken her woolly hat off and her hair was rumpled, her ashen face now attractively suffused with colour from the warmth of the café. 'I just wanted to avoid a whole load more trouble for everybody.' She gave him a warning look. 'And you'd do well to do the same. Giving Syd Bell a good hiding will do you no good at all. Violence never solved anything.'

Ray's expression hardened. 'Despite what you may have heard to the contrary,' he announced soberly, 'I am not a violent man.'

Too late, Ellie realised how easily her words could be misconstrued. 'I'm not suggesting that you are,' she corrected. 'Not you in particular, anyway. But that's how men usually solve their differences, isn't it? By getting physical?'

'Not all men see it as the only solution,' he disagreed.

Remembering what a gentle person her brother was she said, 'No, I suppose not.'

'Anyway,' he said, changing the subject, 'I'm pleased to say

216

that you're looking a bit better.'

'I'll survive,' she sighed. 'I shall get out there and try to sell the little bit of stock I have left, the stuff I'd already taken to the stall before Syd Bell did his damage. What I actually want to do is go home to my daughter and a nice warm fire. But Syd would think he'd won if I did that and he hasn't. It's important I don't let him think he's getting me down.'

'That's the spirit,' Ray said, finishing his coffee.

Putting her hat on and wrapping her scarf around her neck, as they were about to leave, she said, 'So, do I have your word that you won't do anything?'

He put his head to one side, giving her a half-smile. 'I said I wouldn't do anything silly,' he reminded her. 'I didn't promise not to do anything at all.'

'Oh, Ray, please . . .'

'Don't worry, I won't use violence or get myself into any sort of trouble,' he told her. 'I wouldn't give Syd Bell the satisfaction.'

'Be careful,' she urged him.

'Will do.' They left the café together, bracing themselves against the subzero temperature outside.

Despite her warnings to him not to intervene, Ellie was impressed by his chivalry.

Being bigger altogether than the weaselly Syd Bell, Ray towered over him when he confronted him a few minutes later at Syd's stall. 'You and I need to talk . . . in private,' Ray informed him.

'I don't think so,' said Syd.

'Well, I do think so,' insisted Ray, 'So come to the café with me *now*.'

'I'm busy. I do have a living to earn, you know,' mumbled Syd, concentrating on a set of saucepans he was putting out on display.

'Me too, which is why I want us to get our business out of the way before the market opens.' Ray grabbed his upper arm

217

and held it, just firm enough to be persuasive but without breaking his promise to Ellie. 'Be there in two minutes or you'll regret it.'

'OK, OK,' agreed Syd reluctantly; after arranging cover for his stall, he followed Ray to the café.

The two men faced each other across a table.

'This is the deal,' began Ray. 'You leave Ellie Hall alone, or you'll find yourself in intensive care.'

'Oh, yeah,' mocked Syd with unconvincing bravado, 'and who's gonna put me there?'

'Me.'

Syd was full of confidence when it came to talk. But he wasn't physically brave, and he found Ray's superior size and strength somewhat intimidating. He wasn't seriously worried, though, because he had what he thought was a trump card, an absolute beauty. 'With your reputation, you can't afford to step out of line, mate,' he told Ray with a smirk. 'You so much as ruffle my hair and I'll have you put back inside for GBH.'

Ray threw back his head and laughed.

'What's so funny?' Syd frowned.

'Do you really think I would be stupid enough to personally harm a hair on your head?' said Ray, his expression becoming deadly serious. 'I'm not that much of a mug.'

'So, you'd have someone do it for you,' said Syd, a touch less smugly but still sounding confident. 'I could still have you done for it because I'd know it was you. I've got mates on the market who'd back me up. A convicted murderer wouldn't stand a chance in court against an upstanding member of the community like me.'

'Court?' Ray drew in his breath. 'Ooh, I think you're being a bit optimistic there, mate.'

Syd looked at him. 'What are you on about, Brent?' he couldn't resist asking.

'You'll be too frightened to go outside of your front door, let alone go to court when I've finished with you,' explained Ray.

218

Syd shrugged, affecting an air of indifference.

Ray leaned across the table and grabbed him by the collar. 'That prison stretch I did that you're so fond of reminding everyone of –' he ground out – 'do you honestly believe that I spent six years living with villains without getting friendly with some really hard men? Men with contacts?'

'I've never bothered to give it any thought,' said Syd, maintaining a nonchalant manner which didn't ring true because his voice was beginning to quiver.

'Well, I suggest you do so now.' Ray let go of his collar and stared at him with his eyes narrowed. 'There's a special bond between ex-cons. It's us against the rest of the world and we're always there for each other when a favour needs doing – it's part of our code. I only have to pick up the phone and I can get in touch with men all over London, animals who think nothing of putting a man in a wheelchair for the rest of his life, or worse if the situation warrants it. Blood and broken bones don't worry them. That sort of thing gives them a kick.'

'I'd still know it was you who set it up.' Syd was looking frightened now.

'You wouldn't be able to do anything about it, though,' Ray informed him. 'Even apart from the fact that you would have lost the will to live, these men come from nowhere and disappear into thin air after they've done the job. No one knows who they are or where they come from. There would be nothing to link me with your . . . er, shall we call it your tragic misfortune? Your life would be ruined and I'd get off scot-free.'

'You wouldn't dare.'

'I think you know that I would,' Ray speculated smoothly. 'One single phone call is all it would take for me to have you crippled for life.'

'You're just bluffing.' Syd was beginning to look bilious now. 'Trying to scare me.'

Looks as though I'm succeeding too, thought Ray. 'Try me, if you dare,' he challenged.

'You're all mouth,' said Syd.

'There's to be no more warnings, no more negotiation,' Ray continued swiftly. 'One hint of trouble for Ellie Hall in the future and you'll find out that I'm not bluffing. And don't think you can terrorise her into not telling me because I shall keep a close eye to the situation without her even being aware of it. I'll soon know if she's having trouble.'

Syd's hand was shaking as he picked up his mug and moistened his dry lips with tea.

'And not only must there be no trouble for Ellie in the future,' Ray went on, 'you must pay her compensation for that stock of hers you trashed.'

'You'll be lucky.'

'I don't know how much the stock was worth, so shall we say a figure of twenty pounds . . . just as a gesture of your goodwill?' suggested Ray.

'Don't make me laugh,' sneered Syd.

'Laughing is the last thing you'll be doing if you don't do as I say,' Ray warned him with a cruel edge to his voice. 'By the time the market closes today, I want Ellie Hall to have twenty pounds of your dough in her possession. You will tell her that you're sorry for what you've done and you want her to have the money as a token of your goodwill. You don't mention me, *right*?'

'I shan't mention anyone because I won't be doing it,' blustered Syd.

'That's entirely up to you,' said Ray in a neutral tone. 'But you ignore what I'm telling you at your peril.'

'You don't scare me,' muttered Syd lamely.

'I shall know if you've given her the money because I shall make it my business to find out.' Ray stood up. 'Now I must go. There's work to be done.'

He strode across the café to the door, looking back through the window as he passed outside to see Syd staring mournfully into his mug. Confident that the other man had swallowed his story hook, line and sinker, Ray walked back to his stall grinning. He had sorted the problem without so much as a fist being clenched.

Ray didn't mix with hard men who got their kicks from beating people up. He'd always steered clear of them in prison, and he certainly wouldn't know how to contact one now. The whole thing had been pure fiction but it had really got Syd sweating. Ellie was right when she said that violence never solved anything. But the threat of it to a man with a highly developed sense of self-preservation worked wonders.

'Well . . . you're looking cheerful considering what's happened to poor Ellie,' said his father when Ray reached the stall.

'It's all sorted, Dad,' he told Alfie. 'She won't have any more trouble.'

'You didn't waste any time.'

'It was my fault her stuff was trashed, my responsibility to put it right,' he said. 'There's no time like the present.'

'How is she?' asked Alfie.

'She'll be all right now.'

'What are you grinning about?'

'Something's amused me,' Ray chuckled.

'Share the joke, then.'

Ray told him about the yarn he'd spun Syd Bell, and they both had a good laugh.

'Now it's my turn to thank you,' Ellie told Ray.

'What for?' he replied innocently.

It was lunchtime that same day and Ellie had gone over to Ray's stall, which was laden with the most beautiful hand-crafted metal artefacts she had ever seen. Candle holders with a leaf pattern, plant pot holders, and the coffee tables were gorgeous with smoked-glass tops and curly metal legs.

'Don't try and tell me that I received cash compensation and an apology from Syd Bell without your having a hand in it because I simply won't believe you,' she said.

'I didn't lay a finger on him, I swear,' Ray assured her.

'I didn't notice any bruises on him so I'll take your word for that.' She looked from Ray to his father and back to Ray. 'So how did you do it?'

'Let's just say I told Syd a little story,' he smiled. 'That's all you need to know.'

'So long as you didn't hit him, that's all right with me.' She looked at Ray. 'Joe's agreed to look after my stall while I take you for a thank-you drink.' She gave his father a persuasive smile. 'If Alfie will cover for you here.'

'No problem,' agreed Alfie.

'But before we go, I must have a look at these lovely things you've been making,' she said, singling out a coffee table. 'Isn't it beautiful? Glass as well as metal. You're so clever.'

'Not that clever,' he confessed. 'I do get the glass cut to the shape I want.'

'Even so, the metal work is highly skilled and you've put the two together so beautifully,' she complimented him. 'I'll treat myself to one when I get some spare cash. It'll look nice in my living room.'

'In the meantime, let's go to the pub.' His eyes twinkled. 'As you're in the chair I'll have the most expensive drink in the house.'

She laughed because she knew instinctively that the last thing he'd ever do would be to take liberties with her.

If she hadn't actually experienced it for herself, Ellie wouldn't have believed it possible to feel so different in such a short space of time. When she'd seen the damaged stock, she'd felt traumatised and personally violated. It wasn't so much the loss of the garments, but the shock of knowing that anyone could hate her enough to want to hurt her that way had been devastating. But sitting in the pub at a corner table chatting with Ray, the events of the morning might never have happened. In his company she felt soothed and revitalised.

They talked about the market for a while, then got on to

more personal topics. She found herself telling him about Tom's condition.

'Brain damaged,' he said gravely.

'Mm.'

'That's really sad.'

'It's tragic,' she agreed. 'He's virtually a child in a man's body.'

'How do you cope with it?'

'You get used to anything in time,' she said. 'But it still breaks my heart to see him like it.'

'Is he physically disabled?'

'No. They keep him heavily drugged, though, so his movements are slow,' she said. 'He doesn't look much different from before, oddly enough. He's always been very handsome and he still is. But that's about all there is left of the old Tom.'

'How does he react when you visit him?'

'He's very difficult. His behaviour is so unpredictable you never know what he'll do from one minute to the next. He's a danger to himself and other people. That's why he can't live at home.'

'Is there nothing they can do?'

'Not to improve his condition, only his quality of life.' Ellie went on to tell Ray more about Greenlands and how she could afford for Tom to live there.

'It was the best thing you could have done for him. But it must be lonely for you.'

'My daughter is my salvation. But, yes, it is lonely in the way that you mean,' Ellie confessed. 'As you said when we spoke about it before, it's like being a widow as far as everyday living is concerned. Tom doesn't realise I'm his wife. He doesn't even know what marriage is.'

'That's awful,' he sympathised.

'All the more so because Tom is the only man I've ever loved.' She went on to tell him about the close family relationship. 'I adored him from the start. Never had any other boyfriends, never wanted any other man.'

'Were you hurt in the accident?'

She filled him in about that, mentioning the fact that Donna wasn't injured either. 'She was a small baby at the time so wasn't aware of what happened. So at least she won't have any bad memories to cope with as she grows up.'

'You do, though?' he assumed.

'Yes, I was driving the car so I still have a problem with that from time to time . . . guilt, you know.'

'Was the accident your fault then?'

'Oh no, the other driver jumped a red light,' she explained. 'There was never any question of it being my fault, technically. But it's a heck of a thing to live with, being the driver of a car which is involved in an accident which ruins someone's life. There's always the feeling that perhaps I could have avoided it in some way.'

'I'm sure you've nothing to blame yourself for.'

'I've been through it a million times and I know what you say is true, but I suppose there'll always be a little part of me that wants to punish myself for the fact that Tom isn't able to live a normal life and I am.'

'All you can do is constantly remind yourself that it wasn't your fault and that you are doing the very best you can for him by keeping him at this place in Surrey.'

'Yeah, I know.' Ellie sipped her drink. 'How about you? Do you have someone special?'

'Not now. I was courting a girl called Maria before I went in prison. We were really serious. I thought she was the girl for me. We were even thinking of getting engaged,' he told her, looking mistily into space. 'But when I got arrested, she didn't want to know.'

'That must have been a blow.'

'It was, especially coming on top of everything else. It was the worst time of my life,' he said. 'Still, I suppose you can't blame her. She didn't want her reputation blackened by being the girlfriend of an alleged murderer. She couldn't cope with that.'

'Understandable, I suppose,' commented Ellie.

'She did give me a good character reference in court, so that helped me to forgive her,' Ray went on to say. 'Maybe she thought I killed the man – the evidence against me was pretty damning, my actually being with Keith Wilkes when he died, I mean. I think my father was probably about the only person who believed that I was telling the truth when I said I didn't do it. Maria was with me when I was arguing with Keith in the pub. The row came about because he was pestering her. She probably put two and two together, like everyone else.'

'And made five.'

He gave Ellie a sharp look. 'You don't really believe that, do you?' His manner was tentative.

'Well, don't sound so shocked,' she said.

'I'm not used to having my story believed,' he explained. 'Except by my father, of course.'

'I have only my gut instinct to go on, since I hardly know you,' she said. 'But, yes, I believe you.'

His face worked. 'You can't possibly know what that means to me.' His eyes were moist.

'I'm glad I've pleased you.' His obvious emotion spoke volumes about the depth of pain he'd been through. 'I can see that your reputation means a lot to you.'

'It's only natural. No one wants to be thought of as a murderer, do they?' Ray said. 'But I gave up protesting my innocence long ago because I was flogging a dead horse. All that did was bring me a load more aggro and made things worse.'

'Have you never tried to clear your name?'

He emitted a bitter laugh. 'There isn't much you can do when you're locked up in prison,' he pointed out. 'I think my solicitor believed my story but the police weren't prepared to listen. And there was never any question of an appeal because there was no new evidence.'

'Does it still matter as much to you now, after all this time?' Ellie enquired.

'Oh, yeah.'

'Even though you've done your time and it's all water under the bridge?'

'Doing the time doesn't erase the stigma,' he told her. 'The trouble at the market proved that.'

'That seems to have blown over.'

'For the moment, yes it has, thanks to you,' he said. 'But people don't forget. The way they look at me sometimes, I know they're imagining that I have blood on my hands. They wouldn't want to be alone with me in case I strike again.'

'Surely there must be something you can do to prove you didn't do it?' she suggested.

He spread his hands expressively. 'There isn't, believe me.'

'No leads as to the real culprit at all?'

'Not a single clue,' Ray confirmed. 'Keith Wilkes had been in a fight when I found him outside the pub. He was already about to breathe his last when I got there. He was groaning a bit at first, then he lost consciousness. I didn't know what to do except try and make him comfortable. I was about to go for help when some people arrived on the scene.' He paused, spreading his hands in a helpless gesture. 'The rest is history, as they say.'

'Whoever was responsible must have got away quick,' Ellie reasoned.

'Oh, yeah, they scarpered leaving no trace,' Ray told her. 'People are sleeping easy in their beds because they think I did it and have been punished for it, albeit that some don't agree with my early release. And it's no good my trying to convince them otherwise because they just won't believe me.' He drank his beer. 'I've thought about it until it's nearly driven me crazy and there's no way I can find out who killed Keith Wilkes. There were no witnesses . . . none that came forward, anyway. It's a complete dead end. Most of the punters from the pub had gone home when I left; he was probably attacked by a gang of yobs – there's always plenty of them roaming the streets after the pubs close.'

'The truth will out, so they say,' Ellie said to encourage him.

'I'd like to believe that.' There was a note of bitterness in his tone. 'But they never caught Jack the Ripper, did they?'

'There is that,' she was forced to agree.

Why am I telling her all this? Ray asked himself. He didn't normally unload his troubles on to other people. 'Anyway, that's enough gloomy talk,' he said, bringing the subject swiftly to an end. 'I'd much rather talk about you, so tell me some more about yourself.'

Ellie laughed. 'My life doesn't make sparkling conversation, I'm afraid,' she said. 'I work, I bring up my daughter, I visit my husband . . . that's about it.'

'Everything you say is interesting to me,' he blurted out. 'Every single word.'

The mood changed instantly from casual and ordinary to throbbingly intimate. She could feel new energy flowing into her – warm – exciting – *and must be nipped in the bud*. 'It's time we were going,' she uttered weakly. 'We'll have a mutiny on our hands if we don't get back to our stalls soon. The last time I went for a drink with you I was away much longer than I intended.'

'My fault entirely.' He raised his hands as though in surrender. 'I enjoy being with you so much, I don't want it to end.'

'The feeling is mutual.' The words just popped out. She hadn't meant to say it, and added quickly, 'Probably because we have a lot in common, both working on the market, both being in the field of crafts.'

'Yes, that must be it,' Ray agreed with a slow smile.

They both knew there was much more to it than that. But they also knew she wasn't in a position to allow whatever it was to develop. He was respecting that and she admired him for it.

'Come on, back to work,' she said lightly. 'Before this gets really embarrassing.'

'Slave driver,' he chuckled, and they finished their drinks and went back to the market together.

Chapter Eleven

'I thought Tom seemed quite well today, didn't you, dear?' Pat remarked to Ellie.

'Mm. He still appears to be in good physical health,' agreed Ellie. 'And perfectly content.'

It was a Sunday afternoon and they were in the car heading out of Greenlands along a winding, tree-lined drive. Soft, persistent rain dripped through the skeletal branches of the mature poplars, the cheerless skies an unbroken mass of cloud – low, grey and angry.

'Oh, yes, he's happy enough, despite the bizarre circumstances.' The gates were opened for them by the gatekeeper and they continued along a country lane towards Senbridge en route to Dorking to pick up the main road back to London, the tyres splattering through muddy puddles to the monotonous accompaniment of the windscreen wipers sliding to and fro. 'He seems set to have a good Christmas too. The staff do everything they can to make it pleasant for the patients.'

'I'm sure he'll have a whale of a time,' said Ellie in a subdued tone.

'Easier for him than us, eh?' sighed Pat.

'Exactly.'

They wouldn't be seeing Tom on Christmas Day, which was just under a week away. Ellie didn't want to spoil the festivities for Donna by disappearing for a large chunk of the day; it seemed especially pointless as her visits meant nothing to Tom. Ellie and Donna would be joining the rest of the family at her parents' home in Marsh Road. Pat had also been invited.

This would be Ellie's third Christmas without Tom. As usual, the season highlighted the tragedy of his situation. As well as the poignancy of their being apart at such a family time, giving a grown man toys as presents still upset her. But that was what he responded to now.

With a mood of depression settling over her, Ellie observed the countryside. It was an extremely bleak landscape on this wet winter's day but it wasn't without a sombre kind of beauty. A rain mist hung over the fields and everything seemed wrapped in gloom. It matched her mood perfectly.

She was recalled from her reverie by the sound of Pat talking about the shop, in particular her difficulties in finding a suitable assistant who would stay for any length of time. Les hadn't lasted long and there had been a couple more since him, both male, since none of the women applicants had a driving licence, so essential for the deliveries.

'I don't think the latest chap will stay long,' Pat was saying mournfully. 'He's getting fed up already, I think. He always seems to be complaining, anyway.'

'Oh dear.'

'People would rather work somewhere big, with a staff canteen and a social club than a corner shop with only me to talk to apart from the customers,' Pat went on.

They probably take a dim view of having to run the shop on an assistant's wages as well as having to put up with your lofty attitude, Ellie couldn't help thinking. But she said, 'I should think most youngsters would prefer to work at a firm that provides them with a social life and company of their own age. It's only natural.'

'I realise that,' Pat responded.

'Why not try to get someone more mature?' Ellie suggested. 'An older person would probably be more reliable, and you might find it easier to talk to someone nearer to your own age. Working together in a small shop can be a bit stifling. You need someone you feel comfortable with, and so do they.'

'You're quite right. But I have to take who I can get, with so many jobs about,' Pat grumbled. 'People can take their pick of employment these days.'

'But it's a good thing that the country is prospering generally.'

'I wouldn't dream of denying it. It does make life harder for employers, though.'

Which couldn't be a bad thing, in Ellie's opinion. At least exploitation wasn't quite so easy for them in the current 'affluent society', with full employment bringing improvements in wages and working conditions to a lot of employees.

'No chance of your getting fed up with your knitwear business and coming back, I suppose?' Pat enquired hopefully.

'No. Sorry.'

'You'd have less responsibility if you worked with me at the shop,' she tried to persuade, 'as well as a good steady wage with none of the worry and insecurity of running your own business.'

'I'd like to help you but I really want to stay with what I'm doing.' Why did Pat have the power to make her feel guilty simply for earning her living in her own way? 'I enjoy what I do, despite all the hard work and uncertainty.'

'All right, dear.' Pat gave a sigh of resignation. 'Just thought it was worth a try.'

'I'm sure you'll find someone to suit you soon,' Ellie said to encourage her, though she actually had grave doubts about this because of Pat's unfortunate manner.

'I certainly hope so.' Her voice broke and she started to cry. She usually got a bit weepy at some point on the journey back from Greenlands. It was perfectly understandable, Ellie thought. She wasn't far from tears herself.

'Bear up, Pat,' she said, her voice warm with empathy, though she was unable physically to comfort her because she was concentrating on the road ahead.

'I keep thinking of the days when Tom and I ran the business together.' Pat's voice was thick with tears. 'I was happy then, even though I'd lost George.'

'I know . . .'

'I still miss Tom so terribly,' she wept.

'I wish there was something I could say to make you feel better,' said Ellie, a burning sensation pricking at the back of her eyes, 'but I'm at a loss to know what. I comfort myself with the thought that he's happy. At least we can both rest easy about that.'

'Yes, I know. I'm sorry.' Pat was sobbing now. 'It just comes over me every now and again, the awful business of knowing he's never coming back to us as he was.' She blew her nose and sniffed into her handkerchief but her voice was steadier when she spoke again. 'Of course, I realise it must be even worse for you, being his wife. I don't suppose you can ever get him off your mind.'

Ellie reeled from a sharp slap of guilt. Up until recently that had been true. How shocked and hurt Pat would be to know the truth – that someone else occupied her son's wife's thoughts now. It wasn't Tom Ellie couldn't stop thinking about. It was Ray Brent – his dark eyes, his warm smile. The mere thought of him filled her with longing.

'Naturally, I think about him a lot,' she said, comforting herself in the thought that it wasn't exactly a lie.

On the afternoon of the day before Christmas Eve Ellie strode across Shepherd's Bush Green with Donna in the pushchair. It was a crisp, chilly afternoon, with a sharp wind smarting her cheeks as she headed for the market for some last-minute shopping.

Daylight was already fading and the market was ablaze with electric light and colour, fairy lights framing the stalls, Christmas tree sellers out in force. The sweet scent of pine needles was just discernible above the powerful mixture of hot dogs, roasting chestnuts and frying from a nearby café.

'Lights, Mummy, lights,' said Donna, her eyes shining out from her bright blue siren suit that covered all of her except her eyes, nose and mouth.

'Aren't they pretty, darling?' responded Ellie.

At almost two and a half, Donna was just about old enough to appreciate the season and Ellie ached with love for her. She saw Christmas in a new light now, through her daughter's eyes. As they passed the sweet stall, she stopped and bought her two ounces of jelly babies.

Having shopped in Shepherd's Bush market all her life, Ellie knew a lot of the stallholders; some of them had known her since she was Donna's age. They were always pleased to see her and made a great fuss of Donna. Purchasing some seasonal wrapping paper and a few extra decorations for the tree, she packed them into the shopping bag attached to the pushchair, then went to the fruit and veg stall where the greengrocer insisted on giving Donna an apple. Ellie was busy thanking him for it and putting some sprouts and carrots into her bag when a deep voice said, 'Hello. Are you having a busman's holiday?'

Ray was there beside her. All six foot of him, dressed in a casual jacket and light high-necked sweater, his handsome face smiling down at her.

'I hadn't thought of it that way but I suppose you could call it that,' Ellie said, paying for her purchases. 'You doing some last-minute Christmas shopping?'

'No, I'm just taking a break,' he explained. 'My workshop isn't far from here. I wanted to stretch my legs and I always enjoy a stroll down the market.'

'Me too.'

'So this is your little girl, then?' he said, giving Donna a warm smile.

Ellie nodded proudly.

Ray went down on his haunches. 'Well, you're a pretty little thing, aren't you?'

Donna eyed him uncertainly.

'What have you got in the bag?' he enquired.

She chewed on her sweet slowly, sizing him up.

'Come on, tell us,' he coaxed.

'Jelly babies,' she informed him at last.

'Jelly babies, eh?' he said. 'I used to love those when I was little like you.'

Her round blue eyes rested on him; she still wasn't quite sure what to make of him.

'Give us one?' he grinned.

Still she stared at him.

'Go on.'

Ellie watched with interest for the result of his attempt at friendship. Nothing happened for a few moments, then slowly the child opened the bag and handed it to him, her face lighting into a toothy smile.

'Thank you.' He dipped into the bag and popped a sweet into his mouth. 'Mm, yum yum.'

Donna gave him a chuckle. Ray had won her over. He talked to her for a while longer, then stood up as he became aware that people were trying to get past.

'We're causing congestion here,' she said, moving to the side of the road with the pushchair.

'Where are you going now?' Ray stepped through the crowds towards her.

'Home,' she told him. 'I've finished my shopping.'

'Got time for a cup of tea or coffee?' he invited. 'There's a place I know of two minutes from here where they do delicious espresso.' He glanced down at Donna. 'The milk shakes look nice, too.'

Ellie was tempted but decided to be sensible. 'I have to get back,' she said. 'I've work to finish.'

He was clearly disappointed. 'Come on, it's nearly Christmas – surely you can spare half an hour for a cup of coffee with a friend?' he tried to persuade her.

In the end she couldn't resist. 'OK, you've talked me into it,' she said, and they made their way through the crowds together.

The coffee bar was noisy and steamy with Elvis Presley's 'Love Me Tender' resonating from the juke box. Ellie and Ray

234

had coffee and doughnuts, Donna had a strawberry milk shake and a fancy cake she chose from the counter herself.

'You're spoiling her,' admonished Ellie, as her daughter tucked into her treats. 'What with the sweets I bought her and all of this fancy stuff now, she'll think Christmas has come early.'

'It's here all bar the shouting,' Ray pointed out, smiling at the little girl now sitting opposite him beside her mother. 'Isn't that right, Donna?'

She nodded but was too busy taking in the scene around her to pay much attention to what he was saying. She was mesmerised by the garland of tinsel decorating the counter and the brightly coloured paper chains roped across the ceiling, the Christmas tree glowing in the window.

'This is the first Christmas she's been old enough to know what's going on,' Ellie mentioned. 'Even now she's a bit baffled by it all. Next year she'll be just the right age.'

'She's a smashing kid,' he complimented Ellie. 'A real credit to you.'

'Thank you.' She beamed at him across the table. 'You've certainly made a hit with her.'

'Really?'

'Why so surprised?'

'I've never had much to do with small children so I haven't got a clue how to go on with them. My mother died when I was a baby,' he told her, as though an explanation was necessary. 'And I was an only child.'

'Would you like a family of your own or aren't you especially bothered?' Ellie enquired conversationally.

'I'd like kids,' he said without hesitation.

'They do enhance your life,' she told him. 'I wouldn't be without Donna.'

'I might have had some by now, if things had been different,' he said, and she could hear the bitterness in his tone.

'You've plenty of time,' she encouraged. 'You're still in your prime.'

'Thanks for the vote of confidence.'

Ellie opted for a slight change of subject. 'You don't remember your mother, then?'

'No.'

'That's a shame.'

Ray seemed to become spiky suddenly. 'What you've never had you don't miss,' he snapped.

'There is that.'

He made a face, looking apologetic. 'What's the matter with me? Wittering on about having no kids and no mum. You must be thinking I'm a right old whinger.'

'I'd never think that about you,' she said softly. 'These things obviously go deep.'

'You're such a good listener, I always start going on about the bad things in my life,' he told her. 'Sorry.'

'Don't apologise.' He seemed embarrassed so she swiftly moved on to other things. 'Are you doing anything special over the holiday?'

'Nothing wildly exciting,' he told her. 'Dad and I are going to an old friend of Dad's and his wife for Christmas dinner. Apart from that, I'll be loafing about, overindulging probably, this being my first Christmas of freedom for a long time.'

She nodded.

He gave her a questioning look. 'What about you?'

She told him about the family Christmas she would be having.

'Sounds lovely.'

'Yes, I'm looking forward to it,' she said. 'It'll be fun seeing what Donna makes of it all.'

The record came to an end, the same song for the third time running since they'd been there. 'I love that song,' Ellie mentioned casually.

'Would you like to hear it again?' Ray asked.

She grinned. 'I would but I'm not sure the other customers will want another helping.'

'This is Elvis we're talking about.' He looked around at the youngish clientele and made a rash generalisation. 'Everybody under thirty likes him. Anyway, we pay our sixpence, we're entitled to our money's worth.'

'OK, you've convinced me.'

He returned with the news that someone had put a Cliff Richard record on. 'Ours will be on after that,' he told her.

She reminded herself that his use of the word 'ours' had no romantic connotation and was merely a convenient label. She admonished herself for being ridiculously sentimental; if she wasn't careful, she was likely to make a complete fool of herself. She wasn't some teenager, for heaven's sake, but a married woman and a mother, and she'd do well to remember that. She thought of Tom and was immediately sobered.

The conversation began to flow again. They talked about the market. Then Ray spent time chatting to Donna and Ellie was touched by the effort he made with her.

When Elvis came on again, Ellie found herself oddly separated from her surroundings, hearing and seeing everything in sharp, almost dazzling focus: the gaudy paper chains, the hiss of the coffee machine, the rise and fall of conversation, the traffic outside, the smell of coffee and cinnamon toasted teacakes. She saw her daughter sitting beside her happily, and Ray saying something to make her laugh. She knew instinctively that she would never be able to hear the song without thinking of Ray.

It was as though she'd been transported back to a time before her life had become a rollercoaster of misery and guilt, filled with agonising decisions and crushing responsibility. She tasted again those carefree days before the accident, when fun and pleasure had been a natural part of life, not something to be ashamed of because she couldn't share them with Tom.

But it wasn't quite the same as then; it was better. There was a new ingredient now, an adrenaline rush that was sweeter and more thrilling than anything that had gone before. She felt chosen and special and she loved the feeling.

Ray broke into her thoughts. 'Penny for them.' He was smiling at her.

Startled, Ellie was recalled to the present as the song came to the end again. 'I was just thinking that it's time I was going.' She knew she must pull herself together. 'I should get my daughter home before the cold of evening sets in.'

Ray didn't look pleased but he didn't argue. 'Yes, I must go too,' he said.

'Thanks for the coffee and the company,' she said. 'It's been lovely.'

In a sudden action he reached across the table and rested his large hand on her slender one. 'I've enjoyed every moment,' he uttered huskily.

Their eyes met and Ellie felt drawn ever deeper into something beyond her control. OK, she reasoned with herself, maybe you can't stop the feelings coming but you can do something about the way you deal with them. 'So have we.' Including her daughter was intended to negate any romantic slant. She removed her hand and busied herself with Donna, wiping cake crumbs from her face and doing her coat up. Her hands were trembling, though.

Outside the coffee bar, Ellie strapped Donna into the pushchair, said a hurried goodbye to Ray and went on her way. These fanciful notions have got to stop, she resolved.

Ellie threw herself into Christmas with vigour in an effort to forget everything else – Tom, Ray, the recent trouble at the market. It wasn't difficult to capture the spirit of the season with Donna about. She was wild with enthusiasm about everything from the orange in the foot of her stocking to the wrapping paper the presents from Santa were covered in. There were a few tears, inevitably, when the excitement got too much for her, but the special day was a happy one on the whole.

Boxing Day was less emotionally charged but just as hectic for Ellie, who entertained the family and Pat at her place.

Food and drink was in abundance and overindulgence rife. The adults kept the children amused with riotous musical chairs and other games in the afternoon, then slumped exhausted in front of the television after Donna and Matthew had gone to bed, the latter in Ellie's spare bed. Pat was never a cheery soul at the best of times but even she seemed to enjoy herself.

'It's been a smashing day, Ellie,' remarked Ann when she was in the kitchen helping Ellie to prepare a light supper of cold meat and pickles.

'Thank you. I think it went rather well,' Ellie responded. 'I had a fun time too.'

Ann gave her a sharp look. 'You've certainly been on top form. It's good to see you enjoying Christmas again.'

'It makes a difference now that Donna's able to take an interest,' she explained. 'You can't help but get into the spirit of the thing when there's a child about.'

'That isn't all, though, is it?' Ann observed. 'There's something else.'

'What do you mean?'

'I'm not sure,' Ann mused thoughtfully. 'I think it's that you seem different.'

'Do I?' said Ellie guardedly. 'In what way?'

'I can't quite put my finger on it,' Ann pondered as she spooned pickled onions from the jar into a dish. 'But there's a sort of glow about you somehow.'

So the pervasive sense of joy created by Ray Brent was even obvious to other people, Ellie realised with alarm. Despite sobering glimpses of the future reminding her that nothing could possibly come of it, the feeling of euphoria persisted. A sudden urge to confide in her friend overwhelmed her. But Ann was a relative as well as a friend. There was a risk she might let the secret out to Doug in some unguarded moment.

With the family on her side Ellie was unbeatable. But they wouldn't be with her over this. Collectively they would be horrified to know that Ray Brent was playing havoc with her emotions. So she resisted the temptation to share her feelings. 'It must just be a general feeling of optimism for the new year,' she fibbed. 'I've got another talk booked, by the way.'

'Well done,' said Ann. 'When is it?'

'January. It's the monthly meeting of a women's group in Notting Hill Gate.'

'You all right for a baby-sitter?'

'Mum said she'd do it.'

'If you're stuck, let me know.'

'Thanks.'

'It's good that your first talk wasn't just a one-off, isn't it?' enthused Ann.

'I'll say,' confirmed Ellie. 'A recommendation is the ultimate compliment.'

'That must be the reason for your new glow,' Ann speculated. 'The sweet smell of success.'

'Yes. That must be it,' agreed Ellie, arranging some sandwiches on a plate so that she didn't have to meet Ann's eyes.

Alfie and Ray had gone to the local for a Boxing Night drink and were standing at the bar when – without any sort of lead-up – Alfie issued a warning to his son.

'I hope you're bearing in mind the fact that she's a married woman,' he said gravely.

'Who?'

'Don't come the innocent with me, son,' rebuked Alfie. 'I've seen the way you look at her. I've heard your tone of voice when you mention her name. You've been mooning about like some lovesick schoolboy all over Christmas. Miles away.'

So it was that obvious, thought Ray worriedly. 'This is my first proper Christmas in a long time,' he reminded his father. 'I've just been enjoying it in my own quiet way.'

'You've been daydreaming about Ellie Hall,' Alfie corrected, wagging an admonitory finger. 'That's what you've been doing all over the holiday.'

Ray sighed. 'You're a shrewd old devil. I should have known you'd twig. All right, so what if I have been thinking about her?' he admitted, sipping his beer. 'It's nothing to be ashamed of.'

'I'm not saying it is,' Alfie conceded. 'It's the nature of the thoughts that will land you in trouble.'

'She's just so wonderful, Dad,' Ray burst out. 'I can't get her off my mind.'

An eloquent sigh emitted from Alfie. 'You know how much I like Ellie. She's a fine young woman,' he said. 'Lovely to look at, kind-hearted and good company. But she's also married with a child and a husband who isn't in a fit state to keep her on the straight and narrow, the poor devil.'

'OK, so she's married,' Ray was forced to admit. 'But she doesn't have a husband, not in the normal sense, anyway.'

'She's still married, son.'

'She's on her own, though.' Ray's voice was rising. 'Her husband can't be with her as he should be. He isn't capable of adult love now, and he never will be again. Where does that leave Ellie? On her own for the rest of her life? She's still young, Dad. Isn't she entitled to happiness with someone else?'

'What makes you so certain you can make her happy?' Alfie wondered.

'I'm not *certain* of anything except that I want to be with her and I want to try to make her happy,' Ray said heatedly. 'Surely that's a good enough base to work on.'

'Haven't you had enough bother, son?' Alfie could see big trouble ahead if his son followed his heart.

'You know the answer to that.'

'So stop it now while no harm's done.' Alfie was begging now.

'I can't.'

'Don't talk daft, of course you can.'

'She's really important to me, Dad,' Ray went on to say. 'And, as I've said, she might just as well not be married.'

'But she *is* married. Her old man is still very much alive and he's legally her husband,' Alfie pointed out again, his voice almost a shout. 'It doesn't matter how unfair it seems, those are the facts of the matter. I strongly advise you to think carefully about what you would be getting into if you proceed along that road. You start messing about with Ellie and you'll stir up a whole load of trouble for yourself.'

'That doesn't bother me.'

'Then it should do. It's hard enough to get people's trust when you've done a prison stretch, you know that only too well,' Alfie continued. 'You steal another man's wife and everyone will turn against you.'

'Since when have I worried about what people think of me?' he asked.

'That isn't the point.'

'Look, Dad, her husband can't be hurt by anything that happens between Ellie and me because he doesn't even know he has a marriage,' Ray countered. 'I wouldn't kick a man when he's down, you know that. But he wouldn't be affected and that's the important thing.'

'You'd still be seen as a marriage-wrecker by the people around here,' said Alfie.

'If they're shallow enough to make judgements without considering the facts, then they're not the sort of people I'd want to be associated with anyway,' was Ray's answer to that.

'Forget her, Ray,' advised Alfie. 'Find yourself a woman who's free.'

'If only it was that easy.'

'What are you talking about?' Alfie queried loudly. 'A good-looking bloke like you won't have any trouble.'

'I was referring to the fact that wanting someone other than Ellie is impossible,' he explained ardently. 'She's the only woman for me. I mean it.'

Alfie tutted, shaking his head. 'Sounds to me as though you

really have got it bad,' he muttered.

'I'm afraid I have,' confirmed Ray.

'In that case, God help you,' said Alfie, drinking his beer and staring worriedly into space.

All the family went to Ann and Doug's on New Year's Eve to welcome in the new decade. It was a lively party – plenty to eat and drink, and bags of festive cheer. Doug rolled back the carpet and they danced to records, the evening culminating in the usual boozily sentimental 'Auld Lang Syne'.

Ellie enjoyed herself up to a point but was relieved when the celebrations were finally over. Because the previous Saturday had been Boxing Day, there had been no market at Napp's Road. Despite all her common sense and good intentions, she was longing for this Saturday's market with a feverishness that had nothing whatever to do with selling knitwear.

Ray was waiting for her when she arrived in her usual parking place on Saturday morning.

'You're early,' she said as she got out of her car, her manner casual though her heart was beating so loud, she could feel it throbbing in her ears.

'Yes.'

'Where's Alfie?'

'He's gone on ahead.'

'Oh?'

'I wanted to see you on my own.' Ray looked very serious. 'Can you meet me in the pub at lunchtime?'

'Provided I can get Joe to look after the stall for me, I can take a short break.'

'See you in there at one o'clock, then.'

'Fine,' Ellie agreed thoughtfully.

'So what's all this about?' she asked over a ham sandwich and a shandy in the pub. Joe had told her to take as long as she liked. She'd offered to cover for him in return. 'It sounded urgent.'

'It is, *very*.'

'Did something happen to you over Christmas to put you in such a serious mood?'

'Yes, it did.' Ray's expression was tender but grave. 'You happened to me. Maybe I shouldn't be saying this but I was thinking about you the whole time. I can't get you off my mind, Ellie.'

She tried to be cool and detached but the feelings were just too strong. 'That's quite a coincidence,' she said softly.

His features seemed to melt into tenderness for her. 'Oh, Ellie,' he breathed, reaching over and taking her hand, 'you can't know how much I've been hoping you felt the same. I sensed it was mutual but couldn't be sure.'

'Despite my very best intentions, you were on my mind all over the holiday.' She looked at him earnestly. 'You realise it can't go any further, though?' she made herself tell him. 'It's a complete nonstarter.'

'You want it to go further, though, don't you?'

'What I want doesn't come into it.' She shook her head despairingly.

'I'll take that as a yes.'

'And you'd be right to, but I must be honest and tell you that I'm very confused about my feelings,' she told him. 'There's never been any other man in my life except Tom so I don't know how to handle this new thing, whatever it is.'

'We both know what it is.' He was in no doubt.

It was too soon to call it love. Infatuation possibly? But she couldn't deny the power of the chemistry between them. 'But we hardly know each other,' she pointed out.

'We can soon alter that.'

'That's just the point,' she burst out, squeezing his hand tightly in her anxiety. 'To get to know someone you need to spend time together, and we can't do that.'

'There must be a way.'

'There isn't.' She drew her hand away. She was angry because she was so desperately disappointed and he didn't seem to have grasped the impossibility of the situation.

'You're being negative.'

'I'm being realistic,' she corrected. 'I have a young child, Ray. Surely you're not suggesting that I ask one of my relatives to look after her while I go out to have an affair with a man while my husband is locked away in an institution?'

'You're making it sound tacky.' He was hurt.

'And if we did that, it would be,' she replied.

'There's nothing tacky about my feelings for you, I can assure you,' Ray declared with fervour. 'I want to be with you, Ellie, to get to know you. You're making it sound as though I'm looking for some sleazy affair.'

'I don't suppose any affair seems sleazy to the participants. I expect they all tell themselves that theirs is different, theirs is special and therefore justified.'

'I wouldn't know about that. I've never studied such things.' His manner was sharp now. 'I only know how I feel about you. I didn't intend for this to happen. I'm not the sort of bloke who makes a habit of chasing after married women. And it certainly isn't a sordid affair I'm after. I want something far more permanent. Please believe me.'

'I do believe you.' Her tone was softer now, her anger lessened by his obvious sincerity. 'I'm just trying to get you to see the situation as it really is . . . to point out the practical impossibility of us getting together.'

'If we both want it bad enough, we can make it happen,' he told her.

'How?'

'We'll find a way.'

'You're being ridiculously romantic.' She gave him a tender smile. 'It's very sweet but it doesn't change anything.'

'I'm not prepared to give up,' he stated firmly.

'It's different for you, Ray,' she said gently. 'You're single and childless. You can please yourself what you do. It isn't as easy as that for me.'

'I understand that and I'm not saying it will be easy. But you admitted to me yourself that you don't have a husband now, not in any real sense,' he reminded her. 'And Donna isn't a problem as far as I'm concerned.'

'Oh, come on,' Ellie said with a dry laugh. 'You're not expecting me to believe that what you have in mind for us could happen with a child around.'

'You're doing it again.' He was angry now. 'You're making it seem to be all about sex when there's much more to it than that.'

'Sorry.'

'I want to be with you,' he went on. 'And you have a daughter so I want to get to know her better too. She's part of you. And I want all of you.'

His words brought a lump to her throat because it simply wasn't possible. She raked her red hair from her brow with her fingers. 'Oh, Ray, what's happening to me?' she asked him. 'Life used to be so simple. I was a happily married woman, I had a baby and my whole life mapped out for me: Tom and I growing old together and enjoying our grandchildren. Then suddenly—'

'It was like that for me too,' he reminded her. 'I had my life sorted six years ago. I was all set to get engaged to Maria and spend the rest of my life with her.' He shrugged. 'But life is full of surprises.'

'I know you've had a hard time too,' she said.

'I don't want your sympathy. I just want you to do what I've had to do and adapt to the way life is now, not try to hang on to how you thought it was going to be,' he told her. 'Circumstances have changed and you have to change with them.'

'I'm still married to Tom,' Ellie reminded him. 'The circumstances haven't altered that.'

'But do you still love him in the same way?' he asked her. 'That's the question.'

246

'How can I know what I feel when the man I knew isn't there any more?' she said. 'All I am sure of is pity, and I feel plenty of that for him.'

'Of course you do.' He looked into her face. 'But that isn't enough, is it?'

She knew he was right but was ashamed to admit it, so didn't reply.

'We can't let what we have slip through our fingers,' he went on. 'It's too important, we both know that. There must be a way we can see each other.'

Ignoring all her finer instincts, she said, 'I'm giving a talk in Notting Hill Gate on Thursday night. My mother will be baby-sitting for me. I could meet you afterwards if you like . . . just for a little while.'

His face lit up.

'I won't have long,' she added firmly.

'Just tell me where and at what time and I'll be there,' Ray said, his face one big smile.

Ellie was in such turmoil about her arrangement to meet Ray on Thursday night, any tendency towards pre-talk nerves was virtually nonexistent. As a result she sailed through her talk to an enthusiastic response, ending on a high note. She sold three sweaters, took orders for others and was asked by the organiser for permission to pass her telephone number on to a friend who belonged to a different women's group.

Now for the main event of the evening, Ellie thought guiltily, as she walked to Notting Hill Gate station in the heavy rain, wearing a cream-coloured raincoat and black high heels. She'd arranged to meet Ray there, having left the car outside the church hall where she'd been speaking. It was too windy for an umbrella and the rain was beating against her face and soaking her hair, but she barely noticed.

Ray was already there, standing just inside the station. Ellie's heart leaped at the sight of him. Immaculate in a grey overcoat and white scarf, his dark hair gleaming in the station lights, he stood out from the crowd. Magnificent was the only word she could think of to describe him.

'I'm so pleased you came,' he said, walking towards her.

'Me too.'

'What would you like to do?' he asked, taking her arm. 'Go for a drink, or a meal or what?'

'I don't have time for a meal,' she said.

'Just a drink then,' he suggested. 'Somewhere we can talk.'

'I've left my car outside the hall,' she told him. 'Where's yours?'

'Just around the corner.'

'Let's go there then,' she said recklessly.

'There are plenty of pubs around here within walking distance,' he told her. 'We don't need to drive.'

'Let's go to your car anyway.' She knew exactly what she was doing but it was as though someone else was controlling her actions.

He seemed surprised but said, 'Sure. If that's what you really want.'

They walked down the street together to his car, which was parked in a side street out of the light. He opened the passenger door for her and walked round to the driver's door. She managed to retain enough dignity to resist the urge to suggest they get in the back.

'So where to now?' he asked.

'Nowhere.' It was immoral and undignified but she couldn't help herself. She slid her arms around his neck and drew him to her, kissing him deeply again and again.

Nothing had ever felt like this before. It was sweet, tantalising and very frightening. It was also wrong.

'Sorry, Ray, I shouldn't have done that,' she muttered thickly as she pulled away. 'I shouldn't have led you on. Lost control, I'm afraid.'

'It's all right,' he whispered shakily into her hair. 'It doesn't matter.'

'I have to go.'

248

'But you've only just got here,' he said, drawing her back towards him.

'I know I have.' She dragged herself away from him forcefully. 'And look what I'm doing,' she said, her voice shaking with emotion and self-disgust. 'Five minutes alone with you and I'm practically tearing your clothes off in a public place.'

'I know it isn't ideal . . .'

'It's downright sordid,' she burst out.

'It isn't as if—'

'It could have, though, the way I was carrying on,' she interrupted. 'That's what happens when you give in to feelings. You lose all sense of dignity and moral restraint.'

'Ellie . . .'

'It isn't your fault, Ray, it's mine. I'm not being fair, starting something I'm not prepared to finish.' She moved away and reached for the door handle.

'Don't go, please . . .'

'I have to,' she muttered breathlessly. 'I can't bear what's happening to me. I don't like being out of control. I can't let myself go, I have too many responsibilities.'

'At least let's talk about it,' he said.

'No.' She was adamant. 'Please don't pursue this, Ray. If you think anything of me at all, don't unsettle me any more. I just can't cope with it.'

'But—'

'I'm sorry.' And without another word, she turned and leaped from the vehicle. She tore down the street to the car her mother-in-law was kind enough to lend her, tears mingling with rain pounding against her face, the fact that the car belonged to her husband's mother making her feel even worse.

Chapter Twelve

'Everything all right, Mum? Donna OK?' were Ellie's first words when she got home.

'Yeah. Everything's fine,' Mary assured her, knitting needles clacking with piston-like speed. 'I haven't had a peep out of her ladyship all evening.'

'That's good.'

'You're drenched, love,' remarked Mary, casting a concerned eye over her daughter's damp appearance, hair wet and windblown, raincoat sodden.

'It's coming down in stair rods out there,' explained Ellie.

'Long walk from the car to the hall, was it?'

It was nothing more than a casual comment but it registered like a hammer blow to Ellie's uneasy conscience. 'It was too windy to use an umbrella,' was the way she managed to avoid a truthful explanation of her soaked state. 'I'll get my mac off right away.'

'So . . . how did the evening go?' her mother enquired when Ellie returned to the room without her raincoat, and drying her hair with a towel.

'The evening?' Ellie's blue eyes bulged. The incident with Ray filled her mind to such an extent, she thought her mother must be referring to that.

'The talk you were giving at the women's group meeting.' Mary gave her an enquiring look. 'Did you get on all right?'

'Oh . . . the talk.'

'Of course,' confirmed Mary, looking puzzled. 'What else would I be asking about?'

'The talk was fine,' Ellie told her, recovering. 'It went down really well, in fact.'

'What's the matter then?' her mother wanted to know. 'You seem a bit rattled about something.'

'Do I?' Ellie replied innocently, affecting a yawn. 'Must be because I'm tired.'

Her mother didn't look convinced but Ellie eased an awkward moment by launching into an enthusiastic account of her talk. They chatted about other things for a while until Mary gathered her knitting and said it was time she was going.

Ellie got her coat from the hall and thanked her for sitting with Donna.

'Any time,' chirped Mary. 'You know I'm only too pleased to help when you have to go out on business.'

Now Ellie's conscience went into overdrive because the legitimate part of the evening had paled into insignificance against her meeting with Ray, which had, she reminded herself, only lasted a few minutes. Such was her tumult she almost confessed all to her mother. But caution finally prevailed. Mary wasn't narrow-minded but she was fiercely protective of her family and would be horrified to know that her daughter had come close to an adulterous affair with someone Mary saw only as an alleged murderer. Ellie's private life was entirely her own business, of course, but she was much too soft-hearted to disregard the feelings of the people she was closest to.

'Thanks, anyway.' Ellie kissed her mother on the cheek as she saw her out, relieved to be alone with her guilty conscience.

The next day was a hectic one for Ellie as she juggled work at the knitting machine with her maternal duties. A couple of substantial telephone orders created a welcome diversion from the agonising memories of last night.

There was nothing like activity to concentrate the mind, she thought, as she took a break from the machine to help Donna dress her dolls. Having been awake for most of the night reliving every moment of her meeting with Ray Brent, she was exhausted but at the same time fired with nervous energy.

By the end of the day, when she had a pile of finished knitting ready for her mother's expert hand, and had also found the time to take Donna to the park, she was heartened by the fact that the hours had been productive, despite the state of her emotions. It was a good thing she didn't have time to mope about yearning for something she couldn't have.

She gave Donna a boiled egg and Marmite soldiers for tea, then bathed her, finding the strength to make a game of it in the way her daughter enjoyed. She'd just buttoned her into a fluffy pink dressing gown when there was a knock at the front door.

'Ray!' Her legs turned to jelly. 'What on earth are you doing here? How did you find us?'

'I gave Reg Cox a bell,' he explained. 'Told him I needed your address urgently, and it wasn't a lie.'

'I see.' She was smiling, despite herself.

'He had some good news for me, as it happens,' he went on to say. 'He told me that Syd Bell is finishing at Napp's Road market. He's going somewhere else to flog his stuff.'

'Thank God for that.' She was staring at him, still trying to gather her wits and stop this ridiculous grinning. 'Thanks for coming to tell me.'

'That's all right.' He gave her a questioning look. 'Do you keep all your visitors standing outside on the doorstep?' he asked.

'Ray, I don't think it's a good idea . . .' Ellie began.

At that moment, Donna trotted into the hall and emitted a squeal of delight at the sight of Ray. With a bitter cold draught blowing in to the house and her freshly bathed daughter excitedly putting her arms up to Ray to be picked up, Ellie didn't have much choice but to invite him in and offer him a cup of tea.

He'd come armed with persuasive ammunition – Smarties for Donna and chocolates for Ellie. Within seconds of taking his coat off, he was on all fours on the floor, emulating a horse and giving Donna rides on his back. The child loved every moment.

'Don't get her overexcited,' warned Ellie, 'or I'll never get her to go to sleep. It's almost her bedtime.'

'OK, madam,' Ray said to Donna. 'You heard what Mummy said. So let's calm down and do something a little bit quieter now, shall we?'

'More horsey,' she demanded. 'More, more, more.'

'Another time. No more horsey today,' he told her firmly, getting to his feet. 'But I'll read you a story, if you like.'

'Yeth, please,' she lisped.

'Go and get a storybook then,' he requested. 'Go on . . . chop chop.'

Ten minutes later the little girl fell asleep on his lap in the middle of 'Goldilocks and the Three Bears'. With the utmost gentleness Ray carried her up to bed and waited while Ellie tucked her in.

'It won't work, you know,' she said, when they were back downstairs in the living room.

'What won't?'

'Chocolates for me, sweets for Donna and an impressive demonstration of what a wonderful rapport you have with her isn't going to persuade me to dispense with my principles and rush into your arms,' she told him.

He spread his hands, looking at her grimly. 'What do you suggest I do, Ellie?' he asked. 'Walk away from the situation and try to pretend it doesn't exist?'

'I'm sorry about last night.' She spoke with sincerity. 'I should never have let things get that far. But yes, you must walk away from the situation. That's what I want you to do.'

'It isn't what you want me to do at all,' he disagreed. 'It isn't what either of us wants.'

'Stop this, Ray,' she begged him. 'You know how impossible it is for me. So don't try to get to me by winning Donna over.'

'Give me some credit.' He was offended now. 'I wouldn't stoop so low as to involve a child for my own ends. I happen to think she's great. I enjoy making a fuss of her.'

'Yeah, I know, I'm sorry,' she apologised. 'I shouldn't have said that.'

'I should damned well hope you are sorry,' he returned. 'Anyway, I can hardly ignore her when I come to see you, can I? She'd be terribly hurt.'

'Don't come to see me then,' she suggested. 'Then nobody gets hurt.'

'Ooh, not much,' he argued. 'What about us ... you and me?'

'There can't be any us,' she told him. 'We've already been through all this.'

'And I'll keep going through it until you face up to the truth.' He spread his hands again. 'Look Ellie, the last thing I want to do is hurt you or cause trouble for you, and if I thought that leaving you alone was the best thing for you, I'd do it. But I don't think it is. I'm in love with you and I believe you feel the same way about me.'

It was the first time he'd actually used those words and it shook her to the core. The sheer thrill of his declaration wouldn't be stifled. 'You can't be in love with someone you hardly know,' she said but her argument seemed very shaky against the strength of her feelings for him.

'Oh? On whose evidence?'

'You don't need evidence for something so blatantly obvious.'

'Call it mutual attraction then, if you're more comfortable with that,' he suggested. 'But don't try to pretend that there isn't something very special between us.'

Ellie emitted a frustrated sigh. 'Can we change the subject, please?' she requested sharply. 'I really don't want to get into the psychology of it all.'

He didn't reply; seemed to be mulling it over. 'Sure,' he said at last. 'So what would you like to talk about?'

'I wasn't actually planning on talking about anything,' she told him. 'I was thinking of making myself some supper and then relaxing in front of the box.'

'I'll join you,' he announced boldly, 'if you've enough for two. If not I'll go down the chip shop to get us something.'

She laughed; she couldn't help it. He was even more irresistible when he was pushing his luck. 'I was going to have an omelette,' she informed him.

'Big enough for us both?' He was looking at her so appealingly, she couldn't refuse him.

'I think I can manage that.' She paused thoughtfully. 'But only on one condition . . .'

He gave her a slow smile. 'Conditions, eh?' he said. 'I like it. You're even sexier when you're being assertive.'

'I'm trying to be serious, Ray.'

'OK, let's hear it.'

'On condition that there is no talk of affairs or anything at all of that nature,' she informed him. 'Just two friends spending some time together. Right?'

'I'll behave,' he promised.

'In that case you can give me a hand,' she told him. 'You can lay the table while I get busy with the frying pan.'

'Yes, ma'am,' he grinned.

He kept his word and they had a most enjoyable evening, the atmosphere light and full of banter, though Ellie was aware of deeper undertones the whole time. The television – a recent acquisition she'd bought with her earnings now that they were more affordable – wasn't even turned on because they were too busy with conversation. They seemed to have so much to say to each other: food, drink, films, TV programmes and current affairs all came under discussion. The time flew past and suddenly it was almost midnight.

'It's time I wasn't here,' Ray said, looking at his watch.

'I didn't realise it was quite so late,' Ellie admitted. 'I'll go and get your coat.'

But she didn't move, just stared at him, wanting him to stay and knowing she must make him go. 'It's been a lovely evening,' she muttered at last. 'I've enjoyed myself enormously.'

'Me too.' He stood up with a purposeful air. 'If I could have my coat . . .'

As he followed her to the hall, she was surprised by his compliance.

'Thanks for keeping to your word,' she said as she handed him a smart grey overcoat. 'I must admit I was expecting trouble.'

His expression became solemn, dark eyes full of emotion. 'I've decided to leave it up to you, rather than upset you by being a pest,' he told her, slipping into his coat. 'The last thing I want to do is give you grief. You know how I feel about you. When you're ready, let me know.'

'I notice you say "when" and not "if",' she pointed out.

'I'm a positive thinker,' he replied. 'I learned to be an expert when I was in prison.'

'Yes . . . of course.'

'Seriously though, Ellie, there are times when you have to have faith in your own judgement,' he went on. 'And because I believe in our feelings for each other, I know you'll come to me sooner or later.'

'I'm not free to do so,' she reminded him.

'I know.'

'You talk a lot about our feelings when there is so much more to this than that,' she said sadly.

He stepped forward and put his finger to her lips in a silencing gesture. 'I know all about the hideous complications,' he said gently. 'I know exactly how impossible it seems to be. But there's nothing we can't get through together if we both want it bad enough.'

'Some people would call that a selfish attitude.'

'Nobody with a scrap of humanity in them would want you

to spend the rest of your life on your own.' He took one of his business cards out of his pocket and handed it to her. 'So . . . if you change your mind, give me a ring at home or at the workshop.'

'Won't I see you at the market tomorrow?'

'No. Dad's holding the fort for me this week,' Ray explained. 'I'm going to Kent to give someone an estimate on some ornamental gates.'

'Oh!' Up went her brows because she knew how much he wanted to build that side of his business up. 'That sounds exciting,' she enthused.

'Yeah, it is. It'll be a good earner if I get the job, and challenging too,' he told her. 'It's one of these big country houses, apparently. The chap who owns it has a London flat as well. He saw my advertisement in the paper.'

'You won't be working in Kent if you get the job, will you?' she wondered.

'No. I shall have to go there to fit the gates,' he said. 'But I'll make them in my workshop here in London.'

'I hope all goes well for you tomorrow, then.'

'Thanks,' he said. 'It's the break I've been hoping for, to get me started on that type of work.' He paused, looking at her. 'Anyway, we'll just have to see how it goes tomorrow. I should be back by early evening.'

He kissed her lightly on the cheek and headed for the front door. It was as much as she could do not to run after him as he left and hurried to his car.

The market seemed a much duller place the next day for Ellie, knowing that Ray wasn't around. It was probably all for the best, she told herself. Feelings had been running high; this would give them both a breathing space. She hated the feeling, though. The day had none of its usual sparkle; she missed the thrill of knowing she might see him at any moment.

By the time she'd put Donna to bed that night, the ache she'd had in the pit of her stomach since Ray had left the decision to her had become almost unbearable. She thought of doing some work to take her mind off things. But it had been a long day and she was physically tired. Mistakes would be made which would take valuable time to put right.

She turned on the television and tried to concentrate on *The Cliff Richard Show* which shouldn't have been difficult since she was a fan of his. But on this particular occasion, his charm failed to hold her attention under the weight of such strong competition.

What was she to do about Ray? She was a married woman with the life of a single one. She was nearly twenty-five years old and wanted all the things any normal woman of her age wanted: love, warmth, companionship, sex. Was she to be deprived of all of these things for the rest of her life because her husband couldn't give them to her? Was it so wrong to want them with someone else when Tom couldn't have them at all?

The thought of Tom twisted her heart and made her sad. The thought of Ray filled her with desire, happiness and hope for the future. Compunction did nothing to cool her ardour.

But there was much more at stake here than just the satisfying of passion. Ray had made it clear he didn't just want a fling. He would want commitment from her even though she could never marry him. If she did what her instincts were crying out for her to do, there would be no half-measures and no going back.

She got up and paced the room. She wrung her hands and chewed her lip so hard it bled. Then she went to the telephone in the hall and dialled a number.

'Hello, Alfie. This is Ellie . . . Ellie Hall.'

'Hello, love. How are you?'

'I'm fine. You?'

'Not so bad thanks, ducks.'

'Is Ray there?'

Alfie hesitated just long enough for Ellie to feel his disapproval coming down the line. 'Yeah, he's here,' he said at last. 'I'll go and get him for you.'

'Thank you.' Her heart was thumping as she waited for Ray to come to the telephone.

'Happy?' asked Ray later.

'I never thought I could feel this happy again,' she said, snuggling into the crook of his arm as he lay back against the pillow with his arm around her.

'Likewise,' he said, stroking her hair.

'You knew I would make that vital phone call, didn't you?' she suggested to him drowsily.

'I was cautiously optimistic, put it that way,' he confessed. 'I never doubted your feelings for me but was afraid you'd get weighed down by conscience.'

'I did but I called you just the same.'

'And I'm very glad.'

She asked how he'd got on in Kent and he said he'd been given the job.

'Oh, well done,' she congratulated. 'You must be chuffed to bits.'

'I am. It's been my lucky day,' he said, pulling her closer. 'What with that . . . and this.'

They fell into a contented silence until she said, 'Your father doesn't approve of us, does he?'

'What's he been saying to you?'

'Nothing. He didn't have to,' she told him. 'His disapproving silence came down the phone line loud and clear.'

'He thinks it'll cause trouble for us both because of the scandal when people find out,' Ray explained. 'He says that you'll be seen as the heartless wife being unfaithful to the husband who's rotting away in a nursing home and I'll be cast in the role of wicked pervert who stole a sick man's wife.'

'I hope the people who matter will realise that we're both entitled to lives,' she suggested.

'That's what I told Dad,' he said. 'I'm not bothered for myself. People can say what they like about me.'

'I'm not bothered for myself either,' she said. 'But it could have far-reaching effects.'

'Tom can't be hurt by it and, as far as this is concerned, surely he's the only one who really matters.'

'It's a bit more complicated than that,' Ellie explained. 'His mother will be terribly upset about it, and she's a close friend of my mother's. So there could be all sorts of ructions.'

'Surely Tom's mum realises that you will meet someone else eventually,' he suggested. 'You're a young woman. It was bound to happen at some time.'

'I don't think she's ever even considered the idea, to be perfectly honest,' Ellie told him. 'She's a decent enough woman but tends to be a bit narrow-minded. And Tom *is* her only child.'

'I can understand it being difficult for her but you haven't had it easy either,' he reminded her.

'She'll be all right when she gets used to the idea, I expect.' But Ellie wasn't as confident as she sounded. 'She tends to blow her top when she first hears about something she doesn't like, then calms down later on. Once I've explained how I feel, she'll accept it, I'm sure.' She looked up at him. 'For the moment, though, I think it'll be best if we keep our relationship to ourselves.'

'Coward,' he joshed.

'I admit it,' she confessed. 'I'm not ready to let the outside world in just yet awhile. I want to carry on feeling as happy as this, just you and me.'

'It won't be easy to keep it secret,' he pointed out. 'The way I feel I want to tell the world about us.'

'And we will, my darling,' she assured him, looking into his eyes. 'But not just yet.'

One evening a few days later Ellie fancied some crisps and a Babycham so Ray went to the pub to get them for her. He was standing at the bar waiting to be served when someone tapped him on the shoulder.

261

He turned to see an extremely attractive woman in her late twenties. Having not seen her for so long she seemed even more stunning than he remembered, with her dark Italian looks and flashing eyes.

'Maria Dobbs, well stone me.' His reaction to her was nothing stronger than mild surprise at meeting her again so unexpectedly. 'It's been a long time.'

'Yeah, it's been ages,' she said, running an approving eye over his tall frame, casually clad in a T-shirt and slacks. 'I'd know you anywhere, even though you have changed a bit. You look a lot different without the drape jacket and DA haircut.'

He nodded in reply.

'So . . . how have you been?' she asked.

'Pretty good,' he replied. 'Yourself?'

'Surviving, you know.'

'I thought you'd moved away,' he mentioned casually. 'The last I heard you were going away to get married.'

'I did and I was,' she confirmed. 'I went up north to marry a bloke from Leeds. I stayed up there with him but we didn't actually ever tie the knot.'

'You down here to see your folks then?'

'No, I'm back for good,' Maria explained. 'I'm living down the road in Hammersmith. Only a bedsit but it's not bad.'

'What about the boyfriend?'

'He stayed in Leeds,' she said breezily. 'We split up.'

'I'm sorry.'

'Don't be,' she said. 'It had run its course.'

There was an uncomfortable pause. Ray was at a loss to know what to say. 'Can I get you a drink?' he offered to be polite.

'Thanks but I'd better not. I'm with some people.' She stabbed her finger towards a table where two men and a woman were sitting. Ray assumed Maria was the fourth member of the foursome.

'I see,' he said with an understanding nod.

'We heard that the midweek entertainment here was good

so we came to take a look,' she said, seeming to want to prolong the conversation. 'It was a good show, an' all. They had a male singer who was brilliant. Put me in mind of Adam Faith.'

'No wonder you enjoyed the show then. He's flavour of the month with you women at the moment, isn't he?'

'Not half.'

An awkward silence fell. He searched his mind for subject matter. 'I thought you'd be settled down with a couple of kids by now,' he managed at last.

'No such luck,' she told him. 'You got any kids?'

He shook his head.

Maria gave him a guilty look. 'I'm sorry about . . .' Her voice tailed off.

'That's all right.' He knew exactly what she was referring to.

'It was a horrible thing for me to do.'

'I was gutted at the time, naturally,' he admitted. 'But it was all forgotten years ago.'

She looked genuinely regretful. 'I just couldn't . . .' Again she didn't finish the sentence.

'Cope with having a convict as your boyfriend?' he finished for her.

She didn't bother to deny it. That wasn't Maria's way. 'I suppose that's about it,' she confirmed.

'At least you're honest.'

'I usually am, Ray. If you remember nothing else about me you'll remember that,' she said.

'Yes,' he said slowly, thinking back. 'I do remember.'

'Truth of the matter is, I was young then and I just didn't have the bottle to stay with you,' she explained. 'Mean of me, I know, but being good never was my strong point.'

Ray found himself smiling. Until this evening he'd not given Maria any thought for years but now recalled how artless and outspoken she'd been, and such good fun. 'It doesn't matter,' he assured her. 'It's all over and done with.'

'I felt bad about it for ages, you know.' She seemed to need to talk. 'It kept me awake nights, and there aren't many things that do that.'

'Forget it,' he advised her. 'It's past, finished and done with. We were different people back then.'

She thought about this for a moment. 'Yeah, you're right, there's no point in harking back, is there?' she agreed, looking relieved. 'You're a free man now, and looking good for all that you've been through.' She gave him a saucy grin. 'You always were a handsome bugger.'

He smiled, relaxing a little in her company now that a casualness had been established. 'I never got the chance to thank you for speaking up for me in court,' he said.

'I was only telling the truth. I wouldn't lie under oath,' she was keen to point out.

'Of course not.'

'I never thought you'd killed that bloke,' she went on to say earnestly. 'I didn't have the courage to stay with you because everyone else thought you'd done it. But I didn't believe that you were guilty.'

'I remember feeling touched when you said nice things about me in court,' he told her, partly because it was true and also because he thought she needed to hear it.

'That's something anyway.' She looked at him sheepishly. 'It must have been terrible, being arrested like that,' she said, her huge eyes full of sympathy. 'And on top of all that your girlfriend gives you the elbow.'

'Hm.' He wished she'd stop going on about it because it was of no interest to him now.

'As well as not wanting to be known as a criminal's girlfriend, I didn't want all that heavy stuff in my life,' she continued, determined to unburden herself completely. 'I wanted to be out having a good time, you know what I was like in those days. I've often regretted it, though. I've thought about you a lot over the years.' She stared into space, smiling wistfully. 'We had some good times, didn't we, Ray, you and me.'

'We sure did,' he agreed. 'Even if you were the biggest flirt in London.'

'I only did that to keep you interested,' she told him, her dark eyes dancing. 'And it never failed.'

For a moment he was transported back to those carefree, youthful days. He could almost smell the cheap scent Maria had used then, taste the sweet greasiness of her lipstick and the Babycham on her breath. 'Oh, well,' he said briskly, coming back to the present and his wonderful relationship with Ellie, 'all good things must come to an end.'

'Friends again then?' It seemed important to her.

'Sure.'

'You married?' she enquired.

'No. But I am seriously involved with someone.' He looked towards her friends. 'A regular boyfriend?'

'No,' she said, 'he's just a bloke I met at the Palais the other week. We've been out a few times. I don't know if it'll come to anything.'

'You still go to the Palais then?'

'Occasionally. I feel a bit past it among all those teenagers but you've got to make the effort if you want to meet someone new. That's the worst of splitting up with someone – you're back to square one. You've got to go out looking for someone all over again.'

'You don't fancy the single life as a permanent thing, then?' he commented chattily.

'No fear. Being on my own isn't for me.'

'I hope you find someone nice soon then.'

'Thanks. I hope things work out for you too, Ray. I really do.' Maria rummaged in her handbag, took out a stubby pencil and scribbled a number on an empty cigarette packet that was lying on the bar. 'There's a communal phone at the bedsit house where I live so if you're ever at a loose end and you fancy some company, just give me a bell and we'll get together for a chat about old times.'

He took the packet and put it in his pocket out of courtesy.

He had no intention of contacting her. There was no point. She was his past. Ellie was his present and future.

'I'd better get back,' she said, glancing towards her friends. 'Or my date might take umbrage and I'll have to buy my own drinks for the rest of the evening. I can't have that.'

'Oh, Maria,' he admonished.

'Just telling it like it is,' she grinned. 'Ta-ta for now.'

'Ta-ta.' Watching her slink across the bar to join her friends, hips swinging, high-heeled shoes showing off her shapely legs, he remembered how keen on her he'd once been.

Alone again, thoughts of his dear Ellie filled his mind, the meeting with Maria already forgotten.

There were many clandestine meetings for Ellie and Ray over the next few months. Ellie felt as though she were living a double life, and often wondered how she managed to function normally with so much emotional energy flowing through her system. But positively revitalised, wrapped in a rosy glow, she was warm and generous towards her fellow kind collectively. Driven by a massive injection of vitality, she was on top of her work whilst still finding time to spend with Donna.

To the world she was an industrious working mother, totally devoted to her daughter and her business. But when the day's work was done and her daughter asleep in bed, she was a passionate woman, adoring, and adored by her lover, who spared her reputation by not staying the night.

Ray's business went from strength to strength following the Kent job. He was kept busy with a steady flow of orders for new gates and restoration work, which meant the market was no longer essential to his livelihood. But he decided to continue with it, for the time being anyway, until the other side of the business was more firmly established. This gave him and Ellie the opportunity to see each other in public without arousing suspicion. What could be more natural than a couple of market pals having a chat during the working day?

Sometimes they were even bolder and 'just happened' to

meet in Shepherd's Bush when Ellie was out shopping with Donna, and they would go to the coffee bar for a chat. Ray continued to strengthen his bond with Donna; usually made a point of getting to Ellie's in the evening in time to read her a bedtime story.

It was Donna's growing articulateness that made Ellie realise that their secret wouldn't be safe for much longer . . ..

'Who's this Uncle Ray Donna keeps going on about?' Mary enquired one Saturday in the early summer when Ellie got back from the market. Mother and daughter were having a sociable cup of tea at the kitchen table; Donna was outside in the back garden 'helping' her grandfather to weed the flowerbeds.

Ellie's heart palpitated horribly. 'What's she been saying?' She tried to appear normal.

'Oh, her Uncle Ray plays horsey with her and reads her stories,' Mary said. 'It's Uncle Ray this, Uncle Ray that.'

'She means Ray Brent,' Ellie blurted out, desperately searching her mind for some plausible explanation as to how Ray had got on to such pally terms with Donna, because she wasn't ready to go public about him yet.

'*Ray Brent!*'

'There's no need to look quite so shocked,' admonished Ellie as her mother stared at her in astonishment. 'We are sort of workmates, after all.'

'Yes, but—'

'He pops in sometimes, if he's passing, for a chat about the market,' she cut in swiftly. 'And he and Donna seem to have taken a shine to each other.'

'Ray Brent,' Mary said again, in a furtive whisper as though merely uttering his name carried some kind of shame. 'Ray Brent comes to your house?'

Ellie was deeply offended on Ray's behalf. 'Yes, and why shouldn't he?' She was so fiercely protective, she almost let the cat out of the bag in her eagerness to defend him.

'Well, no reason, I suppose,' Mary replied, her tone indicating the opposite.

'None at all,' Ellie stated. 'Ray's a nice bloke. He's settled in at the market now and people have accepted him. He's welcome at my house any time he cares to call.'

'I see.'

Giving her mother a shrewd look, Ellie said, 'Don't panic. Donna and I are quite safe; you won't come round one day to find that he's done us in.'

Mary gave her daughter a sharp look, then swiftly changed the subject. Ellie guessed that she suspected something. But although Mary was the sort to speak her mind, she was also wise and sensitive and had obviously decided to wait until Ellie was ready to confide in her. Having always had a close mother-daughter relationship, Ellie felt bad about keeping something of such importance from Mary, and lying to her into the bargain. This was why she decided that the situation couldn't continue as it was.

'We can't go on with all this secrecy,' Ellie told Ray later that evening when they were ensconced on her sofa, she having told him about the conversation with her mother.

'I quite agree,' he admitted.

'So it has to stop right now,' she continued. 'Time to bring things out into the open.'

'Hear, hear!' he heartily agreed.

'I can't wait to have you accepted as my other half.' Having made the decision her enthusiasm was growing, despite the problems she knew she must face.

'You won't get any arguments from me about that,' Ray told her. 'You can tell who you like as far as I'm concerned. I wanted to be straight about it from the start. I've only kept quiet because you preferred it that way.'

'Only because I couldn't face all the trouble. I didn't want to spoil things,' Ellie confessed. 'There's bound to be an explosion of general disapproval because of Tom. But we can't keep our relationship hidden now that Donna's getting so chatty.'

'No.'

'I'd rather have the family hear it from me than have them start to speculate or hear gossip from the neighbours,' she went on to say. 'Even apart from Donna getting to be such a chatterbox, now that the evenings are light and people see you come to the house, there's bound to be talk. We've been so wrapped up in each other, we probably haven't been as careful as we might have been.'

'Once you've told your family, I'll tell my father,' he said. 'Or rather, I'll make it official. He and I carefully avoid the subject but he knows what's going on.'

She sighed. 'I love you so much, Ray, I don't want anything to wreck it.'

'It's up to us not to let that happen.' He slipped his arm around her.

'It won't be so simple—'

'I know that,' he cut in. 'But what we have is strong enough to withstand anything, in my opinion.' He paused thoughtfully. 'Anyway, we're not committing a crime.'

'I'm committing adultery, though,' she pointed out.

'Yes, but under justifiable circumstances.'

'I don't know if other people will see it that way.'

'The ones we care about will.' He paused before adding, 'Eventually.'

'You're right.'

Ray pondered the situation for a moment. 'I've had an idea.' He sounded excited.

'Ooh, what is it?' she said, picking up on his mood.

'Before we face the firing line, how about a day out tomorrow?' he suggested. 'A day at the seaside, the three of us.'

'Because you think this will be our last chance of happiness?' she suggested lightly.

'No,' he corrected. 'Because the weather's lovely and I

think it will do us all good and I want us to celebrate the fact that I've got another big job.'

'You have?' She was delighted for him.

'Another big house,' he said.

'In the country?'

'No, this one's in Kensington, and it isn't gates,' he explained. 'They want metal banisters and a gallery rail in a fancy pattern.'

'Wow! You're getting on in leaps and bounds,' Ellie beamed.

'Things are pretty good on the work front,' he confirmed. 'But, anyway, what about this day out?'

'I'm all for it,' she enthused. 'It's rather short notice, though. We haven't made arrangements.'

'No preparation necessary,' he told her breezily. 'We just get into my car and go. No picnic needed because we'll eat out. All I require is the company of you and Donna.'

'Where shall we go?'

'Brighton's about the nearest,' he said. 'We don't want to go too far as it's only a day trip. If we get away early we'll have plenty of time there.'

'Suits me.' She frowned suddenly. 'I'm supposed to be going to Mum and Dad's for lunch tomorrow, though. I usually go there on Sundays.'

'It won't hurt to miss it for once, will it?'

'No, of course not. But I was going to break the big news then, because Ann and Doug will be there,' Ellie explained. 'The idea being to get it over in one go, except for Tom's mum. I was planning on going to see her straight afterwards, so that they all get to know at more or less the same time.'

'You can do it next Sunday,' Ray suggested. 'Another week isn't going to make much difference.'

'Mm.' She pondered for a moment. 'I'll have to let Mum know I won't be going there for lunch tomorrow, though.' She bit her lip. 'Trouble is, they're not on the phone and they won't be up when we leave in the morning. If I go round there now, they'll want to know all about it.'

'We'll put a note through their letter box on the way out tomorrow morning, just saying you've gone out for the day,' he suggested eagerly. 'You can give them the details afterwards.'

'Brilliant,' she praised him. 'We'll have this day out, then face up to what must be done.'

'That's the spirit,' he said, kissing her.

Brighton seafront was crowded, sunny and sparkling with gaiety. Day-trippers were out in force with their saucy hats and determination to have a good time, the pebbly beach a sea of deck chairs. At almost three years old, Donna was just the right age for a day out like this and she entered into the spirit with gusto.

When they took her for a paddle in the sea, she squealed at the icy water on her toes but begged for more. She shrieked with a mixture of fear and pleasure on the rides in the funfair, and giggled rather uncertainly at the distorted image of herself in the House of Mirrors. They ate fish and chips and ice-cream cornets in the sunshine, watching fishermen at the end of the pier.

Later they took a respite from the boisterous masses to wander through the historical squares and crescents of which the town was so proud. Ray was full of admiration for the beautiful iron-work so ubiquitous on the balconies and railings of Brighton's old houses, their walls of cream and pale yellow evoking the seaside town image perfectly.

Back to noisier parts, a visit to one of the town's rock shops was essential to choose something to take home for each member of the family.

It was down-to-earth enjoyment but the day was tinged with magic for Ellie; she knew that the memory of it would be ingrained in her mind. Not every man would want to spend a day out with somebody else's demanding three-year-old but Ray appeared to enjoy every moment.

By the time they got back to Ellie's it was late and Donna

was already asleep. Ray carried her inside and Ellie managed to put her to bed without her waking up.

When they were alone at last, Ellie said, 'I've had the most wonderful day, Ray. Thank you so very much.'

'Thank *you*.'

'Tomorrow I'll have to tell a fib,' she confessed with a wry look. 'Mum's bound to ask who I went out for the day with as I didn't mention that in the note. If I tell her it was you, the secret's out before I'm ready.'

'So what will you say?'

'I'll just tell her it was a friend from the market,' she decided. 'I'll tell her the truth when the rest comes out, which is only a week away, thank God. I hate all this deceit.'

'Might she guess it was me?' Ray suggested. 'Given what Donna's been saying?'

'Maybe she will,' Ellie speculated. 'But she won't come right out and say so because she knows that I'll tell her about it in my own good time.'

'So the secret's safe until you're ready?'

'That's right,' she confirmed. 'Then next Sunday, over lunch, I'll make the announcement and there'll be no more need for secrecy or lies. What a relief it will be.'

'I hope you won't go off me when our relationship's out in the open,' he teased her.

'Why on earth would I do that?'

'Some people get a thrill from the illicit, don't they?' he remarked playfully. 'When everybody knows and the shock has died away, you might find it a bit too ordinary.'

'No chance of that,' she assured him. 'I'll get a thrill from having you around more.'

'I hope so.'

'You never know, the following Sunday you might be invited to lunch with the family,' she suggested hopefully.

'Ooh, I think that might take a little more time,' Ray said with a sage shake of his head.

'Being realistic, so do I,' she agreed.

'But we'll get there, don't worry.' He was in a very buoyant mood.

'Next Sunday is the first step towards it, anyway,' Ellie said in a positive manner.

'And meanwhile, there's something more immediate that needs attention,' he said, taking her in his arms.

'Mm,' she murmured happily.

As it happened Ellie's announcement had to be postponed on account of an infectious tummy bug that attacked her mother a few days later and subsequently made its miserable way through the entire family. Donna and Matthew had particularly nasty bouts and were poorly for almost a week. So, what with nursing the sick and coping with her own symptoms, Ellie's secret remained intact.

By the time everyone had recovered and normality was restored, a month had passed. And Ellie had something even more dramatic to tell her family then.

Chapter Thirteen

The Sunday morning shift at the Chad Street corner shop was coming to an end and Pat was using the time until one o'clock to do a spot of shelf-filling. She opened from ten o'clock until one on Sundays and never closed a moment before time because there was usually a last-minute rush.

Opening on a Sunday morning was a tradition at this shop. As it was for such a short time, Pat managed on her own to save paying overtime rates to her assistant. It was all small trade anyway, and most of the customers were regulars who didn't mind waiting to be served if she was busy. They were the sort with a tendency to linger for a chat too. While this wasn't something Pat always encouraged during the week, it was a lifeline to her on a Sunday, which was the loneliest day of the week.

She had an open invitation for Sunday lunch at the Scotts' but she didn't take it up too often for fear she might visit more than she was welcome, and not get invited at all. Ellie often called in with Donna on a Sunday afternoon. And, of course, there were the times when she and Ellie drove out to Surrey to see Tom. But, without the normal shop routine to supply her with a constant stream of company, a feeling of isolation always hovered.

Tom. Poor Tom. Tears burned at the back of her eyes at the thought of happier times and the misery of knowing that they could never return. She'd sunk into a mood of deep self-pity when the tinkle of the shop bell recalled her to the present.

'Thank Gawd I've caught you,' burst out one of Pat's regulars, a stout, middle-aged woman in a wrapover apron and carpet slippers, her hair worn boldly in curlers without even a headscarf to conceal them. 'I've only just realised that I'm out of Oxos and I'd have a riot on my hands if I were to serve up the gravy for Sunday dinner without a couple of those in it.'

Pat took a packet of Oxos off the shelf and put them on the counter. 'Anything else, Mrs Green?' she asked.

The woman cast an eye around the shop. 'Yeah, I'd better take some biscuits while I'm here – ginger nuts and digestives will do,' she told her. 'You've never seen biscuits disappear as fast as they do in our house at the weekends. They're a right crowd of gannets.'

'I can imagine.' The Greens were a family of five children, all young adults now. Pat had known them for years.

'Anyway, how are you keeping?' enquired Mrs Green, handing Pat a shilling piece.

'I'm all right, thanks. It's a case of having to be, isn't it?'

The other woman gave a wise shake of the head. 'You've hit the nail on the head there,' she sighed. 'These things are sent to try us, so they say.'

Pat nodded and handed her her change.

Putting her purchases into the large pocket of her apron, the woman said chattily, 'How is Tom now?'

'About the same.'

'Still, it'll be a comfort to you to know that he's in the best place, I expect,' Mrs Green said in a kindly tone.

'It does help.'

'His wife is looking a lot better now, isn't she?' remarked Mrs Green. 'I saw her going into her mother's house the other day and she looked full of beans.'

Pat never actually gave Ellie's health or appearance a thought but said, 'Yes, she's much better now.'

'She looked very thin and drawn for a long time after the accident – and understandably so,' Mrs Green continued. 'It must have been very hard for her.'

'I'm sure it was,' agreed Pat in a perfunctory manner.

'Still, I suppose she couldn't have stayed in the doldrums for ever,' the other woman went on, 'not with a little one to bring up.'

'No.'

'A lovely little granddaughter you've got. She's the image of her mother with all that gorgeous red hair.' The customer sat down on a chair Pat kept by the counter, looking set for a lengthy discourse. 'Do you see much of her?'

'Oh, yes,' Pat told her proudly. 'Ellie brings her to see me regularly, and I look after her every Wednesday afternoon when the shop's closed. It gives Ellie a chance to work, and I enjoy having Donna to myself.'

'Aah, that's nice.' Mrs Green smiled. 'And how does the little girl get on with her mother's new man?' She studied Pat's reaction with interest.

'New man?' Pat looked blank.

'Oh dear,' mumbled the other woman, rising as though to leave but remaining where she was and looking at Pat with feigned regret. 'I hope I haven't said anything out of turn.'

'What are you actually implying?' demanded Pat sharply.

'Forget it,' replied Mrs Green. 'It's none of my business anyway.'

'You're right, it isn't,' snapped Pat, her cheeks turning scarlet. 'But as you seem to be making some sort of insinuation, you might as well finish what you've started.'

The woman shrugged. 'OK. They say your daughter-in-law has got herself a new bloke,' she informed her. 'I'm surprised you don't know about it, as you're so friendly with her.'

'I think you must be mistaken,' said Pat, the colour now draining from her face.

'There's no mistake,' Mrs Green declared with authority. 'My sister's friend lives in the same street as your Tom's wife. It's common knowledge around there that she's seeing someone. They see him going in and out on a regular basis.'

'Probably a tradesman.'

'No, he's definitely a boyfriend, apparently. She's been spotted seeing him off at the door, and it isn't how you'd say goodbye to the gas man,' Mrs Green said, enjoying herself enormously. 'Not that anyone blames her for it. She's got too many years ahead of her to be on her own.'

'You'll be telling me next you know the name of this man,' said Pat artfully.

'I do, as it happens.' This was the bit the woman had really been looking forward to; Pat Hall was going to be completely floored. 'It's Ray Brent. You know, him who was in prison for murder a few years back.'

Pat flinched as though she'd been physically slapped. 'I don't believe you,' she told her. 'Ellie wouldn't do a thing like that.'

'She's only human,' Mrs Green pointed out. 'And Ray Brent is a very good-looking bloke.'

'Ellie and another man . . .' muttered Pat, finally having to accept the truth.

'Me and my big gob,' said the customer, clamping her hand to her mouth in a convincing show of remorse. 'I should have kept it shut.'

'Don't worry about it.' Too late to hide the fact that she was upset but Pat was damned if she'd let the other woman see the extent of her humiliation. 'I'm glad you've told me.'

'You'd have got to know sooner or later anyway, I suppose. I just hope I haven't upset you too much by blurting it out like that.' Mrs Green was having a wonderful time watching Pat squirm. The stuck-up cow needed taking down a peg or two.

'I'll be all right.' All Pat wanted was to get away from the woman's blatant gloating. 'But it's time for me to shut up shop now. My dinner is cooking on a low light upstairs in the flat.'

'Yeah. I must go, an' all,' Mrs Green said. 'Our dinner will be burned to a cinder if I don't get back to see to it, as no one else in the house will think to turn things down, the lazy buggers.' She walked across the shop and turned at the door. 'Ta-ta, dear.'

'Ta-ta,' replied Pat, following her to the door, turning the open sign to closed and locking the door after her. She was so distressed, she didn't even stop to cash up, but fled upstairs to her flat and sat in the armchair shaking.

Enfeebled by the shock, the thought of Ellie betraying Tom making her feel physically sick, she sat there for a long time, trembling and trying to still her pounding heart. Eventually, she got up and turned everything off in the kitchen because she had lost her appetite. Still feeling weak and shaky, she went downstairs to the shop to do the cashing up.

Anger was beginning to take over, making her feel strong. Her earlier mood of sadness and self-pity had dissolved completely. She was driven by fury now, almost enjoying the new energy it gave her and the vicious thoughts she now felt entitled to have about her rival for her son's affections.

As she went back upstairs with the shop takings, she felt positively fearless.

Lunch was over at the Scotts' and they were all sitting around the table chatting. It was a fine day and the children were playing outside in the back garden.

Ellie's palms were damp with nervous perspiration, her blood pounding in her ears. She'd been waiting with dread for this stage in the proceedings.

'Listen up, everybody,' she said during a suitable lull in the conversation. 'While we're all here together, I've got something to tell you.'

'Let me guess,' joked Doug, grinning. 'You've just made your first million.'

'I'm trying to be serious, Doug,' she admonished.

'Sorry, sis.' He didn't look particularly contrite because the general mood was light-hearted. 'Carry on.'

She cleared her throat nervously. 'The fact is,' she began through dry lips, 'these past few months I've been seeing someone, someone who has become very special to me.'

There was a surprised silence.

'You kept that dark,' said Ann eventually.

'I'll say you did,' agreed Doug.

'I could hardly shout it from the rooftops as I'm married to Tom, could I?' Ellie pointed out. 'But keeping it from you all has been a terrible strain. I've hated being secretive.'

'You're not obliged to report every detail of your private life to us,' Doug said kindly.

'I know. But we're not the sort of family to have secrets from each other, are we? Anyway, now that me and . . . this person are really serious about each other, I want you all to know about it.' She paused, looking grave. 'I'm hoping you'll be pleased for me.'

Her mother didn't say a word and her face was expressionless because, Ellie guessed, she knew exactly to whom her daughter was referring.

But her father said, 'Come on then, tell us who he is.'

Ellie braced herself for the explosion she knew would come. 'It's Ray Brent.'

Silence rocked the room.

'Oh, Ellie,' said her father in a tone of fierce rebuke. 'I thought you'd have more sense. We warned you about getting mixed up with him when you first started at the market.'

'I know you did, Dad.' Ellie felt his disapproval like a physical pain. 'But you can't choose who you fall in love with, can you?'

'Love?' scorned Bob. 'How can you talk about love? You haven't known the man five minutes.'

'I've known him for more than six months,' she corrected. 'Quite long enough to know how I feel.'

'The man killed someone, Ellie,' he said, his voice rising with anxiety.

'He did not,' denied Ellie. 'He didn't kill Keith Wilkes any more than I did.'

'You can't be sure of that.' Her father was shouting now. 'He's hardly going to admit to something like that, is he?'

'I think he would if he'd done it,' she insisted. 'He's that sort of a bloke. But that's irrelevant anyway because I love him and he loves me. I know that I can never marry him but I want us to have a future together.'

'Ray Brent, though,' mumbled her father almost to himself. 'All right, I accept the fact that it's only natural you would find someone else, given the circumstances with poor Tom, and I don't blame you for that. But surely you could have chosen someone a bit less dodgy?'

She was angry now, absolutely furious. 'He isn't dodgy,' she yelled. 'He's one of the straightest and most gentle men I've ever met. He's told me he didn't kill that man and I believe him.'

'You're too gullible.'

'Calm down, Bob,' interrupted Mary. 'We don't know the truth about that. Anyway, Ellie has a right to live her own life.'

'Exactly.' Ellie's cheeks were bright, her lips dry and cracked. 'I don't need your blessing about this. I'm old enough to form my own opinions and make my own decisions. But because I'm part of a family, I was hoping that you'd find it in your hearts to make him feel a part of it too, as he's the man I've chosen to share my life with. If you don't feel able to do this, that's up to you. But it won't stop me seeing him. He's going to be a part of my life from now on – mine and Donna's, whatever your feelings are about him.'

'All right, I accept that it's none of my business since you're a grown woman,' conceded Bob, 'but you're still my daughter and naturally I'm concerned when you take up with someone who's been in prison for murder. I know he says he didn't do it, and perhaps he didn't, but we can't be sure of that, can we?'

She told him she was absolutely certain about that, and was about to impart the rest of her news when there was an intervention from Doug, who was sitting beside her.

'Try to understand, Dad, the man's done his time,' he said reasonably. 'Ellie has chosen him and that's good enough for me.' He fixed his gaze on his sister. 'I can't speak for Ann but as far as I'm concerned, Ray Brent is welcome to come to our house any time you want to bring him.'

'That goes for me too,' added Ann.

Ellie smiled at them gratefully. Doug and Ann had always had a more open-minded outlook than Bob. 'Thanks to you both,' she said. 'That means a lot to me.'

Her father's conscience must have been nudged by Doug's reasonableness because he began to look a little sheepish. 'I haven't said he won't be made to feel welcome here,' he mumbled.

'I got the impression he wouldn't exactly be greeted with open arms,' returned Ellie.

'What do you expect when you drop a bombshell like that on us?' he defended. 'People say all sorts of things when they're in shock. But maybe I was a bit too hasty.'

'Do you think I'd bring him here, knowing your attitude?' Ellie challenged.

'Your dad's just concerned for you,' Mary intervened. 'Anyway, when have we ever not made a friend of yours feel welcome in this house?'

'Never,' Ellie was forced to admit, 'but you've never been so much against anyone before.'

Mary gave her daughter a sharp look. 'Look at it from our point of view,' she appealed to her, spreading her hands. 'We don't know Ray. We only have what we've heard to go by. You can't blame us for having doubts. But if he's the one you want, you'll have our full support.'

'Course you will,' added her father.

Ellie softened towards them. They weren't vindictive, just a bit overprotective of their offspring. 'You'll like him once you get to know him,' she said.

'We'll certainly do our best,' announced Mary, getting to her feet with a purposeful air. 'So, now that that's settled we'd better start clearing away or it'll be teatime and we'll still have the dinner things on the table.'

Ellie made an interjection. 'Er . . . I think you'd better sit down again for a minute, Mum,' she said, making a face, 'because I haven't quite finished. There's something else . . .'

Mary sat down slowly, looking almost frightened.

They all stared at Ellie with puzzled expectation. She took a deep breath and exhaled slowly. 'I'm pregnant. I'm having Ray's baby.

'Well, say something, somebody, for goodness' sake,' Ellie urged them as a tense silence drew tight around them. 'Don't just sit there looking at me.'

'Does he know?' asked Mary weakly.

'Yes, he knows. I found out for sure this week and told him right away. He's absolutely delighted,' Ellie said. 'He wants kids and I never wanted Donna to be an only child.'

'You've really fallen into a trap now, haven't you?' Bob blurted out in the heat of the moment. 'I thought you'd have had more sense than to get yourself knocked up.'

'I don't see it as a trap because it's what I want,' she put him right. 'I admit we didn't plan to have a baby quite this soon but it's happened and I'm thrilled to bits. We can't get married, of course, but we'll be like a proper family in every other respect. We'll move in together and bring the two children up.'

'You'll be the talk of the neighbourhood,' her father warned her, shaking his head.

'I realise that,' she said. 'But it'll be a five-minute wonder. People will soon get bored with the subject.' She paused, looking at her parents. 'I'm sorry that you're going to be embarrassed but gossip doesn't worry me.'

Before they had a chance to respond, Doug said, 'You really are pleased about this baby, are you, Ellie?'

'Very.'

'In that case, congratulations,' he smiled, giving her a hug.

'Yeah, congratulations, Ellie,' added Ann. 'I'm really thrilled for you.'

'Well,' followed Mary, 'I'd be lying if I said that this is what I was hoping for, for you, but as you're so happy about it, then so am I.' She turned to her husband. 'We're going to have another grandchild, Bob, and that has to be good news.'

Bob was more circumspect. 'As long as he stands by you and doesn't bugger off as soon as he realises how much it's going to cost him,' he said gloomily.

'No worries there,' Ellie told him with confidence.

'Stop putting the mockers on everything, for goodness' sake, Bob,' his wife admonished.

'Just being cautious.'

'You're taking it too far,' she warned. 'Our support is what Ellie needs now.'

The conversation was interrupted by a knock at the front door. Mary went to answer it and the others made a start on the clearing up. Ellie and Ann began stacking the plates, while Doug and Bob went to the kitchen carrying the vegetable dishes.

'Well, you've certainly spiced things up around here,' grinned Ann.

'Not half,' Ellie agreed. 'It's a relief to have it out in the open at last, though.'

'Your dad will soon get used to the idea,' encouraged Ann. 'I suppose it must have been a bit of a shock for him.'

'Once he gets to know Ray, he'll be fine, I'm sure, because Ray is a very difficult man to dislike,' Ellie said. 'I guessed Dad would be more difficult than Mum about it initially. Mum adapts to situations quickly.'

'I can't believe that it's all been going on and I didn't have a clue,' Ann said.

'Many times I've almost blurted it out to you, I've been that happy,' Ellie confessed. 'And that's something I never thought I'd be able to say again, after the accident.'

'Terrific news about the baby too,' Ann enthused. 'Before the accident you always used to say you wanted more than one child.' She scraped a plate and put it on top of a pile of others.

'Now that I've got Ray, I realise just how bleak my life has been these last few years,' Ellie told her.

'I'm sure you must do.'

Ellie was about to go to the kitchen with some crockery when her mother-in-law charged into the room, followed by Mary, looking extremely harassed.

'I tried to prevent her coming in while she's in this mood,' Mary explained, 'but there's no stopping her.'

Pat marched up to Ellie, who swiftly put the crockery down on the table for fear of dropping it. 'You slut,' Pat said through clenched teeth. 'You dirty little slut.'

The colour drained from Ellie's face and she shook from head to toe. 'Oh dear,' she muttered, biting her lip nervously. 'I take it you've heard.'

'I'll say I've heard,' Pat ranted, her voice quivering with rage. 'And I bet I'm the last one in the neighbourhood to find out.'

'No—' began Ellie.

'I've just had the humiliating experience of being told by one of my customers that my son's wife has been sleeping with some jailbird,' Pat raged on. 'While my poor son is shut away from the world in some institution that she put him in to get rid of him because she couldn't be bothered with him once he got sick.'

'Don't you dare say such things,' objected Mary.

'You watch your mouth,' added Bob, who had come back into the room with Doug to find out what all the noise was about.

But Pat was incandescent with rage and out of control, her neck and face covered with plum-coloured blotches. 'The customer had a whale of a time telling me, knowing I hadn't a clue about what's been going on.'

'I was going to tell you,' explained Ellie, 'once I'd told Mum and Dad.'

'Liar!' accused Pat, her voice rising to a shriek.

'Ellie isn't lying, Pat,' intervened Mary hotly. 'It's a coincidence your turning up now because she's only just finished telling us. We had no idea until a few minutes ago.'

'I might have known you'd defend her,' was Pat's harsh reaction.

'I'll defend any member of my family against anyone to the ends of the earth,' Mary admitted frankly. 'But that doesn't alter the fact that what Ellie says is true.'

'Be that as it may,' Pat went on in a shrill voice, 'I didn't come here to quibble about that.'

'What did you come here for then?' Bob wanted to know. 'Other than to make trouble?'

'I came here to tell your precious daughter what I *really* think of her.'

'That's enough, Pat.' Mary took the other woman's arm in a restraining gesture. 'I can understand your being upset but throwing insults at Ellie isn't the way to solve anything.'

'Course it isn't,' agreed Bob, uniting with his daughter against an outsider, despite his own concerns. 'Don't you dare come barging in here, slinging abuse at our daughter. If you're going to carry on like this you can leave – get out.' His voice rose. 'Go on, clear off.'

Ellie raised her hands in a halting gesture. 'No, Dad, let her have her say.'

'But—'

'Please, Dad,' she entreated. 'I want to hear everything she has to say.'

'I'll go and make sure the kids are all right,' said Ann diplomatically.

Ellie nodded gratefully.

Ann departed to the garden. Doug didn't follow. He stayed where he was, standing beside his father just inside the door to the hall.

'Before you go on, Pat,' began Ellie. 'I really am *very sorry* you had to hear about Ray and me from someone else. The last thing I wanted was for you to be hurt in that way.'

'Don't make me laugh.' Pat's voice was distorted with bitterness. 'You don't care who you hurt as long as you're all right.'

'That just isn't true,' denied Ellie's mother.

'Yes it is,' insisted Pat, fixing her malicious gaze on Ellie.

'You left me in the lurch at the shop when you wanted to go into business for yourself, without a thought as to how I would get on. And now you've been flaunting yourself in front of the whole neighbourhood with another man, and you a married woman. You should be hanging your head in shame, my girl, not standing there as though you've got something to be proud of.'

'She hasn't been flaunting herself,' Bob put in. 'If she had been, we'd have got to hear about it and we knew nothing until just now. She's been very discreet.'

'Anyway, Pat,' said Mary, 'you must have considered the possibility of her meeting someone else at some point.'

'Of course I haven't,' snapped Pat. 'Why would I when she's married to my son, the mother of my grandchild?'

'I didn't plan to fall in love,' Ellie tried to explain with a sad shake of her head. 'It was as much a surprise to me at the time as it is to all of you now.'

'Sentimental rubbish,' scorned Pat. 'There's only one man you're entitled to love and that's your husband.'

'And I do still have strong feelings for Tom . . . love of a kind,' said Ellie soberly. 'But I'm never going to be able to be a wife to him again, am I?'

'And whose fault is that?' Pat shouted, angry tears now running down her cheeks.

Ellie froze. She knew exactly what Pat was getting at. 'The car crash was an accident,' she told her.

'It was your fault, though,' was Pat's venomous reply. 'My son would be leading a normal life today if it wasn't for you and your careless driving.'

'Bloody cheek!' retorted Bob.

'Stay out of it, please, Dad.' Ellie turned to Pat. 'You're blaming me for the accident?'

'That's right.' She was adamant. 'You should have seen the other car and avoided it.'

'The other driver was to blame and it's official!' roared Bob, almost beside himself now.

'I don't care what the official verdict was,' continued Pat, her voice ragged with emotion, eyes still brimming with tears. 'If Ellie hadn't been driving the car my son would be living a normal life today.'

'Right, that's it,' Bob exploded. 'I'm not having my daughter insulted in my own house.'

'Shut up, Dad, please.' Ellie's face was grey, her legs about to buckle in the aftermath of hearing the accusation she had aimed at herself so many times now uttered by someone else.

'All right,' said Bob, raising his hands in defeat.

'You've blamed me all along, haven't you?' Ellie met Pat's eyes in a steady gaze.

'Yes, that's right,' Pat admitted bitterly.

'I didn't want to drive the car that day, you know,' Ellie informed her.

'And she only did it because Tom bullied her into it,' said Doug, entering into the discussion. 'He forced her to do it like he forced her to do everything else.'

A shocked silence fell on the room, seeming to vibrate with intensity.

'I see,' said Pat cynically, at last. 'So now that it suits you, you're all going to turn against Tom. It's all too easy to kick a man when he's down and can't defend himself.' She glared at Doug. 'I thought you were supposed to be his best friend, yet all you can do is sling mud at him.'

'Don't you think my sister has been through enough since the accident, without you coming here making false accusations?' uttered Doug without replying to her criticism of him. 'Have you been too busy feeling sorry for yourself that you've never stopped to think what it's been like for her?'

'She's been having a high old time, from what I've heard,' declared Pat. Her eyes were dry now, her mouth set in a harsh line.

'Well, in that case you've been misinformed,' Doug pointed out sharply. 'She's not made a fuss about it but we all know how much she's suffered. And as for your snide remark about

Ellie having Tom put away because she couldn't be bothered with him – well, I can tell you that it broke her heart to do it but she sent him to Greenlands because she knew he would have a better quality of life. She was thinking of him, not herself.'

'Huh!'

'Count yourself lucky she didn't leave him in the hands of the NHS as a long-stay patient in St John's where they don't have the means to give the patients special attention,' he went on. 'Every penny of that insurance money has been put away for Tom, yet Ellie was perfectly entitled to use some of it to help her bring up his daughter. But she didn't do that; she went out working to earn the money to keep herself and Donna.'

Pat didn't seem to have a reply to this argument.

'Surely she's entitled to make a life for herself,' Doug carried on. 'Did you expect her to stay on her own and become a self-pitying old crone like you?'

'Doug,' admonished Ellie.

'That's enough, Doug,' added his mother.

'All right, I'm sorry, I know I've been rude,' Doug apologised, looking at Pat.

'I'm amazed to hear you admit it,' was her answer to that.

'But I was rude with good reason,' he continued. 'You can't expect me to keep quiet when you're saying such terrible things about my sister.'

'I don't care what any of you think of me,' Pat responded. 'You can call me what you like and it won't touch me because I'm immune to pain, having lost my son as he was. My life ended on the day of the accident.'

'Well, it shouldn't have done,' Doug told her.

'And how do you suggest it could have been otherwise?'

'You should have had the courage to do what Ellie's done – accept that life has to go on and make the best of things.' His tone became softer because he wasn't naturally a malicious man. 'Look, I know how hard it must be for you to cope with what happened to Tom. We were all devastated by it. But being miserable about it isn't going to bring him back to how he was. We just have to be glad that he's happy and well looked after.'

Pat shrugged indifferently, her eyes dull, mouth downturned in disgust.

'I'm sorry you think so badly of me,' said Ellie, still smarting from Pat's accusations.

'No, you're not . . .'

'For heaven's sake give me some credit.' Ellie couldn't allow this vicious attack on her to continue unchallenged. 'I really am hurt that you think ill of me and I don't want to quarrel with you. But I've suspected all along that you blamed me for the accident, even though you didn't have the guts to come out and say so.'

'Oh, so I'm a coward now, am I?'

'I'm not saying that,' Ellie told her, 'but I will say that you kept quiet because it suited you.'

'Don't start accusing me of things just to take the attention off yourself.' Pat was defending herself by attack now. 'You're the one who's done wrong.'

'Now that I know your true feelings for me, at least I know where I stand,' Ellie told her.

'Yes,' was Pat's stiff response.

Ellie looked at her, wondering if she should say more and deciding that she must. 'And to put you fully in the picture,' she began, hesitating for a moment before getting to the point, 'I have to tell you that I'm having Ray's baby.'

Pat's thin face seemed to shrink as it drew tight in disapproval, her wrinkled lids closing over her small grey eyes for a moment. 'I suppose I shouldn't be surprised after what you've been getting up to these past few months,' she said in a tight voice. 'Now you're well and truly in the cart, aren't you? And it serves you right. I hope he leaves you in the lurch.'

'There's no chance of that. We are both delighted about the baby, as it happens,' Ellie informed her. 'He doesn't have any children and I always wanted more than one.'

Pat looked at Ellie with undisguised hatred. 'Well, I never want to set eyes on it.' She stalked across the room to the door, turning when she got there to have another stab at Ellie. 'And I never want to set eyes on you again either.'

'If that's the way you feel, then good riddance to you,' Bob told her.

'But, Pat—' began Ellie, her manner becoming conciliatory. Despite everything, her heart ached for this embittered woman. She knew she must be in a state of mental torture to have emitted such an outpouring of venom.

'Oh, and by the way,' interrupted Pat, focusing her gaze on Ellie. 'I'll be making my own way to Greenlands in future.'

'As you wish,' was Ellie's sad response.

Pat looked at her intently, her little eyes glinting suddenly with malice as she came up with yet another way to hurt Ellie. 'And you'll have to find another means of transport for your general use too, because the shop car will no longer be available to you. I want it back outside the shop first thing in the morning . . . cleaned and with a full tank of petrol.'

'Sure.' This was the least of Ellie's worries.

'Why, you mean-minded bitch!' exclaimed Bob.

'Leave it, Dad,' urged Ellie. 'The car doesn't matter.'

'As I've already told you, insults are like water off a duck's back to me because I'm beyond pain, Bob Scott,' said Pat.

'Because you're as hard as nails, more like,' he burst out.

'Oh, think what you damned well like,' was Pat's parting shot before she marched from the room, followed by Mary, who saw her off the premises in stony silence.

'You'll be better off without her in your life if that's her attitude, Ellie,' pronounced her father.

'You certainly will,' supported Doug.

Ellie nodded in agreement but her heart was like lead. The last thing she wanted was a rift with her husband's mother. And she couldn't believe that Pat wanted it either, not really. Ellie felt utterly wretched.

Chapter Fourteen

'Well?' enquired Ray when he arrived at Ellie's on the evening of the same day. 'Do I get an invitation to Sunday lunch with the family or what?'

She promptly burst into tears; something she wouldn't have allowed to happen if Donna hadn't been safely out of sight in bed.

His arms were immediately around her, strong, warm and reassuring. 'Shush,' he soothed. 'They'll come round to the idea; they need a bit of time, that's all.'

'It wasn't my family who were the problem.' Her voice was thick with tears but she was already struggling to compose herself. 'Not once they got over the shock, anyway.'

'Who then?'

'My mother-in-law,' she explained. 'She burst in and went bananas. She'd heard about us from one of her customers, apparently.'

'Oh dear.'

'You just wouldn't believe some of the things she said, Ray. It was awful.'

'Tell me about it,' he urged her gently.

So, cosily ensconced with him on the sofa, she gave him, more or less, a verbatim account.

'The wicked bitch!' he exploded, fired up and ready to take action. 'I'll soon sort her out. How dare she upset you like this? I've never seen you in such a state. I'll go round there and tell her a thing or two—'

'No, Ray,' interrupted Ellie. 'That will only make things worse.' She'd stopped crying now and felt more in control. 'The woman is hurting enough as it is.'

'*She's* hurting?'

'Yes, that's why she's being so horrid.'

He thought about this for a moment. 'Mm, maybe it is. But that still doesn't give her the right to do what she did.'

'Pat isn't all bad,' Ellie went on to tell him. 'She's just very unhappy and set in her ideas. She's had a hard time, what with her husband's sudden death and then having Tom's injuries to contend with.'

'Even so . . .'

'The problem is,' continued Ellie, 'she simply can't view Tom's situation with any other eye than that of his mother. It's understandable, I suppose, given that he's her only child and she's always idolised him.'

'You've still got a good word to say for her after what she's put you through today?' Ray was astounded.

'I'm no angel, make no mistake about that,' she was keen to point out. 'I hated her today for the things she said, and many times in the past I've wanted to throttle her. But there's always a reason for people to behave as they do.'

'I suppose there might be some truth in that,' he conceded.

'Anyway, I have so much more going for me than she has,' Ellie continued. 'I've got you and Donna, our new baby to look forward to, and a loving and supportive family. Pat has none of those things. We've all done what we can to ease her loneliness over the years but when it comes down to it she's on her own with no one to give her any close support.'

'Is it any wonder, if that's the way she treats people?' Ray shrugged.

'She does tend to alienate people with her abrasive manner, I must say,' Ellie had to admit. 'But it all comes down to the way she's feeling inside, in my opinion.'

'You mustn't let her get to you.'

'Too late. She already has,' she confessed. 'The thing that

upset me most was actually hearing her say that she blames me for the accident. Suspecting it is one thing; actually hearing it said is quite another.'

'She was just saying anything she could think of to hurt you,' he suggested.

'Not about that. She was doing plenty of mud-slinging about other things just to get back at me, but I think she meant what she said about the accident,' Ellie told him. 'I've blamed myself often enough so knowing that she blames me too really twisted the knife. It gave my thoughts on the subject credibility.'

'You've told me what happened that day and there's nothing you could have done to avoid the accident.' He gave her hand a comforting squeeze. 'The other driver jumped a red light, for goodness' sake.'

'I know. My common sense tells me you're right,' she said, 'but my heart keeps reminding me that Tom is in Greenlands while I'm having a normal and – just lately – a happy life.'

'Tragic for Tom – I wouldn't dream of saying otherwise. But at least he isn't suffering, is he?' Ray reminded her. 'You've told me that yourself.'

'He isn't having much of a life either,' she pointed out sadly. 'He's just surviving from day to day. Trapped in never-ending childhood.'

'Not your fault.' He was very firm.

'Maybe I could have avoided that car, somehow,' she pondered, almost to herself.

'I could murder that woman for putting such silly ideas into your head,' he said.

'They were already there, Ray,' she corrected.

'Reminded you of them, then,' he amended. 'You don't need all this hassle, especially in your condition. Pat is completely wrong, so put what she said out of your mind.'

His assurance was a comfort, but it didn't remove the nagging ache of compunction. Ellie knew nothing ever would. But enough had been said on the subject to Ray. It wasn't fair to burden him with it any more than she had already. She turned to look at him. 'Don't worry about me and my condition.' She smiled in the hope of lifting the atmosphere. 'I'm as strong as a horse.'

'You still need to look after yourself, though . . .'

'Enough about my awful day,' she halted him. 'Tell me how you got on. How did your dad take the news?'

'He's glad it's out in the open, I think,' he told her. 'He gave me his blessing anyway, even though he doesn't think this is the cleverest thing I've ever done.'

'So long as he's OK about it.'

'He's tickled pink about the baby, loves the idea of being a grandad,' Ray grinned. 'He's very fond of you too. Still thinks we're in for trouble, though. He's right if your mother-in-law is anything to go by.'

'As I've said before, the local gossip doesn't bother me,' Ellie told him. 'But a major bust-up with Pat does. We haven't always seen eye to eye about things but she's been a part of my life for as long as I can remember.'

'If she felt so strongly that you were to blame for the accident, why didn't she say anything before?' he wondered.

'I think it's because Donna and I are all the family she's got, now that Tom's out of the picture, so to speak. She didn't want to lose us so she kept shtoom about it,' Ellie explained. 'I suppose when she heard about you and me, she just couldn't take it so decided to cut all ties. Once she didn't have anything to lose, out it all came.'

'The blame wasn't so strong that she couldn't sweep it under the carpet for her own ends,' Ray pointed out.

'Exactly.'

'She sounds like a right nasty cow to me,' he said.

'She was today, and that's a fact.'

'You'll just have to try and put her out of your mind,' he advised.

'I can't do that, Ray.'

'No, I don't suppose you can,' he said sympathetically.

Turning her attention to a more practical matter, she said,

'One thing I must put a priority on is finding a cheapish car now that the shop car is no longer available to me. I can't run my business without something to shift the goods about in.'

'If you're stuck for cash I can help out.'

'It's kind of you to offer but I should be able to manage the deposit,' she told him. 'I should have got my own wheels long before this, but it seemed to please Pat to let me use hers so I went along with it.'

'She wanted to make sure you stayed grateful,' he suggested.

'Oh, yes, there's no doubt in my mind about that.' She gave him a smile. 'Thanks for offering, anyway.'

'No problem.' He seemed to be mulling something over. 'Look – I know a few people in the car trade. I'll make some enquiries, if you like – to save you shopping around.'

'That would be a great help. Thank you.'

'A pleasure,' he assured her. 'We're a team, you and I.'

'I hope it'll always be that way.'

'It will if I've got anything to do with it,' he said, holding her close. 'It'll take more than the disapproval of a bitter old woman to drive us apart.'

'Course it will,' she said, snuggling up to him. 'I'm not going to let it get me down.'

'That's the spirit.'

But the trauma of Pat's attack had taken its toll on Ellie's health and she didn't feel well. Her nerves were on edge, she felt sick and she had a terrible headache.

Alfie was still up when Ray got home.

'You don't look very happy,' the older man remarked from his armchair in front of the TV. 'Didn't the news of you and Ellie go down well with her folks?'

'It isn't that.' Ray told him about Pat. 'She sounds like a right old horror to me,' he said in conclusion. 'Left to my own devices, I'd go round to that shop of hers and give her a piece of my mind. But Ellie's dead set against it and I don't want to upset her any more than she is already.'

'It's probably best to let the dust settle, anyway,' Alfie opined. 'Pat Hall has a wicked tongue. But she isn't as bad as she seems. She'll come round.'

'You know her?'

'I did once, a long time ago.'

'I didn't know that.'

'You'd have no cause to know about friends I had before you were even born, would you?' Alfie pointed out. 'Pat was just a girl when I knew her.'

'She wouldn't have been a mouthy cow in those days, I suppose,' mumbled Ray aggressively.

'There's no need for that sort of talk,' admonished his father sternly. 'She doesn't deserve to be bad-mouthed by you, no matter what she's done.'

'You wouldn't be defending her if you'd seen the state Ellie was in tonight,' asserted Ray. 'That woman's really been having a go at her. She's even got the cheek to accuse Ellie of being to blame for the accident, would you believe?'

'She probably doesn't mean it,' suggested Alfie. 'It's just an outlet for all that anger and pain.'

'It doesn't do much for Ellie, though, does it?' said Ray. 'She looked really ill when I left there.'

'You won't help her by getting all steamed up,' his father advised him. 'You need to calm down and let things blow over.'

'How can I calm down, knowing that Ellie's so upset?'

'I don't know but you'll have to do it for her sake,' his father insisted. 'She needs a soothing influence, in her condition.'

'You're right,' conceded Ray, reminded of the pregnancy. 'I'll do my best.'

It was just turned midnight and Ann lay in bed, conscious of the nervous thud of her heart as she anticipated her husband's next move. He was restless, rolling this way and that; obviously thought she was asleep, which she had been until he'd woken her with his tossing and turning. Any minute now he would get out of bed, careful not to disturb her, as though he hadn't already, and make his lonely way to the kitchen for a lengthy smoking and tea-drinking session. His sleepless nights went to such a pattern, she knew every move he would make. She'd heard no evidence of a bad dream this time, probably because he hadn't yet slept.

He'd seemed more settled for a while after Matthew was born, taking an active part in the upbringing of his adored son. But he'd been troubled again just lately. She'd known he would have a bad night tonight after the trouble at his parents' place at lunchtime. He'd been very quiet and morose ever since.

Predictably, he got out of bed and she could hear him fumbling into his dressing gown and feeling his way across the room in the dark, trying not to disturb her. She lay there staring into the darkness, tension mounting. The fact that he excluded her still hurt and angered her but didn't lessen her concern for him. She loved him and wanted to help.

Unable to lie still any longer, she got up, put on her slippers and dressing gown, and went downstairs to the kitchen. Doug was standing by the worktop in their small, Formica-rich kitchen, waiting for the kettle to boil on the cooker.

'Sorry.' He turned as she entered the room, looking pale and haggard. 'I tried not to wake you.'

'It doesn't matter.'

He turned away from her towards the stove.

'It does matter that you're not sleeping again, though, Doug,' she added.

'I'll be all right, love,' he assured her, swinging round to look at her with that closed expression she had come to know so well. 'You go back to bed. I'll be up in a few minutes.'

'No you won't,' she disagreed. 'You'll be down here for hours; you always are when you have these bad nights.'

'I'll be up when I'm tired enough to go to sleep,' he said with an edge to his voice; he was standing near the cooker with his arms folded.

She sat down at the table with her fists on her chin. 'You can't go on like this, you know,' she warned him. 'Managing on so little sleep. You need to be alert for your job.'

'Leave it, Ann, please,' he said irritably. 'Go back to bed and forget about me.'

'What a ridiculous suggestion,' she snapped. 'How on earth can I sleep when I'm worried sick about you?'

'How many more times must I tell you, there's no need for you to worry about me?' he insisted.

'Anyone who's driving a heavy lorry all day needs a good night's sleep,' she pointed out. 'It's dangerous to be at the wheel when you're half asleep, which you must be during the day after you've had a bad night.'

'I'm one of these people who can get by with very little sleep,' was his dull reply. 'You ought to know that by now.'

'Getting by isn't enough in your line of work,' she stated categorically. 'You need to be on top form for the sake of other road users as well as yourself.'

'For Pete's sake, stop fussing.'

She brushed a tired hand over her furrowed brow. 'Don't you think it's time you told me what's behind all this?' she told him wearily. 'I am your wife – surely I have a right to know what it is that causes you such torment?'

'I don't know what you're talking about,' he bristled. 'I get insomnia from time to time, that's all.'

'And bad dreams,' she reminded him.

'All right, so I have the occasional bad dream,' he admitted with reluctance. 'So what? Disturbed sleep patterns are very common. Lots of people have them. It's just part of my make-up. You should be used to it after all this time.'

'I am used to it. I also know that something in particular is troubling you and it comes to the surface every so often, and gives you a hard time.'

'Rubbish.'

'You seem to get upset whenever anyone says a bad word about Ray Brent,' she went on. 'I know you have strong feelings about victimisation and so on, but what it is about him in particular?'

'Now you're just being stupid,' he accused, his voice rising angrily.

His overreaction confirmed her theory that Ray Brent struck a raw nerve in her husband for some reason. 'I'm not a fool, Doug,' she argued. 'It's obvious to me that that man affects you. What I want to know is why.'

He shut his eyes for a moment as though in pain. 'I'd feel the same about any ex-con who wasn't being allowed to forget his past. But some people at work know Ray and they say he's a really decent bloke. I don't like the way some people write him off as no good, that's all,' he explained, his voice quivering. 'He should be left alone to get on with his life in peace. What my sister was put through today just because she's involved with him is enough to make anyone angry. And as for that mother-in-law of hers – what right did she have to spoil everything for Ellie when she's found someone she can be happy with at last?'

'Pat would have behaved in exactly the same way whoever Ellie had taken up with. It's nothing to do with Ray having been in prison. She just can't cope with Ellie being with anyone except Tom.'

'Well, it's time she faced up to the fact that it's going to happen,' Doug declared grimly. 'What sort of a life is it for Ellie bringing up Donna on her own?'

'You don't have to convince me, Doug,' Ann said. 'I agree with you.'

'She finds someone she can be happy with and that woman tries to ruin everything,' he ranted on. 'It isn't only her, either. My parents were ready to do Ray down.'

'They were all right later on, though,' she pointed out.

'Only because I shamed them into it,' he said with an angry sigh. 'People are too keen to judge him.'

'Everything you say is true, Doug,' she said gently, slipping her arms around him. 'And I agree with you that it's wrong.

But you mustn't take it all on your own shoulders. It's not your place.'

Pulling away from her, he looked at her, his eyes bleak and haunted. 'You don't understand,' he blurted out.

It seemed to Ann as though he was reaching out to her, as though he was ready to confide. 'I want to understand, I really do,' she said, seizing the moment. 'So tell me what I need to know.'

He opened his mouth to speak but changed his mind.

'How can I understand when you won't tell me what it's all about?' she implored him. 'Your shutting me out hurts more than you could possibly know. I'm your wife, we're supposed to share things.'

He turned away from her and she could see his shoulders shaking.

'Just tell me what to do to help you come to terms with your demons,' she pleaded with him. 'Let me in, Doug. Please let me help you.'

He didn't reply; just stood with his back to her by the cooker.

'Doug?'

At last he turned round and looked at her. 'What?' he said blankly.

'What is the matter, Doug? Please tell me.'

'Nothing.' He looked grim. 'There's nothing wrong, nothing at all. Everything is fine and dandy apart from a spot of insomnia every so often. Now please go back to bed and leave me alone, or you'll be tired tomorrow.'

Now she was angry. 'You're not being fair,' she said through gritted teeth. 'If there's something bothering my husband I've a right to know what it is. I want to help.'

'Go to bed, Ann, please,' he requested, his tone dull and lacklustre.

'All right, I'll go and leave you to wallow in self-pity,' she said in a tone of sad resignation. 'But frankly I think you're being unreasonable as well as hurtful.'

'Sorry.' He turned away and began pouring water from the kettle into the teapot.

'If you were really sorry, you'd stop shutting me out,' she said, and marched from the room.

Back in bed, she thrashed about, sleep impossible. She was still awake when Doug finally came back to bed. She didn't say anything, though – just lay with her back to him, pretending to be asleep.

When Ellie got back from taking Donna to the playgroup the next morning – after leaving the car outside the Chad Street shop and handing the keys to a silent and hostile Pat over the counter – she went straight to her knitting machine, glad to have something absorbing to do to blot out the awful memories of yesterday. Luckily, Ray was looking after her transport problem, which saved her the tedious task of searching for a suitable vehicle within her limited price range.

Fortunately the morning sickness had been quite mild with this pregnancy so far. There was the usual queasiness when she first got up but it wasn't bad enough to be debilitating, which was just as well because she was in the middle of a large order of children's cardigans for Rene Morris.

Seated at the table in the back room, Ellie worked with dexterity, pulling the cam box to and fro. She didn't feel on top form, though, and found herself dropping stitches, which was unusual for her. They were eventually retrieved with the aid of a latch tool but it was a fiddly operation and cost her time she could ill afford.

Having completed a garment in white, she needed a break from the machine, so ironed the different pieces and settled in the armchair in the living room to sew it up. She still made a point of doing a large proportion of the embroidery herself too, because she enjoyed it. Her mother had more than enough to do, anyway, because Ellie had recently supplied her with a batch of knitting for sewing up and embroidery.

They had been so busy lately. Mary had cut her hours at the wool shop to cope with Ellie's work; she was planning on resigning from the shop if things continued as they were.

Now, having sewn the cardigan up, she started on the embroidery. Working with a deft hand, a large needle and an eye to the pattern she had worked out on graph paper, Ellie weaved a bunch of coloured balloons into the corner of the garment. The finished effect was lovely.

But although her work soothed her to a certain extent, her stomach was still churning horribly, the scene with Pat refusing to go away. Towards the end of the morning she was feeling so dreadful, she decided to do something about it.

She left early to collect Donna from her playgroup and called to see Ann, whose offspring wasn't quite old enough to go yet. Having made an arrangement with her sister-in-law, collected Donna and deposited her into the safe care of her Auntie Ann for an hour or so, Ellie headed purposefully for Chad Street.

'What are *you* doing here?' demanded Pat as Ellie walked up to the counter, having waited outside until the shop was empty.

'Well, I haven't come to buy anything,' Ellie replied meaningfully.

'I thought I made my feelings clear yesterday.'

'You did. Abundantly clear,' Ellie confirmed. 'But I need to talk to you so can we have a chat?'

'I've nothing to say to you,' Pat scowled.

'Maybe not. But I have things I want to say to you,' persisted Ellie.

The conversation was halted by a customer, who Pat served with a tin of oxtail soup, some bread rolls and a quarter of tea.

'In case you haven't noticed, I'm trying to run a business here,' Pat reminded Ellie when they were alone again. 'And I'm on my own because my assistant has phoned in sick.'

'You'll be closing for lunch in a minute, though, won't you?' Ellie pointed out.

'Well, yes . . .'

'Can I come upstairs to the flat for a talk?' she requested. 'It won't take very long.'

Pat didn't look pleased but, heaving an eloquent sigh, she stamped across to the shop door, turned the sign over and locked the door. She then led the way to the stairs through a door behind the counter.

'So, what's this all about?' she asked coldly when they got into the living room. No mention of a cup of tea or coffee; she didn't even invite Ellie to sit down.

Ellie was so tense, she felt dizzy. 'I couldn't leave things as they were when you went yesterday,' she explained, perching nervously on the edge of an armchair.

'Why not?'

'Because I can't bring myself to believe that you really meant all the things you said.'

'I wouldn't have said them if I didn't mean them,' was Pat's uncompromising answer to that.

'You were angry and upset,' Ellie suggested hopefully. 'I thought you might be able to see things more clearly now that you've had a chance to calm down.'

'I can see things clearly all right,' Pat said curtly. 'And I don't like what I see.'

'I would never do anything to hurt Tom, you must know that.' Ellie was desperate to reach the humanity she knew must be in Pat's nature somewhere.

'Oh, please . . .'

'I can't love him as a husband now,' Ellie went on to say. 'Surely you can understand the reason for that.'

'You married him for better or worse,' Pat pointed out coolly.

'I haven't forgotten that, and I'm still there for him,' she told her. 'But he no longer needs me as a wife. He's a child, Pat. Lovable in his own way but not as an adult. He's still very important to me but not in the same way as before.'

'Don't insult my intelligence with a load of claptrap.' Pat's eyes were darkly shadowed in her ashen countenance.

'It isn't claptrap,' said Ellie, appealing to her, 'and I think you know that in your heart.'

'You're glad to have him out of the way.' Pat was admitting nothing. 'And as for that criminal you're knocking about with – have you no sense of responsibility towards your daughter, exposing her to such riffraff?'

She'd really overstepped the mark now and Ellie wasn't having it. 'Don't you dare speak about Ray like that,' she cried. 'He's a thoroughly decent man.'

Pat almost choked on that one. 'Oh, yes,' she sneered. 'So decent that he goes around killing the first person who upsets him.'

Ellie was so angry it was as much as she could do not to strike her. 'I didn't come here to argue with you about Ray's character,' she said in a tight voice, managing to restrain herself. 'But just for the record, he has never killed anyone.'

'That's why they found him guilty, is it?' Pat said with a withering look.

'It isn't the first time the courts have got it wrong.'

Pat shrugged her shoulders to evince disinterest. 'Is that it then?' she asked. 'Have you said what you came to say?'

'No.'

'Get on with it then.'

'I came to try and patch things up between us, actually,' Ellie explained.

'You must be joking.'

'No. I'm perfectly serious,' said Ellie. 'No matter what you say, I can't believe that you truly want me out of your life.'

Pat's face worked as though it had been slapped but she quickly composed herself. 'You've made me want it. It's you who's wrecked everything,' she said with a wobble in her voice. 'There's no going back after what you've done.'

Still Ellie didn't believe that the words were coming from

Pat's heart but from the narrow-minded values she couldn't break away from, and an obsessive love for her son. The woman was lonely enough as it was – surely she didn't really want to lose Ellie's friendship. If nothing else Ellie was her link to happier times with Tom.

If pride was a problem Ellie was prepared to offer the olive branch and let Pat accept it without appearing to lose face. But there was something she had to know before she went any further. 'Do you really believe that I was to blame for the accident, Pat, or did you just say that to hurt me because you were so upset about my relationship with Ray?'

Pat looked at Ellie for a long time in silence, her mouth trembling slightly. 'You can't possibly know what it feels like to lose a son in the way that I lost Tom,' she said at last, her voice barely more than a whisper.

'We both lost him,' Ellie reminded him.

'Your loss is quite different,' Pat stated harshly. 'You can't replace a son in the same way as you can a husband. You're a mother yourself, you know how strong the feelings are.'

'I do,' Ellie told her. 'But in saying that you've lost Tom as a son, you are admitting that I've lost him as a husband, that I might just as well be a widow.'

'If you're looking for justification for your affair with Ray Brent, you won't get it from me,' Pat was quick to point out.

'So you think I should spend the rest of my life alone, then?' Ellie challenged her.

'Would that be so terrible? I'm on my own and I have no intention of changing that.'

'But I've met someone and fallen in love with him,' Ellie reminded her.

Pat winced, leaving Ellie in no doubt as to the depth of her feelings about this. 'You can't alter the fact that you're married to Tom, Ellie,' she said. 'No matter how much you tell yourself that what you're doing with Ray Brent is justifiable, the fact is, you are still betraying your husband.'

'But he can't possibly be hurt or even mildly affected by

anything that I do. Surely that counts for something.'

The older woman mulled this over for a few moments. 'My mother is dead and can't be hurt by anything that I do,' she said, fixing Ellie with a stare. 'But I still wouldn't do anything I know she wouldn't approve of.'

'There's no answer to that sort of reasoning,' said Ellie.

'Because it's rock solid, that's why.' A fleeting moment of despair was visible in her eyes before her expression hardened again. 'And getting back to your original question – yes, I did mean what I said about the accident. In my opinion, none of this would have happened if you'd been more careful.'

'If I'd not been driving the car, I'd be where Tom is now,' Ellie pointed out sadly. 'Because I'd have been in the passenger seat. Is that what you wish had happened?'

'It wouldn't have happened if Tom had been driving the car,' Pat persisted in a subdued manner.

The sudden mildness of her tone was far more cogent than all the shouting she'd done yesterday. Now Ellie knew that this was her true opinion and not just the ranting of an hysterical woman.

'There's nothing to be said then, is there?' Ellie looked at her, still hoping she might find it in her heart to be more understanding.

'No . . . I don't think that there is.'

Ellie didn't feel angry or irritated or imbued with any sense of injustice. She just felt terribly sad. She walked slowly to the door, turning when she got there. 'Don't bother to come down. I'll see myself out,' she said dully. 'You'll be pleased to know that you won't be seeing me again. Unless, of course, we meet by accident and I shall do my utmost to make sure that doesn't happen.'

Pat nodded stiffly.

Making her way down the stairs, Ellie was assailed by symptoms of stress. This latest meeting with Pat had made her feel physically ill. Her heart was beating erratically and she felt light-headed and sweaty. For a minute she thought she was going to faint and paused for a moment, gripping the stair rail, her head swimming. But the feeling passed so she left the building and headed for Ann's to collect her daughter.

'I just popped across to tell you how pleased I am about you and Ray,' smiled Alfie, the following Saturday morning when Ellie was setting up her stall.

'Thanks, Alfie,' she said, looking at him warmly. 'I know you've got your doubts about it.'

'No doubts about you, love,' he was keen to point out. 'You're the best thing that ever happened to Ray. I thought you might be letting yourselves in for a whole load of trouble, that's all.'

'And you were right,' she told him, hanging up some women's sweaters on a rail.

'Yeah. Ray's been telling me that you've had a bit of bother with your mother-in-law.'

'That's an understatement,' she said. 'Everyone else was fine about it.' She glanced towards the market where the stallholders were all busy setting up for the day. 'The people here have been great. They guessed anyway. I think Ray's had a few snide remarks from people in The Bush who know I'm married to Tom but it's nothing he can't handle. Pat's the only one to seriously disapprove and she went potty.'

'Take no notice,' he advised.

'I'm trying not to,' Ellie said. 'But it isn't easy. She is Tom's mother, after all.'

Seeing her eyes moisten Alfie effected a swift change of subject. 'Good news about the baby, isn't it?' he said, coming closer to her and lowering his voice so that he couldn't be overheard by Joe on the next stall.

'I'm glad you're pleased,' she said. 'You're not mad with us for making you a grandad, then?'

'You're joking,' he laughed. 'I couldn't be more delighted. And Ray's up there on cloud nine.'

309

Ellie managed to smile, though she was feeling quite ill – nauseous, and achy. She'd been feeling out of sorts ever since the upset with Pat, but the thought of the baby kept her spirits up. She wanted it so much. 'Yes, I know he is,' she said. 'We're both really excited.'

They talked some more about the baby, then moved on to other things. 'I hear you've got fixed up with a motor,' Alfie commented chattily.

'That's right. Ray found me a Ford estate car,' she said. 'It's just right for me.'

'You'll be all right with anything Ray found for you,' he said. 'There are a lot of crooks in the second-hand car business. But Ray knows who to trust.'

'I know.'

He gave her a concerned look. It was a fine summer's morning and she was as pretty as ever in a cotton dress. But she didn't look well. Her face was paper white against her red hair. 'Are you feeling all right, love?' Alfie asked. 'You're looking a bit peaky.'

'I'm not feeling too good, as it happens,' she admitted.

'What's the trouble?'

'Just a bit off colour. Nothing to worry about. All part of being pregnant, I should think. Women expect discomfort when they're having a baby.'

'Would you like me to finish setting up your stall for you while you go to the café for a sit-down and a cup of something?' he offered. 'Ray can manage without me for a while.'

'I'll be all right, Alfie, don't worry,' Ellie assured him. 'But thanks for offering.'

They were interrupted by Ray. 'What's all this?' he said, grinning at his father. 'You're supposed to be helping me, not skiving off and chatting up my girlfriend.'

'Leave him alone, you big bully,' joshed Ellie. 'He happens to be a friend of mine.'

With a beaming smile, Ray moved towards Ellie and put his

arm round her, brushing his lips against her cheek. 'I can see I'm going to have to watch the two of you,' he joked.

Alfie watched Ellie come to life, her whole being seeming to light up at Ray's touch. Ray seemed to radiate new energy too. It gave Alfie a poignant reminder of his dear departed wife and how they had been together. He knew in that moment that these two were right for each other, his earlier doubts dissolving completely. What they had was priceless.

But you could see that Ellie was hurting inside, despite her cheery manner. The pain was there in her eyes and Pat Hall was to blame for it. Anxiety wasn't good for a woman in the early stages of pregnancy, Alfie found himself thinking.

'Well, I'll leave you two lovebirds together and go and get on with some work,' he told them.

'About time too,' teased Ray.

'Enough of your cheek,' Alfie retaliated good-humouredly.

'Just kidding,' said Ray. 'I'll be back in a minute.'

'OK, son.'

Leaving the two of them chatting happily, Alfie walked back to Ray's stall, mulling over the unhappy situation between Ellie and her mother-in-law and wondering what could be done about it.

Chapter Fifteen

Whenever Mary and Pat had a falling-out, a speedy reconciliation was always initiated by Mary because Pat was too proud to make the first move. Mary knew she ought to take a firmer line, of course, but she was the sort of person who would rather put things right than have to endure the misery of lingering hostility.

However, they had never had such a serious argument as the one that took place at Mary's house on Sunday. She was profoundly hurt by Pat's vicious attack on Ellie and believed most passionately that her daughter was owed an apology. So she did nothing; just waited in the faint hope that Pat might do the decent thing.

Predictably there was no word from Pat, and the sad ache that had been lodged in the pit of Mary's stomach ever since the altercation turned to simmering umbrage. So on Sunday evening, with all guns blazing, she headed for Chad Street.

Pat looked somewhat daunted when she opened the door and saw Mary standing there. But she soon recovered sufficiently to evince a superior air.

'Oh, it's you,' she said dully.

'I've waited all week to hear from you.' Mary knew how difficult it was for someone like Pat to back down and had hoped that her visit might prompt an apology and spare them both more heartache. But it was obvious that remorse was the last thing on Pat's mind. 'But if Mohammed won't come to the mountain . . .'

'You'd better come in.' It was said more as a complaint than an invitation. 'I don't want my private business discussed in full view of the neighbours. I'm the talk of the street as it is because of your daughter.'

Mary didn't say anything; just followed her upstairs and into the living room.

'Tea, coffee or anything?' offered Pat formally.

'No thanks.'

Pat lifted her bony shoulders in an indifferent shrug, sat down in an armchair and waved her hand airily towards a chair for Mary to do the same.

But Mary preferred to remain standing while she said her piece. She felt stronger that way. 'You and I have had our disagreements in the past, Pat, but you've really overstepped the mark this time,' she said.

'*I've* overstepped the mark? That's rich.'

'You've really upset Ellie and I think you should apologise to her,' Mary went on.

Pat's eyes bulged. '*Me* apologise to *her*?' She was incredulous at the suggestion.

'Yes, that's right.'

'After what she's done to me?'

'Oh, for heaven's sake,' said Mary impatiently. 'She hasn't done anything to you.'

'Oh, not much. She's only ruined my son's life, that's all.' Pat's eyes were hot with malice.

'What happened to Tom wasn't Ellie's fault and if you weren't so stubborn you'd be able to admit it,' Mary told her straight. 'You're just being bloody-minded.'

'No I'm not.' Pat's face was set in a harsh expression, her mouth a grim line. 'In my opinion it was her fault. And when she hurts my son, she hurts me too.'

'Same here,' retorted Mary. 'You hurt my daughter and I feel the pain.'

'That makes you and me quits then, doesn't it? But Ellie deserves a lot worse than the trouncing I gave her,' she tutted, raising her eyes, 'after the way she's behaved.'

'She deserves some happiness after what she's been through,' contradicted Mary, her voice rising. 'And now that she's found someone who can give her that, I won't have you spoiling it for her just because you're all screwed up inside and feel like taking your spite out on her.'

'I don't know what you're getting at,' denied Pat with a guarded look.

'Come on, Pat,' said Mary. 'You know in your heart of hearts that Ellie wasn't to blame for the accident, in the same way as you know that she isn't hurting Tom by having a relationship with Ray Brent. But having someone to blame and disapprove of helps you to cope with the anger that's eating away inside of you because of what happened to Tom, anger you seem determined to hang on to indefinitely.' Her tone softened slightly. 'Look, I can imagine how terrible it must be for you. Any mother would feel for you. But you have to let go of the rage, Pat. Stop letting it poison you and start trying to make the best of things. It isn't fair to take your fury out on Ellie just because she's the most convenient target.'

'You're talking out of the back of your head.' She was full of indignation.

Physically weakened by the trauma of these confrontations, Mary sank down in an armchair and put her hands to her head in a brief gesture of despair. 'You and I go back a long way,' she began, dropping her hands and looking at Pat. 'We've had our differences over the years as all close friends must do. But we've always come through them before.' She shook her head gravely. 'But I have to tell you that if you don't change your attitude about this, I'm afraid we've come to the end of the line.'

She saw Pat wince but her tone didn't soften. 'If that's the way you want it,' she said drily.

'Of course it isn't the way I want it.' A bolt of anger shot through Mary and she leaped to her feet. 'You can't just write off a friendship as long as ours. You might be too wrapped up in yourself to care about anyone else but I still care about you. So why can't you break the habit of a lifetime and show some humanity?' she entreated through dry lips.

Pat didn't reply; just stared at the floor in silence.

'All right, strictly speaking Ellie is being unfaithful to Tom,' Mary continued in the absence of any input from Pat. 'But is it so dreadful under the circumstances?'

'Don't make excuses for her.'

'She's a young woman and it's nearly three years since Tom was able to be a husband to her,' Mary went on.

'In sickness and in health,' was Pat's scathing reminder.

'But there's nothing more Ellie can do for Tom,' Mary tried to reason with her. 'He doesn't need her now . . . isn't capable of loving her. So why can't you find it in your heart to keep your personal feelings to yourself and be glad she's found someone to care about her and Donna?'

'You can't possibly expect me to condone this scandalous affair she's having.' Pat was completely unrelenting.

Mary looked at her sadly. 'No, I don't suppose I can,' she sighed. 'I should have known better than to expect such a thing from you. You'd rather be friendless than open your mind to anything outside of your own narrow horizons.'

'As long as we know where we stand with each other,' was Pat's harsh reply.

Angry and deeply hurt that Pat couldn't bring herself to make a compromise, for the sake of their friendship if nothing else, Mary walked slowly to the door. 'It's bad enough you calling my daughter a slut,' she said, turning. 'But to accuse her of being to blame for the accident is downright evil.' She sucked in her breath. 'One of these days you'll realise how cruel you are being and want Ellie back in your life. But by the time you come to your senses she won't be willing to listen to anything you have to say.'

'If anyone needs to apologise, it's her,' Pat persisted. 'But I wouldn't accept it anyway. As I said on Sunday, I want nothing to do with her.'

'In that case you won't be seeing me again either,' declared Mary. 'Our friendship is over, as from now.'

The two women stared at each other, shocked that it had come to this. Mary saw her own regret mirrored in Pat's eyes; she saw fear there too. Her expression softened a little and Mary thought for a second that she might relent. But the moment passed. 'Fair enough,' she said in a cracked voice.

Mary turned and hurried down the stairs and let herself out of the side door. Outside in the street, she rummaged in her pocket for a handkerchief to mop the copious flow of tears. Her friendship with Pat hadn't always been a pleasure by any means, but its end still came as a bitter blow. It didn't help to know that Pat was probably even more unhappy than the people she was hurting.

Alfie left work early on Monday evening and went straight to the Chad Street corner shop, arriving a few minutes before closing time. Pausing for a moment outside to read a notice on the door – informing customers that there would be no grocery deliveries until further notice because of staff problems – he took a deep breath then went inside.

Pat was behind the counter talking to a female customer of advanced years, and didn't look at him as he entered. 'I'm sorry, but I just don't have anyone to do the deliveries this week,' she was saying to the woman in an appeasing manner. 'Could somebody come and collect your order for you, perhaps?'

'No, somebody can't.' The customer was obviously not prepared to tolerate the drop in the standard of service. 'I don't know anyone who has a car.'

'In that case I'll have to bring any urgent items to you myself,' Pat ground out in a tone of seething impatience, still too involved in what she was doing to look at Alfie, who was passing the time by looking at a display of Lyons fruit pies and Wagon Wheels on a stand near the door.

317

'Don't bother yourself, as it's obviously too much trouble,' snapped the customer.

'I didn't say it was too much trouble.' Pat sounded harassed now as well as angry.

'You didn't have to say it,' the other woman informed her. 'Your tone of voice says it all.'

'I didn't mean to sound—'

'I'll go somewhere else for my groceries in future,' the other woman cut in. 'If I'm not having them delivered I might as well go to the self-service store in town. It's cheaper there anyway.'

And with that she marched across to the door.

Pat clamped a tired hand to her furrowed brow. 'Don't be like that, Mrs Fish,' she called after her, her manner noticeably more conciliatory. 'I really am sorry for the inconvenience but I don't have an assistant to do the deliveries.'

'It's no wonder you can't keep staff with your stuck-up attitude,' opined Mrs Fish. 'Nobody wants to work with someone who looks down their nose at them.'

'There's no call to be insulting,' returned Pat.

'You're supposed to be giving a service,' Mrs Fish pointed out tartly. 'And until you start doing that again, I'll do my shopping elsewhere.'

The door was closed with a resounding crash.

'Sounds as though you're having a bad day,' remarked Alfie, walking up to the counter.

'The understatement of the century,' Pat mumbled absently, still staring at the door with a worried expression.

'Would you like me to go after her to try and talk her round?' he offered.

Pat looked at him now, her eyes widening in a face that suddenly became suffused with pink. 'My God. Alfie Brent, as I live and breathe,' she gasped.

'I haven't aged beyond recognition, then?' he said.

Ignoring his comment, she asked, 'What on earth are you doing here?'

'This is a shop, isn't it?' he mentioned casually. 'I thought the general idea was for people to come in.'

'If they're going to buy something, yes, of course it is,' she said coolly.

'Give us a tin of baked beans then, please?' he requested, casting an eye over her.

Avoiding his eyes, she took a tin from the shelf behind her and put it on the counter. 'Anything else?'

'Yes, there is, as a matter of fact.'

'Tell me what it is then, so I can close the shop,' she said briskly. 'I've been standing behind this counter all day and I want to put my feet up.'

'I'm surprised you've got any customers left to serve with that sort of attitude,' he told her. 'I've watched you see one off, now you're doing the same thing to me.'

'Because it's closing time,' she tutted. 'And as for Mrs Fish, she's just a cantankerous old biddy. I mean, I can hardly operate a delivery service without an assistant, can I, since I can't drive the shop car? The wretched man walked out on me without a moment's notice; left me high and dry.'

'I'm not surprised if this is the way you carry on,' he said with brutal candour.

'How I conduct myself is none of your business, Alfie Brent,' she said acidly. 'And the reason you got the sharp edge of my tongue is because I don't believe that you're a genuine customer.'

'I've bought a tin of beans,' he pointed out, putting a shilling piece on the counter.

She gave him a shrewd look. 'I've worked in this shop for more years than I care to remember, and I've never seen you come through that door before,' she pointed out, operating the cash register and putting his change on the counter. 'So why have you appeared on the scene now?' She paused, her eyes narrowing as the penny dropped. 'As if I didn't know.'

'Just a friendly chat . . . in private,' he explained. 'Which is why I came at closing time.'

They were interrupted by a flurry of last-minute trade, which Pat dealt with swiftly. As the last customer left, she marched purposefully to the door, turned the sign to closed, pulled the blind down and locked the door.

'Right,' she began, going back behind the counter and facing him with her arms crossed, 'as it's obvious that this *friendly chat* is going to be about your son and my daughter-in-law, say what you have to and sling your hook.'

Ignoring her demand, Alfie said, 'A lot of years have passed since you and me were . . .' he paused, his brows rising, mouth curling into a smile, 'close friends.'

She lowered her eyes so that he couldn't see the memories his appearance evoked. 'I think that's best forgotten, don't you?' she said frostily. 'It never had any substance anyway.'

'I wouldn't say that.'

'We were just kids.'

'We were old enough . . .'

She fiddled with her pearl choker nervously, her cheeks flaming. 'Yes, well . . . the least said about that the better,' she said in embarrassment.

'It could have come to something between you and me, you know,' he went on, undaunted.

'Hardly likely as you married someone else,' she said, recalling her pain when she heard he'd got married.

'You chucked me, remember,' he was quick to remind her. 'You got rid of me because I wasn't good enough for you. So why shouldn't I marry someone else?'

'No reason at all, and it really doesn't matter anyway,' she said with an impatient sigh. 'It's all in the past.'

'It doesn't matter *now*,' he agreed. 'But it did at the time. We had something good and you threw it all away because I was too rough for you.'

'I ended it because I wanted someone more serious-minded than you were,' she corrected haughtily. 'All you ever wanted to do was lark about.'

'That's what people do when they're young,' he pointed out.

'Most people, anyway. Not you, though. You were far too busy looking after the future to enjoy your youth. You were obsessed with finding a reliable husband, as I recall.'

'There's nothing wrong with that,' she defended. 'Getting a husband was important to every decent girl in those days.'

'And the fact that this shop was in George Hall's family didn't make any difference, I suppose,' he suggested with irony.

She started to deny it but faltered. Alfie had always been able to see right through her, had always spoken his mind to her in a way no one else ever had. The direct manner that had disconcerted her as a girl still did so now. But she wasn't about to be defeated by it. 'So what if I wanted a man with a few bob in his pocket, someone who could be relied on to pay the bills?' she said. 'There weren't many of those about back in those days.'

'True.'

His cool gaze made her defensive. 'I was a good wife to George,' she informed him as though an explanation was necessary. 'He had nothing to complain about in me.'

'I'm sure he didn't. You'd have been very correct about everything,' he conceded. 'You were a very serious-minded person. In fact, you were the only girlfriend I ever had who seemed older than my mother.'

She winced. 'Thanks very much,' she snapped.

'You were a good-looking girl, Pat,' he continued, explaining his remark. 'But you were old in your ways and always bossy. Could never let yourself go. Seemed to think fun was some kind of sin.'

'Whereas all you wanted was fun,' she said.

'It's only natural when you're young,' he pointed out. 'There's nothing wrong with wanting a few laughs before you get tied down with responsibility.' His expression darkened. 'God knows, life gets serious enough later on.'

'Yes, it does.' She sounded subdued.

'The trick is not to let it grind you down.'

'You obviously haven't,' she commented. 'I suppose you still treat life as one big joke.'

'It isn't my way to go about with a long face.'

'No, it never was.'

He looked at her thoughtfully. 'Whereas you . . . you must be in your forties now, the same as me. But your attitude to life is that of a bitter old woman.'

'How do you know what my attitude is?' she demanded, her voice rising. 'You don't know me at all. We haven't seen each other for years.'

'I've heard a lot about you, though. I've heard how you're trying to destroy what my son has with Ellie,' he said, getting to the purpose of his visit. 'The poor girl is distraught because of what you said to her.'

'She got what she deserved.'

'There you go again, judging people by your own standards,' he rebuked.

'She shouldn't be sleeping with someone else when she's married to my son,' Pat insisted.

'Her personal life is her business and not yours.' Alfie's tone was hard now, his eyes dark with anger. 'It's a private matter between herself and her conscience. She's married to your son, not to you, Pat. Don't you think it's time you accepted that?'

'All right, so it's her business what she does,' she agreed with reluctance. 'But by the same token it's my business what I say to her, and it has nothing to do with you. Free speech isn't against the law. You should know, you're an expert at speaking your mind.'

He gave her a close look, observing the thin face, the staid hairstyle, the tight-lipped expression. 'I don't believe you're really as hard as you pretend to be, you know,' he said, his manner softening slightly. 'I remember a woman who could be warm and loving . . . not to mention passionate. Surely some of that must still be in there somewhere.'

Pat heaved a pitiful sigh. 'Life has made me hard. It isn't

322

exactly a barrel load of laughs when you lose your husband, then have your son's life wrecked.'

'I lost my wife. And my son was sent to prison for something he didn't do,' he informed her. 'But I don't take my misery out on other people.'

'Neither do I.'

'I haven't seen much evidence of the milk of human kindness around here today and I haven't heard about it either,' he told her frankly. 'And as for your accusing Ellie of being to blame for the accident, that really was out of order.'

'Shut up,' Pat said, clutching her head. 'Just go away and leave me alone.'

'Somebody's got to talk some sense into you,' he went on. 'If you don't change your ways, you'll turn into a lonely old crone, spoiling your own life as well as other people's.'

Her face was ashen, her neck red and blotchy. 'Get out of here,' she said, grabbing the keys from the counter and marching to the door with them.

Alfie raised his hands in a gesture of defeat. 'OK. I'm going.' He picked up his change and the tin of beans from the counter and walked to the door, which Pat was now holding open. 'I don't believe you really want to spend the rest of your life alone, being disliked by everyone around you?'

She shrugged indifferently.

'It's what will happen if you continue as you are,' he persisted. 'You'll end up with no one to talk to except the few customers you'll have left. So go and see Ellie and her mother and put things right before it's too late. You'll feel better for it, believe me.'

'Get out,' she told him again.

He finally did as she asked and she locked the door after him and pulled down the blind, glad to shut out the outside world which she'd had quite enough of for one day.

Later that evening she sat in an armchair drinking a cup of tea and wondering why she felt so shaken by Alfie Brent's reappearance in her life. She hadn't seen him to speak to since they'd both been eighteen years old. She'd heard about him, of course, and seen him around the town occasionally, but this was the first personal contact they'd had since then.

Their youthful romance had been brief but intense; much more emotionally and sexually vibrant than the relationship Pat had subsequently had with her husband. George had given her security, Alfie had given her passion. He'd had the ability to take life by the throat and didn't give a damn what people thought of him. She'd always envied him that.

He was still a very handsome man now, she was forced to admit, but he'd been stunning when he was young. He could have had any girl he wanted and he'd chosen her when she'd caught his eye at a local dance. They had been hard times, back in the depressed 1930s, but Alfie had always had a sparkle in his eye and a spring to his step. His gift of the gab and good looks had made him irresistible to a girl as inhibited as she'd been.

Looking back on it, it was a miracle she hadn't got pregnant, she thought, blushing at the memories she'd pushed to the back of her mind for so long. How shocked people would have been to know what prim and proper Pat used to get up to in secluded dark corners of West London late at night. Even Mary didn't know about that. Pat had never dared tell anyone. People didn't admit to that sort of thing much in those days. But despite her shame she'd been excited and happy too, for a while, because she and Alfie had been smitten with each other.

Then it had started to go wrong. She'd wanted him to settle down and put a ring on her finger. He'd said he would when he was ready but wouldn't be rushed into it. He'd refused to have her dictate to him. She'd said he wasn't serious about her, or about anything, and had ended it and set her cap at the less dynamic George Hall. Maybe he hadn't set her heart racing in the same way as Alfie had but they'd had a good marriage.

Now she had nobody at all. She'd even lost her dear friend Mary, who she'd thought could be relied on to stand by her through anything. But she'd taken her daughter's side so that was the end of the friendship because Pat was damned if she was going to apologise to Ellie when she had nothing to be sorry for. She'd stifled her feelings for long enough about where the blame for the accident lay. The Scotts weren't worth having as friends if they couldn't see how hurt she was by Ellie's behaviour.

Why couldn't they understand how it felt to have a son's life destroyed and then to discover that his wife was sleeping with someone else? It was cruel of them to turn against her when she already had enough problems trying to run this shop on her own because she couldn't get reliable staff.

Steeped in self-pity, she got up and walked heavily to the kitchen and rinsed her empty cup under the tap. She'd felt bad enough after Mary's visit yesterday. She felt even worse now, having been thrown into turmoil by Alfie Brent. Although she refused to pursue this train of thought any further, she suspected he'd done the unthinkable; he'd made her question her judgement.

But she wouldn't let the doubts take root. She refused to be influenced by someone of no importance, a mere factory hand and the father of an alleged murderer. His opinion wasn't worth anything; he was a nobody. He didn't seem insignificant when you were with him, though. He never had. Alfie Brent was the sort of man who would maintain a certain presence whatever his station in life.

She dried her solitary teacup and put it away in the cupboard. Then she went back into the other room and turned the television on to drown out the silence. The flat had never felt emptier than it did tonight.

'It's going really well, don't you think?' Ray remarked to Ellie when they managed a few words alone together in Ellie's parents' back garden.

'An unqualified success,' she agreed happily.

'The more I get to know your family, the better I like them,' he told her.

'Good. I think they feel the same about you,' Ellie was pleased to tell him.

'My dad seems to be enjoying himself too,' Ray added.

'Yes, I noticed that.'

It was a month later. Having already extended the hand of friendship to Ray by inviting him to Sunday lunch a few weeks ago, today Mary and Bob had compounded their approval by inviting his father too. The meal was over and Ray had followed Ellie into the garden where she'd gone to check on Donna and Matthew, who were playing out there.

It was a warm summer's day and the small, narrow garden was bathed in sunshine, the flowerbeds a colourful tangle of pansies, marigolds and hollyhocks. The children were busy on the lawn. Donna was putting the covers on her doll's pram with great concentration. Cousin Matthew, who was now turned two, was enjoying himself with a push-along cart full of wooden building bricks, watched by a neighbour's cat, which was dozing in the sun nearby.

'Do you think the fact that our fathers already knew each other helped to smooth our path?' asked Ray.

'It certainly didn't do any harm,' Ellie replied.

'Your mum's trying hard not to show it but I think she still has doubts about me,' he mentioned.

'Maybe a few,' Ellie admitted. 'You've had a lot of people doing you down. It's bound to have had an effect. She'll get over it. She's already warming to you, I can tell.'

'Yeah, I know.' He slipped his arm around her, casually kissing the top of her head. 'I don't have any trouble with your brother and his wife. I think they're a smashing couple.'

'The best,' Ellie agreed.

'In fact, I thoroughly approve of the family I'll be coming into,' he said, adding quickly, 'I know that I can never be family, as such, but you know what I mean.'

326

'You're my other half,' she swiftly assured him. 'So you'll be family in every way that matters.'

'And while we're on the subject of families, we ought to start making decisions as regards our living arrangements,' he said. Although they'd agreed to live together, they hadn't yet decided when this would take place or where it would be, though they both favoured a fresh start in accommodation without memories.

'You're right; we ought to get that sorted.' Ellie put his hand on her stomach. 'I'm turned three months now; it's time we did something definite.'

'We'll go and visit a few estate agents to start the ball rolling, shall we?' he said. 'See what's available?'

She nodded enthusiastically. 'Do you know something, Ray?' she said, waxing sentimental. 'I can't remember ever feeling this content before. There were happy times with Tom, of course, but I feel so complete now, somehow.' She was still troubled by compunction, especially when she remembered Pat's accusations. But she was managing to keep things in perspective, for Ray's sake as much as her own. 'Despite all the gossip and complications, I still want to be with you for the rest of my life.'

'Likewise,' he said, their eyes meeting.

'Love you,' she said.

'You too.'

The magic of the moment was shattered by a sudden uproar on the lawn as Matthew picked up the visiting tabby and tried to stuff it into Donna's doll's pram. She shrieked; the cat, spitting and hissing, made a hasty retreat over the fence to safer regions next door, leaving Matthew wailing loudly.

Ellie and Ray were immediately on the scene, Ray trying to calm Matthew while Ellie soothed Donna.

'I don't want that pussy in my pram,' the little girl sobbed. 'It'll squash my dolly. Matthew is a bad boy. Tell him, Mum.'

'Shush, shush,' said Ellie, picking her daughter up and wiping her eyes. 'The cat's gone now. So no more crying, eh?'

327

Meanwhile Ray had plucked the screaming Matthew from the ground. 'Now, now, little chap,' he was saying soothingly, 'how about you and me putting all your bricks back into your cart? Would you like that?'

At that moment Ann appeared followed by Doug, both looking worried. 'Sounds as though you've got a major riot on your hands out here,' said Ann.

'Only a minor one, and it's all under control,' Ellie told her, smoothing Donna's damp hair from her brow.

Ann put her arms out to relieve Ray of her tearful son but Matthew turned his head towards Ray's chest and snuggled there, not to be budged.

They all laughed.

'Looks as though you've got the knack, mate,' grinned Doug.

'You'll need it when your own arrives,' added Ann. 'And if you haven't already got it, you'll learn fast.'

Ray beamed proudly, cuddling his charge close to him. 'Small children were uncharted territory to me until I got to know Donna,' he confessed.

'Now he reckons he's an expert,' joshed Ellie.

'This is all good practice for you,' said Ann.

'You'll get plenty of the real thing soon enough,' added Doug.

'I can't wait,' said Ray.

'I'll remind you of that when the bags under your eyes are weighing you down because the nipper's had you up all night,' laughed Doug.

There was more ribbing and plenty of laughter. Matthew wanted to go back to his cart so Ray put him down. Ellie lifted her now smiling daughter down on to the ground. It was as she straightened up that she felt the first stab of pain right across the lower part of her stomach. It was so violent, she cried out instinctively, clutching her abdomen.

'What's the matter, Ellie?' asked Ray worriedly.

'What's up, sis?' Doug was concerned too.

'I'm not sure.' She didn't want to alarm them unnecessarily but the pain was so strong she felt winded by it. 'I must have eaten my lunch too fast, or something. I've got a bit of a stomach ache.'

'Let's go inside so you can sit down,' suggested Ray, taking her arm with infinite tenderness. 'Come on. Lean on me.'

'It's probably nothing,' Ellie told him, still trying to make light of it.

'Probably just one of those harmless pregnancy twinges that come and go,' said Ann to encourage her.

The two men were both a ghastly colour, though. 'There's no need to look so terrified,' Ellie told them. 'I was perfectly all right a minute ago and I will be again. A touch of wind, that's all it is.'

In the house the parents were unable to hide their concern.

'There's no need for you all to panic,' said Ellie in mild admonishment.

'No one's panicking,' Ray assured her, gently helping her into an armchair, his love for her manifest. 'We're just concerned about you, that's all.'

'Should I call the doctor?' suggested her mother.

'No,' replied Ellie. 'I know you mean well but we can't bother the doctor with every little twinge.'

'Are you sure?' said Ray. 'Because it'll only take me a minute to go to the phone box.'

'It'll probably go off in a minute so will you all stop fussing?' Ellie was very tense.

'Is there anything I can get for you?' offered Ray.

'A warm drink,' suggested Mary.

'No, nothing at the moment, thanks,' said Ellie. 'It's only a touch of indigestion. It'll pass.'

But it didn't pass and it wasn't just a touch of indigestion. Fifteen minutes later Ellie was on her way to hospital in an ambulance, its emergency bells clanging.

Chapter Sixteen

It was around eight o'clock in the evening of that same day and Ray and Mary were sitting in a corridor at the West London Hospital outside the ward where Ellie was seriously ill with complications following a miscarriage. Bob and Doug had gone outside for cigarettes and Ann was at home looking after the children. The family and Ray had been allowed to see Ellie briefly but she'd been barely conscious.

Frantic with worry, Ray was pacing about, hands in his pockets, head down.

'You aren't half getting through some shoe leather with all that walking about,' warned Mary. 'You must have done miles up and down this corridor these last few hours.' She patted the seat beside her in a friendly manner. 'Come and take the weight off your feet before you get blisters on them.'

Distractedly, he did as she asked, leaning forward and resting his elbows on his lower thighs. 'I feel like a nervous wreck,' he confessed. 'I hope I'm not upsetting you.'

'You're not bothering me,' she told him. 'But you must try to keep a grip.'

'It isn't easy with Ellie being so ill.'

'And don't I know it. But you have to do it, Ray.' Her tone was warm but firm. 'You don't want to be in a state of complete exhaustion when she comes through this crisis, do you? She'll be very weak and need you to be strong.'

'Once she's out of danger I'll be Tarzan himself, I promise you,' he assured her.

She smiled at his analogy and rested her hand on his for a moment. 'I'm really sorry about the baby,' she commiserated. 'I know how very much you both wanted it.'

'I'm disappointed, of course,' he admitted with a sigh. 'But it just wasn't meant to be.'

'That's a very sensible attitude,' she told him. 'Unfortunately, some people find it difficult to see it that way when they've lost a child.'

'To be perfectly honest, at the moment all I can think about is Ellie.' He shook his head slowly, too distressed to hold anything back. 'She's come to mean everything to me. I just don't know what I'll do if—'

'Don't even think about it,' she cut in.

He sat up and turned to look at her, seeing the terror in her eyes, despite the stoicism she had displayed throughout this whole ordeal. 'This must be awful for you too,' he said. 'And my being so jumpy can't have helped.'

'It hasn't worried me,' she told him. 'You've been there for Ellie, that's the important thing. You were a rock for her when she was taken bad at home, keeping her calm while we waited for the ambulance. I think a few nerves at this stage can be forgiven.'

Warming towards her even more, Ray found himself speaking from the heart. 'You're a good sort, Mary. It must have been difficult for you, having someone with a reputation like mine brought into your home. But you've made me feel welcome, whatever your true feelings, and I appreciate that.'

'I admit I wasn't pleased when Ellie told us about the two of you,' she told him frankly. 'And the doubts haven't been easy to shake off. But seeing you together these past few weeks has been a real eye-opener to me. And after today I don't think any of us are in doubt as to how much you care for her.' She paused and when she spoke again her tone was imbued with respect and affection. 'You'll do.'

His emotions already highly sensitised, his vision blurred. 'Thanks, Mary,' he said, staring at the floor to hide how close he was to breaking down. 'I've never felt for anyone with the same depth as I feel for Ellie. That's why I'm in such a state.'

'She'll come through this,' said Mary, her voice breaking. 'We're a tough lot, us Scotts.'

A doctor bustled up to them, looking grim. They both stared at him in terror.

'Mrs Hall is stable now,' he informed them in an expressionless tone.

Ray leaped up. 'You mean she's going to be all right?'

'She's very weak because she's lost such a lot of blood,' the doctor told them wearily. 'But the bleeding is under control and she's out of danger.'

'Oh, thank God,' said Ray.

'She's sleeping now and she isn't likely to wake up for a while because we've given her a sedative,' the doctor continued. 'So I suggest you go home and come back to see her in visiting hours tomorrow.'

As the doctor hurried away, Ray impulsively threw his arms around Mary and hugged her. They were both crying with relief. 'From the look on his face, I thought we were about to hear the worst, didn't you?' he muttered.

'He didn't look very happy, I must admit. Hospital doctors work long hours; the poor man's probably worn out,' she said, her voice muffled with tears. 'Come on then, let's go and tell the others the good news.'

Together they walked to the hospital exit to find Bob and Doug. Although it wasn't mentioned, both Mary and Ray were aware of having passed through some sort of a watershed in their relationship and emerged from it as friends.

'Maybe we could have a night out on Saturday, Ellie,' suggested Ray. 'We could go to the West End, if you fancy it. I'll try to get tickets for a show. We could have a bite to eat out as well. I'll ask Ann or your mum to baby-sit for us.'

'It's nice of you to offer, Ray,' said Ellie, perched tensely in an armchair in the living room, working swiftly with her embroidery needle to weave the image of a yellow teddy bear on to a child's jumper, 'but I'm always so shattered after the market on a Saturday, the last thing I want to do is go out for the evening.'

'What about Friday night then?'

She hesitated for a moment, biting her lip. 'To be perfectly honest, Ray, I'm not really in the mood for a night out at the moment,' she told him, without looking up.

'You know what they say about all work and no play,' he persisted gently.

She looked at him, her pale lips tightening. 'I have to work hard to make up for the time I lost while I was ill,' she snapped. 'I do have a child to support, remember.'

'I've offered to help you out financially,' he reminded her. 'There's no need for you to work yourself into the ground like this when you've got me to look after you.'

'Leave it, Ray . . .'

Glancing at his watch, he continued, 'It's turned nine o'clock and you're still working. You should be taking things easy after what you've been through.'

It was a month since Ellie had lost the baby and she seemed to have lost all her zest for life along with it. She was painfully thin because she had no appetite, her face was paper pale and her eyes dull and lacklustre. The worst thing was that she was so cold and detached now; Ray just didn't seem able to reach her.

'I appreciate your offer of help but I don't need it at the moment,' she told him. 'Anyway, my work isn't a chore but an enjoyment.'

'But you just said you have to work hard—'

'And I do,' she cut in, 'but I'd want to do it even if I didn't have to. I used to knit and sew for pleasure long before it became my means of earning a living.'

'Yes, I know that, Ellie,' he said patiently. 'But surely it doesn't have to be your only pleasure.'

'At the moment it suits me to work hard,' she said dully.

'A night out together might do us both good.' He was nothing if not persistent when it came to her wellbeing.

'Another time,' she said, digging her needle into the garment even more determinedly.

He looked at her sadly. Her head was bent over her work, red hair bright against her pale complexion, but hanging limply over her rigid shoulders. Before the miscarriage she and Ray used to snuggle up on the sofa together of an evening. Since she'd been home from the hospital she made a point of sitting in the armchair – to keep him at a distance, he suspected.

'Don't exclude me from your grief, Ellie,' he entreated. 'I love you and I want us to go through this together. We've both lost something precious. Don't push me away.'

'I'm sorry, Ray.' She looked at him soulfully. 'I'm just not very good company at the moment.'

He went over to her chair and sat on the arm. 'Put your work down for a minute and come and sit with me on the sofa,' he urged her affectionately.

She fastened the needle to the garment and put it down on a small table, then went to sit on the sofa in a stiff, dutiful manner. He sat down beside her. As he slipped his arm around her, she shrank from him so noticeably it sent a bolt of panic through him.

'What's all this about?' he wanted to know. 'Why have I become so repugnant to you?'

'You haven't,' she denied. 'Don't be silly.'

'Why won't you let me touch you then?'

She stared at her hands. 'I just don't feel like it,' she told him guiltily.

'All I want to do is be near you, just to feel you close to me, nothing else,' he wanted to make it clear. 'I know you need more time to recover after being so ill and I wouldn't dream of expecting more from you at this time. What do you think I am, some sort of an animal?'

She put her hand on his arm in a swift conciliatory

335

movement. 'Of course I don't. That's the last thing I would ever think about you,' she tried to assure him.

'That's what it seems like.'

'It's something inside me, Ray. It has nothing to do with you personally,' she tried to explain, genuinely distressed by her feelings and the awful thoughts that had plagued her recently. 'I seem to want to be on my own after Donna's gone to bed.'

'On your own to dwell on what's happened?' He was really worried about her.

'Not necessarily.'

'I think that's the reason even if you don't realise it yourself,' he said. 'And all that will do is make you feel worse.'

'Ray, please—'

'I won't let you do that, Ellie,' he interrupted. 'I care too much for you to let you sink ever deeper in this downward spiral. Losing the baby was a blow to us both and we'll never forget it. But you must concentrate on getting well now.'

'I'm sorry if I seem to be thinking only of myself,' she apologised. 'I know how much you wanted the baby. I realise that I've disappointed you.'

'You haven't disappointed me in the least. A quirk of nature was the reason you lost the baby. It wasn't your fault,' he corrected, eager to reassure her.

She shrugged in reply.

'Anyway, we're still quite young,' he went on. 'There's plenty of time to think about trying again if you feel like it at some time in the future.'

She fiddled with her fingernails and didn't reply straight away. 'Yeah, course we can,' she said at last, taking his hand and managing a watery smile. 'Sorry, I've been a bit offhand lately when you've been so good to me. I don't deserve you.'

'That's a silly thing to say.' He was relieved to see her relax a little as she moved closer to him, albeit stiffly. 'So don't let's have any more of that sort of talk.'

'OK,' she agreed, snuggling up to him and forcing a lift to her voice for his sake. 'And I'll really try not to be such a misery guts in future.'

After Ray left, about half an hour afterwards because he thought she needed an early night, Ellie returned to her armchair and sat staring blankly at the vase of flowers in the hearth in front of the firescreen she had embroidered when she'd first moved into this house with Tom. With thoughts of her husband, prior to the accident, filling her mind, guilt and self-loathing consumed her with such power, it was as much as she could do not to pummel her head with her fists.

Ray wanted to share her grief but how could she burden him with her complex inner feelings? She couldn't expect him to understand what a failure she felt as a human being. Because he loved her he would deny that she'd lost the baby as the result of some biological weakness in herself. Nor would he take the view that she was to blame for the fact that her mother and her mother's oldest friend had parted company, and that because of her own inexperienced driving Tom was living in an institution instead of having a normal life at home. And if all of that didn't make a big enough stick to beat herself with, there was adultery to give it an edge.

Because Ray was a kind-hearted man and wanted to spare her feelings, he tried to convince her that these things had happened through no fault of hers. But that viewpoint was an easy one to have when you weren't the one actually involved in the string of disasters so damaging to the lives of other people. Quite why the events of the past had come back to haunt her with such ferocity, Ellie wasn't sure, and could only assume it had something to do with the shock of losing her baby.

But for whatever reason, the recalcitrant mood of self-castigation was unliftable. The only peace to be had was in meeting the demands of her adored daughter, which kept Ellie's emotions under control, and working manically at her knitwear. No matter how hard she tried, she couldn't respond to Ray physically as she had before the miscarriage; it just didn't happen. She loved him but couldn't warm to him even though she'd pretended to just now because she didn't want to go on hurting him.

There seemed to be a dichotomy in her personality now. She couldn't bear him to touch her while at the same time wanting him with a ferocious ache. She felt trapped and alone in a maze of confusion. What could you do when you felt frozen towards the man you loved? There didn't seem to be an answer.

She did know that she wouldn't sleep if she went to bed, though, so picked up her work and continued with the embroidery, working with fast jerky movements.

Still tense and anxious about Ellie, who hadn't fooled him for a moment with her sudden show of cheerfulness, Ray felt the need to unwind so stopped off at a pub on the way home.

Lost in thought, Ray barely noticed what was going on around him. He nodded to a few familiar faces then ordered a pint and stood at the bar with it, mulling over the situation with Ellie. He could feel her slipping away from him and he didn't seem able to do a damned thing about it. It was terrifying.

He mustn't panic. She hadn't gone off him but was thinking baby not boyfriend just now, that was all. It was only natural after going through the miscarriage, the emotional upheaval as well as the physical pain and weakness. By the mere biology of it, a woman was bound to be more deeply affected than a man. All he could do was be patient and supportive. He must give her time to let nature take its course. But he longed for some other way to help her on to the road back to normality.

'Oh no, not you again,' complained Pat when Alfie came into the shop one wet evening in early autumn just as she was about to turn the sign on the door to closed. 'I thought I made 'it clear last time that I didn't want you to come here again.'

'Just thought I'd drop in to see how you were doing,' explained the indomitable Alfie, wearing a beige raincoat dripping with rain, his greying hair soaked.

'I'm doing fine, so now you know that, can you please leave?' she demanded. Although she was careful not to show it, his rough charm did actually warm her heart, which in turn made her feel vulnerable. She disliked the feeling so felt compelled to discourage him from coming here.

'That's gratitude for you,' was his cheerful riposte.

'I don't have to be grateful to you,' she pointed out. 'I didn't ask you to come here.'

'I know you didn't,' he grinned. 'But I thought you might like to see a friendly face.'

'Not particularly.'

'Oh well, I'm here now,' Alfie said. 'And it would be bad manners on your part to chuck me out straight away.'

'I want to close the shop and go upstairs to relax,' she said pointedly.

'Looks to me as though you can do with a hand.' She was standing by a pile of large cardboard cartons which he could see from the labels contained heavy canned goods.

'The delivery man just came in and dumped them there,' Pat explained with disapproval. 'He was in too much of a hurry to take them out the back to the stockroom and I was busy serving so didn't get the chance to insist.'

'That's not good enough, is it?'

'It certainly isn't,' she agreed wholeheartedly. 'You wouldn't believe the way some of these delivery men do their jobs. It's a wonder they don't just stand in the back of the lorry and throw the stuff on to the pavement outside.'

'Where do you want them?' Alfie asked, looking at the boxes.

'It's all right,' she assured him. 'I'll shift them myself in my own time.'

'They're too heavy for a woman to lift,' he pointed out.

'I'll manage.'

'You still haven't got an assistant then?' he assumed.

'If I had I wouldn't be here on my own, would I?' she said with a withering look.

'You might be, if it was their day off, or they'd already knocked off,' he countered.

'Mm, there is that, I suppose,' she said grudgingly. 'But no, I haven't got anyone.'

He tutted. 'It's a lot of work for you, running this place on your own.' His manner was sympathetic.

'Tell me something I don't already know.'

'Anyway, you want these in the stockroom,' he said purposefully, taking off his jacket and moving towards the cartons.

'I've told you I'll do it.' Accepting any sort of help from him seemed tantamount to letting him get a foot in the door to an inhibited woman like Pat.

'You'll do yourself an injury lifting those,' was his reply.

'I won't do them all at once,' she told him. 'I'll open the boxes and move a few tins at a time. I'd have had to do it myself if you hadn't happened to call in.'

'But I did call in, and it'll be quicker if I do it.' He gave her an enquiring look. 'The stockroom's at the back behind the counter, yeah?'

Pat nodded and before she could object any further, Alfie lifted one of the cartons as though it weighed nothing, and headed for the stockroom.

By the time she'd closed the shop and done the cashing up, he'd shifted the lot.

'Thanks very much,' she said gratefully.

'Glad to be of help.'

She opened the till and took out a two-shilling piece. 'Have a drink on me,' she said, handing it to him.

Now he was the one with the sharp tongue. 'Are you trying to insult me or something?' he objected strongly.

'No, of course not. I just thought—'

'All I did was shift a few boxes,' he interrupted sharply.

Pat's cheeks flamed. 'I didn't mean to offend you,' she told him with uncharacteristic meekness.

He shrugged. 'It'll take more than you on your high horse to offend me,' he assured her. 'But you'd do well to realise that not everyone needs paying for doing a favour.'

'Delivery men usually expect a tip if they do something over and above the minimum expected of them,' she informed him.

'Maybe they do but I'm not a delivery man,' he reminded her firmly.

'All right, you've made your point.' She reverted to her normal snappy manner.

'Anyway,' he said, changing the subject, 'have you tried that new cash and carry that's opened over at White City?'

'I've heard it mentioned but I've never been there,' she said. 'Some sort of a wholesale warehouse, isn't it?'

'Yeah, but with a difference. Retailers can buy the stuff at a cheap price for resale and take it with them instead of having it delivered, so you can buy in quite small amounts if you want to,' he explained. 'It's a new idea. The chap in our newsagent's was telling me about it. He uses it for confectionery some-times if he runs low on stock and isn't due for a delivery from the wholesaler. It isn't open to the general public. You have to prove that you're in business and they give you a card. I should think it would be useful to a small business like yours, just to tide you over when you need it.'

Despite herself Pat was interested in what Alfie had to say. 'It would be useful, I must admit,' she agreed. 'It's no good to me, though.'

'Why not?'

'I don't drive,' she told him.

'You've got an estate car, though,' he pointed out. 'I've seen it outside.'

'And a fat lot of good it is to me without anyone to drive it,' she said.

341

'I don't have a car but I do have a driving licence,' he mentioned. 'I learned to drive when I was in the army and I quite often borrow Ray's car. I'll drive you to the cash and carry, if you like. They stay open late in the evenings, apparently, so we could go when I get home from work, after you've closed the shop.'

'It's kind of you to offer, but I don't think so.' She looked embarrassed.

'Leave it until the dark nights are here if you'd rather not be seen with me,' he grinned.

'It isn't that,' she said, her cheeks burning because she took him seriously. 'I'm set in my ways, I'm used to having everything delivered.'

'Oh, well, suit yourself,' he said breezily. 'It was only a suggestion.'

'Thanks anyway.'

''S'all right.' He paused, looking at her over the counter. 'I suppose you heard that Ellie lost the baby,' he mentioned soberly.

She nodded. 'You can't keep something like that quiet around here, not when someone's rushed to hospital, anyway,' she said. 'There were complications, I believe. I understand she was very poorly.'

'Extremely.'

'How is she now?'

'Not too good.'

'Still not better?' said Pat in surprise. 'And it must be a couple of months ago.'

'I'm not saying she isn't better physically but she isn't her old self by any means. She seems very down,' he explained. 'Still, I suppose it takes a while for a woman to get over a thing like that.'

Pat felt a gnawing ache in the pit of her stomach, similar to the feeling she'd had as a child when she'd been sent away to stay with an aunt and had been grindingly homesick. She'd sooner die than admit it but she missed Ellie and Donna terribly, and Mary even more. She felt very alone without them in her life. 'Oh, yes, it's sure to,' she said in a subdued tone.

They fell silent until he asked, 'Have you done anything about getting some help in the shop?'

'Yes, I've advertised in the local paper and the notice is a permanent fixture in the shop window,' she explained.

'No response, I take it?'

'Not a great deal. I've had a few applicants but no one I'd feel happy about working with. People prefer to work in large establishments with a social club and staff benefits.'

'The younger element would be attracted to that, I suppose,' he agreed.

'I don't want a youngster, anyway, and especially not some slip of a girl,' she told him. 'I need someone with plenty of muscle, someone who can drive a car so that I can resume my delivery service again.'

'Didn't I hear that Ellie worked here for a while?' Alfie mentioned.

Pat's expression hardened but she couldn't hide the pain in her eyes. 'That's right,' she said.

'She's young, and definitely not muscular,' he remarked.

'She looks as though a puff of wind might blow her over but she's tough and not afraid of hard work, and of course . . .' She faltered. 'She was family and I've known her all her life. You have to work closely together in a small shop like this and it's difficult with a stranger. I've been on edge with everyone I've employed since Ellie left. That's why I'm being careful about who I take on. No point in giving someone the job out of desperation and then feeling uncomfortable with them.'

She'd been caught off guard and had allowed him to see how deeply she felt about the split between herself and the Scotts. Alfie felt a surge of compassion for her even though she'd brought it on herself. 'No. But at the same time, you need someone to help you rather urgently, don't you?' he said.

'Yes, that's true,' she sighed. 'But I manage to keep going somehow.'

'Anyway,' he said, 'I'd better be going. My belly's telling me it's teatime.'

Up went Pat's brows and she gave an expressive tut. 'Do you have to be so crude?'

'It isn't compulsory, no,' he teased her.

'You always were very basic,' she said in disgust.

'You didn't used to object.'

'I didn't used to object to an outside lavatory when I didn't know any better,' was her sharp retort.

Their eyes met fleetingly. 'Yeah, well, I'm off,' Alfie said, walking to the door without any further reference to the subject. 'Just called in to see how you are, and as you're obviously fine I'll go home for my tea. See you.'

'Cheerio.'

She followed him to the door to let him out. The windows were steamed up and the shop felt damp and chilly – and incredibly lonely suddenly. Having closed the door after him, she went to pull the blind down and lock up but didn't. Instead she opened the door and called after him.

'Yeah?' he said, turning and standing there in the rain, his hands sunk deep into his raincoat pockets.

'Er . . . I was thinking that perhaps it might be a good idea to go and have a look at that cash and carry one evening, after all,' she said uncertainly.

'Sure I won't be too common for you?'

'I'm only going to the warehouse with you,' she said, 'not moving in with you.'

'Thank God for that.'

Pat gave an exasperated sigh because his humorous manner was difficult to deal with and she found it impossible to find a suitable reply. 'When shall we go then?' she asked in a serious tone.

'Which day did you have in mind?'

'Whenever it suits you,' she heard herself say.

'My word, we are being considerate,' he smiled. 'I hope you're not sickening for something.'

Her face twisted into a scowl. 'If you're going to be downright rude, you can forget it altogether,' she snapped. 'I won't bother to go at all. I've managed to run this business successfully without a cash and carry warehouse for a good few years. So I'm sure I can continue.'

He sucked in his breath, shaking his head in an admonitory manner. 'You really must learn to take a joke,' he told her, 'and stop taking every single thing so seriously.'

She lowered her eyes, ashamed of her lack of humour. No one had ever been able to embarrass her in the way that he could. 'How about Wednesday?' she suggested quickly, to gloss over the awkward moment. 'The shop's closed in the afternoon so I can be ready when you get here.' She didn't add that Wednesday afternoons were desolate for her now that she didn't look after her granddaughter, and an outing in the evening might help to ease the crippling loneliness. She'd cut herself off from Ellie and that meant not seeing Donna either, because the two of them went together as far as she was concerned.

'Wednesday it is then,' Alfie agreed cheerfully. 'About the same time as I got here tonight?'

'Right.'

She watched him head off down the street, the puddles splashing around his feet. He still had the same swaying gait he'd had as a young man, a touch of devil-may-care about him despite a troubled life. Unexpectedly she found herself seeing his visit in a new light. He'd bothered to come and see her in this miserable weather after a full day's work in a factory when he could have gone straight home for his tea. She was hateful to him but he was still willing to drive her to the cash and carry.

Compunction wasn't something she had any truck with as a rule because it was a nuisance; it interfered with logic and made things less clearly defined. But her conscience was troubling her now. She was also aware of something else: for the first time in years she felt a flicker of warmth inside her as she recognised true human kindness.

Chapter Seventeen

'I'm surprised you're willing to put yourself out for Ellie's mother-in-law,' remarked Ray to his father one evening in late September, 'considering the way she treated Ellie.'

'It was because of the way she treated Ellie that I went to see her in the first place,' Alfie explained. 'I've told her exactly what I think about that and tried to persuade her to put things right. I'm still working on it.'

Ray gave him a shrewd look. 'Doing her shop deliveries for her is all part of your master plan, is it?' he suggested waggishly.

'No. I'm doing that because I feel sorry for her,' his father told him straight.

'After what that woman's done to Ellie and her mother,' disapproved Ray, 'you must be bonkers.'

'I know I'm soft,' Alfie admitted, 'but she doesn't seem to have a friend in the world now that she's fallen out with Ellie and her family. It must be lonely for her.'

'And whose fault's that?' Ray was combing his hair in front of the mirror above the fireplace near where his father was sitting in the armchair. Wearing a smart brown leather jacket, Ray was all ready to go to Ellie's.

'Her own, of course,' his father conceded. 'Pat Hall is a very difficult woman to get on with, I won't deny that.'

'Difficult!' exploded Ray. 'I can think of stronger adjectives to describe her.'

'You can call her what you like but you won't alter the fact that she feels pain the same as the rest of us,' said Alfie. 'She is still a human being.'

'Not a very nice one from what I've heard.' Ray turned away from the mirror, slipping his comb into his top pocket.

'That's the general impression she creates,' Alfie told him. 'She's obviously feeling wretched within herself and it's making her behave like some sort of a monster. Someone has to save her from herself. And, I think I do actually get through to her even though she's at pains to hide it.'

'All sweetness and light with you, is she?' Ray teased him.

'That'll be the day,' corrected Alfie, raising his eyes and puffing out his lips to emphasise the point. 'But I do think she takes notice of what I say, even though she'd never admit it in a million years. If I keep chipping away at her, she might actually do something about it eventually.'

'I wouldn't bank on it.'

Alfie had a sudden thought. 'I hope Ellie won't think that by helping Pat I'm being disloyal to her in any way.' He looked worried.

'Course she won't,' Ray was quick to assure him. 'Ellie isn't like that. Knowing her, she'll be pleased that you're taking the trouble. Even after the damned woman had given her such a tongue-lashing, she was still making excuses for her. That's the way Ellie is.'

'You're a lucky man.'

'You don't have to tell me that,' was Ray's wholehearted agreement. He crossed the somewhat cluttered living room and picked up his car keys from the top of the sideboard.

'I'm only helping Pat out with the deliveries until she gets a new assistant, you know,' Alfie pointed out. 'It's just a temporary thing.'

'There's no need to explain yourself to me.' Ray paused on his way to the door and turned to his father, grinning. 'I can't help noticing that you seem to be getting your feet under the table there, though. First the cash and carry warehouse, now you've giving up your Friday evenings to do her deliveries.'

'Just a favour,' he insisted. 'She's losing a lot of customers because she had to stop her delivery service. That was the one thing she had to offer that the big stores didn't. The least I could do was offer to do some driving for her until she gets somebody full time.'

'It's a job of work, though,' Ray pointed out, in a more serious tone. 'So I hope she's paying you.'

'I was willing to do it for nothing but she wouldn't hear of it.'

'That's all right then.' Ray's mind was already moving on to other things. He jangled his keys and headed for the door with a spring in his step.

'Give Ellie my love and tell her I'll see her on Saturday at the market,' Alfie mentioned.

'Will do.'

His father gave him a sharp look. 'You're looking very pleased with yourself tonight, son,' he commented. 'Any particular reason?'

'Yeah. Ellie's been a bit brighter lately,' he explained. 'So I'm feeling positive. I want to take steps to put our relationship on to a more permanent footing.'

'Oh?'

'Before Ellie lost the baby we were planning to move in together – a new start for us both,' Ray said. 'But for a long time after the miscarriage she was so weak and low in spirits I didn't feel able to bother her with it.'

'That's understandable.'

'But now that she seems so much better I think it'll be all right to bring it up again so I'm going to talk to her about it tonight.' He cast his eye around the room, which was comfortable enough but old-fashioned, and rather small. 'It's high time I got out from under your feet, anyway.'

'You're welcome to stay here for as long as you like but it's only natural you should want to move on,' said Alfie. 'Good luck with Ellie, anyway.'

'Thanks, Dad, I'll see you.' And whistling a popular tune, Ray left the flat.

Ellie had allowed Donna to stay up to see Ray and within seconds of his arrival, he was into his second childhood, on the floor doing the horse game to loud shrieks of delight from the little girl. Eventually, he and Ellie put her to bed together, leaving her cuddling a fluffy rabbit and almost asleep.

It was when they came downstairs Ray sensed that something was wrong. Ellie seemed edgy and overanxious to please him, asking how he was and what sort of a day he'd had. She was looking particularly attractive this evening, he noticed, in a pale blue jersey dress, her hair shining with vitality again, her countenance glowing from a light dusting of make-up. None of this could hide the fact that she was extremely tense, though.

She didn't join him on the sofa but remained standing, fiddling nervously with a lock of hair. 'I've got something to tell you,' she blurted out.

'Snap,' he said, 'but you can go first.'

Whatever she had to say, it was making her uncomfortable, he noticed, watching her shift from foot to foot, unnecessarily combing her hair back from her face with her fingers. 'Get on with it, then,' he said uneasily.

'There's no easy way to say this, Ray,' she burst out, turning his mild uneasiness into heart-stopping dread. 'So I'll get straight to the point.' She paused, taking a deep breath. 'The fact is, I have to stop seeing you.'

'I don't understand.'

'It's over, Ray,' she clarified, her voice barely a whisper. 'I'm so sorry.'

Stunned into silence, he stared at her, breathless with shock, his heart beating so loudly it throbbed right through to his fingertips. 'I don't believe I just heard that,' he said at last, looking at her with a bemused expression.

'You did hear it, I'm afraid.'

He stood up and looked into her sad eyes, realising with a horrible ache that she meant what she said. All the signs had been there but he hadn't wanted to face up to their meaning. Anyway, she'd seemed more like her old self lately. 'You've seemed warmer towards me this last couple of weeks,' he muttered, hardly aware of what he was saying. 'So I thought everything was all right between us.'

'Knowing I had to end it heightened my feelings for you,' she explained dully. 'I felt as though I never wanted to let you go. I should have told you as soon as I made the decision. I just kept putting it off because I didn't want it to happen.'

'This is all to do with the miscarriage, isn't it?' he guessed. 'You haven't been the same person since then. You didn't want to know about me after that.'

'It isn't like that,' she tried to explain. 'My feelings towards you haven't changed.'

'Oh, do me a favour,' he said with a hard edge to his voice. 'They must have or you wouldn't be doing this.'

'That just isn't true, Ray.'

'In God's name why then?'

'I was so low when I lost the baby, feeling such a failure, I took a long hard look at myself and my life,' she explained, 'and I didn't like what I saw.'

'Why?'

'I'm a walking disaster,' she stated categorically. 'I do nothing but cause trouble for other people.'

'Of course you don't,' he denied. 'No more than anyone else, anyway. We all hurt people from time to time. It's just part of being alive.'

'It's a bit more than that in my case,' she insisted. 'My affair with you has caused my mother to end a long and valued friendship. My careless driving has put my husband in an institution—'

'That just isn't true, Ellie,' he cut in. 'All right, if you must torture yourself about our affair and its effect on your mother's friendship with Pat, then go ahead. But there is no way on God's earth you can be blamed for what happened to Tom.'

'I'd like to agree with you but I can't,' she told him, her

351

voice ragged with emotion. 'I just can't.'

He paced up and down, face flushed, perspiration shining on his skin. 'It's all an excuse,' he accused, through tight lips, 'because you don't have the guts to tell me straight that you don't want us to be together.'

'It isn't an excuse.' Ellie was on the verge of tears now. 'I'm married to Tom and having an affair with you. That isn't right, whatever the reason for the accident.'

'Most people would think the circumstances make a difference to the morality of the situation,' he told her, standing still now with his hands clenched tightly by his sides.

'What other people think isn't an issue,' she said. 'If it had been I'd never have got involved with you in the first place.' Shining with tears, her eyes were a vivid shade of blue in her ashen face. 'This has nothing to do with the gossips. It's about me and how I feel inside.' She spread her hands in a helpless gesture. 'I'm so tired of all the guilt. I just can't take it any more.'

'And you think giving me up will give you absolution?' he said harshly. 'Make you feel clean and righteous?'

'Of course not.'

'Why do it then?'

'Because I think it's right,' she informed him. 'And let's face it, I'm no good to you as I am at the moment, all screwed up inside and not responding to you properly.'

'Oh, please, spare me the bit about it being better for me.' He was very bitter.

'I know I'm hurting you, Ray,' she said in a tone of sad resignation. 'It's what I do to people, I've told you.'

'Don't do this,' he begged.

'I need to get myself sorted.' She was very subdued.

'You can do that with me around,' he pointed out. 'I can see no purpose to your ending our relationship whatsoever.'

'At least I'd be doing something that was right.' Her voice was shaking now.

'Right by whose standards?' he queried. 'The local gossips',

352

your narrow-minded mother-in-law's?'

'By my standards,' she said thickly. 'Maybe I can do more for Tom if I'm on my own.'

'What more can you do, for God's sake?' Ray blasted, his voice guttural with emotion. 'The man is beyond your help. He doesn't know what your name is from one visit to the next, let alone that he's a married man with a daughter.' He raised his hands, appealing to her. 'Think about it, Ellie. What more can you possibly do for him other than ensure that he has the best care you can afford. He's happy – why don't you leave it at that and get on with your life?'

'I can't, Ray,' she told him. 'I just can't go on feeling like this day after day. It's draining the spirit out of me.'

'You, you, you.' His voice was almost a growl now. 'What about me in all this? While you're taking the moral stance and luxuriating in a glow of righteousness, I'm left out in the cold. What do you think this is doing to me?'

'I won't be feeling righteous, and not having you in my life will be hell,' she tried to make him understand. 'But I've got to do it, Ray. I've got to try and work through this on my own. I'm sorry.'

'Sorry just isn't good enough.' His expression was sheer granite. 'You dump me after all we've been to each other, and all you can say is sorry and goodbye?'

'What else can I say?' she implored him, tears falling now.

'How about something like, "I'm going to behave like an adult and face up to the reality of the situation which is – I no longer have a husband as such, so I'm going to get on with my life with you, the man I love." ' He paused then added, 'All supposing, of course, that I am the man you love.'

'You know perfectly well that you are.'

'I thought I knew that,' he said. 'But now I'm not so sure. You don't do something like this to someone you love. It isn't the way it works.'

She wiped her eyes. 'Not normally, I agree,' she said thickly. 'But my circumstances are not normal.'

'OK, so you're a married woman with a disabled husband,' Ray conceded. 'I can see that you might have a moral dilemma. If I thought Tom could be hurt by our relationship in any way at all, you wouldn't see me for dust. But he can't possibly be affected. And he is the only one who matters in this, apart from you and me. His mother and everything that's happened because of her unreasonable disapproval is incidental. Tom isn't affected so that leaves you, me and Donna and a good future together. Don't throw it away.'

'There's no point in your going on about it, Ray.'

'What do you expect me to do?' he demanded. 'Sit back and accept it?'

'It's the only thing you can do.'

'I still can't believe this has happened,' he went on. 'I came here tonight with the idea of putting a seal on our relationship. I was going to suggest that we start looking for a place to live. And all the time you had this little bombshell up your sleeve.'

She was crying silently, head bent, shoulders shaking.

Raking his fingers through his hair distractedly, he said, 'That's right, turn on the tears . . . Make me feel guilty for trying to make you see sense.'

'I'm not trying to make you feel guilty,' she sobbed. 'You've every right to be angry.'

He went to her and put his arms around her, feeling her stiffen against him. 'I'm sorry I've made you cry,' he told her, his own eyes moistening.

'You haven't made me cry,' she told him. 'I'm crying because I'm unhappy.'

'Don't do it then.' Gently he put both hands on her face and turned it up so that their eyes met. 'Stop this before it goes any further.'

'No matter how much I want to, I can't do that.' She wiped her eyes again and tried to compose herself. 'So go, Ray, please leave.'

He moved back as though he'd been slapped. 'If I go out of that door, I'll be out of your life for good,' he told her gravely.

'So make sure it's really what you want because I won't be back.'

'Just go,' she said, staring at the floor.

There was a brief hesitation, then he left, closing the front door quietly behind him so as not to wake Donna. That final thoughtful gesture pierced at Ellie's heart.

So it was over. She'd done what her conscience dictated and it felt like hell. When her tears had finally subsided, she went upstairs to her daughter's bedroom, watching her sleep in the glow from the landing light. She looked utterly perfect, lying there on her back, ginger curls spread over the pillow, one arm still cuddling the rabbit, the other splayed by the side of her head. The storybook from which Ray had been reading to her was on the cupboard by the bed.

The thought of how much Donna was going to miss Ray tore at Ellie's heart and caused fresh tears to form. She comforted herself in the knowledge that her daughter was too young for any lasting memories. It might be days, possibly weeks even, but she'd soon forget him.

She bent over and kissed her warm face, then covered her up and went downstairs to the back room and sat down at her knitting machine. She continued work on the garment in progress. But as she pulled the cam box to and fro and watched the knitting grow, she experienced none of the usual satisfaction. In this particular instance, peace of mind didn't lie in activity. She searched for consolation in having done what she thought was right about Ray. But there was none.

When he left Ellie, Ray drove home, parked the car outside his father's block of flats and walked to the nearest pub, knowing he wouldn't be in a fit state to drive when he came out. He stayed only until he'd had enough to numb the pain, then staggered home.

His father was watching the television when he got in.

'I'm drunk,' announced Ray, his speech slurred, his manner belligerent.

'So I gather,' said Alfie.

'My girlfriend's ditched me and I don't want to talk about it so I'm going to bed,' he declared.

'Good night then, son,' said Alfie, knowing better than to ask questions while Ray was in this mood.

'G'night.'

Ray made his way slowly and laboriously up the stairs and fell drunkenly asleep on the bed, fully dressed. When he woke up the next morning with the father of all hangovers, and remembered what had happened, he put his head under the covers and wanted to stay there for ever.

He hadn't had that feeling since the early days of his prison sentence. Having overcome it then, he'd thought he was impervious. He hadn't expected to come up against anything else that would make him low enough to experience it again.

'So, what's been happening here while I've been away?' asked Doug of his wife over their evening meal a few days later. He'd been on a long-haul trip with the lorry to the north of England and had been away for a couple of nights.

'Nothing much. Matthew hasn't been very well, though,' she mentioned, forking some shepherd's pie into her mouth.

'Aah, bless him.' Doug was immediately concerned. 'What was the trouble?'

'Just a tummy bug that's been doing the rounds with the local kids. He's all right now, though. Sleeping like a top. He'll be pleased to see his daddy in the morning.'

'Likewise.' Doug concentrated on his meal. 'Have you been all right while I've been away?' he asked.

'I managed.' Neither of them liked it when he was away from home. 'I missed you, though.'

'Same here, love.' He smiled at her fondly. 'It's such a relief to be home.'

'Missed my cooking, did you?'

'Not half as much as I missed you,' he said. 'And Matthew, of course.'

'That's nice.'

They continued with their meal in comfortable silence for a while, the atmosphere warm and affectionate. 'Are the family all right?' Doug enquired eventually.

'Your mum and dad are fine.' Her brow creased into a frown as she remembered something. 'Your sister's had a bit of a setback, though.'

'Ellie?' He held his knife and fork poised. 'Why? What's happened?'

'She and Ray have split up.'

'What!' Doug dropped his cutlery on to his plate with a clatter, looking horrified.

'I could hardly believe it either,' she told him. 'But it's true. Ellie told me about it yesterday.'

'But they seemed so settled.'

'I know,' agreed Ann. 'I thought they seemed perfect for each other. But Ellie decided she couldn't continue, so she told him she couldn't see him again.'

'*She* ended it?'

'That's right. And she's in a pretty rotten state about it, I can tell you. Even though she's making out she's fine.'

'What on earth possessed her to do such a thing?' Doug wondered aloud.

'Tom's the main reason, as far as I can make out,' Ann said. 'She's been burdened with guilt about several things for ages but finishing with Ray is down to Tom, I think, and the fact that she blames herself for the accident.'

'Not still,' uttered Doug disapprovingly.

'Yeah, still. She could probably have coped with the adultery and all the trouble it's caused if it wasn't for that, given the circumstances. But because deep down she thinks she's to blame for Tom being in Greenlands, in the end the affair with Ray was just too much to take.'

'Poor old Ray,' tutted Doug. 'He must be devastated.'

'Bound to be, I should think,' Ann agreed.

'Ellie's completely out of order on this one,' said Doug,

357

becoming angry. 'She shouldn't have done that to Ray. That's nothing short of cruel.'

The harmonious and loving atmosphere that had been so strong only minutes before, vanished completely. The news about his sister had soured Doug's mood.

'It's hurting her too, you know,' Ann said quietly.

'Why do such a stupid thing then?'

'That's her business,' she replied curtly. 'It's nothing to do with us.'

'It isn't right, Ann.' Doug was vehement about it.

'Hey, calm down,' she urged him, astonished by the violence of his reaction. 'There's no need to get so worked up about it. You can't live your sister's life for her.'

'And I wouldn't dream of trying,' he told her. 'But it's ridiculous for her to feel guilty about what happened to Tom. Everyone knows it wasn't her fault.'

'I quite agree with you, as it happens, but this is between her and her conscience,' Ann pointed out. 'Only Ellie knows how she feels. And if she doesn't feel able to continue seeing Ray, that's entirely up to her.'

Doug pushed his plate away.

'You're not leaving your dinner?'

'I'm not hungry . . .'

'Oh, Doug . . .'

'Sorry, love, but I've lost my appetite.'

But Ann wasn't having it. 'Look, Doug, I'm as sorry about Ellie and Ray as you are but you're taking it too far,' she reproved. 'I spent a lot of time cooking our meal. I've been looking forward to your coming home and us spending the evening together, having been on my own for a few days. And you let somebody else's love-life affect you to the extent that you can't eat your food. I know you care about your sister but this is ridiculous.'

He gave her a sheepish look. 'I'm sorry, love.' He put his plate back in front of him. 'You're right. I shouldn't spoil things for us because of something that's not our business.' He was obviously still thinking about it, despite his apology. 'It just seems so pointless for Ellie to punish them both over something that wasn't her fault. Maybe I should try and talk some sense into her.'

'No. I really don't think you should interfere.' Ann was very definite about it. 'It was a difficult decision for her to make, apparently, and having gone through agonies over it, the last thing she needs now is someone telling her that she's done the wrong thing.'

'Mm. I suppose you're right.'

'So eat your meal and let's talk about something else,' she suggested.

'OK.'

But although Doug entered into a conversation of sorts with her, she knew his heart wasn't in it. He was miles away and gloomy, obviously still mulling over the situation with Ellie. Ann guessed he would have a disturbed night . . .

At times like this, she felt as though she was married to a stranger, and it was a bleak feeling. But what could she do? If she tried to talk to him about his worries, he just refused to discuss it. Because she loved him she had no choice but to put up with his mood. But it was painful to know that her husband didn't feel able to share his worries with her. Ann wasn't the clinging sort of wife who thought couples should be immersed in each other to the point where they lost their own individuality. But she did believe they should share their troubles.

Most of the shepherd's pie ended up in the bin that night.

Many women have times in their lives when they feel the need of a female friend, some trusted person outside of the family circle in whom they can confide.

Mary was experiencing such a time in the aftermath of Ellie's break-up with Ray, when her daughter was desperately unhappy and expending a great deal of energy pretending otherwise. There was no shortage of cheery chatter. Ellie uttered plenty of it through lips fixed into a smile. But anyone could see it was false, and that she was actually miserable inside herself. She couldn't be persuaded to talk about it either. All she would say on the subject was that she had made her choice and wanted to put the whole thing behind her and get on with her life. Mary was worried sick.

There was no one in the family she could talk to about it. Bob just said it was Ellie's choice, Ann said very little out of loyalty to her friend, and Doug seemed very emotionally involved, for some reason. He became irritable if she tried to broach the subject and launched into a diatribe about his sister's error of judgement. So Mary needed someone outside to discuss it with.

Had things been different between herself and Pat, she would have headed straight for Chad Street. But as they weren't speaking and Pat's attack on Ellie was probably partly to blame for the split, anyway, this option wasn't open to Mary. Pat was still greatly missed by her. For all that their friendship had been more of an irritation than a pleasure at times, its absence left a void in her life.

Still, she was going to have to get used to it because it wasn't likely to change since a reconciliation required a change of heart on Pat's part, and she was stubborn when she thought she was right about something. Mary still couldn't remember their bitter parting without pain. It was a sad fact of life that her friendship with Pat Hall was well and truly over.

Ellie listened to the matron of Greenlands intently as she responded to what Ellie had had to say.

'I can understand your feeling that you should be more involved with your husband's care,' she said in an even tone. 'It's only natural that you should.'

'I suppose it is.' Ellie found her very easy to talk to.

She was quietly spoken and kind-hearted but Ellie knew from past experience that she also had the tough edge necessary to do this job; the ban she'd imposed on Ellie visiting

Tom was one example. 'But what you have to remember is that he's perfectly content in his life here with us at Greenlands so there's no need for you to worry about him, or feel that you are neglecting him in any way.'

'That's something, anyway,' said Ellie.

'His physical health is quite good considering the injuries he sustained in the accident, and his mental condition is reasonably stable at the moment,' the matron went on to say. 'We seem to have found the right combination of drugs for him.'

It was a Sunday afternoon, a month or so after her break-up with Ray. Since then Ellie had given a great deal of consideration to the question of how she might add something to her husband's life. Having drawn a complete blank, she'd driven to Greenlands in the hope that the matron might have some suggestion.

'I understand what you're saying and I have complete faith in what you do here at Greenlands,' Ellie assured her. 'It's just that I feel so distanced from him. And feel I ought to be doing more for him.'

The woman's intelligent brown eyes rested on Ellie. 'This is a very common problem with relatives of patients as severely disabled as Tom is,' she told Ellie.

'Is it?'

'Oh yes. It's actually much harder for their loved ones than it is for the patients themselves,' she explained. 'They are protected from any regret about their plight by the condition itself, and completely oblivious to the suffering of their relatives.'

'Yes, I understand that.' Ellie distractedly pushed her fringe from her brow with her fingers, an idea beginning to form. 'As you've said he's fairly stable at the moment, I was wondering . . . might it be possible to have him come home for a visit?' she suggested tentatively. 'Just a short one, perhaps a weekend or something?'

Matron shook her head without a moment's hesitation.

'No, that wouldn't be a good idea, Mrs Hall,' she stated categorically. 'It would be far too unsettling for him. As I've mentioned to you before, Tom needs the security of a regular routine. Being away from here would disturb and upset his behaviour pattern when he came back to us, as well as him possibly being difficult for you to handle at home.'

'I see.' Being brutally honest, Ellie was relieved. On the one hand she wanted to assuage her guilt by doing something positive for Tom, something that would give him pleasure. On the other hand, she'd suspected that having him home might be stressful and possibly dangerous for them all, especially as she had a lively young child in the house.

'There is one thing we could try, though,' Matron mentioned thoughtfully.

Ellie looked at her expectantly.

'I think maybe now that we have him settled on these particular drugs, you could take him out for an hour or so, one Sunday afternoon perhaps during visiting time,' she suggested.

'For a run in the car?'

'Oh, no. Being enclosed in a car might get him too excited and lead to trouble,' Matron pointed out. 'I was thinking in terms of something simpler, just a walk down to the town to buy an ice cream or something.'

'Sounds like a good idea,' approved Ellie, brightening.

'There's a rather nice ice-cream parlour in Senbridge that the staff take some of the patients to on the odd occasion for a treat,' she went on. 'There's a teashop too, but I think a sit-down tea out would be too taxing for Tom. He might get fidgety and start wandering around, which is a little disruptive for the other customers, and in turn disturbing for him. Just an ice cream, I think.'

'You've never suggested anything like this before,' Ellie remarked in an enquiring tone.

'No, because his behaviour was always so unpredictable. I still can't guarantee that the trip will be a success,' Matron warned sternly. 'But as it would only be short, I'm prepared to allow you to do it. An hour away from here shouldn't do him any harm.'

'I'm willing to give it a try, anyway,' Ellie told her.

'Good.' She leaned back in her chair, looking at Ellie thoughtfully. 'It's only a small thing but it might help you to feel a little more involved.'

Ellie's mind had moved on. 'Do you think I could bring my little girl along?' she asked.

'What age is she now?'

'Nearly three and a half.'

'She hasn't been here before, has she?' Matron said, looking into space as though thinking back.

'No. We decided not to risk it the last time the subject came up, if you remember,' Ellie reminded her. 'We thought the noisy and unpredictable presence of a small child might trigger off one of Tom's rages.'

'Yes, I remember.'

'But as he's more stable now, perhaps this is a good time to introduce them?'

The matron didn't reply at once; she seemed to be mulling the question over, tucking an escaping curl from her tight perm under her cap.

'She's still too young to wonder where her daddy is, of course,' Ellie explained. 'But if you approve, I'd like to bring her with me when I come to take Tom out. At least it would be some contact with her father. Of course, if you don't think it's wise, I'll leave her with my mother and come on my own.'

'No. You bring her along,' Matron decided at last. 'But obviously Tom won't respond to her as a daughter.'

'Of course not,' she said. 'Should she call him Daddy, do you think?'

'I'll leave that to you. It won't make any difference to Tom one way or the other. It's just another word to him.'

'But you think he'll be able to cope with having a child around?' Ellie needed assurance.

'I think so,' Matron affirmed, 'as you'll only be away for a short time. If he's upset by her we'll know before you leave so she can stay here. If he's unhappy for any reason at all while you're out, come straight back. You'll only be a few minutes' walk away.'

'We'll come next Sunday afternoon then, shall we?' suggested Ellie.

'Right you are, my dear,' smiled the matron. 'Let's hope the weather is fine for you.'

It was nigh on impossible to avoid someone completely when you both worked on the same market. Ellie studiously avoided the places she knew Ray might be, such as the café and the pub. She even changed her parking place to a side street she knew he didn't use, and she didn't go near his stall, not even to say hello to Alfie, who solved that particular problem by coming over to her stall for a few friendly words.

For the first few Saturdays after the break-up Ellie didn't see sight of Ray. But on the fourth one she was so distracted by nervous apprehension about what she had planned for Tom the next day, she didn't have all her wits about her on her way back from the greengrocery stall where she'd gone to get some apples, and bumped into him – literally.

'Sorry,' she apologised without looking up.

'You ought to look where you're going.' He hadn't been paying attention either and didn't realise it was her.

Her head shot up at the familiar sound of his voice. 'I had no idea it was you,' she said, standing there staring at him, clutching a brown paper bag full of apples.

'Likewise.'

They stood still, their gazes locked, oblivious to the jostling crowds and the market bustle around them.

'How are you?' he asked, mouth dry with nerves.

'Fine. You?'

He shrugged, fixing her with a steely stare, having composed himself after the initial shock of this unexpected confrontation. His eyes were brilliant and very fierce. 'Oh, I'm

364

wonderful,' he informed her with withering sarcasm. 'I'm bound to be on top of the world, aren't I, having been dumped by my girlfriend!'

'I'd better get back,' she said.

'Don't want to be reminded, eh?'

'Ray, please.' She bit her lip. 'There's no point in going over it again.'

'No, you're right.' His expression was ice hard. 'There's no point at all.' He looked in the direction he'd been going. 'See you around, then.'

'Yeah, see you.'

He disappeared into the crowds, leaving her reeling from the effects of the meeting for the rest of the day. Unfortunately this sort of incident was going to happen all too often while they both worked on the market. Maybe it was time she stopped doing the stall and concentrated all her energy into knitting for the shops and her personal customers. She'd only ever intended the market to be a temporary thing anyway, and the other side of her business was doing well enough now. If anything, she had too much work.

She decided to give the matter some serious thought when she was feeling calmer and more capable of rationalising. She needed to get tomorrow at Greenlands over first.

Ray was still feeling shaken by the meeting with Ellie that evening as he stood at the bar in a Shepherd's Bush pub. His father had gone to the Rose and Crown to play dominoes with his cronies so Ray was alone.

The situation at the market couldn't continue. On Saturdays he was in emotional turmoil, knowing that Ellie was at such close proximity. He had to restrain himself from going over to her stall and begging her to change her mind. He'd never get over her while he still had the stall.

'Wotcher, Ray,' said a female voice.

'Maria,' he said, turning. 'You're getting to be quite a regular in here.'

'Yeah, I am, aren't I? We thought there might be some sort of entertainment,' she said, glancing towards the same friends she'd been with the last time he'd seen her; they were standing at the other end of the bar. 'But they don't have anything on at the weekend, apparently.'

'They don't need entertainment to pull the punters in on a Saturday,' he pointed out, 'as the pubs are full anyway.'

She gave a casual nod. 'On your own on a Saturday night?' she asked. 'Or have you stopped off for a quick one on your way to see your girlfriend?'

'We split up,' he blurted out.

'Oh.' She seemed surprised. 'I thought you were fixed up permanent.'

'I thought so too,' Ray said glumly.

'Oh dear, it sounds as though she gave you your marching orders, not the other way around,' she probed.

Because Maria was of no special importance to him, there was no loss of pride to Ray in admitting the truth. 'Yeah, she did, as a matter of fact.'

'What is she, some sort of lunatic?' was Maria's forthright response.

Ray knew it was meant to be a compliment but his natural instinct to defend Ellie blotted out the much-needed boost to his ego. 'No, not at all,' he said, frowning. 'Far from it.'

'Ooh, we are touchy tonight. No offence intended,' she apologised, picking up on the admonishment in his tone. 'You know what I meant.'

'It's all right,' he said, soothed by her cheery candour. 'No offence taken.'

'I know that if I had my chance again I wouldn't let you go,' she went on to inform him.

Their eyes met fleetingly. He was aware of the chemistry between them but shunned the idea of taking it further because it wouldn't be fair to use her merely as a diversion. 'Shouldn't you be with your friends?' he said pointedly.

'Yeah, I'll go back in a minute,' Maria chirped. 'Just

thought I'd pop over and say hello. I'm glad I did, an' all. Seems to me you need some cheering up.'

'I'll be all right,' Ray assured her. 'But I'm a miserable old sod at the moment. So you go and enjoy yourself.'

'I suppose I'd better.' She looked up at him through thick, sweeping lashes. 'I meant what I said just now, though. I really do regret letting you go.'

'Well, it happened and there's no harm done.' Her interest in him was flattering but it wasn't reciprocated.

'This bloke I'm with tonight's only casual, you know,' she informed him.

Ray decided to be straight with her. 'I'm not looking for a reconciliation, Maria, if that's what you're hinting at,' he informed her.

'I can understand that, Ray, after the way I treated you,' she said in a soft, persuasive voice. 'But if you ever feel like a chat, just give me a call. You've got my number.'

'Thanks.' He had no intention of contacting her and had thrown away the cigarette packet she'd written her telephone number on.

But Maria was one step ahead of him. 'Just in case you've lost it, I'll give it to you again,' she said, rummaging in her bag and taking out a pencil and a screwed-up envelope. Writing her number on the back, she slipped it into his jacket pocket.

'It's nice of you but I meant what I said,' Ray insisted.

'No harm in having the number of a friend when you're feeling low, is there?' She put her head at a saucy angle and winked.

She was nothing if not persistent, he thought. 'Go on with you,' he said, grinning. 'Go back to your friends and enjoy yourself.'

'You know me. I've never been known not to.' Her eyes danced as they rested on his face. 'See you,' she said, and walked away.

Ray found himself smiling after her. She was totally hedonistic and out for her own ends. But she wasn't without a certain charm. He turned to the bar, ordered another drink and let his thoughts drift back to Ellie and the abysmal state of his life.

'I've made a decision, Dad,' Ray said later that same evening, when both the men were back home.

'That sounds ominous,' said his father. 'What is it?'

'I'm going to finish with the market and concentrate wholly on making and marketing the big stuff,' Ray announced, standing with his back to the fire while Alfie sat in the armchair. 'The ornamental gates and stair banisters.'

'Because of Ellie working on the market, I assume?' Alfie guessed.

'That's part of it,' admitted Ray. 'It isn't easy seeing her, the way things are between us. But I never intended the market to be permanent.'

'True.'

'So this is as good a time as any to change tack,' he said in a positive manner.

'Yeah,' nodded Alfie absently.

'I'll be sorry in a way,' Ray went on. 'The market's been good for me. It got me started and gave me the confidence to have my own business. Now I must progress onwards.'

'Mm.' Alfie was thoughtful.

'I've enjoyed the stall but it'll be nice not being tied to it every week,' Ray went on. 'I shall spend the time in the workshop on a Saturday if I've got a lot of work in. If not, maybe I'll relax a little, might go to a football match now and again.' He looked at his father in concern. 'I hope you won't miss the market too much, Dad. I know you enjoy it on a Saturday as a change from the factory.'

Alfie was actually delighted by this turn of events. Having Saturdays to himself set him free to pursue plans of his own that he'd been thinking about for some time. But he wasn't ready to discuss them with his son yet so he just said, 'I'll soon find something to do, son, don't worry about me.'

'That's good.' Ray studied his fingernails for a moment before looking up. 'Actually, Dad, there's something else I have to tell you too,' he said.

'Go on.'

'I'm going to start looking for a flat, even though Ellie and I aren't together. It's time I had my own place.'

'All right, son,' was Alfie's amiable response. 'I'll miss you but I can understand how you feel.'

'Being able to stay here has been a lifeline, and I really appreciate it,' Ray added with deep sincerity. 'You've been brilliant.'

His father gave a careless shrug because the Brents weren't the sort of people who went in for sentimental talk. 'I've enjoyed having you around,' he told him.

'Likewise,' replied Ray.

Giving his son a careful look, Alfie said, 'So you're giving up the market and you're moving out of here, all at the same time. You're obviously in the mood for a change.'

'I certainly am,' confirmed Ray. 'A new attitude and a new life, that's my motto. It's time to stop hankering for something I can never have and get on with other things.'

'As sorry as I am about you and Ellie, I think you're right, son,' agreed Alfie.

'What is it people say in this sort of situation?' Ray put his hand in his pocket and closed his fingers around the envelope with Maria's telephone number scribbled on it. 'Tomorrow is the first day of the rest of my life.'

'I think it goes something like that,' said Alfie. He wasn't fooled for a second. His son was still carrying a torch for Ellie no matter how hard he was trying to convince himself otherwise.

Chapter Eighteen

Senbridge was a charming country town at the foot of the rolling downs. Quintessentially English, it was traditional and pretty, with a selection of small shops and a beautiful gilt-faced town clock at the end of the High Street.

Although a busy shopping centre during the week, the centre was quiet on a Sunday afternoon, the activity focused around the only two establishments that were open for business: the Georgian tea-rooms and the ice-cream parlour, both of which were bustling with people; there was a queue at the serving window of the latter.

Following the matron's advice not to subject Tom to the formalities inside, Ellie joined the queue outside, clutching Donna's hand and keeping a watchful eye on Tom. The weather was gloriously autumnal, with hazy sunshine and a chill in the air to remind them that summer was over.

Although Ellie was too much on edge to enjoy herself, the outing did seem to be going rather well. Donna's lively presence helped to ease the strain. She had maintained a constant flow of chatter so far, seeming unperturbed by the fact that Tom's behaviour wasn't quite that of other adults. She didn't seem to have much trouble with his mangled speech either. Not that he'd said much.

'Can I have a cornet, please, Mummy?' she asked now excitedly. 'A pink one.'

'If they've got it, yes, darling of course you can,' agreed her mother.

'Are you having a cornet or a wafer?' Donna asked of Tom.

'Cornet,' was his garbled reply.

'Say please then,' chirped his daughter authoritatively. 'You must always say please, Mummy says.'

Obediently he uttered a noise which seemed to satisfy her.

Licking their ice creams, they ambled to the edge of the town. By the time they reached Berry Lane, a country road that led back to Greenlands and was flanked on either side by woodland, the cornets were finished. Beginning to relax a little now that they were on the homeward stretch with no disasters to report to the matron, Ellie was able to take notice of their surroundings and was struck by the simple beauty of the autumn day. From a misty blue sky the sun filtered through the trees that arched the lane in places, the air so still the russet leaves didn't stir, though a few were moved by the season and floated to the ground.

'Are there animals living in there?' enquired Donna, looking towards the woods.

'Sure to be,' replied Ellie.

'What kind?'

'Rabbits and squirrels, I should think,' guessed Ellie.

'Ooh . . . can we go and find them?' requested the little girl excitedly.

Noticing the density of the trees and fearing that Tom might wander off, Ellie felt compelled to say, 'No, that isn't a good idea, love.'

'Is it 'cos there are scary wild lions and tigers in the woods as well?' Very much an urban child, Donna's imagination was running riot at this close encounter with the countryside.

'No, those sort of wild animals live in the jungle, and this is just a wood,' explained Ellie.

'Why can't we go and see if we can find rabbits and squirrels then?' she asked, a threatening note of recalcitrance creeping into her tone.

'Because we have to take Tom home and then drive back to London,' Ellie said gently.

'But I want to go in the woods.' She was whining now. 'I want to have a look.'

'Not today.'

'Oh Mummy, please?' She had the bit between her teeth. 'I want to see some animals.'

'No, Donna.'

'Not fair,' she huffed.

'Don't keep on about it, there's a good girl,' said Ellie in mild admonition. 'I've said no and I mean it.'

But the idea of actually seeing the creatures of her picture books was too much for Donna and she let go of her mother's hand and ran towards the woods.

'Donna!' shouted Ellie, instinctively putting a restraining hand on Tom's arm. 'Come back here . . . at once. Come on now. Don't be a naughty girl.'

The small red head was tossed towards her mother defiantly. 'I want to go in the woods.' Her rebellious blue eyes were fixed on Ellie. 'Please let me . . . just for a little while.'

'No. Just come here this minute,' Ellie ordered.

With a look of devilment the child turned and headed away. Forced to let go of Tom's arm, Ellie tore after her and caught her in a firm grip. 'You bad girl,' she reprimanded, raising her voice, nerves stretched even more by the responsibility of a second 'child'. 'Don't you dare to defy me.'

Usually a most sweet-natured child, some demon had got into Donna today and she wriggled away, forcing Ellie to struggle with her quite forcibly. A sudden guttural roar rent the air and Ellie felt herself being dragged away from her daughter with a strength that left her powerless, Tom's grip on her arms making her cry out in pain. Once clear of Donna, Tom knocked Ellie to the ground with a blow to the head so forceful a shower of stars exploded in her vision.

'Tom . . . no.' Still dazed, she managed to scramble to her feet, horrified to see him sweep Donna into his arms and shrink back from Ellie as though she was an enemy. 'Put

373

her down, you're frightening her.'

Having obviously misunderstood the situation completely, he backed away from Ellie, as though he thought she intended to harm Donna. Some long-forgotten protective instinct must have mistakenly resurfaced.

The child let out a wail. 'Mumm-ee!' she shrieked, clearly terrified. 'Mumm-ee . . . I want my mumm-ee!'

'It's all right, darling,' said Ellie, having to shout to make herself heard above her daughter's screams. 'I'm here.'

'Make him put me down,' came Donna's pleas, muffled by sobbing. 'I don't like it. I'm scared.'

'He won't hurt you, darling,' Ellie tried to soothe her.

Fearing that Tom might accidentally harm Donna if he panicked, Ellie decided that her best bet was gentle persuasion. 'Come on now, Tom,' she said in a mild tone, moving towards him warily and holding her arms out to Donna. 'Put her down. I'm not going to hurt her, I promise you.'

He moved closer to the woods, looking at Ellie fearfully.

'I had to shout at her when she ran off in case she got lost in the woods.' She doubted if he could comprehend a word she was saying but was desperate enough to try anything. 'I was doing it for her own good.'

But her words fell on deaf ears, as she'd suspected they would. He moved backwards with the screaming child, clutching her to him even tighter. Ellie was afraid to go after him too quickly in case he took flight in fear and went deeper into the woods with Donna. He didn't know his own strength. He was a big man, Donna a small child. He could crush her to death without even realising it, or trip and fall on top of her. This was a dangerous situation and needed careful handling.

Donna's screams had turned to heart-rending sobs, her face wet with tears, and pale and blotchy. The more she cried the more Tom tightened his grip. Ellie daren't take her eyes off him for a second for fear he would turn and run.

But at the sound of a car in the lane, she knew she was going to have to risk it. With heart pounding and breath coming in short gasps, she ran out into the road and flagged the car down.

'Could you get someone from the nursing home down there?' she asked the astonished couple in the car, pointing down the lane and refusing their offers of help because anything other than specialist assistance could put Donna in even more danger than she was already. 'Tell them Tom Hall's wife needs help urgently. Tell them where I am, they'll know exactly what to do. Please hurry.'

Back in the woods, Tom hadn't moved, much to Ellie's relief. He was still clutching Donna, who was sobbing quietly now, her head resting on his shoulder in sheer exhaustion. Ellie noticed with alarm that Tom was trembling, which meant he was frightened and probably out of control. Heaven knows what he'll do next, she thought. She had to do something to calm him until help came from Greenlands. What though? she wondered, as he stared at her, his blue eyes wide and manic.

'Your arms must be aching like mad, Tom,' Ellie said at last, trying not to show her fear. 'Donna's getting to be quite a weight these days.'

He replied with a grunt.

'Why don't you sit down and take the weight off your feet for a minute?' she suggested in a friendly tone. 'It'll take the strain off your arms too.' She took off her coat and spread it on the shaded ground. 'There you are, that'll keep the damp off.'

Without taking his eyes off Ellie, Tom put the weeping child down while retaining a hold on her. Then he sank to the ground pulling his daughter down with him and holding her close. This didn't bring a rescue for Donna any nearer but Ellie felt safer in the knowledge that it wouldn't be easy for him to run off with Donna from this sitting position; neither could he trip and fall on top of her.

She kept talking to him in a companionable manner – about the weather, the animals in the wood, anything – just to keep him where he was until help came. After what seemed like for ever, two members of Greenlands' staff arrived. One was an orderly called Will, the other a nurse called Ruby.

'You'll catch your death of cold sitting there, Tom,' said Ruby in her soft Irish brogue.

Ellie saw Tom relax immediately.

'You'll get a damp bum if you sit there for too long,' added Will calmly.

Tom became noticeably more at ease in the presence of these professionals. His trembling lessened and he loosened his grip on Donna, though he didn't let go altogether.

'Come on, Tom,' persuaded Ruby in a warm tone, moving closer to him and offering her hand to help him up. 'Let's go home now and have some tea, shall we? It's your favourite today, toasted teacakes with butter and jam. I think there's some of that fruit trifle you like too.'

There was only a brief hesitation before Tom let go of Donna and took Ruby's hand, Donna and Ellie apparently forgotten. He stood with the nurse in a docile manner with a benign smile on his face, seemingly unaware of the suffering he had caused.

Ellie rushed to her child and gathered her in her arms, stroking her hair and gently wiping her tears.

'Mummy,' Donna sobbed, holding on to Ellie as though she would never let go.

'It's all right, darling,' Ellie said. 'You're safe now.'

'Your husband will be fine with us, Mrs Hall,' said Ruby as Will led Tom away. 'I'm sorry you've had trouble with him. What happened?'

'He got the wrong end of the stick about something,' Ellie explained.

'And got into one of his states.' Ruby looked at Donna. 'I hope your little girl isn't too upset.'

'She's very shaken up, naturally.' Ellie herself was weak with relief, her head still throbbing from Tom's blow.

'You can give her your full attention now,' said the nurse, 'because we'll take care of Tom.' She nodded her head towards Greenlands. 'See you back at the house.'

And she hurried off to catch up with the others. Ellie watched her and Will walk down the lane towards Greenlands with Tom between them, the incident already forgotten by him. Ellie didn't go after them right away but stayed where she was with her child; the more distance there was between her daughter and Tom the better. There must be no more of these outings, no more experiments. Standing there on the edge of that Surrey wood, Ellie finally accepted that she and Donna had no place in Tom's life at all now, and to pretend otherwise was dangerous for them all.

As the others moved out of sight, she took Donna's hand and they walked down the lane to Greenlands to see the matron and collect the car. Ellie thought this must surely be the saddest day of her life.

Alfie rang Pat Hall's front doorbell in the early evening of the same day.

'What do you want?' she asked, her eyes widening in surprise to see him there.

'I knew I could rely on you for a warm welcome,' he said with a wry grin.

'Cut the cracks and get to the point,' she told him.

'There's something important I want to talk to you about.'

'Oh?' Up went her brows. 'What sort of something?'

'Something I believe will be to your advantage.'

'Oh, for heaven's sake, Alfie, do get on with it,' she said irritably. 'Don't keep me standing here in the cold.'

'You want me to discuss private business with you here on the doorstep?' Now his brows were raised.

Pat emitted an eloquent sigh. 'I suppose you'd better come in then,' she conceded, and led the way upstairs to her living room.

'Nice place you've got,' he commented, looking around and helping himself to a seat in an armchair. 'Not very up to date but homely.'

'I like it,' she said in a manner to suggest that she didn't give a damn about his opinion. 'Now will you please get to the point? I've got things to do.'

'Such as?'

'Never you mind.' In actual fact she had nothing to do at all. The weekly paperwork was done, the shelves in the shop filled, domestic chores up to date. The evening ahead was to consist of watching television on her own and a lonely cup of cocoa at bedtime. But being sharp with people had become such a habit she did it instinctively, especially to Alfie, even though she'd been feeling warmer towards him since he'd been helping her out with the deliveries. She guessed it was some sort of a defence mechanism because he made her feel vulnerable, yet safe too, paradoxically. But she'd never let him know the effect he had on her. 'Now will you please get on and tell me why you're here?'

'You're looking for someone to help you run the shop, aren't you?' he said.

'You know perfectly well that I am.'

'I'm your man,' Alfie grinned.

'You want to work for me?' Pat was astonished.

'Not you especially,' he put her straight. 'But I fancy that sort of job and you just happen to have a vacancy. I'm not keen on my job in the factory and I'm good with people. Working on the market has proved that to me. Now that my son's giving up the market I'll be free to work on a Saturday, which I know would be needed if I worked for you.'

'It's a bit drastic, isn't it?' she commented. 'Giving up a job you've done all your life?'

'I've always fancied shopwork but I got stuck in the factory – the devil you know and all that,' Alfie explained. 'I reckon I'd suit you down to the ground, what with having a driving licence and plenty of muscle. Most importantly of all, I'm a hard worker and you can trust me with the money because I would never do you out of so much as a penny piece.'

'That isn't in question.' She stroked her chin, looking

doubtful. 'But we'd have to work together and we're not exactly harmonious, are we?'

'I agree that you'd have to curb your temper,' he told her frankly, 'or it would never work.'

'Me?' She was shocked at his effrontery.

'That's right.'

'You're telling me that I must curb my temper to suit *you*?' she gasped.

'Oh, yes.' He was quite definite about it but struggling to keep a straight face. 'That's at the top of my list of job conditions. I'm not the one with the bad temper.'

'Bad temper, job conditions.' Pat looked utterly bemused. 'You've got a nerve.'

'All part of my charm.'

She ignored that completely. 'You're planning on stipulating job conditions when you're the one who's asking me for a job!' she exploded.

'Actually, it was more of a suggestion than a job application.' He was looking at her sternly but there was a smile lurking in his eyes that anyone, except someone as lacking in humour as Pat, would have seen. 'I thought it would benefit us both, since you need someone like me to help you and I'd get to do a job I think I could enjoy.'

'But you want it all on your terms.'

'No,' he corrected, 'I just want a fair deal and I'm in a strong negotiating position because I don't need the job as much as you need a reliable assistant.'

'Oh, really . . .'

'It's true,' he told her. 'I can stay at the factory until I retire if I want to. Whereas you can't go on indefinitely without full-time help. Even if you were to find someone who suited your criteria, they wouldn't stay long because people simply aren't prepared to put up with your snooty attitude. That won't be a problem for me because I'll soon put you in your place.'

'How dare you?' she objected, looking flushed.

'I'm only saying what's true and you know it.' He'd bring

her down off her high horse or die in the attempt. By the time he'd finished she wouldn't be miserable and isolated; she'd have friends like everyone else. 'Even if you can't bring yourself to admit it.'

Her lips were pressed tightly together, beady eyes narrowed on him challengingly. 'You say you want me to curb my temper. Just out of interest, what are the other job conditions?' she couldn't resist asking.

'That you allow me some responsibility,' he informed her cheerfully. 'I wouldn't want to be just your lackey, fetching and carrying like a shop boy and shelf-filling between customers. I would want more from the job than that.'

'Such as?'

'Once I've learned the ropes I'd like to be allowed to take a general interest in the business,' he explained. 'Be able to make suggestions and have my ideas treated with respect. I would also like you to feel that you can leave the place in my charge if you want to go out or take the day off, or even go away on holiday.'

'I never take time off,' Pat stated categorically.

'You can't at the moment, can you, because there's no one to cover for you?' he pointed out. 'But you would be able to if I worked for you because you could go away safe in the knowledge that your business is in good hands.'

She sat rigid in the chair with her arms folded. What would she do with time off? She had no friends and she didn't see her granddaughter now. But it would be nice to know that she could have a day off to be lazy if she fancied it and to know that she wouldn't have to struggle on in the shop when she wasn't feeling well. 'Anything else?' she asked.

'That's about it,' he said. 'Except that I would like to get things straight about our working relationship.'

'Go on.' She could hardly believe she was allowing this to happen.

'Your spikiness doesn't bother me when we're on our own.' He paused, giving her a thoughtful grin. 'In fact, I rather like a spirited woman and you wouldn't be Pat without your sharp tongue.' His expression became deadly serious. 'But I won't stand for you putting me down in any way in front of customers. If you try that you'll get much worse back from me, and I won't be the one who's made to look foolish, I promise you.'

'In a nutshell then, you want everything your own way,' she snorted.

'Not at all,' Alfie corrected. 'In return for a little respect and consideration, you will have the most loyal and hardworking assistant you've ever had in your shop.' He stood up. 'Anyway, that's the deal. I'll go away and leave you to think about it.' He was halfway across the room when he paused. 'If you do decide that there might be some sense in what I've been saying, give me a ring. I'm in the phone book.'

Pat nodded, her head spinning. The shop was too much for her on her own, there was no doubt about that. And although she would never admit it to Alfie, he was right when he said she couldn't keep an assistant. Alfie Brent was too unnervingly outspoken for her taste. But she knew instinctively that he was right for the job; the idea of sharing the responsibility and working *with* someone instead of over them was very appealing. She was so tired of doing it all alone.

'Don't bother to come down,' he said, heading for the stairs. 'I'll see myself out.'

He was halfway down the stairs when she called out after him. 'How much notice do you have to give at the factory?' she enquired.

'A week.'

'You'd better come up so that we can talk about wages and get everything settled,' she said. 'Then you can give your notice in tomorrow.'

A short pause, then: 'I hope you're going to put the kettle on,' he said.

'Well, I—'

381

'Two sugars for me, please,' he cut in, smiling as he made his way back upstairs.

'I'm giving up the stall,' Ellie told her mother a few days later. She'd called in to see her after taking Donna to playgroup and they were having coffee at Mary's kitchen table.

'That's a coincidence,' said Mary.

'Why?'

'Because I was about to tell you that I've decided to give in my notice at the wool shop so that I can concentrate on your work,' Mary explained. 'I can't comfortably manage the two now that we're so busy with the knitwear. I seem to be permanently chasing my tail. But if you're giving up the market, you might not have so much for me to do.'

'I will.' Ellie was confident. 'As it is at the moment, it's a permanent nightmare trying to find the time to make enough stock for the market as well as meet deadlines on our other orders. Like you, I've been finding it too much. Not having the stall will make life easier for us both. And I don't expect to be short of work because we've got a solid customer base now. I'm also aiming to strengthen that by getting more made-to-order business. As well as increasing my advertising, I'm going to do more talks and demonstrations to spread the word. So you can go ahead and give in your notice at the wool shop with an easy mind.'

'Good,' smiled Mary.

'It'll be nice having Saturdays to myself again,' Ellie mentioned casually.

Mary threw her a shrewd look. 'And your decision is purely a business one and has nothing to do with Ray, I suppose?' she said.

'Of course it has,' Ellie admitted. 'I'll never get over him if I keep seeing him. But the stall was only ever meant to be a temporary thing and I wouldn't hesitate about going back to it if we hit another bad patch. But for the moment, I want to concentrate on made-to-order stuff. And the shops, of course, are our bread and butter. I won't have to keep personal customers waiting so long without the market to knit for.'

'How are you going to get more talks and demonstrations,' Mary wondered, 'since you have to wait to be invited?'

'By making my services better known,' Ellie explained. 'I'm going to the public library to get the names of all the women's groups in London and surrounding areas, then send out a standard letter telling them that I'm available as a speaker. They're always looking for people to talk at their monthly meetings.'

'You've certainly been doing some hard thinking,' Mary commented.

'I need a new challenge,' Ellie confided. 'To keep my mind occupied.'

Her mother sipped her coffee, looking at Ellie over the rim of the cup. She wasn't quite as skinny as she'd been after the miscarriage but she was heading that way again. It wasn't surprising, having found it necessary to inflict more suffering on herself by parting from Ray. And as if that wasn't enough, there was that terrible business with Tom on Sunday. Ellie had come straight here afterwards, very shaken up. The whole thing sounded horrific. From what Mary could gather, it was nothing short of a miracle that neither Ellie nor Donna had been seriously hurt. Still, at least it had brought things to a head as far as Tom was concerned. Ellie had finally admitted that she must stop believing she ought to play a significant part in his life; she knew now that she must keep her distance, for his sake as well as her own. It seemed harsh but it was a relief to Mary.

Personally, she thought Ellie had made a mistake in ending her relationship with Ray. Tom had never let her be herself or made her happy in the same way as Ray had. It had always been a one-sided thing with Tom, whereas she and Ray had seemed like equal partners. 'Might you consider going back to Ray, now that you've accepted that there's nothing more you can do for Tom?' Mary enquired.

'No, definitely not,' Ellie said without hesitation.

'It seems a shame.'

'It is a shame but you can't have everything you want in life, can you?' Ellie said briskly. 'I've come to my senses and realised that I must let Tom go. But all the other demons are still there.'

'Surely you and Ray can work something out,' said Mary, pushing her luck.

'If it was that simple, I wouldn't have given Ray up,' was Ellie's curt reply.

'Oh well, I suppose you know your own mind,' Mary conceded sadly.

'Anyway,' Ellie moved on hastily, not wishing to linger on such a painful subject, 'let's see if we can come up with some ideas for my promotional letter to the women's groups, shall we? All suggestions welcome.'

'I'd better get my thinking cap on then, hadn't I?' smiled Mary, pleased to be involved.

Ray moved into his own place early in the new year. He bought a flat in a small block just off the Uxbridge Road near the Shepherd's Bush borders with Acton. It was a newish property and contained a few luxuries that were new to him such as central heating, fitted cupboards and a lounge with double-aspect windows. It was very smart.

He furnished it in contemporary style with fitted carpet and sleek modern furniture, plain walls and boldly patterned curtains. It wasn't particularly spacious – bordering on the poky, in fact – but it was light, bright and comfortable, and suited his bachelor lifestyle perfectly. Given the choice, he would prefer a family home with a garden and Ellie and Donna living in it with him. But since that wasn't possible this was fine.

'Wow!' enthused Maria, whom he'd been seeing on a regular basis since last autumn. 'This really is something else.'

'Glad you like it,' he smiled. 'I must say I'm pleased with it.

And it's so good to be in my own place.'

'Good for me too,' she blurted out. 'Now that you've moved out of your dad's place, I won't have to go there any more.'

He raised his brows. 'You never said you didn't like going there.'

'Well, I didn't want to say anything but I hated going there. Always felt on edge with your dad,' she explained. 'I know he doesn't like me.'

'Probably something to do with the fact that you walked out on me before,' Ray suggested. 'Anyway, I don't think he dislikes you, exactly. It's more that he's very keen on Ellie and no one else will ever be right for me, in his eyes.'

'That's plain stupid,' she scorned. 'Does he expect you to live like a monk or something, just because he happened to like your last girlfriend?'

'Of course not.'

'It isn't even as though you were the one who ended it, is it?' she went on.

Ray winced. 'All right, don't rub it in,' he admonished. 'The fact that she gave me the elbow doesn't stop Dad wishing it was otherwise. He's got a soft spot for Ellie.'

'Silly old git.'

'Hey, that's enough of that. I won't have you talking about my father like that,' he rebuked, eyes simmering with offence. 'He's an absolute diamond and I won't hear a word against him. Not from you or anyone.'

'All right, I'm sorry,' she apologised. 'There's no need to burst a blood vessel over it.'

'Well, he means a lot to me,' Ray emphasised. 'Nobody could have done more for me than he has.'

'I know.' She was full of contrition. It had been a mistake to criticise his father and she was keen to gloss over it. 'I shouldn't have said that.'

'No, you damned well shouldn't.' He wasn't going to let her off lightly.

'But you must admit, he didn't exactly lay the red carpet out for me, did he?' Maria reminded him, begging his approval.

'He was never rude to you, that I know of,' he said. 'Dad wouldn't do that.'

'Never rude, no,' she conceded. 'But I could feel his ill will.'

'You hardly ever went to his place when I lived there, anyway,' Ray pointed out. 'We usually went to yours.'

'However few times, it was enough for me,' she told him. 'I don't like having to compete with your ex.'

'You shouldn't even try,' he advised her.

'Bound to, aren't I?' she said. 'It's only natural.'

'Not necessarily,' Ray disagreed. 'You were in a long-term relationship before we got together again, but I don't try to compete with him.'

'There'd be no competition,' she declared. 'He wasn't a patch on you.'

Maria tended to be overly generous with her flattery and Ray found it rather cloying. 'Don't start all that again,' he said, keeping it casual. 'You know that flattery embarrasses me.'

'I'm only saying what's true,' she said, 'but as you get narky about it, I'll stop paying you compliments. You should think yourself lucky somebody wants to say nice things to you.'

'I do, I do,' he grinned.

'You'd better.'

Since the night last autumn when he'd decided to put the past behind him and get on with his life, Ray had thrown himself into everything he did, including his relationship with Maria. He wasn't in love with her – and had never led her to believe otherwise – but she was entertaining company and she helped to assuage the pain of losing Ellie.

He'd made the first move by calling her on the phone. After that the initiative had been hers entirely. She'd taken him by the hand, as it were, and led him into a relationship. He was fully aware of the fact that he was being manipulated but didn't put up any resistance. What was the point? Maria didn't want to be alone and neither did he. So they suited each other.

He hadn't been able to recapture the magic she'd held for him in his youth, but she was by no means abhorrent to him. As for her character, he was under no illusions about that: she had deserted him once and she would do so again if it suited her. But he was happy to let things drift on as they were.

Giving up the market had proved to be an extremely wise move. He'd increased his advertising for made-to-order gates, banisters and balcony rails. This, added to personal recommendations, produced a steady workflow. This type of work was not only more financially beneficial, it was also more creatively challenging.

The nervous energy he'd inherited from the trauma of losing Ellie had been channelled into his work. Gates and banisters made by Ray Brent – Decorative Metals now adorned the homes of the wealthy and élite. He got on well with his customers. One thing his new line of work had taught him was that the appreciation of good craftsmanship transcended the classes. With so many goods being factory-produced these days, anything hand-made had a special appeal and automatically bestowed respect upon its maker.

'So you like the new gaff then?' he said to Maria now.

'Not half,' she enthused, casting an envious eye around the room. 'It makes my place seem like a tip.'

'Your place is all right,' he said. 'It's quite comfortable and pleasant.'

'Hardly in the same league as this, though.'

He couldn't deny it. Her bedsit was cosy enough but it *was* just a bedsit and didn't match up to this. Her wages as a general clerk in a factory office didn't run to this sort of accommodation. 'You don't begrudge me this after living in a prison cell for six years surely,' he said lightly.

'Of course not,' she was quick to assure him. 'But I can't help comparing it to mine. It's only natural.'

'Yeah, well, we all have times when things work out, and times when they don't,' he said. 'And things are going very well for me at the moment.'

'I can see that.'

'Strange as it may seem, though, if I'd not done a stretch in prison, I probably wouldn't have this place now.'

'How come?'

'I wouldn't have been able to afford the mortgage on a place like this if I was still working at the factory,' Ray explained. 'Through learning a new trade while I was inside, I've been able to start my own business.'

'Mm, there is that.'

'I don't make a fortune but I make a damned sight more than I did in a factory,' he mentioned chattily. 'But the important thing is that I enjoy the work. I love being creative with metal.'

'It was worth going inside then,' she suggested lightly.

'Oh, no, Maria,' he corrected, his mood becoming grim. 'Nothing on earth was worth that.'

'Just kidding,' she hastily pointed out. 'There's no need to go up in the air about it.'

'Sorry,' he said. 'I suppose I'm still a bit touchy about prison, even though some good has come from it.'

'It didn't just happen, you know. You made the most of an opportunity,' she praised. 'You built something worthwhile from a bad experience.'

'Thanks.'

She sighed wistfully, looking around the room at the pictures, the wall lights and glass-topped coffee table. 'Anyway, you're certainly doing well for yourself now. I won't want to go back to my place after being here.'

He knew exactly what she was after; she wanted to move in with him, as his wife. She made that abundantly clear at every opportunity. Although outgoing and unsubtle, Maria could be a very determined and persuasive woman. Ray sometimes wondered how long he would manage to hold out against her wishes, given that there was no incentive to resist.

'Come on, let's go out for a drink now that you've had the grand tour.' He wanted to keep the mood casual.

388

'I'd rather stay in,' she said, running her avaricious eye around his new home again.

'Stay in, you?' he said in astonishment.

'Why go out when you've got a place like this to stay home in?' she said.

'Maria Dobbs wanting to stay at home,' he teased her, shaking his head. 'You must be ill.'

'You could call it that,' she said with a particular look in her eye which he studiously ignored.

'I fancy going out, anyway,' he told her. 'A couple of drinks and a few laughs?'

She didn't put up any more opposition. 'OK, then,' she agreed.

He helped her on with her coat and they headed for the nearest pub together.

Chapter Nineteen

'I was wondering,' began Alfie tentatively, 'if it might be a good idea for us to stock a small selection of greetings cards.'

'This is a grocery store, not a stationer's,' was Pat's dismissive response.

It was early spring and they were having a quiet few minutes in the shop without customers. Looking spruce in a starched white grocer's overall, face scrubbed and clean-shaven, hair slicked back with Brylcreem, Alfie was putting the time to good use by stacking tinned fruit on to the shelves while Pat attacked the counter top with a cleaning cloth.

He hadn't expected a positive reaction to his suggestion because Pat was naturally circumspect and had to be coaxed into any new venture, no matter how small. 'We're also known by some people as a convenience store,' he amended.

'Meaning?'

'Meaning that we would be even more convenient if we were to stock a few more lines outside of actual grocery,' he replied.

She stopped what she was doing and looked at him, cloth in hand. 'We need all the space we have for standard grocery,' she pointed out.

'Most of the space is accounted for, I grant you,' Alfie agreed, 'but we could easily find room for a few new lines.'

'There's no necessity for it.'

'I think there is.' He was warming to his theme and becoming more determined. 'I mean, how many times in the course of a week do we get asked for something we don't have in stock, especially greetings cards? Someone always wants a card of some sort – birthday, anniversary, get well. You can get them for all sorts of occasions these days.'

'Hmm.' Pat didn't sound convinced.

'As well as giving another service to the customers, it wouldn't do the shop profits any harm because there's a very good mark-up on cards.'

'Ah.' Pat's eyes lit with the gleam of understanding. 'Now I know what's brought this on,' she announced triumphantly. 'You've been got at by one of the greeting cards reps.'

He chuckled. 'He called while you were upstairs having your tea break,' he confessed.

'You'll have to learn not to be so susceptible to reps, you know,' she lectured. 'They're trained to be persuasive and they'll talk you into anything if you let them.'

'I wouldn't be persuaded unless I thought what he said made sense,' Alfie told her. 'And I really believe it would be a good idea to stock a few bits and pieces beside grocery. It would mean a better all-round service.'

'We're a small shop,' she reminded him.

'Not so small that we can't carry a few more lines if we juggle things around a bit,' he pointed out, casting a speculative eye around the shop. 'And the card manufacturers will supply us with a carousel stand so we won't have to use any of our existing display space.'

'Another line, another supplier and more paperwork for us.' Pat wouldn't be persuaded.

'There's always the thought too,' Alfie battled on, 'that if someone calls in for a card – once word gets around that we sell them – they might buy something else while they're here.'

'No, Alfie, I don't think so.'

'There you go again, writing something off without even seriously considering its possibilities,' he admonished.

'And there *you* go again, telling me how to run my business,' she retorted.

'I see. So, I'm just the shop boy when I get a good idea, but the manager when you want to take the day off.' Alfie sounded more than a little peeved.

'All right, calm down,' Pat said, becoming reasonable in a way that would have once been unthinkable. 'We'll have a proper chat about it after the shop's closed.'

'I shall hold you to that, an' all,' he declared in a firm tone. 'I came to work here on the understanding that you'd listen to my ideas.'

'Listen being the operative word,' came Pat's sharp reminder. 'There was nothing said about my automatically putting your ideas into practice.'

'We'll see,' he said, with a resolute glint in his eye. He'd discovered during the past six months or so that he could usually win her over in the end.

Although Pat would never admit it to Alfie, his coming to work for her had changed her life. It was soothing to know that she no longer had to plough her lonely furrow in the business. If being a little less rigid in her ideas stopped him from leaving, then so be it. There was a certain tenderness beneath the surface of their spiky dealings with each other which they both tacitly acknowledged. She thought it was probably the reason they were able to work together, given their disparate personalities.

It was true to say that Alfie was more shop manager than assistant, and had made a point of familiarising himself with the entire administration from the start. Versatility was something else he excelled in. He'd turn his hand to anything, from trawling around the cash and carry warehouse for stock to washing the shop floor if necessary.

As she had known he would be, he was a great favourite with the customers. He joshed with them and they loved it. His sauciness didn't cause offence because he was entertaining and warm-hearted with it and never overstepped the mark. He might be a bit rough around the edges for her taste but he was good for business. Although theirs was just a working association which didn't continue outside of shop hours, she didn't feel so lonely within herself now. Even the fact that he was the father of a convicted murderer who had stolen her son's wife slipped easily to the back of her mind in the light of so many advantages.

But now he was saying, 'Hello, Mrs Fletcher, and how are you today?'

'Mustn't grumble, thanks, Alfie,' replied the customer. 'How's yourself?'

'All the better for seeing you,' he beamed. 'What can we do for you?'

'I'll have a piece of that Cheddar . . . about half a pound, please,' she requested, pointing to some cheese in a glass cabinet on the counter, 'and half a dozen rashers of streaky bacon. As fast as you can, if you wouldn't mind, Alfie. I'm in a bit of a hurry.'

'Coming up, my dear,' he said, putting a sheet of grease-proof paper on the marble slab then fixing a large joint of bacon in the slicer and turning the handle.

'You're rushing about a bit today,' Pat remarked to the customer sociably.

'Yeah. But only because I've just remembered it's my neighbour's birthday and I haven't got a card for her,' Mrs Fletcher explained. 'So I've got to go haring right down to the Green to get one and I have to be back before the kids get in from school.' She tutted. 'It's a damned nuisance.'

'It would be handy for you if you could get a card here, then?' suggested Alfie.

'Not half,' she agreed heartily. 'If I had a pound for every time I've had to go all the way to the Green just for a card, I'd be a rich woman today.'

Alfie didn't say a word; just concentrated on wrapping the bacon rashers.

'All right,' said Pat when the customer had gone, 'I'll admit you have a point and we'll have a serious talk about stocking some cards at the first opportunity. But if I see so much as a hint of a gloat, I'll throw something at you.'

'I wouldn't dare,' he told her.

Looking extremely smart in a blue jersey suit and high-heeled shoes, her hair taken back into a chignon, Ellie packed her knitting machine into the back of her estate car, which was parked on the street near the White Hart on the outskirts of Shepherd's Bush towards Acton. It was a fine spring evening, the air warm, the dark sky clear and bright with stars.

She was feeling rather pleased with herself, having just given a talk and machine demonstration to the members of a local women's guild who held their monthly meetings in the function room upstairs in the pub. The promotional letter she'd sent out last autumn had brought in a regular flow of speaking engagements.

Some went better than others and she could never tell in advance how it would go on the night. It was all about giving. You had to give to an audience to get something back, to speak *to* them not *at* them. Tonight she'd felt the communication like a living thing, warm and uplifting.

This kind of work was so enjoyable she would gladly do it for nothing. But the fact that she usually received a fee, as well as the chance to promote her knitwear, made it a valuable addition to her business. Her decision to finish at the market had proved to be a wise one. It gave her time to produce quality knitwear and work on new embroidery designs.

But now she locked the back doors of the car and got into the driver's seat, pausing before switching on the engine as pleasurable memories of the evening washed over her, making her feel warm inside. She was recalled to the present by a car drawing up in front of her. Absently she watched as the occupants got out, vaguely noticing that it was a youngish couple. She was about to turn the ignition key when her heart did a sudden somersault. The man was Ray, his dark hair shining in the glow from the streetlight.

Frozen, she watched him lock his car before walking over

to the woman and slipping his arm round her. She looked up at him as he lowered his face to hers. The sound of their laughter echoed in the night air as, with arms entwined, they walked towards the pub entrance.

Ellie couldn't move. She just sat there, the talk forgotten, her evening in ruins. It was the natural way of things, she told herself as the pain welled up. She hadn't expected him to spend the rest of his life alone. But neither had she expected to feel this bad when she saw him with someone else. Not a day had passed in the six months they'd been apart when she didn't think of him and wish things could be different. But they couldn't so she must accept the fact that he'd fallen in love with someone else.

With blurred vision and a shaky hand, she started up the engine and headed for home where her mother was looking after Donna. The mental image of Ray and the new woman in his life filled her mind to the exclusion of all else. She didn't think she would ever forget the sound of their laughter or the look of intimacy about them.

Ann called round to Ellie's for a social visit one evening a few days later after the children were in bed; she'd left Doug baby-sitting. She had a message from her neighbour who'd asked her to enquire if Ellie could knit matching cardigans for her two little girls.

'She thought you might be snowed under at the moment,' explained Ann as Ellie made coffee.

'Fortunately I am busy but I'll fit them in as she's a friend of yours,' said Ellie. 'Tell her to give me a ring to arrange to bring the girls round so that I can measure them, and discuss exactly what she wants.'

'Will do.'

'I'll have to start paying you commission,' smiled Ellie. 'All these jobs you get for me.'

'It's your reputation that brings in the orders,' Ann pointed out. 'I'm just the messenger.'

'Thanks anyway.'

'A pleasure.'

Ellie put some coffee and biscuits on to a tray and they went into the living room. 'So . . . how are things?' she asked when they were settled in armchairs.

'Fine. You?'

'Fine.'

Ann gave her a sharp look. 'Are you really, though?' she enquired. 'You look a bit heavy-eyed, as though you haven't been sleeping.'

Ellie made a face. 'Ray's got a new woman,' she explained. 'I saw them together and I've hardly slept since.'

'I see.'

'It's tearing me apart, Ann.'

'I'm really sorry,' she sympathised. 'It was bound to happen, I suppose. He knows he can't have you, and he's only human.'

'That's what I keep telling myself but it doesn't make it hurt any the less.'

'Perhaps you'll feel better once you fully accept the idea of him being with someone else,' Ann suggested kindly. 'This could be a blessing in disguise. Just what you need to get him out of your system altogether.'

'Maybe,' said Ellie, not sounding convinced. 'But let's change the subject before I start blubbing all over you.'

'OK,' agreed Ann. 'Let's do what we usually do and talk about the kids.'

A conversation ensued but Ellie's heart wasn't in it.

Ellie's parents asked if they could take Donna out for the day one Saturday in April to see Bob's cousin in Ilford. Guessing they wanted their granddaughter to themselves, to spoil her and show her off to a relative, Ellie was happy to agree.

'I'll make the most of the time and get some work done,' she told them. 'I'll have a wander around the shops and a walk down the market too.'

And so it was that she was out shopping on her own that sunny Saturday. Casually dressed in a shirt and black slimline trousers, hair worn loose and casual, she indulged in some window shopping in the dress and shoe shops opposite the Green, then walked the length of the market, buying fruit and other sundries. Heading back across the Green in the glorious spring weather, she decided to take a break and sat down on a bench in the sunshine, feeling its gentle warmth on her face.

'Well, well, now there's a sight for sore eyes,' said a male voice nearby.

Looking up, she was treated to a most welcome sight, looking very smart in a suit and tie. 'Alfie!' Ellie cried, leaping up and hugging him. 'Oh, it's so good to see you.'

'Likewise,' he beamed. 'I've missed you, ducks. How have you been?'

'Not so bad, thanks,' she said. 'You?'

'I'm all right, dear.'

They were united in the pleasure of this unexpected meeting. Ellie sat back down on the bench and Alfie made himself comfortable beside her.

'I've heard through the local grapevine that you work for Pat at the corner shop now,' she remarked.

'That's right.'

She threw him a querying look. 'Working at the corner shop means going in on Saturdays so I presume you don't help Ray on the stall now.'

'Ray gave up the stall soon after you two split up.' He told her briefly what Ray was doing now in the way of work. 'I met Joe in a pub and he told me that you packed it up too at about the same time.'

'How ironical,' Ellie said with a dry laugh. 'Had either of us known the other was going to leave, only one of us needed to go.' She paused. 'Still, it's worked out for the best for me, as it happens.' She went on to tell him what she was doing. 'And at least I don't have to get frozen to death on winter Saturdays now.'

'I'm glad it's worked out well for you,' he said, leaning back on the bench and shading his eyes from the sun with his hand. 'Ray's business is doing well too, now.'

'I'm pleased.' Ellie cleared her throat nervously. 'How is he in himself?' she asked.

'He's very well,' Alfie told her. 'He doesn't live with me now. He's got his own flat. Very nice too.'

'I know he's seeing someone else,' she forced herself to say. 'I saw them together.'

Alfie leaned forward with his hands on his knees. 'Yeah, her name is Maria.'

The name rang a bell. 'Not the same Maria who—'

'Deserted him when he got arrested,' he finished for her. 'Yep, that's the one.'

'It doesn't sound as though you approve,' Ellie said quietly.

'I don't. But not because of what she did to him back then,' he explained. 'That's all water under the bridge. It was a big thing to expect any woman to take on and Maria was still quite young at the time.'

'Why so glum then?'

'They're not right for each other,' he stated categorically.

'They looked right enough together when I saw them,' she mentioned grimly.

'They get on all right together but there's nothing there of any substance.' He paused, sitting upright and staring ahead thoughtfully. 'After you two split up, he threw himself into everything with great enthusiasm, putting on a show of cheerfulness, when it was obvious to me that he was as miserable as sin.'

'A natural reaction,' she remarked. 'I did the same thing.'

'Anyway, he took up with Maria on the rebound,' he continued. 'But he doesn't love her any more than she loves him.'

'How do you know?' Ellie asked. 'Surely only they know how they feel about each other.'

'You only have to be with them for any length of time to

know that the spark isn't there,' he explained. 'Maria's looking after her own interests. She's on her own and wants a man, any man who'll give her a nice home and a decent standard of living. Ray fits the bill perfectly.'

'Ray's too cute to be fooled, though,' she pointed out.

'He isn't fooled,' Alfie told her. 'He knows exactly what she's after. He admitted that when I tried to talk some sense into him. But it doesn't bother him. He and Maria are both on their own so why shouldn't they try and make some sort of life together, that's his attitude. He can't have you so he doesn't have any motivation to fight back. He still loves you, Ellie.'

Tears burned at the back of her eyes. 'I still love him too,' she confessed.

He looked at her, putting his hand on hers briefly. 'I know you had your reasons for doing what you did,' he said. 'But it seems such a terrible waste.'

'It seems like that to me too,' she admitted. 'But ending our affair was something I had to do.'

'It doesn't seem right to me–' Alfie told her – 'two people being miserable when they could be happy together.'

'Doing what's right and being happy aren't always compatible,' she said quietly.

'I suppose not,' he agreed. 'Anyway, what's done is done. It's too late to change anything now.'

'Yes.' She thought he was just making a casual reference to Ray's new relationship.

'Anyway,' Alfie said, looking at his watch, 'I must go.'

Something dawned on her and she gave him a close look. 'I mentioned your having to work Saturdays but I was so thrilled to see you I forgot to ask why you're not at the shop today.' She ran an approving eye over his smart apparel. 'You've obviously got the day off for something special. Going somewhere nice?'

He looked uncomfortable. 'Not really,' he told her.

'Not a funeral, is it?'

Scratching his head and avoiding her eyes, he said, 'No, it's a wedding actually.'

'But that's nice,' she responded, puzzled by his lack of enthusiasm. 'Anyone I know?'

His next words shook her so profoundly she flinched visibly. 'It's Ray's wedding, Ellie,' he informed her gravely. 'He's marrying Maria at two o'clock at Hammersmith Register Office.'

When she'd recovered sufficiently to speak, all she could utter was, 'Oh, Alfie.'

'Sorry, love.' He patted her hand in a fatherly manner. 'It hurt me to have to tell you.'

'No need to apologise. I'd have got to hear about it eventually anyway.' She stared at the ground, a grinding pain settling in the pit of her stomach. 'I shouldn't be shocked, I know. I just didn't think it had gone that far with Maria.'

'Neither did I,' he told her gloomily. 'But it has. In less than an hour, Maria will be my daughter-in-law. Talking of which, I really must go. I want to be there in plenty of time.'

They both stood up and he gave her a peck on the cheek before heading off across the Green.

'Oh, Alfie,' she cried to herself, watching him walk away with the same purposeful stride as his son. 'What have I done?'

'Ah, there you are, Tom,' said Ruby in a rousing tone when she found him sitting in the television lounge on his own. 'I've been looking all over the place for you. Didn't you realise it was lunchtime?'

No reply.

'The others are already sitting down in the dining room,' she went on. 'So come on, boy, or there'll be nothing left.'

He remained where he was in the armchair, putting a hand to his head.

'Headache?' she asked.

He nodded, his face a ghastly shade of grey.

'Hmm, you do look a bit pale,' she observed. 'I'll get you something for it in a minute. In the meantime, come and have something to eat.'

He stood up and promptly threw up all over the floor, soiling his shirt and splashing their shoes.

'Never mind, Tom,' comforted Ruby as he started to cry. 'You couldn't help it. I'll see to the mess later. I'll get you cleaned up and into bed first. That's the best place for you as you're not well. It's only a bilious attack but still not very nice.'

Taking him by the hand, she led him to his room, managing to get him to the basin before he was sick again, complaining the whole time about his headache. She settled him in bed, then went to the matron to report him sick.

Watching Alfie out of sight, Ellie started walking home. She had no heart to stay out now. The news about Ray's wedding had sapped all her energy and broken her heart all over again. She'd had no choice but to let him go. It had been the right decision, she kept reminding herself. There was too much guilt, too many complications. She tried to be charitable about his new love. At least Maria was free to be a legal wife to him.

So why did it feel so wrong? *Because it was wrong.* This sudden revelation was so strong, she was shaken to the point of immobility, standing there on the pavement, thoughts racing. Ray shouldn't be marrying Maria because he belonged with her, Ellie. No matter how strong the case against her and Ray, the fact of the matter was that they were right for each other. Logic and wisdom were swept aside by the voice of her heart. She broke into a run, tearing through the streets of Shepherd's Bush.

At home she stayed only long enough to grab her car keys. Without even stopping to comb her hair, she left the house, got in her car and headed for Hammersmith.

Ruby was humming a tune as she walked towards Tom's room to check on him. He was only having a bilious attack but

Matron insisted on regular checks when any of the residents was the slightest bit off colour.

Her mind was filled with thoughts of the evening ahead. She was off duty tonight and her boyfriend was taking her out on his motor bike. They'd probably go into Dorking to a pub. Or to a café with a juke box. They might even go to the cinema. She'd have a good time whatever form the entertainment took. Ruby was a compassionate woman and a dedicated nurse but it was a very demanding job and she was always ready to go off duty when the time came.

Noticing that Tom was asleep, she was pleased. It's the best thing for him with that headache, the poor lamb, she thought, gently stroking his brow. She paused, frowning. Something wasn't right. He was *too* still, sleeping *too* deeply. She nudged his shoulder. He didn't stir. She felt for a pulse. Found one. Thank God for that. But this was no ordinary sleep.

Trained to stay calm in an emergency, she none the less felt her heart pumping as she pressed the bell on the wall and kept her finger on it.

It was turned two o'clock when Ellie arrived at the register office, having battled through the usual Saturday afternoon traffic jams. She was fraught with panic, heart racing with the fear that she might be too late.

Driven by the urgency of her emotions, she rushed up to the building. All she could think of was getting him back. But a sudden stab of conscience halted her at the entrance. What was she thinking of? She couldn't go in there and wreck his wedding just because of her own selfish feelings. That wouldn't be fair to Ray or Maria. Ellie had given him up and now she must have the courage to accept the consequences.

Whatever's happening to me? she asked herself, realising that she could barely remember driving here, she'd been so traumatised. Slowly she walked away, then turned and stood looking towards the door from which Ray would soon emerge with his bride, torturing herself with the thought that it was probably all over by now. Civil marriages didn't take long, she'd heard. Combing her untidy hair back from her brow with her fingers, she couldn't bring herself to move away.

Given the serious nature of marriage, it was only natural for a bridegroom to look solemn when the nuptials began. But Ray's expression was more one of blind panic than quiet contemplation as he stood by Maria's side in front of the registrar.

Behind those grave dark eyes, self-castigation was in full flow. The fact that he was so obviously making a mistake was no longer negotiable. He'd gone beyond that. The ceremony had started and he had to go through with it whether he liked it or not.

This was a mess of his own making; he'd let it happen when it was the last thing he wanted. He'd never proposed marriage to Maria or anything as formal as that. As far as he could remember she'd suggested it, casually at first, then behaving as though it was an established fact. He'd gone along with it because he couldn't have Ellie. What a fool he'd been even to consider the idea. You couldn't replace the woman you loved with someone else. It just didn't work that way.

Now he could feel Maria's eyes on him, and turned to be fixed with a beaming smile. She looked lovely in a cream-coloured suit with a big green hat, a porcelain glow to her skin. She was indisputably beautiful. But she wasn't Ellie. Her great dark eyes rested on him, willing him to give her a smile of reassurance. His mouth felt frozen; he was incapable of forcing his lips into a smile.

The walls seemed to close in on him as his longing for escape grew ever more urgent. 'Do you take Maria Sophia . . .' The voice droned on. Ray opened his mouth but not a word was uttered. The silence in the room thundered in his ears. He stared at Maria. She looked worried now, her eyes pleading with him to continue with the ceremony. There was a communal holding of breath among the guests.

He could feel the level of tension in the room rise to breaking point.

He couldn't do it. To marry a woman he didn't love was a recipe for disaster. She would be hurt even more in the end if he went through with it.

'I'm sorry, Maria,' he choked out, 'so very sorry.'

And he turned and rushed from the room.

Outside, he stared in disbelief at his beloved Ellie, standing there in the spring sunshine looking forlorn, cheeks flushed, hair all over the place.

The matron of Greenlands dialled Ellie's number again. Still no reply. She replaced the receiver, emitting a worried sigh. She'd been trying to get hold of Mrs Hall for some time. This being a Saturday afternoon, she was probably out shopping and would be back soon. Matron did hope so because something had happened that Tom's wife needed to know about right away. Tom was unconscious in hospital with a suspected blood clot on the brain.

She leaned back in her chair, mulling over events since lunchtime. There was never a dull moment in a place like this where people were brain damaged and on high drug doses. One minute they'd thought Tom was suffering from nothing more harmful than a bilious attack, the next he was in a coma. She tapped her pen on the desk anxiously. She'd leave it for a few minutes, then try his wife's number again and keep trying until she did get hold of her. Mrs Tom Hall needed to get to the hospital as soon as possible.

'I just can't believe what happened back there at the register office,' said Ellie, later that same afternoon; she was snuggled up in Ray's arms in his bed.

'I can hardly believe it either.' He gave her a wry look. 'It was a bit dramatic.'

'That's like saying that ice is a bit cold,' she quipped.

'I know,' he agreed. 'I didn't mean to be flippant.'

Ellie sighed in disbelief. 'It was a major drama, the stuff of films,' she said. 'You were meant to be marrying one woman and you end up in bed with another.'

'Let me rephrase that so it doesn't sound quite so tacky,' he suggested. 'I was marrying the wrong woman and I ended up in bed with the right one.'

'It might sound a bit less sleazy but it doesn't alter anything.' Her expression was grave. 'Maybe if I wasn't outside you'd have gone back in and finished the ceremony.'

'I wouldn't have,' Ray said. 'Definitely not.'

But she still felt bad. 'I don't even remember driving to the register office. One minute I was talking to Alfie, the next I just seemed to be there,' she told him. 'It was as though I was in a sort of dream with no control over my actions after Alfie told me you were getting married.'

'Seeing you outside was like the answer to a prayer.' He made a face. 'God, what a cruel thing to do, though – to say sorry to Maria and rush out in the middle of the ceremony.'

'It was awful,' she said.

'But marrying Maria wouldn't have been right,' he told her. 'It wouldn't have lasted six months.'

'Even so,' she chewed her lip, 'it was awful for Maria to be so publicly humiliated.'

'I know,' he agreed. 'I should never have let things go that far. Maria and I weren't meant to be life partners and I think she knows that.'

'Do you?'

He nodded. 'She knew all along that I was still in love with you,' he explained. 'But I was weak, I just went along with what she wanted because it was easier. It was unforgivable of me.'

'Yes, it was,' Ellie couldn't deny, 'but I suppose everybody does something they're really ashamed of at some time in their life.'

'I suppose they must do, as we're all only human,' he said.

'We're just making excuses now,' said Ellie.

'One thing I am certain of that might make you feel less bad about what happened,' he went on, 'is, if it hadn't been me she was getting married to, it would have been someone else. She was determined to find a husband.'

'Your dad said something similar.'

'Maria doesn't like the single life. She was looking for company and security more than love,' he explained. 'She was quite open about it.'

'That's something, anyway.'

'One of her greatest charms is her openness,' he continued. 'She's tough too, so don't spend too much time torturing yourself about her. She's been around the block a good few times, and she isn't the type to sit about moping. She'll pick herself up, dust herself off and go out looking for someone else.'

'I hope so,' said Ellie.

'I'll go and see her when the dust has settled,' he said. 'I'll probably get a broken jaw but still . . .'

'You deserve it,' she said.

'Yeah, I know.' He paused, kissing her hair. 'But as the dreadful deed is done and there's no going back, let's forget about Maria for the moment.'

'We can try,' she said. 'But I can't help thinking that if I'd not let my complicated emotions come between us in the first place, none of this would have happened.'

'Don't start feeling guilty about that, for goodness' sake,' Ray urged her lightly. 'Your conscience has caused us enough trouble already. And all's well that ends well.'

'Not for Maria,' Ellie reminded him. 'The poor woman's heart must be broken, no matter how tough she is.'

'I know Maria and her heart isn't broken, believe me,' Ray assured her. 'Her pride's a bit dented, that's all.'

'Mm, well, whatever the truth about that, I'll have to go home soon,' she told him. 'It's getting towards evening and Mum and Dad will be back from Ilford. We've arranged for them to go straight to my place to drop Donna off and I want 'to be there when they arrive, to greet them, you know.'

'I'll go with you . . . I can't wait to see Donna again. I've missed her too.' Ray drew her closer.

'She'll be pleased to see you.'

'But in the meantime,' he began, 'we still have some adult time left.'

'Wonderful,' she whispered into his face.

The ringing tone sounded repeatedly in the matron's ear. Eventually she put the receiver back on its cradle, her expression grim. Mrs Hall still wasn't home and Matron really did need to contact her urgently. She'd just have to keep trying.

The shrill sound of the telephone startled her. She picked up the receiver and listened to what the caller had to say.

'Yes, this is the matron. Oh . . . I see.' She listened intently. 'Thank you for letting me know.'

When the call was over she took a handkerchief from her pocket and wiped her eyes. Then she dialled the number of the local police station.

Ellie and Ray got back just before the others arrived so were there to welcome them. It was a happy reunion. Mary and Bob were delighted at the news that Ellie and Ray were back together. Donna flung herself at his legs, shrieking with delight when he lifted her up and swung her round.

'Had a good day?' Ellie asked her parents.

'Lovely, thanks, dear,' said her mother, taking off her coat and sitting in the armchair because Ellie had said something about making tea. 'And Donna was a little poppet. Madge was very taken with her. She sends you her love, by the way.'

'That's nice.'

'So, are you two back together again for good this time?' Bob wanted to know.

'I'm not letting her go again,' said Ray, who now had Donna sitting on his shoulders.

'When did this happen?' asked Mary.

'Earlier today,' replied Ellie.

'So you wait until we're out of the way before you come to your senses?' Mary teased them.

'It wasn't your not being here that made me see sense, it was something quite different,' Ellie said mysteriously.

'Do we get to know what it was?' probed her mother.

A knock at the front door interrupted the conversation. 'I'll just answer that,' said Ellie. 'Then we'll have a cup of tea and a good old natter.'

Opening the front door she was confronted by the alarming sight of two police officers who asked her if she was Eleanor Hall, wife of Tom Hall.

'Yes, that's me.' Shakily, she ushered them into the hall. 'It's my husband, isn't it?'

'The matron of Greenlands has been trying to contact you all afternoon, apparently,' said one of the officers, his tone determinedly unemotional though he wasn't quite able to hide a slight breathlessness. 'But your phone hasn't been answered. So she got through to her local police station and they contacted us.'

'I've been out,' she said in a nervous whisper. 'Has Tom been taken ill?'

The officers looked at her gravely. The younger of the two betrayed his nervousness by scratching his cheek. 'I think you should sit down,' he suggested.

'No, no, it's all right.' She was trembling now, her heart beating so fast she thought it would burst. 'Just tell me what's happened – now . . . please.'

The older officer paused for only a moment. 'I'm sorry to have to tell you, Mrs Hall, that your husband died just after four o'clock this afternoon,' he informed her.

'Oh my God . . .'

Hearing voices in the hall, Ray came to see who was there. He was just in time to catch Ellie as her legs gave way.

Chapter Twenty

Grief-stricken – her own personal sorrow combined with compassion for Tom's mother – Ellie stood by Mary's side in Pat's living room, watching her face turn scarlet then become bloodless in reaction to the dreadful news. Old grudges forgotten in the drama of the moment, Mary had thought it fitting she be the one to break it to her. Ellie had come with her to offer moral support.

'Tom dead?' Pat muttered in a whisper, her expression one of utter bewilderment. 'I didn't even know he was ill. He seemed all right last week when I visited him.'

'It was quite a sudden thing, apparently, dear,' Mary told her kindly.

'Just came out of the blue,' added Ellie. Although it was a long time since she and Tom had been together, she had once loved him and his death was a terrible blow. But she'd forced herself to be strong. As soon as she'd been sufficiently composed – having collapsed into a fit of uncontrollable weeping after the policemen left – Ellie had telephoned both Greenlands and the hospital for details, then come straight here. So she was still feeling extremely shaky. 'He wasn't ill for long. A nasty headache this morning, that's all.'

Whey-faced and bemused, Pat nodded. Having ignored their suggestion that she sit down, she'd remained standing, looking stiff and tense.

'I'm so sorry to bring such awful news,' Ellie told her.

'Me, too.' Mary moved towards Pat and tried to embrace her but Pat drew back sharply.

'Thank you for coming to tell me,' she said, as though they were strangers. 'I appreciate that.'

Ellie couldn't bear to see Pat withdraw into herself. 'We're hurting with you, Pat,' she said, moving towards and putting her hand on the other woman's arm. 'Please don't push us away.'

Pat stood rigid; she didn't reply.

'Let's forget what happened in the past and help each other through this awful thing,' Ellie persisted in a gentle tone.

'I'm grateful to you for coming to tell me,' Pat's voice was flat and expressionless, 'but I'd like to be alone now.'

'Don't be on your own at a time like this, for goodness' sake, Pat.' Mary was horrified at the idea. 'We're here for you. Either come to our place or we'll stay here with you.'

'I'd rather be on my own, thanks.'

'But, Pat—'

'Leave her, Mum,' Ellie cut in sadly.

The two women exchanged a look, knowing they must respect Pat's right to privacy in her grief. With great reluctance, Ellie and her mother made their way down the stairs and closed the front door carefully behind them.

Alone in the flat, which seemed achingly silent after she'd heard the soft click of the front door closing behind her visitors, Pat sank into an armchair, staring emptily ahead of her; she stayed there for a long time. The shock seemed to have weakened her legs to the point where she didn't feel able to stand. But the urgency of something she needed to do finally galvanised her into action and she forced herself up and walked shakily to the telephone in the hall.

With a trembling hand she dialled a number. 'Hello, Alfie. It's Pat, Pat Hall.' Her voice was muffled with emotion. 'I was wondering if— Do you think you could come over . . . right away. I need you. Please come.'

412

Without so much as a query or hesitation, he said, 'I'm on my way.'

When Ellie and her mother got back to Ellie's house, Ray had put Donna to bed and Doug had arrived, his father having been round to tell him what had happened. Ann had stayed at home with Matthew.

First thing tomorrow morning Ellie, Ray and Doug were going to drive to the Surrey hospital where Tom's body was in the mortuary, but now they all sat around in Ellie's living room, talking and drinking tea.

'The awful part about it is,' confided Ellie, ashen-face and drawn, 'while my poor husband was taking his last breath, I was having a passionate reconciliation with Ray. You can imagine how that makes me feel.'

'You weren't to know what was going on at Greenlands.' Ray was sitting beside her on the sofa, and gave her hand an encouraging squeeze. 'There was nothing you could have done, anyway.'

'I could have been with him at the end if they'd been able to contact me,' she pointed out, turning to him sharply. 'And they could have got hold of me if I hadn't been with you because I'd have been at home.'

'Please don't torture yourself, Ellie,' Ray begged her. 'It would have made no difference if you had been there. Tom was already unconscious when the matron started trying to get hold of you.'

'Ray's right,' put in Mary. 'He wouldn't have known whether you were there or not.'

'I'd have known, though,' cried Ellie, fresh tears forming. 'If I'd known in time, I'd have got into the car and driven straight down there, taking Pat with me. As it is, my husband died alone.' She put her hands to her head in despair. 'That's one hell of a thing to have to live with.'

'For pity's sake, Ellie, don't start tormenting yourself about that,' intervened Doug, becoming surprisingly heated on the

413

subject. 'You've punished yourself enough over the years because of Tom. It's time to call a halt to it.'

'I should have been there,' she insisted.

'What were you supposed to do? Stay at home by the phone every second of every day, just waiting for something to happen to Tom?' he asked her.

'What your brother says makes sense,' approved Bob.

'He was a young man,' Doug went on. 'He could have lived to a ripe old age, brain damaged or not.'

'I understand everything you're saying,' she said thickly. 'But that doesn't make me feel any better.'

'Well, it should do.' Her brother seemed very fired up. 'You'll have to be very firm with yourself on this one, Ellie, for Ray's sake as well as your own. What's happened is bad enough. Don't make it worse by burdening yourself with guilt that you don't deserve.'

'All right, Doug, I'll try not to,' she said to pacify him. 'Anyway, I'm lucky. I have all of you to help me through.' She held Ray's hand very tight as though to illustrate the point. 'Poor Pat has no one now that she's turned us all away.'

'Not quite no one,' corrected Ray.

'Oh?' she enquired.

'Nothing,' he replied. 'Just thinking aloud.'

And they were all far too upset about Tom's death to press him on the subject.

'Whatever's the matter?' asked Alfie when Pat answered the door to him, her face paper white, lips so pale they seemed almost to have disappeared. 'Are you feeling poorly?'

She didn't say anything; just turned and went back up the stairs, leaving him to follow her.

'What is it, Pat?' he asked, as she stood facing him in her living room. 'There's obviously something wrong.'

Still she didn't reply. 'Tell me, Pat,' he urged her gently. 'Tell me what's happened.'

She opened her mouth to speak but not a word emerged.

414

Instead the room was filled with the sound of her screams, piercing the air with their shrillness and quickly turning to laughter, terrible manic shrieks that convulsed her whole body.

A sharp slap across the cheek ended her hysterics, and she stood before him looking bewildered. Then her face seemed to crumple and she bent over and wept. Gently he held her in his arms while she told him in between sobs that her son was dead. When her tears finally subsided it wasn't because she was any the less grief-stricken, just cried out.

Ellie tried to discuss the funeral arrangements with Pat so that she wouldn't feel excluded. As Tom's mother she was important, and Ellie wanted her to feel part of things; she even suggested that Pat have the hearse go from the shop as that was where Tom had been brought up. But Pat had gone right into herself and told Ellie she didn't feel up to making the arrangements.

So the funeral party went from Ellie's house in Fenleigh Gardens. It was quite a small gathering but there was a crowd at the cemetery because Tom had been a well-known, if not particularly well-liked, local man. A neighbour of Ellie's offered to look after Donna while Ellie attended this sad function. Matthew stayed with a friend of Ann's.

Much to the concern of Ellie and her mother, Pat made her own way to the church with Alfie, sat apart from everyone else and left immediately after the burial, despite Ellie's attempts to persuade them both to come back to the house for something to eat.

'Poor Pat,' said Ellie to Ray when they arrived back at her home. 'She must be going through hell, shutting herself off from us all like that.'

'Dad'll look after her, don't worry,' he assured her.

'I understand now what you meant when you said she wasn't quite alone. I didn't realise she and Alfie were that close until I saw them at the funeral together.'

'I don't know if they're what you could call close exactly,'

Ray said. 'It is just a working relationship, but he's got a soft spot for her, I think.'

'You can tell that from the way he looked after her at the funeral,' said Ellie. 'And if anyone is in need of a friend right now, it's Tom's mother.'

A short time later Ellie found her brother in the back garden; he'd retreated from the social gathering for a cigarette and some peace and quiet in the spring sunshine.

'I suppose you and I were closer to Tom than anyone, apart from his mother, when we were all growing up,' she mentioned chattily, perching next to him on the low wall between the paved area and the lawn.

'Yeah.'

'I know he hasn't been around for a while but now that he's actually gone it's like having a chunk of our childhood wiped out, isn't it?' She was very sad.

'Mm.' Doug was standing staring absently into space. He seemed exceptionally tense.

'He was like a brother to you, wasn't he?' she mentioned in reminiscent mood.

'Suppose so.'

'There was never anything sisterly about *my* feelings for him,' she went on wistfully. 'I loved him in that special way all my life. I just couldn't believe it when he loved me back.' She sighed. 'Who would have thought it would end like this?'

'Your life is with Ray now,' Doug said with such sharpness it was almost an order.

'That seems rather a brutal thing to say on the day of Tom's funeral.'

'Maybe it is but it's something you need to keep in mind,' was his return.

'Doug . . .' Ellie took his arm, worriedly, 'what's the matter with you? Why are you so worked up about it?'

'I know what you're like when it comes to Tom,' he told her gruffly.

'He *was* my husband,' she reminded him. 'What do you expect me to be like when I've just buried him?'

'Sad and reflective, of course,' he conceded. 'That wasn't what I meant.'

'What then?'

'I was referring to the fact that you always put yourself in the wrong when it comes to Tom. You blame yourself unnecessarily.' He seemed particularly angry about this, and she wasn't sure why. 'Knowing you, Ellie, you'll let the fact that you were with Ray when Tom died fester in your mind. Then you'll add the accident to it and punish yourself all over again.'

The process had already begun so she couldn't deny it.

'I know this might sound callous,' Doug continued, 'but Tom is dead and that stage in your life is finally over. You must move on with Ray with no guilt about any aspect of your life with Tom.'

'You *are* in a mood today,' she responded, put out. 'I know you're grieving for the loss of your best mate but there's no need to be quite so cross with me.'

'Things aren't always what they seem, you know,' he told her grimly.

'Oh?' She looked at him questioningly. 'And what do you mean by that?'

He studied her face, drawing hard on his cigarette and seeming about to explain. But then he just lowered his eyes and said, 'Nothing. Forget it.'

'Come on, you must have meant something.'

He opened his mouth to speak but changed his mind for the second time.

'Doug . . .?' she coaxed.

'It was just a generalisation. I wasn't referring to anything in particular.'

She didn't believe him but the conversation was cut short by the appearance of their mother. 'Ah, there you are, Ellie,' she said. 'I've been looking for you all over. Have you got any

417

more sherry? We've almost run out.'

'There's another bottle at the bottom of the larder but I'm coming in now,' said Ellie, and followed her mother into the house, leaving Doug alone with his mysterious thoughts.

On the way back from the cemetery to Pat's place, Alfie stopped at the off-licence and bought a bottle of brandy. As soon as they got indoors he poured two glasses while she took off her coat and sank down into an armchair. She didn't even bother to take off her black hat and that made her face look even more gaunt and colourless. They'd closed the shop for the day as a mark of respect, so neither of them had to go on duty.

'I don't normally drink brandy,' she told him.

'Today isn't normal,' he said, handing her a glass with at least a treble in it.

'Drowning my sorrows in drink isn't the answer,' she muttered, but it was only a token protest because she needed something to ease the pain.

'Stop fussing and drink it, woman.' He wasn't prepared to take no for an answer.

She did as he said, making a face. 'It tastes foul,' was her verdict. 'I never have liked spirits.'

'It'll calm you, though.'

'Yes, I know,' she sighed. 'I can feel it warming me already.'

Alfie sat down in an armchair opposite her, sipping his drink and stroking his chin meditatively. 'Alcohol will only give you temporary relief, though,' he pointed out. 'You need something that will give you more lasting comfort to help you through this awful time.'

'Are you suggesting that I get tablets from the doctor or something?' Pat asked.

'Oh no, nothing like that,' he was keen to make clear.

'You've got something definite in mind, though, haven't you?' she said with a questioning look. 'I can tell by your tone of voice.'

His sheepish look confirmed her suspicions. 'Look, Pat, I know you won't thank me for saying this—'

'But you're going to say it anyway, so get on with it.' She sounded weary but the alcohol had put some colour in her cheeks and her voice was a little steadier.

'I think you're making things even harder for yourself by cutting yourself off from Ellie and her family,' he blurted out. 'You need your friends at a time like this.'

'They aren't my friends now, though, are they?' was her sullen reminder.

'They could be again with a little effort on your part,' he was at pains to point out. 'I think it would help you to be on good terms with them.'

Pat looked at him, her eyes full of sorrow. 'I've just buried my son,' she reminded him dully. 'Don't you think I've had enough punishment for one day?'

'I certainly do,' he replied. 'Which is why I think you should stop making things even worse for yourself. Make it up with the Scotts. And the sooner the better. You should have been with them today at the funeral, not standing apart from them. You need each other at a time like this, especially Ellie.'

'No, Alfie,' was her flat response.

'Surely Tom's death has made you realise that life's too short to be at war with people.' He was blatantly persuasive now. 'You know you didn't mean those terrible things you said to Ellie.'

'Didn't I?' she sighed wearily. 'You seem to know more about it than I do.'

'I'm on the outside looking in so I get the broader view,' was his answer to that. 'I can understand your being upset initially about Ellie and Ray, but you're an intelligent woman; you must have known she would meet someone else eventually. I think once you'd made a stand about it, you were too proud to back down.'

The alcohol had mellowed her. 'There probably is some truth in what you say,' she admitted tiredly. 'You always could see right through me.'

'You didn't really think Ellie was to blame for the accident, did you?' he went on. 'You just needed someone to blame because you were hurting so much yourself.'

She didn't reply, just sat perfectly still, staring ahead of her. 'Tom was such a beautiful child,' she said, almost to herself. 'I probably loved him more than was good for him.' She put her empty glass on the coffee table and clasped her hands together on her lap, her eyes glazed in thought. The brandy had relaxed her and made her want to talk. 'I never loved George in the way a wife should. I was good to him, though. What I lacked in passion I made up for in duty. He gave me security and in return I attended to his every need. Maybe if I'd loved him as I ought, I wouldn't have been so obsessive in my love for Tom. But I just worshipped the ground he walked on.' Her voice softened at the memory of her son in happier times. 'I couldn't help it.'

'What it is to be a parent, eh?' Alfie said.

'I've never been able to let go and have fun,' she said, straying off the point again, 'and I've always envied people who can.' She gave him a sad smile. 'I always admired your happy-go-lucky ways when we were young, even though I pretended to disapprove.'

'It was easy for me to be carefree in those days,' he told her. 'A lot of water has flowed under the bridge since then.'

'You haven't lost your sense of humour, though,' she pointed out. 'Despite losing your wife . . .' She paused for a moment. 'And all that trouble with Ray.'

'Some of it's just front, you know,' Alfie admitted. 'No point in making other people miserable by going about with a long face, is there?' He paused, wagging his finger at her. 'But don't change the subject. We're supposed to be talking about you.' He looked at her, willing her to carry on.

'Because Tom was my life, it was hard for me when he got married because I didn't want to share him,' she continued. 'But at least he married someone I already knew so I didn't have to cope with a stranger.' She fell silent, thinking back, her face tightening with the agony of the memories. 'When Tom had his accident, the pain was unimaginable. And yes, you're quite right, I did need someone to blame and the driver of the car was the obvious target. But I kept my feelings to myself because I didn't want to lose Ellie. She and Donna were the only family I had left, in any real sense.'

'But when you heard about her and Ray, that didn't matter any more?' Alfie suggested.

'Exactly. I was so devastated, I let it all out – everything I'd been holding back all that time. I was hurt and I wanted to hurt back. Of course it was wrong of me to blame Ellie for the accident, I knew that in my heart all the time. And, although it hurts even now to face up to it, I suppose I also knew it was only natural for her to fall in love with someone else eventually.'

'But pride wouldn't allow you to put things right?'

Pat looked thoughtful, as though trying to analyse her own feelings. 'I think it was more than pride. Pain can seriously impair your judgement and there was an awful lot of that eating away inside me,' she told him. 'That terrible day when I parted from Mary and Ellie, I felt utterly destroyed. Everything hurt so much . . . thoughts of poor Tom in an institution while Ellie was enjoying herself with someone else – the terrible things I'd said to her. I couldn't bear to think about any of it so I tried to shut it out of my mind.'

'Do you feel better for finally admitting the truth to yourself?' Alfie asked.

'Yes, but only up to a point.'

He knew exactly what she meant. 'Why don't you go round to Ellie's now?' he suggested.

'Oh, Alfie, don't be daft,' she said. 'There's a funeral gathering going on there.'

'And you should be there at that gathering,' he told her. 'You snubbed them by not going to the actual funeral with them, or back to the house afterwards. Don't let this sad day pass without putting things right.'

'They won't want to see me after the way I've behaved, the

things I've said.' He'd never seen her looking so vulnerable. 'Not today of all days.'

'Especially today,' he argued. 'I reckon they'll welcome you with open arms. And if I'm wrong, at least you'll have made the effort to put things right. That in itself should give you some comfort.'

'I can't, Alfie.' She looked utterly defeated.

'Yes, you can,' he encouraged. 'And when you've done what you know you must, you can let your son rest in peace.'

She bit her lip. Baring her soul to Alfie had had a cathartic effect and she finally felt able to right a wrong. Needed to, in fact. 'If I do go,' she began uncertainly, 'will you come with me?'

'Course I will.'

'Thank you, Alfie.' She managed a stiff smile. 'You're a good friend to me.'

'Thank you.' He stood up with a purposeful air. 'Come on then. Let's do it.'

'What now?' It was all moving a bit too fast for Pat.

'There's no time like the present,' he said, holding her coat out for her.

Ellie answered the door. 'Pat, Alfie. How nice to see you both,' she said, her initial look of surprise quickly changing to a welcoming smile. 'Come on in, both of you.'

'Ellie, I . . .' began Pat, tears rushing into her eyes as she stepped into the hall. 'All those things I said . . .'

'It doesn't matter now.' Ellie was startled by this unexpected attempt at an apology but warmed by it too.

'But it does matter,' insisted Pat, and Alfie noticed a glimpse of her old spirit. 'Please let me apologise.'

From behind Pat, Alfie nodded at Ellie. 'OK,' she said. 'If that's what you really want.'

'I'm so sorry, Ellie, about everything,' Pat blurted out, 'I didn't mean all those awful things.'

'I was very hurt, Pat.' Ellie felt it needed saying. 'I'm not going to deny it.'

422

'You must have been, I can see that now. Please forgive me,' she entreated with humility, something that was almost unprecedented for Pat. 'I so much want us all to be friends again.'

Out went Ellie's arms to encircle the thin, rigid body. 'And so do I,' she said, hugging her and feeling a real response from Pat for the first time ever. 'So do I.'

'Well, it's taken you long enough, Pat Hall,' declared Mary appearing on the scene.

Pat drew back from Ellie. 'Mary, I—'

'Don't say anything,' said Mary, her voice quivering on the verge of tears. 'Just come here, you daft bat.'

The two older women wrapped their arms around each other, sobbing with a mixture of sadness and joy, allowing Pat a glimpse of light on this darkest of all days.

Ann was just drifting off to sleep when the sound of move-ment woke her with a start. It was Doug getting out of bed and feeling his way across the bedroom to the door. As usual when this happened she lay there staring into the dark, listening to his careful steps on the stairs. He hadn't had a decent night's sleep since Tom's death.

It was only natural that he would be upset at the loss of such an old friend, and the funeral today must have been traumatic for him, but there was something more than just grief bothering him, she was sure of it.

Making a sudden decision she got up purposefully, slipped into her dressing gown and went downstairs. She found him sitting at the kitchen table, smoking.

'This has gone on for long enough, Doug,' she declared without preamble.

'What has?'

'Don't come the innocent. You know exactly what I'm talking about,' she told him. 'These depressions of yours and my exclusion from whatever it is that causes them. For years I've been forced to stand aside while you've gone to your own private hell and back, every so often. I've lain awake at nights worrying about you when you've been downstairs smoking when you should have been in bed asleep. And quite frankly, I've had enough. I'm sick and tired of being left in the dark.'

'An old mate of mine was buried today,' Doug said, staring straight ahead and carefully avoiding her eyes. 'Surely you don't expect me to be full of the joys of spring.'

'No, of course not. But this current mood of yours isn't just about Tom's funeral,' Ann stated categorically. 'There's something wrong and I want to know what it is – something you've kept locked up inside yourself for years. Whatever it is we can sort it. But you have to tell me, Doug.'

Expecting another denial, she was astonished when he looked at her gravely and said, 'I'm sorry, Ann, for all the hurt I've caused you over the years. Yes, you're right. There is something I haven't told you. Something I should have brought out into the open a long time ago.' He inhaled on his cigarette, then stubbed it out slowly in the ashtray. 'The reason I haven't told you is because I'm so terribly ashamed.' He drew in his breath, his eyes never leaving her face. 'The truth is, I've done something shocking and you're going to hate me when you know what it is.'

Breathless with fear at what she was about to hear, she sat down and faced him across the table. 'You'd better tell me what it is then, hadn't you?'

The next morning Ann and Doug arrived at Ellie's house, having telephoned first to tell her that they needed to see her urgently. They had also arranged for Ray to be there. The children were at playgroup so there were just the four of them.

'This is all very mysterious,' said Ellie, ushering them into the living room.

'What's it all about?' enquired Ray, who was perched on the edge of the sofa. 'I've got a lot to do at the workshop. I can't afford to take time off during the working day.'

'Sorry about that,' Ann apologised, sitting on a hardback

chair, looking tense. 'But when you hear what Doug has to say, you'll realise how important it is for you to be here.'

Ellie and Ray exchanged puzzled glances. 'Get on with it, then,' urged Ellie, sitting down next to Ray on the sofa, 'before we die of curiosity.'

'I wanted you to be here together,' began Doug hesitantly, 'because although what I have to say mostly affects Ray, it affects you too, Ellie.'

'Spit it out, mate, for God's sake,' demanded Ray. 'I've got work to do.'

Doug focused his gaze on Ray. 'The fact is, I've done you a terrible injustice,' he told him. 'You served six years in prison for something you didn't do, because of me.'

Ellie's eyes widened with shock. Ray gave Doug a hard stare. 'Oh, Doug,' gasped Ellie in disbelief. 'Are you saying that you killed Keith Wilkes?'

'You?' echoed Ray incredulously. 'You are Keith Wilkes's murderer?'

'If you'll let me finish,' Doug said, raising his hands in a silencing gesture, 'I'll tell you exactly what happened that night.'

Ellie and Ray nodded for him to continue.

'On the night that Keith Wilkes died, Tom and I were on a boys' night out together. We had a few drinks at the Flying Goose, then went on to the billiard hall and had a few more while we were having a game. So we were quite squiffy when we walked home. As we passed the Flying Goose, this bloke – who we later knew to be Keith Wilkes – came out of the pub and tried to pick a fight with us. He was drunk and in the mood for a bundle. I ignored him and walked on but Tom let himself be provoked. I heard a scuffle and turned round to see the two of them fighting. I went back and tried to stop the fight but Keith Wilkes kept coming at Tom – he was mad with drink. To defend himself Tom gave him a really hard punch that knocked him to the ground.'

A shocked hush fell over the room.

'Anyway,' Doug continued, 'I was on my way to the pub to get help when Tom panicked and dragged me back. He said we'd have to make a run for it. He reckoned no one would believe he'd hit the man in self-defence. Of course at that stage we didn't know the man would die. Tom was worried about getting done for GBH.'

'And you went with Tom and left the man dying and me to take the blame,' accused Ray bitterly.

Doug didn't even try to defend himself. 'That was how it worked out, yeah. Of course I didn't know then that that was what would happen. Someone came out of the pub just as Tom was trying to persuade me. It must have been you, Ray, so I knew that help was on its way. We were in the shadows. No one saw us slip away.'

'You didn't even stay around to see what happened.' Ray's tone was scathing.

'I panicked,' Doug admitted. 'I was awake all night worrying about it and the next morning, when I heard that Keith Wilkes had died and you'd been arrested, I was sick, though the family thought I was just hungover. I told Tom we must go to the police but he wasn't having that. He said they'd be even less likely to believe it had been self-defence as we'd made a run for it, and if I went to the coppers he would tell them it was me who'd struck the fatal blow. It would have been my word against his as the only witness was dead.' He paused for breath, his skin pallid, eyes heavy with remorse and lack of sleep. 'There was nothing at all to link us with the crime because we'd left the pub hours before it happened. We were both due back off leave on that Sunday. Tom said we should go back as though nothing had happened, but if I breathed a word I would be the one on trial for murder, not him. Coward that I was, I went along with it.' He hung his head. 'I'm so ashamed.'

'I should bloody well hope you are,' growled Ray.

'I know this won't be much consolation, but I can honestly say that not a day has passed since that night when I haven't been tormented.'

'I can vouch for that,' added Ann. 'I've had to live with his sleepless nights, his black moods, always knowing something was wrong and never being told what it was . . . until last night.'

'When Tom was so badly injured in the accident,' Doug continued, 'I thought that was his punishment and I felt even worse about it. Although I wasn't guilty of the actual crime I thought I should have been punished for not coming forward and telling the truth. I actually did think about going to the police then and getting you out of prison, Ray. Tom was no longer in a position to put the blame on me, and the police were unlikely to do anything to someone in such a feeble state.'

'Why didn't you do it, then?' asked Ellie.

'It would have been like kicking a baby,' he explained. 'I also thought it would destroy his mother to know the truth about her beloved son.'

'And never mind about me rotting away in prison,' said Ray, his eyes black with rage.

Doug pushed his fingers through his hair, his face white and shining with nervous perspiration. 'I suppose it was a question of looking after my own,' he said. 'I'd known them all my life. You were a stranger to me then.'

'Bloody coward,' roared Ray in disgust. 'You should have had the courage to go to the police.'

'There's nothing you can say that can possibly make me feel worse than I do already,' Doug assured him solemnly. 'I should think your first instinct is to beat the living daylights out of me.'

'I'm too sick even to do that,' muttered Ray.

'I'll go to the police right away,' Doug told him quickly. 'I'll do whatever it takes to clear your name; make sure it gets in the papers so that no one is left in any doubt about it. Maybe you'll get compensation for wrongful imprisonment. I know I'll get done for withholding evidence and perverting the course of justice.'

Ray said nothing, just looked at him icily.

Ellie looked at her brother. 'Now I know why you leaped to Ray's defence every time his name was mentioned,' she said. 'It was your guilty conscience.'

'Don't lose sight of the fact that it was Tom who actually did the deed, and not you, Doug,' Ann was keen to point out to her husband. 'The way you're carrying on, anyone would think that you killed Keith Wilkes yourself.'

'Not coming forward with the truth and letting Ray do a prison stretch seems almost as bad,' he said.

'It does to me too.' Ray was in no mood to let Doug off lightly.

Doug lowered his eyes. 'Yes, I can imagine it would do.' He paused, looking at his sister. 'Before I finish, there's something I want to say to you, Ellie.'

'Go on then.' She was dreading what she might hear next.

'I know we're not supposed to speak ill of the dead but I also think it's wrong to remember them untruthfully,' he began. 'If you want a future with Ray, you must open your mind to reality and remember Tom as he really was, a cruel bully who controlled us both for the whole of our childhood and beyond. You even blamed yourself for the accident when it was proved to be the other driver's fault. Even without that there would have been no blame attached to you because Tom forced you to drive that day when you didn't feel ready. You've never said as much, but reading between the lines I know that's what happened. I knew Tom; I know what he was like.'

Ellie didn't say anything, just listened as he continued, 'He bullied and humiliated us both and had such power over us we let him get away with it. I honestly believe that he never lost a wink of sleep about the death of Keith Wilkes or Ray going down for it. He was very cold-blooded. I am only telling you this so you will stop feeling guilty about any aspect of your life with him and move forward with Ray, unburdened by the past.'

'This is all very well but I lost six years of my life because of you,' said Ray, standing up and stepping towards Doug in a threatening manner.

'Ray, calm down,' cried Ellie, leaping up and putting a restraining hand on his arm as he seemed about to strike her brother. 'I know what you've been through but Doug knows he's done you a terrible wrong. He can't ever put it right but he's going to clear your name.'

Ray turned away from Ellie and faced Doug. 'Have you any idea what prison life is like?' He put his face very close to Doug's. 'Have you any idea how demoralising it is being locked up in a stinking cell with no sanitation, or what it's like to be beaten by cons who want to make sure you know who's running things when you first arrive? Can you imagine what it feels like not to have respect or liberty?' He grabbed Doug's jacket lapel and pulled him even closer. 'No, of course you can't imagine it because you've never had to do it. Well, I think you should go to jail so that you know what I went through because you were too yellow to come forward and tell the police what really happened.'

'I'm so sorry, Ray,' said Doug meekly. 'What else can I say?'

'And if prison wasn't enough,' Ray ranted on as though Doug hadn't spoken, 'I even had the humiliation of people thinking I was guilty when I came out.' He let go of Doug suddenly. Ray's face was tight and pale, his lips set in a grim line. 'You make me so sick, I can't even bear to look at you. I hope I never have to again.'

Without even glancing at Ellie, Ray turned and marched from the room, heading for the front door.

'Ray!' cried Ellie, going after him.

Doug grabbed her arm and pulled her back. 'Leave him, Ellie,' he advised.

'But I can't just let him go.' She was distraught.

'You must,' he said commandingly.

'But I love him, Doug.'

'Do you think I don't know that,' was his anguished reply. 'The last thing I want to do is come between you and Ray, on top of all the other misery I've caused. But you are my sister and Ray is very angry with me at the moment. People get funny about blood ties at times of stress. You might get hurt if you go after him now because he isn't thinking straight and he'll say things he doesn't mean. Give him time to calm down, then go looking for him.'

'Doug's right, Ellie,' Ann agreed. 'You're too closely involved with Doug. You need to leave Ray alone for a while.'

'You think he'll turn against me because I'm your sister?' Ellie was horrified.

'He might well, initially, but only while he's in shock,' Doug tried to assure her. 'He probably feels sore towards the whole family because he's upset and won't be rational. But if he holds it against you permanently then he isn't the man I believe him to be.'

But for all his words of reassurance, he was worried about this aspect of the whole miserable business. If Ellie lost the man she loved over this, Doug really didn't know how he would live with himself.

Chapter Twenty-One

Ray was too angry for rational thought as he drove through the back streets of Shepherd's Bush, furiously muttering the foulest expletives he could think of. The wrath of knowing that he'd paid the price for Tom Hall's crime consumed him to the exclusion of all else. And if that wasn't bad enough, he couldn't even vent his anger on Tom Hall because the bastard was dead.

Finding himself near the centre of the town, he decided not to continue on to his workshop, which was situated near the market. Trying to work while he was this angry wouldn't be a good idea because he would make mistakes. So instead he parked the car in a side street and walked across the main road to the Green, where he sat down on a bench, far too immersed in his own fury to feel the sun on his face or notice the fresh new leaves in bud on the trees.

Housewives plodded by, weighed down with weekend shopping, this being Friday. A couple of tramps dozed under the trees while a dog sniffed around them unnoticed. It was just coming up to midday and shop assistants and office girls were beginning to appear in force, taking their lunch break alfresco.

Vaguely observing all of this, Ray felt the steady rhythm of everyday life cooling his temper. But the respite was brief. As soon as he remembered the injustice he'd suffered, his temper flared again. He admonished himself for idling away the time on Shepherd's Bush Green when he had a living to earn.

Thoughts of his work lingered in his mind soothingly. He had a challenging project currently in progress – a set of ornamental internal doors consisting of decorative metal on clouded glass, the metal shaped to a pattern he'd created especially to the customer's requirements. The doors were for a town house in Chelsea, and would do wonders for his reputation if he got them right.

As he lingered on the technicalities of the job, his anger began to dissolve, his mood lightened by thoughts of his craft. He reminded himself of the fact that had he never been to prison he wouldn't be a craftsman at all. He'd probably still be spending his days on the assembly line at the factory.

Now that he was calmer and his mind began to clear, Ellie came sharply into focus. He began to feel ashamed of the way he'd rushed off without so much as a word to her. None of what had happened was her fault. She couldn't be held responsible for her brother's actions.

In a moment of introspection, he realised that part of the reason for his anger was his profound disappointment in Doug. He'd taken an instant liking to the man, had thought he was a genuinely decent bloke. Who would have thought he'd been harbouring such a cruel secret all those years?

And now the cause of all the trouble was dead. With the emphasis so strongly on grief and death this past week or so Ray hadn't focused his mind on the other aspect of Tom's death, which was that he and Ellie were now free to marry. The thought pleased and softened him. But reality soon put a stop to that. What chance would he and Ellie have now that there was such bad feeling between himself and Doug? Even if she did agree to marry him under those circumstances, which was doubtful, their relationship would be doomed. Given her love for her brother, it couldn't be otherwise. If Doug had killed Keith Wilkes in cold blood, she would have stood by him.

And Doug hadn't killed the man in cold blood or in any way at all. He'd done wrong by not coming forward with the

432

truth, had actually broken the law by withholding evidence, but he hadn't done the crime for which Ray had been blamed. Nothing would ever convince Ray that Doug was justified in protecting Tom, and he doubted if he would ever be able to forgive him, but there was no need for his original opinion of Doug to change; he was basically a good man who'd had a moment of weakness into which he'd become trapped.

Now that he was in a more reasonable frame of mind, Ray could see how difficult it must have been for him to do the right thing later on, having made that fatal error of judgement at the time of the killing.

No word or deed could alter what had happened. Doug had done wrong and he knew it. Ray had done the time and it was in the past.

Things were good for Ray now. He had the love of a woman he adored, and they were free to marry. He had a good business and a lot to look forward to. What was the point of wrecking the future by clinging on to old injustices? Doug had obviously punished himself over the years. Why not just leave it at that?

He took a deep breath and let it out slowly, feeling the tension knots loosen. Then he lifted his face to the sun and let its rays warm his skin. After a little more cogitation, he got up and walked back to his car.

Doug was on his way out of the front gate when Ray drew up in the car outside Ellie's house.

'Where are you off to?' he asked, poking his head out of the car window.

'The police station, where else?' Doug told him, coming closer. 'I'd be there already if it wasn't for Ann going on at me. She's terrified I'll get done for withholding evidence and go to prison for a long stretch. She might be right too.'

'Go back inside,' said Ray. 'I've things to say.'

'I have to put things right,' insisted Doug. 'And the police station must be my starting point.'

'No, Doug, you're going back inside and listening to what I have to say,' Ray ordered. 'You owe me that much.'

Doug looked sheepish. 'Yeah, OK,' he agreed, turning and walking towards the front door.

'Right,' began Ray, standing with his back to the window and addressing Ellie, Ann and Doug who were all sitting down. 'You'll probably all be very relieved to hear that I have decided not to go public with the truth about the death of Keith Wilkes.'

There was an astonished gasp.

'But you've dreamed of clearing your name and you can't do that without making the truth public,' Ellie reminded him. 'Ever since I've known you, you've wanted that – *so much*.'

'Yes, I have wanted it,' he confirmed. 'And I still do. But it's a question of priorities. There are other things that are more important to me now.'

'But you must have your name cleared,' Doug persisted. 'It's only right.'

'I will have it cleared – to all the people who matter, anyway,' Ray informed them gravely. 'And I'd like you, Doug, to be the one to tell them.'

'Them? What exactly do you have in mind, mate?'

'I want my reputation restored to your parents and certain other trusted people that I shall list for you in due course,' Ray explained. 'If you tell them the truth, rather than me, there can be no doubt about it. But there'll be no police and no newspapers involved in this. I want it kept among ourselves.'

'It's very good of you.' Ann couldn't remember ever feeling this grateful to anyone.

'Don't make a saint of me because that's the last thing I am,' he was quick to point out. 'I'm just being realistic. If this thing gets official a lot of people will be hurt, not least Ellie.' He looked at her brother. 'Anything that hurts you, Doug, hurts her.'

Doug nodded, waiting for Ray to continue.

Ray directed his next comments to Doug. 'I'll probably never be able to forgive you for costing me six years of my life,' he said solemnly.

'I can understand that,' was Doug's sober response.

'But I'm going to do my damnedest to put it to the back of my mind,' Ray went on to say. 'And the reason I am willing to try is because what we all have together is too good to throw away because of one mistake.'

Ellie was deeply moved. She knew how much this decision had cost him. She got up and went over to him. 'You're quite something, do you know that?'

'I'll second that,' added Doug.

'Don't go all soppy on me,' Ray objected, looking bashful. 'I've told you my reasons. You know they are based on common sense.'

'We're all grateful, just the same,' Ann told him.

Visibly embarrassed now, Ray scratched his cheek and swiftly moved the conversation on. 'Before you say a word about it to anyone, Doug,' he said, 'there is someone I must tell myself, a man who never lost faith in my innocence – my father. He deserves to know that his faith was not misplaced before anyone else does.'

'You just say the word,' said Doug, 'and I'll put the record straight to whoever you want.'

'I think I'll go and see Dad right away,' decided Ray suddenly. 'I'll be back later, Ellie.'

'I'll be here waiting for you.'

He kissed her and hurried from the house.

'You've got yourself a really good man there,' said Doug, looking at his sister.

'You don't have to tell me that, Doug,' she beamed.

'No, I don't suppose I do.' He stood up. 'Well, as I'm going to be a free man after all, I'd better go to work and make my excuses for being late.'

'And we have to collect the kids from playgroup,' said Ellie, looking at Ann, who was positively radiant with relief.

Alfie was so shocked at what his son had to tell him, he spilled beer all over his trousers. 'Well, stone me,' he said, dabbing his beer-soaked clothing with a handkerchief. 'Tom Hall killed Keith Wilkes and he let you take the blame. Why, that wicked bugger. I'd like to—'

'I know, Dad. If he wasn't already dead you'd want to kill him,' Ray said. 'I felt exactly the same when I first found out.'

Ray had arrived at the shop just as Alfie was closing it for lunch, so persuading him to join him for a drink hadn't been difficult. Now he went on to tell his father more details of what had happened and what he had decided to do about it.

'It can't have been an easy decision for you to make, son,' he commented. 'I know how much you want the world to know that you're innocent.'

'It's only natural that I would,' Ray said. 'But you can't have everything. And as long as the people in my world know the truth, that'll do for me.' He paused, looking awkward. 'There is one person I think should know the truth. But you might not agree.'

'You mean Pat,' guessed Alfie.

Ray nodded. 'It isn't that I want her to know that Tom wasn't quite the paragon she thought he was,' he explained. 'It's more that I feel she ought to know that I'm not the villain she believes I am. I'm quite prepared to spare her the humiliation of other people knowing. But I do feel she must know that I didn't kill anyone.'

'You can't protect everyone at the expense of your own reputation,' agreed Alfie.

'For your sake too, Dad,' Ray added, 'I think she should know that it was her son and not yours who killed Keith Wilkes.'

'Oh, yes, she must be told, there's no doubt about that,' said Alfie. 'But will you let me be the one to tell her?'

'Sure.'

Finishing his drink, Alfie stood up. 'And the sooner I get it over with the better,' he announced.

Ray was about to leave his flat to go to Ellie's that evening when the doorbell rang. Answering it, he was confronted with Pat Hall and Alfie. She looked very austere, dressed in dark clothes, her face pale and grim. Ray found himself slightly nervous about what was to come.

'Pat's got something she wants to say to you, son,' announced his father.

With more than a little apprehension, Ray ushered them inside and led them into the lounge. Alfie sat down, Pat remained standing, a frail figure, for all that she was awesome.

'I've just come to thank you,' she said to Ray.

Thank him? For having asked his father to tell her that her son had killed a man and let someone else take the blame?

'Really?' he said in a questioning manner.

'For not going public over the Keith Wilkes killing, I mean,' she explained, her lips trembling slightly. 'Your father has told me everything. I'm so shocked I hardly know what to say.'

She looked so forlorn, Ray felt pity for her. 'I'm sorry you had to know but—'

'Of course I had to know about something as serious as that,' she said sharply. 'I understand that my son acted in self-defence but it was a terrible thing he did, letting you go to prison for something you didn't do.'

'Well, yes . . .'

'You've every right to make the information public to clear your name, and I wouldn't blame you if you did.' She paused, seeming weak and breathless. 'But I'm very grateful to you for not doing so. It's hard enough for me to come to terms with the fact that my son would do such a terrible thing. Being spared the disgrace of everyone else knowing too will be a great help to me. It's an extremely generous gesture on your part.'

He shrugged, noticing how tired she looked and warming to her. 'You look worn out, Mrs Hall,' he commented, waving a hand towards a chair. 'Why don't you sit down?'

'Pat, please.'

He nodded and repeated his invitation for her to sit down.

'But we don't want to impose,' she said considerately. 'You look as though you're about to go out.'

'I am, but I'll give Ellie a call and tell her I'll be a bit late,' he offered.

'Are you sure?' said Pat.

'Yeah, course I am,' he assured her. 'You sit down and make yourself comfortable.' He looked at his father. 'I'm sure Dad won't mind keeping you entertained while I go to the phone. He might even be able to find something half decent to drink in the sideboard. I won't be a minute.'

He strode across the room en route for the telephone in the hall. Turning at the door, he caught his father's eye. Alfie gave him a grateful wink.

One Sunday a year or so later there was quite a gathering at Mary and Bob's for Sunday tea. Ellie and Ray were there with Donna; Ann, Doug and Matthew; and Alfie and Pat, who had surprised everyone by getting married recently.

'Another sandwich, Pat?' offered Mary.

'I don't think I could manage another morsel,' she declined politely. 'I'm saving some room for the trifle.'

'It's lovely, Gran,' Donna informed her paternal grandmother. 'It's got lots of tinned fruit in it.'

'Peaches,' added the observant Matthew, now a lively four-year-old with the same gentle nature as his father. 'You can see them through the glass bowl.' He rested his big brown eyes on Mary persuasively. 'Can I have some, please, Gran?'

'Not until you've finished your sandwich,' his mother cut in.

'Oh, Mu-um,' he groaned.

'Stop being cheeky and eat it up,' said his cousin, who was nearly five.

'All right, Bossy Boots,' admonished her mother. 'Stop pulling rank on your cousin just because you're the eldest.'

The two children bickered happily, while everyone else talked among themselves, the warm roar of friendly conversation filling the room. The sound of a spoon banging on the table produced immediate silence. Ellie was astonished to see that Pat was responsible.

'If I can have your attention I'd like to say a few words,' she announced.

Silence fell. Even the children were quiet.

'I just want to say how pleased I am to be back in the Scott family fold,' she told the gathering. 'I know I gave you all a bad time when I first heard about Ellie and Ray.' She paused, seeming breathless. 'Who would have thought then that I would end up marrying his father and become Ellie's mother-in-law for the second time?'

A murmur of agreement.

'Anyway,' she went on. 'I never thought I would be able to say this but I'm glad that Ellie and Ray are safely married.'

A cheer went up.

Pat swallowed hard, her eyes moistening with tears. 'I don't suppose I'll ever stop missing Tom. No matter what he'd done, he was still my son.' She pointed to her heart and cleared her throat. 'It hurts right here, knowing I'll never see him or hear his voice again.' Her voice was trembling. 'But having you all as friends . . .' she paused to look at Alfie, 'and my dear Alfie by my side makes it so much easier to bear.'

There was an awkward silence before Mary said thickly, 'Aah, isn't that nice?'

'Lovely,' agreed Bob, though he wasn't a sentimental man and looked more than a little embarrassed.

It was as much as Ellie could do to hold back the tears. Ray gave her hand a reassuring squeeze under the table. Across the table she met Ann's gaze. Ann nodded and both women stood up, having made an arrangement earlier.

'While we're in the mood for speeches,' began Ellie, 'Ann and I both have something to tell you all . . .'

'Matthew and I are having a brother or sister, one each,'

439

chimed in Donna, pre-empting the situation with childish triumph, then clamping her hand over her mouth and giggling. 'Oops, I wasn't supposed to say that.'

There was a short silence followed by a burst of hilarity. 'Oh well,' laughed Ellie, 'so now you know.'

'Both of you?' questioned Mary.

Ellie nodded.

'Blimey,' grinned Bob, 'there must be something in the air.'

'The babies are due within days of each other,' Ann informed them.

There was a lot of kissing and congratulations before the meal resumed. Ellie perceived so much heart here today, such warmth and camaraderie. There had been a time when her life had seemed beyond repair. Now she was happily married to Ray and expecting his child. Because she felt so much more relaxed with this pregnancy, she was quietly confident that nothing would go wrong. She'd not felt right from the start last time. This time it was different.

She and Ray had both sold their properties and bought a house in Shepherd's Bush, a new start in a home without memories. She had no plans to give up her business when the baby was born, though obviously she'd take time off, and take fewer orders for a while when she went back. The break in continuity would mean a certain amount of rebuilding but Ray was doing well so money wouldn't be a problem.

But now she was struck by the smile on Pat's face. She'd never thought she'd see Pat rejoin their family circle, but here she was like in the old days, but all the better for having lost a lot of her superciliousness. Most of that was down to Alfie in Ellie's opinion. He was more than a match for her and had brought her right down to earth.

Out of the blue, Ellie had a sudden vivid recollection of Tom as he'd been before the accident – strong, commanding, articulate. The image was so strong he might almost have been there in the room with her. Despite his bullying ways and the wicked thing he'd done to Ray, she was still able to remember him with affection, and often thought of the happy times they'd had together. She supposed it was inevitable. He'd played such a large part in her life for so long, a tiny corner of her heart would always belong to him.

She was recalled to the present by the sound of Ray's voice. 'Are you all right?' he was asking. 'You seem a bit sad all of a sudden.'

'I'm fine.'

'Sure?'

Looking into his dark eyes, she was filled with love for him. She would always have a fondness for Tom's memory. But that's all it was – a memory. Ray was the love of her life now. He was the man with whom she wanted to spend the rest of her life.

'Yes, I'm sure. In fact I've never felt better,' she told him.

'That's good,' he said, smiling at her and holding her hand. 'I feel just the same.'

Now you can buy any of these other bestselling books from your bookshop or *direct from the publisher.*

FREE P&P AND UK DELIVERY
(Overseas and Ireland £3.50 per book)

My Sister's Child	Lyn Andrews	£5.99
Liverpool Lies	Anne Baker	£5.99
The Whispering Years	Harry Bowling	£5.99
Ragamuffin Angel	Rita Bradshaw	£5.99
The Stationmaster's Daughter	Maggie Craig	£5.99
Our Kid	Billy Hopkins	£6.99
Dream a Little Dream	Joan Jonker	£5.99
For Love and Glory	Janet MacLeod Trotter	£5.99
In for a Penny	Lynda Page	£5.99
Goodnight Amy	Victor Pemberton	£5.99
My Dark-Eyed Girl	Wendy Robertson	£5.99
For the Love of a Soldier	June Tate	£5.99
Sorrows and Smiles	Dee Williams	£5.99

TO ORDER SIMPLY CALL THIS NUMBER

01235 400 414

or e-mail <u>orders@bookpoint.co.uk</u>

Prices and availability subject to change without notice.